*W*inning over a lady was a matter of strategy, of patience. The first contact must not be skin-to-skin, nor even glove-to-glove, but solely eye-to-eye. Toby moved forward to bow to her, his gaze riveted to hers. Her eyes were remarkable. Wide-set, almond-shaped, and fringed with sable lashes. So large and serious, they seemed to swallow up the rest of her face. For a moment, he let himself sink into those dark, placid pools.

He had a devil of a struggle fishing himself back out.

A few bars later, he was still recovering when the pattern compelled him to take her hand. He seized her gloved fingers firmly. The soft fabric heated between them as they circled, becoming warm and pliant as skin. Her bare flesh would feel like this, he thought. Satin-smooth. Supple. Hot to the touch as his hands glided under that cool silk to explore her every enticing curve. It would have the texture of cream against his tongue.

Lord. Toby hauled on his mental reins before those thoughts carried him away. Never before had he felt such a thrill simply taking a lady's hand. But then, never before had he seduced a woman straight from the arms of his enemy.

Also by Tessa Dare

Goddess of the Hunt
Surrender of a Siren

A LADY OF PERSUASION

A Novel

Tessa Dare

BALLANTINE BOOKS • NEW YORK

A Lady of Persuasion is a work of fiction. Names, characters, places, and incidents are the products of the author's imagination or are used fictitiously. Any resemblance to actual events, locales, or persons, living or dead, is entirely coincidental.

A Ballantine Books Mass Market Original

Published in the United States by Ballantine Books, an imprint of The Random House Publishing Group, a division of Random House, Inc., New York.

BALLANTINE and colophon are registered trademarks of Random House, Inc.

ISBN 978-0-345-50688-7

Cover illustration: Doreen Minuto

Printed in the United States of America

www.ballantinebooks.com

9 8 7 6 5 4 3 2 1

For my husband,
who is the best kind of hero—
one who doesn't mind
being called "Lance Romance" by his coworkers.

CHAPTER
ONE

Sir Tobias Aldridge was contemplating an act of cold-blooded murder.

Failing that, an act of barbarous incivility.

By nature, Toby wasn't one to hold a grudge. As a gentleman of rank, wealth, and unarguable good looks, he'd never received a slight he couldn't simply laugh off. He called every man friend, and no man enemy.

Until now.

"So that's him." Toby glared at the man twirling a fair-haired beauty across the gleaming parquet—Benedict "Gray" Grayson. The scoundrel who'd stolen Toby's bride, his future, and his very respectability, then returned to a bloody hero's welcome.

"That's him. Here, have a brandy." His host, Jeremy Trescott, the Earl of Kendall, extended a glass.

Toby accepted the drink and downed a quick, blistering swallow. "I could call him out," he murmured behind the glass. "I could call him out and shoot him dead tonight, in your garden."

Jeremy shook his head. "You're not going to do that."

"Why not? You don't think I have it in me?" Toby gave a bitter laugh. "Don't you read the papers, Jem? That affable Sir Toby is a phantom of the past, and good riddance to him. Where did honor and decency get me, I ask you? Jilted, and replaced by a thieving, unprincipled bastard."

"Gray's not a bastard. He's the legitimate nephew of a duchess."

"Oh, yes. And now a knight, as well. What isn't he? If you listen to the talk, *Sir* Benedict's a shipping financier, a West Indian planter, a feared privateer, a paragon of valor . . ." Toby shook his head. "I know the truth. He's the thieving bastard who seduced my intended bride. It's within my rights to call him out."

"Even if you *could* do it," his friend said tersely, "you're not going to do it. This is Lucy's first ball. She's been planning it for months. If you turn it into scandal-sheet fodder, I'll take you into the garden and gut you myself."

"Well, if you didn't want scandal, you shouldn't have invited me. So long as I have the devil's own reputation, I might as well live up to it."

"You ought to rise above it." Jeremy lowered his voice. "Listen, you're bound to meet with them at some point. Gray's bringing out his younger sister this year, and they'll be at every major social event. Best to make your public reconciliation now and quell the gossip. Why do you think Lucy and I planned a ball so early in the Season?"

"Because if you waited a few months she'd be too round?" Eager to change the subject, Toby clapped his friend on the shoulder. He had no intention of reconciling with Grayson, publicly or otherwise. Ever. "Congratulations, by the way."

"How did you know Lucy's with child?"

Toby made eye contact with his friend's wife across the ballroom, as she weaved through the crush of guests. For years, Lucy Waltham Trescott had dogged their annual hunting excursions at Henry Waltham's estate. She'd harbored a girlish infatuation for Toby but had forgotten him quickly enough when Jeremy captured her heart last autumn.

He said, "I've three older sisters, and ten nieces and nephews to date. I can tell. A woman's face gets a bit rounder, her hair shines. And her bosom, it . . ." Jeremy shot him a glare, and Toby sipped his brandy. "Right, well. I can just tell."

Lucy reached them, and Toby fortified his smile. He'd be damned if he'd let this assembly catch him wearing any expression other than his usual rakish grin.

"Toby!" Lucy exclaimed, taking his hands. "I'm so glad to see you."

"Look at you, Luce." He gave her a sweeping gaze and an appreciative wink. The once-hoydenish twig of a girl had blossomed into the lovely, confident Countess of Kendall. "Stunning. Most beautiful lady in the room."

Lucy made a dismissive wave of her hand, but behind the gesture she blushed to the ears. Just as he'd known she would. Toby leaned in to kiss her cheek, ignoring Jeremy's forbidding glare.

"I know you say that to all the ladies," Lucy said. She gave him a cautious look. "Sophia looks well, doesn't she?"

"Oh, she's radiant." Toby forced his grin wider as the Graysons waltzed by, Sophia's flaxen hair and porcelain complexion an elegant ivory blur. "Incandescent, even. She has the look of a woman in love."

Sophia had never looked incandescent with him.

Lucy seemed to read his thoughts. She laid a hand on his sleeve. "Toby. You weren't in love with her, either."

He shrugged. Lucy spoke the truth, but the truth didn't help.

"What's done is done. You've got to move on." Jeremy nodded toward the crush of guests. "It's a new Season, man. There's a fresh crop of debutantes just waiting to experience the renowned Sir Toby charm. Surely one of them has caught your eye."

Toby considered. True, a fresh conquest might provide a welcome diversion from murderous rage. He'd always been a favorite with the debutantes. But lately, there was scarcely any challenge to it. His scandal-sheet notoriety as the "Rake Reborn" had the mamas on alert and the young ladies in a flutter. All he had to do was appear.

"Now that you mention it, there was one . . . just one." Toby scanned the ballroom for a glimpse of vibrant emerald silk. There was only one lady who'd caught his eye even briefly since he'd made his entrance. He knew he'd never seen her before—he certainly wouldn't have forgotten her if he had.

Ah, there she was. An intriguing dark-haired beauty unlike any other lady in the room. Unlike any lady he'd ever seen. Until now, he'd caught only glimpses of her through the churning sea of dancers—a flash of emerald, a cascade of raven hair, a swatch of honey-gold skin. Now she lined up with the ladies in preparation for a reel, and he had his first opportunity to study her in full view.

She was tall. Not nearly so tall as he, but taller than the ladies she stood amongst, and possessed of a lushly proportioned figure. The cut of her gown was modest, but she was the kind of woman who managed to look indecent, even fully clothed. Hers was a body plucked straight from some harem fantasy—full breasts, flared hips, long legs.

Toby watched as she favored her dance partner with the hint of a smile. That subtle curve of her lips was somehow more sensuous than any other curve of her body. Desire sparked through him, surprising him with its intensity. His whole body thrummed with that base, ineloquent instinct in which every seduction, no matter how suave, took its root:

I want that.

Who was she? She was in her first Season, most certainly. With her beauty, she could not last more than a few months on the marriage mart—even if her dowry were made up of cockleshells.

Toby shifted to view the row of gentlemen lined up

opposite, to discern the identity of her partner. "Bloody hell."

It couldn't be. She was partnered with Grayson, the thieving bastard. It wasn't enough he'd already stolen the woman Toby had planned to marry—now he had to strut and impress the debutantes, too? Damn it, they were Toby's territory. Now what had begun as vague, lustful inclination firmed into a plan:

I want that.

And I'm going to take it.

"Fancy a reel, Luce?"

"Why, I had not—"

Without waiting for her answer, Toby took Lucy by the hand and tugged her onto the dance floor, wedging their way into the queued-up dancers just instants before the music began. He'd positioned himself at Grayson's shoulder, and though he bowed to Lucy as the first chords were struck, he kept his gaze slanted toward the beauty in green silk beside her.

The dance was one patterned in groups of three couples, requiring much interchange between adjacent partners, just as Toby had hoped. At regular intervals, he would have occasion to take his emerald-clad vision by the hand, exchange a few words, twirl her dizzy, and—if all that failed to render her breathless—flash his most winning smile.

But all in good time.

Winning over a lady was a matter of strategy, of patience. The first contact must not be skin-to-skin, nor even glove-to-glove, but solely eye-to-eye. Toby moved forward to bow to her, his gaze riveted to hers. Her eyes were remarkable. Wide-set, almond-shaped, and fringed with sable lashes. So large and serious, they seemed to swallow up the rest of her face. For a moment, he let himself sink into those dark, placid pools.

He had a devil of a struggle fishing himself back out.

A few bars later, he was still recovering when the pattern compelled him to take her hand. He seized her gloved fingers firmly. The soft fabric heated between them as they circled, becoming warm and pliant as skin. Her bare flesh would feel like this, he thought. Satin-smooth. Supple. Hot to the touch as his hands glided under that cool silk to explore her every enticing curve. It would have the texture of cream against his tongue.

Lord. Toby hauled on his mental reins before those thoughts carried him away. Never before had he felt such a thrill simply taking a lady's hand. But then, never before had he seduced a woman straight from the arms of his enemy.

"*Toby.*" Lucy beckoned him with a twitch of her fingers, and Toby realized they'd fallen behind in the pattern.

"Right. Beg pardon." He leapt forward to claim Lucy's hands and sweep her down the dance. "And I apologize in advance, for what is about to occur."

Her eyes flared. "Toby, no. You can't make a scene."

"Oh, but I could. I could denounce Grayson and Sophia in front of the entire ballroom. Everyone thinks they're the golden couple, the freshly knighted hero and his beautiful, innocent bride? I could expose the truth."

"And I could expose your innards." Lucy's fingernails dug into his arm, proving a fierce huntress still prowled within that elegant exterior. "You wouldn't dare. I've been planning this evening for months, Toby."

The dance parted them before Toby could respond. Then the lady in green silk smiled, and something in his chest pulled tight. He couldn't have spoken if he'd tried. It was perfect, that smile, composed of full, sensuous lips the color of fine Madeira. Lips designed for sin, framing an innocent row of pearly teeth. And about the corners of her mouth, the slightest hint of melancholy—just enough to intrigue the mind, stir the heart. Those lips defied mere admiration; they wanted a kiss.

There was only one thing wrong with that smile.

It wasn't directed at him. That bastard Grayson was its lucky recipient, and it was all Toby could do not to thrust out his boot and trip the man as he moved forward to take the beauty's hands.

Tempting, that idea—but inconceivable. Toby might scuff his boot.

No, he would exact his revenge more subtly, more justly. No messy duel, no public denouncement. Did not the Bible advise an eye for an eye, a tooth for a tooth . . . or, in this case, a lady for a lady?

When the pattern brought them together again, he pulled his dark-haired temptress close—so close the green silk of her gown tangled with his legs. Her scent teased him: a crisp, fresh-smelling blend of verbena and citrus.

Tightening his grip on her arm, he whispered just as they parted: "I must tell you a secret."

He squeezed her fingers before releasing them, allowing his thumb to brush the sensitive center of her palm. He fancied he heard her gasp.

Grayson cast him a wary look. Toby's arrogance made a feast of it.

He turned back to the lady in green. "You will be shocked," he murmured as they brushed by one another again, "but it cannot be helped."

He did not imagine her gasp that time, nor the flush that bloomed from her hairline to her bosom. Lord, she had the most magnificent bosom, and now it was lifting slightly with her every breath, straining the seams of her bodice. Tearing his eyes from the sight was quite possibly the most difficult thing he'd ever done.

An eternity passed before the pattern reunited them. Toby dutifully twirled and promenaded, avoiding Lucy's inquisitive glances by watching *her* instead. Within him, bitter envy twined with lust. Admiration glowed on her face as she regarded her partner. He despised Grayson more every moment.

When at last he rejoined the lady in green, it was with profound, bone-deep relief. As though he'd journeyed to the Holy Land and back to earn her favor, rather than circling a ballroom. If he'd tried, he couldn't have explained the sense of purpose and destiny that gripped him. This jaunty reel had become a mission, more serious than any undertaking of his life.

He kept up a low, seductive rush of words as they traced a tight spiral, denying her any opportunity to respond. "I am drawn to you. I haven't taken my eyes from you all evening. I am enraptured."

He was a liar.

Isabel Grayson trembled as she resumed her place in the line. Her heart pounded a wild rhythm, twice the tempo of the reel. Fortunately, the pattern now afforded her a few bars of rest. She ventured a furtive glance in the gentleman's direction, only to encounter the disquieting appraisal in his eyes.

Blushing, she dropped her gaze to the floor.

I am drawn to you, he'd said. *I haven't taken my eyes from you all evening.*

A lie, a lie. His eyes had most definitely *not* followed her all evening. If they had, Bel would have noticed—for she'd been staring at him the whole time.

How could she not stare? He was, quite simply, the most handsome man she'd ever seen, despite the fact she'd grown up in the company of three exceedingly handsome men: her father and two brothers. But their rugged, roguish appeal drew as much from their imperfections as from their well-formed features. By contrast, this man—this man was an ideal. Sculpted profile, light brown hair threaded with gold, and a lean, confident grace to all his movements, grand or small.

She'd observed him since the moment he entered the room. While he'd circled the assembly with a lithe, easy step; as he'd chatted with their hosts. Even when courtesy forced her to direct her eyes elsewhere, she'd been aware of him, in some tingling notch at the base of her spine.

And now, this dance. His bold glances, the stolen caresses, and those devastating murmured words: *I am enraptured.*

Her whole body hummed with a foreign, forbidden thrill: desire.

Oh, this was a disaster!

Bel did not want to be feeling desire. She did not want to be *feeling* anything. Any other young lady in her place might dream of just this—a divinely handsome man to sweep her away on a giddy tide of emotion.

But not her. She had come to this ball for one reason only: to select a husband from among the eligible lords. Her choice would be a wholly rational decision, made on the basis of reflection, prayer, and a well-informed portrait of the man's moral character and sphere of influence. In aid of the process, she knew that a measure of physical attraction on the gentleman's side would be beneficial; hence, this lavish, formfitting gown. But for her part, Bel would not be influenced by capricious flutterings of sentiment, or worse—by sinful stirrings of desire.

And it must be desire, this plague of sensation rendering her feverish and lightheaded. It certainly felt sinful. And stirring.

"You dizzy me."

The words were a whisper as the pattern shifted and the handsome gentleman wove past. Reeling from an unwelcome frisson of pleasure, Bel missed a step.

Her brother gave her a look of concern. "Come now," Gray said, guiding her back into the pattern. "Don't trust me to lead. You know I'm just learning this country-dance nonsense myself." He lowered his voice. "I don't dare cease counting under my breath, or I'll lose my place completely."

Bel gave a nervous laugh and willed her molten-wax knees to solidify. *Behave normally,* she told herself. *One, two, three. Dance, laugh, smile.*

"For God's sake, don't smile."

He'd passed behind her again, that seductive phantom, trailing his serpentine whispers that wormed in through her ears and coiled low in her belly. And here he came once more.

"When you smile, I can't breathe."

Oh dear. This was not good. Not good at all.

She knew, because *she* was good. She *was.* She was a good, good girl. Not at all the type of lady to be tempted by a golden-haired, silver-tongued devil in fitted broadcloth.

Yes, she'd been raised by a degenerate father, a lunatic mother, and two brothers who had rebuilt the family fortune through violence and theft—but Bel refused to follow that path. She'd devoted her life to service and charity, although she'd grown frustrated with the limits of her good work on Tortola. Visiting the infirm, teaching children to read, even supporting the sugar cooperative— she was only sticking plasters on a rifle wound. She couldn't decrease unfair tariffs; she couldn't abolish slavery. The only people with the ability to effect meaningful change were here, in London: the lords, with their wealth and power and voices in government. Bel could not become one of them, but she could become one of the wealthy, powerful ladies at their sides.

It was a simple plan, really. She would marry a lord. She would become a lady of influence. And then she would make the world a better place. *One, two, three.*

But first she must get through this dance without disgracing herself completely. The task was proving easier conceived than accomplished.

"Right," the man whispered as they crossed paths again.

Right? What did he mean, *right?* Now irritation bubbled inside her. There was nothing right about his presumptive behavior. There was most certainly nothing right about the surreptitious touch that glanced off the base of her spine—*there.* A firm brush just above her left hip that had her startling, quivering, pivoting . . .

Turning to the right.

"Then left," he murmured. "Mind the feathers."

Bel turned to her left, ducking to avoid a sudden onslaught of ostrich plumes as she circled a dour-faced matron. Her mind whirled. He was helping her through the dance. It wasn't enough that he already had her intrigued, thrilled, angered, and just a little bit afraid. Now, to this stew of emotion inside her, he was adding gratitude.

He was making her *like* him.

"Now back," he whispered. "Nicely done."

Oh, this just became worse and worse. They stood at rest again, and Bel felt his gaze burning over her skin. In a desperate effort to discourage him, she lifted her chin and shot the handsome stranger a haughty, quelling look.

In return, the man winked. Winked!

More distressed than ever, she averted her eyes. She should have known it wouldn't work. She had no talent whatever for haughtiness or quelling.

But she was an expert at following rules.

This dance had rules. A pattern. There was a right way to step, and a wrong way. The thought calmed her. If she adhered to the pattern, followed all the right steps, perhaps she could subdue this tempest of sensation within her—all these inconvenient feelings stirred by a gentleman whose name she did not even know and whose fine profile she would never forget, should she live to the age of ninety-four.

Bel squared her shoulders. *I have a mission,* she reminded herself as she took her brother's hand and moved numbly through the pattern. Turning first left, then right, then releasing his hand to circle back round. *I have a purpose, a cause.*

"You have me utterly bewitched."

The words set her trembling anew. How did the man keep passing so close to her, so indecently near, without drawing attention?

Bel looked to her brother, whose forehead was wrinkled with concentration. As Gray danced, his lips moved ever so slightly. *One, two, three . . .* He was too absorbed in the pattern to notice a thing.

Perhaps she ought to flee. Would it draw a great deal of attention, if she simply turned on her heel and ran? She sighed. Of course it would. And as much as she hoped to draw society's attention, she didn't want to attract it that way. If she wanted to change the world, or even some small corner of it, these people must respect her and follow her example. Her comportment must be above reproach.

No, she could not flee. She must stay. She must follow the pattern of the dance. She must move toward this unnervingly handsome man and allow him to take her hand once again.

"Give me a word." His hand slid up to clasp her arm just below the elbow. Just above her glove. His thumb stroked her bare flesh, and Bel quivered with exquisite fear. "One word."

Together they halted in the center of the dance. His eyes held her captive, warm copper alloyed with insistent steel. His voice was low, for only her ears. "Forgive me, but there is something between us. Some force I can no better explain than resist. I am faint with it, feverish. Give me a word. Tell me you feel it, too."

Bel made a feeble attempt to retract her arm, but his

grip tightened, his thumb pressing against the racing pulse in the hollow of her elbow. She couldn't think what to do. There were no more thoughts in her head, only riotous, mad sensation pounding in her blood.

"Do you? I beg of you, speak the truth."

Her eyes squeezed shut. She was a good girl. A good, good girl.

She did not lie.

"Yes."

CHAPTER
TWO

"Then you belong with me."

Toby slid one arm around his lady's waist, grasped her other hand in his, and danced her right off the parquet, twirling her toward the row of glass-paned doors that opened onto the terrace. They were almost to the door when that oaf Grayson finally looked up from his feet and noticed his partner had gone missing. He scanned his immediate circle in vain. The dancers around him stopped, their bemusement certain to become amusement soon enough.

With a laugh, Toby swept his temptress and her yards of green silk straight out into the night. Now there was a story the *ton* would remember, when the names Sir Toby Aldridge and Sir Benedict Grayson bumped against one another in conversation. Grayson might have eloped with Toby's intended bride, but now Toby had stolen an admirer straight from Grayson's own arms.

He could not call it complete revenge, but he could call it a solid beginning.

And now, he could turn his attention to the gorgeous creature he held in his arms. Could it possibly have been just minutes he'd been yearning for this embrace? It felt like years. A lifetime. Or here, in this Greek-styled colonnade, he could imagine it an eternity. It was as though an enchantment had been cast around them, binding them together with some primeval, pagan magic.

"Remarkable," he whispered.

She froze in his arms, though she made no attempt to pull away. The rush of cool night air surrounding them only emphasized the heat building between their bodies.

"What, precisely, is remarkable?" Her voice was melodic, and flavored with some foreign spice.

"You," he answered honestly. "Do you realize, your hair is actually a shade darker than the night sky?" He wound a jet-black tendril around his finger, enjoying the way her lower lip quivered in invitation. Oh yes, he was in fine form tonight. "And softer than moonlight. How is that possible?"

"It's not," she said. "Dear heavens. You do this often, don't you?"

"What?"

"Sweep ladies onto secluded terraces and pay them nonsensical compliments."

"Er . . . perhaps," he said, chastened.

"Perhaps," she echoed. Her look went from one of skepticism to one of dismay.

"Don't fret, darling. With you, I actually mean them." Toby gave her his most disarming grin—that lopsided, mischievous boyish smile he'd honed on a mother and three older sisters, then polished to a seductive gleam. It was a grin that said, *I know I'm impossible, but it's useless to resist. We both know you can't help but love me.*

Except—evidently, this lady could. Her look of dismay became one of despair. She swallowed, then released a flurry of words. "Please tell me you are a lord."

Toby's involuntary burst of laughter increased the distance between them. "A lord?"

"Duke, marquess, earl, viscount, baron . . ." Her eyes were grave and pleading. "Please tell me you hold one of those titles."

"Sorry to disappoint you, but the arms holding you belong to a baronet. I'm not a lord, but a sir."

"Ah!" She pushed away from him, flinging her hands

wide. The exasperated cry she made, the dramatic gesture—so unreservedly passionate, so deliciously un-English. What other cries of passion might she produce, if expertly provoked? A man could not help but wonder.

"What have I done?" She leaned against a marble column, framing her brow with her fingertips. "Not a lord, but a sir. And a rake, to top it. This . . . this is a disaster." Her accent grew more pronounced as her agitation increased, her vowels tilting at interesting angles. Toby was almost too enthralled to take offense.

Almost.

"A disaster?" he repeated. "Surely it isn't so—"

"Such behavior . . . such impropriety. I'll never find a suitable husband now. What honorable man would have me?" She dropped her hands and looked up at him. "And I couldn't possibly marry *you*."

And that timeless, pagan enchantment? Popped like a soap bubble.

Toby was tempted to point out that he didn't recall proposing anything, and that the notion of marrying her had not even formed in his mind. But neither of those facts mitigated the innumerable insults contained in her declaration. "Let me understand you. You couldn't possibly marry me, because I am neither a lord, nor even suitable, nor do I qualify—by your estimation—as an honorable man." He ran a hand through his hair, muttering, "Right, well. Doesn't *that* sum up public opinion nicely?"

"I'm sorry. So sorry. I'm not thinking. You . . . you make it so I can't think at all." She turned and paced away from him. "I must go back inside. I'm a waste of silk, standing out here."

"To the contrary," Toby said, enjoying the sight of her nubile form in motion. "I'd say you're putting that silk to excellent use."

She gave him a horrified look as she moved for the door. "I must return, before my reputation is completely destroyed."

"Wait." He caught her arm. She couldn't go back inside yet, not before everyone noticed their absence. What sort of revenge would that be? He made his voice soothing. "Please, calm down. Truly, you've done nothing so scandalous. You merely became dizzied by the dancing and the closeness of the room, and I've brought you outside for some fresh air." He tugged her over to a bench and motioned for her to sit. "Now, what you need is a bit of refreshment. Allow me to bring you a glass of champagne."

"Oh, no. I never take spirits, not even medicinally."

"Lemonade, then."

"No. No, thank you." Her hands fluttered in her lap. "You know I am not truly ill."

"Aren't you?" He crouched before her. "I distinctly remember you trembling. I told you I felt faint, feverish. You said you felt the same." It didn't seem possible that her eyes could widen any further, but widen they did. "You must have been ill. God knows, the attentions of an unsuitable, dishonorable, lowly baronet could not possibly bring you to such a state."

"You are teasing me." The words were an accusation, spoken in a wounded tone. As though teasing were an offense tantamount to stealing bread from beggars. "And we shouldn't be alone."

"We're not in hiding. Anyone could come by at any moment." Toby tilted his head toward a cluster of guests down the colonnade. "And a few minutes in a secluded corner with me are hardly a barrier to marrying well. Just ask half the ladies in that ballroom."

She turned a puzzled glance toward the glass-paned doors and the colorful blur of dancers beyond them. "Really, I should be—"

"No, you shouldn't," he said, scrubbing the teasing tone from his voice. He needed her to trust him. He needed her to stay. "You've nothing to fear from me."

"I'm an unmarried woman with a reputation to guard, and you are clearly the worst sort of rake." She touched a hand to the lone ornament she wore: a slender gold pendant in the shape of a cross. "I have everything to fear from you."

"Have you been reading that nonsense in *The Prattler*?" Toby rose to his feet. "My dear, don't believe everything you read in the papers. You ought to thank me for whisking you out of that ballroom and rescuing you from your partner—now there's a true scoundrel. That Grayson's the one you ought to fear."

"But . . ." She shook her head, her black curls inky against the gleaming marble. "Why should I fear my own brother?"

"Your . . ." He stepped back, stared at her. "Your *brother*."

"Yes, my brother."

Toby returned to a crouch before her. He braced his hands on the bench, one on either side of her skirts, and stared hard into those dark, solemn eyes. "Tell me your name."

"Miss Isabel Grayson. I thought everyone knew. True, we've only just arrived from Tortola, but the gossip . . ." Toby bent his head, and her tone sharpened. "Are you laughing?"

When his shoulders stopped shaking, he wiped a tear from the corner of his eyes. What an ass he was, congratulating himself on his revenge. Drawing a lady's eye from her own brother, what a triumph. "Miss Isabel Grayson. Good God," he said, laughter quaking his chest anew. "Have you any idea who I am?"

She lifted her eyebrows. "Other than a baronet? No."

"I'm Sir Toby Aldridge."

He waited for recognition to dawn in her eyes. He waited in vain.

"Sir Toby Aldridge," he repeated. Still nothing but blank indifference. "Did Sophia—Did Lady Grayson never speak of me?"

"Never. Should she have?"

Toby flinched inwardly. How quickly she'd forgotten him. "No, I suppose there is no real reason she should. And you don't read *The Prattler*?"

She shook her head. "I abhor it. I despise rumor and innuendo, though it seems these people think of little else." She waved toward the ballroom—another of those expansive, impassioned gestures. "These are the leaders of government and society, yet they seem hopelessly shallow. Children starve in the streets, free men live in chains—but their attention is absorbed with illicit liaisons, marital disputes . . ."

"Broken engagements," Toby added bitterly. "Elopements."

"Yes, precisely."

"Revolting, isn't it?" He clucked his tongue. "Insupportable. I'm quite weary of scandal myself."

She perked with enthusiasm, a pretty flush warming her complexion. "Do you know, I've been in London over a month. I've attended dinners and card parties, my brother's fête, and this ball. I've heard ever so many words from these people's mouths, and all of it scandal and nonsense."

"And this disappoints you."

"Of course!" There went her vowels again, lilting and stretching. "It seems no one has any ideas or opinions worth the breath to speak them aloud."

"But you, Miss Grayson? Something tells me you are full to bursting with ideas and opinions. Not only worth your breath to speak them aloud, but worth the silence of others, to be heard."

"Oh." Her lashes trembled. "Truly?"

Such wonderment in her voice, as if he'd divined the very key to her soul. No, he'd done nothing so impressive. He'd merely paraphrased what he knew to be every girl's desire: someone willing to listen.

Toby was a very good listener.

"Believe me, I come from a family rife with opinionated females." He felt himself sinking back into those wide, dark eyes, and there he perceived an inner depth to rival her fathomless gaze. Not every girl had that. "I know an intelligent, principled woman when I meet with one."

Blushing deeper, she looked away. God, she truly was beautiful.

"Feeling feverish and faint again?" he teased. "I know I am."

A smile pulled at the corner of her mouth.

"Oh, no. Don't smile. You'll kill me. I stop breathing when you smile." Those sensuous lips curved wide, and all teasing aside, Toby's heart gave his lungs a deflating kick.

The irony did not escape him that here sat the sole lady in London who had no knowledge of his recent jilting, nor his outrageous reputation. The only lady who would not regard him as her entrée into the scandal sheets, or a delicious brush with infamy. With her, he could simply be his old, carefree self.

He hadn't realized, until this moment, how much he'd missed that. Just one more thing Grayson had stolen from him. How the same parents had produced both that scoundrel and this angel, Toby couldn't comprehend.

A thought struck him. Smacked him, really, with all the force of a brick. Of course. This was Grayson's sister. If he wanted an opportunity to exact revenge, well then . . .

Here she sat.

Good God, he could—

"You could what?" she asked.

Had he said that aloud? *Damn.* "I could . . ."

I could seduce you. I could take your virtue. I could live up to my infamous reputation and make you a public scandal. I could refuse to marry you and leave you heartbroken and ruined, with no prospects. I could take all your brother's hopes for your future and dash them just as thoroughly as he destroyed my own.

"I could . . ." His voice trailed off again as he stared into those wide, lovely, innocent eyes.

No. No, he really couldn't.

It simply wasn't in him, no matter what the papers said. And if the only respect left to him was his self-respect, Toby would cling to it. Grayson had already taken his bride and his reputation. He'd be damned if he'd surrender his last shreds of honor, too.

Besides, he liked this girl. She deserved better treatment than that.

"I could escort you back inside now," he said at length. "Or fetch our hostess, if you prefer. Or perhaps you've changed your mind and would like some refreshment?" Smiling, he covered her gloved hand with his. "Can I be of no service to you?"

"Perhaps there is a way you can help me."

"Anything, my lady." He knelt at her feet, mimicking a gesture of fealty. "You've only to say the word."

"Sir Toby," she whispered, her fingers clutching his. "Find me a husband."

"A husband?" He cocked his head slightly and quirked one eyebrow. "You want *me* . . . to find *you* . . . a husband?"

Bel's stomach flipped. In some unjust, inexplicable way, confusion rendered him even more handsome. If she did not recall her priorities quickly, she was in danger of forgetting them altogether. "Yes," she replied. "A husband. Tonight, if possible."

"Tonight?" He laughed. "What a mission you're setting me. You're determined to net a husband this very evening?"

"Well, I do not expect a proposal tonight. But I would like to identify a suitable candidate for marriage. Why else would I attend a ball?"

"Oh, I don't know. To enjoy yourself, perhaps?"

"To *enjoy* myself?" Bel suddenly realized she was still holding his hand. She released it abruptly.

She had not thought herself the sort of woman who would be susceptible to seductive, charming rakes ... but here she was with one. Alone. On a darkened terrace. The warmth of his skin still dancing on her fingertips ...

"It's not such a preposterous suggestion," he said. "These events are typically considered enjoyable, I believe." He rose from his knee and sat on the bench next to her—too close for Bel's comfort. The masculine scent of his cologne surrounded her, intrigued her. Oh, dear. She could close her eyes to his handsome face, but how could she block out his scent? Much less close her ears to his rich, soothing voice.

"Come now," he said. "Can you honestly tell me you have not enjoyed yourself at all this evening?"

She wilted in silence. They both knew she could not.

He inched closer on the bench. "I know I'm finding the night more enjoyable by the minute."

Not good, not good at all. Bel shot to her feet. "I have but one purpose in attending this ball," she insisted as much to herself as to him, "and that is to find a husband. I must marry a lord."

"You *must* marry a lord?" he echoed from the bench. "Don't tell me. Your brother's bartering you for connections? I would believe it of him."

"No, no." She briefly wondered how Sir Toby had formed such an ill opinion of her brother, when Sir

Benedict Grayson was London's current *cause célèbre*. Evidently he did pay little heed to rumor. "Dolly has given me an obscenely large dowry, expressly so I might select a husband without regard to title or fortune."

"Dolly?" Sir Toby chuckled.

Bel cringed at her mistake. She knew her brother hated the pet name, but how could she erase her habit from girlhood? "Shortened from Adolphus, his middle name. I know everyone calls him Gray. At any rate, *Gray* wishes me to marry for love, as he did."

"I see. As he did."

Did she detect bitterness in his tone?

"Marrying a lord is my own wish," she rushed on. "Not just any lord, mind, but a worthy one. A man of honor and principle." She gestured toward the ballroom full of elegant guests. "But how can I discern a gentleman's moral character in this setting? Dancing, cards, gossip, and drink—a ball is all vice, and no virtue."

She turned back to Sir Toby, who was wearing his becoming expression of puzzlement once again. "I've only recently arrived in England, but you have lived among these people all your life. You know their titles, their characters, their spheres of influence. So long as you've spirited me out onto the terrace, you can assist me in identifying a suitable match."

He stared at her intently. It seemed an age before he finally spoke. "You have the most intriguing accent. I can't place it at all."

"My . . . my accent? My mother was Spanish. She was our father's second wife."

"Ah. That explains it, then."

Still he stared at her. Bel grew self-conscious. "Is it so hideous to the ear?"

"No, not at all. I find it enchanting. I could listen to you all night."

"Oh." Now "self-conscious" did not begin to describe

her state. Heat built low in her belly, melting her center of gravity. She felt unsteady on her feet. "So, will you help me?"

He rose from the bench. She had not remembered him being so tall.

"Why don't you wish to marry for love?" he said.

Bel swallowed hard as he approached.

"Everything about you—your voice, your gestures, your opinions . . . even the way you dance. So passionate." He reached out, brushing the backs of his knuckles against the bare flesh of her arm. "So warm. And yet, you would choose a husband in this cold, calculated manner? For a title and status? It hardly seems in your nature."

"You would presume to know my nature? I am not—" She stiffened. She could not claim to be without passion. That would be a lie.

She continued, "If I have passion, it is for God. If I marry for love, it is for love of His children in their hour of need. From my father and brother, I am burdened with this ill-gotten dowry, gold tainted with blood. From my mother, I inherit *this*." She swept an impatient gesture down her curvaceous form. "How can I live with myself, if I barter those advantages for my own pleasure, or for something so transitory as romantic love? No, I will redeem them instead—by trading them for a title and status, as you say. For the opportunity to do good."

She shut her eyes and took a deep, steadying breath. Sir Toby didn't deserve her anger. After all, he was right. Her mother's unpredictable passions did simmer in her blood, and something about this man brought them to a boil.

Perhaps she had been born with a fiery nature, but she also had the choice to control it. As her mother's example proved, wild, emotional outbursts did not earn a woman respect or influence.

They earned her a padlocked room, and years of derision and neglect.

"Please forgive me," she said, once she'd banked her inner fire. "It's just . . . What can you know of my nature?"

"I know it is human." He gave her a little smile that only stoked the flames. "And I know it will be some undeserving man's great fortune to explore."

Without giving her time to respond—not that Bel had any coherent response to make—he linked his arm with hers and steered her toward the windows. "Well, then. Let us begin our search for Lord Honorable." After a moment, he said, "Ah. I've spotted an earl who is, by all accounts, a very excellent man and a respected landlord, if a bit stern in his demeanor. Impeccable aristocratic lineage, pots of money, and a burgeoning political career."

"Why, he sounds ideal."

"Yes. There's just one snag, you see."

"What's that?"

Sir Toby smiled down at her. "Lord Kendall is already married, to Lucy."

With a cry of reproach, Bel attempted to withdraw her arm from his. He had already tightened his grip, in anticipation of just such a retreat.

She asked, "Why must you insist on teasing me?"

"Because you are in dire need of it, my dear. Don't worry, you'll learn to enjoy it."

"I shall not." She was, however, learning to enjoy the warm press of his arm against hers, the solid support it afforded her. Charming devil of a man. "Surely there are other honorable lords in the assembly, apart from our host. Other gentlemen with burgeoning political careers."

"Well, if it's political acumen you seek, look no further. Here we have Lord Markham, the renowned orator." He directed her attention toward a lean, silver-haired gentleman. A great deal older than she, Bel thought, but perhaps his maturity boded well for her purpose.

"Is he very influential?" she asked.

"Oh, very. Legislation passes and fails on the wave of feeling generated by his speeches."

"Truly?" Bel perked. This Lord Markham sounded promising.

"Yes, I understand he was instrumental in turning the majority against the abolition bill a few years back."

She gasped. "Then he will not do at all."

"But I thought you sought political clout."

"I do, but it must be in aid of justice, not oppression. That is my entire design in marrying a lord—to further charitable causes as a lady of influence."

"A lady of influence." He gave her an amused look. "Over society? Or over a well-connected husband?"

"Ideally, both." Bel rued the blush warming her cheeks. It had nothing to do with shame over her motives, and everything to do with the way he brushed aside a strand of hair that had fallen over her brow. So casually, as if it were the most natural thing in the world for him to do. Her brow tingled where his skin had grazed hers.

"I see. So all this time we have been searching for Lord Honorable, when the man you truly seek is Lord Malleable." She attempted to protest, but he interrupted. "Lord Whittlesby would be an excellent candidate. He's a marquess, recently widowed. Rather stolid sort of man. A member of my club, though I never see him in his cups or sitting down to cards. His opinions are rarely solicited when conversation turns to matters of politics. He mostly speaks of puddings."

"Puddings?"

"Hm. Great connoisseur of puddings, Whittlesby. Goes on and on about them." He drew her close and turned her toward the window. "He's just there. By the potted palm."

Bel followed the line of his arm. There, by the aforementioned palm, stood a squat, balding man spooning custard from a flute. She watched as he withdrew a linen square from his breast pocket and proceeded to wipe first his mouth, then his glistening pate.

"An influential title, and possessed of opinions easily influenced," Sir Toby said. "Surely you can find no cause to reject him."

"He's . . . why, he's shorter than I."

"I did not realize your definition of 'upstanding' encompassed actual physical stature. Must I add 'tall' to the list of qualifications, then? And handsome, as well? This task you've set me becomes more and more difficult."

"Fine looks are of little importance," she replied, irritated with herself for her petty remark. "As is stature. Beauty of character is often at odds with physical appearance. A tall, handsome man may very well make the least desirable husband."

"Yes, yes. You ruled me out some minutes ago, remember? I've everything against me. Tall. Handsome." He pulled a face and made a dramatic shiver. "Not a lord," he repeated, mimicking her accent, "but a lowly *sir*. This is a disaster."

This time Bel succeeded in wrenching her arm away. "I did apologize. And I never used the word 'lowly.' My own brother is a sir, and I know him to be the equal of any duke."

He smiled. "How very loyal of you. But if that be the case, then why are you so set on marrying a lord?"

"For his influence in Parliament, of course. Knights and baronets have no seats in the House of Lords."

"Parliament has two houses, darling. Don't neglect the House of Commons. That's where all social debate and progressive bills originate, before Markham and his followers shout them down. Perhaps it's an MP you ought to marry."

"Are MPs more honorable, as a rule?"

"Of course not. This is government, my dear." He shook his head, chuckling. "You are like Diogenes with his lantern, roaming the earth in search of an honest man. Admittance to the House of Commons is only marginally more selective than that of the penny theater. Anyone with a few thousand pounds to spare might buy himself a rotten borough, and the fairly elected members are largely chosen out of habit or by default."

At his description, Bel suffered a pang of disappointment. She had hoped to marry an honorable, principled man with a seat in Parliament. A man for whom she could feel . . . not passion or love, but perhaps friendship, and a temperate sort of esteem. But what if that man simply didn't exist? She'd have to settle for one like Whittlesby, she supposed. She caught sight of the cream-puffed, balding lord through the window and stared at him long and hard, taking careful assessment of her emotions.

Nothing. He stirred nothing within her, save a mild flutter that resembled indigestion.

Sir Toby continued, "Why, even I could secure a seat in Commons whenever I wished. Lowly, disastrous, unsuitable *sir* that I am."

"I never said those things," she argued. "I would never say such things, and it pains me to be accused of them. Kindly stop twisting my words."

He inched closer to her. "Which words am I twisting? I clearly remember hearing 'disaster,' and a pursuant discussion of my unsuitability." He chucked her under the chin, and his thumb lingered on the edge of her jaw. "Don't worry, I'm not one to hold a grudge."

"Then why do you tease me so?"

"Because, as I said, you need teasing. You're taking yourself so seriously. Too seriously. It's a grave condition, solemnity. Causes ill humor, indigestion. And it's bad for the complexion. Teasing's one of two proven remedies."

"One of two?" Bel sighed. "If you're so concerned for my complexion, may I implore you to switch to the other?"

His hand framed her jaw. "Very well."

And then his lips were on hers.

CHAPTER THREE

Oh.

She was being kissed. Kissed, for the first time in her life, in a moonlit colonnade, by a man with the beauty of a Greek god and the morality of a satyr. It was everything right and everything wrong all at once, and Bel didn't know what to make of it. She was so used to placing actions in one category or the other.

She was too shocked to move, so she just—stood still.

His lips brushed over hers in a series of slow, teasing caresses. Tender, gentle . . . extending every invitation but making no demands. She caught the unmistakable scent of brandy on his breath—a familiar aroma, but an as yet untested flavor. She never took spirits, and here this man's lips were giving Bel her first taste of sin. It savored of fire. Not bitter, as she'd always imagined it would taste, but raw and potent. The flavor opened all her senses, awakened her entire body to the light pressure of his mouth against hers, the gentle stirrings of the breeze around them, the spar of whalebone pressing between her breasts.

She felt *everything*.

He whispered something against her mouth, something Bel could not hear through the roar of blood pounding in her ears—but she felt it, rushing over her lips. His hand slid from her jaw to the back of her neck, tilting her head to meet his. And now he kissed her again, more firmly this time, his lips slightly parted as they covered hers. Once more, the flavor of brandy flooded her senses, intoxicating and dark.

She might have pulled away at any moment. But she didn't. She remained still, so still as his thumb traced a lazy circle over her pulse. She did not move. She dared not breathe.

But inside, her blood danced. A frenzied, pagan dance that resembled a minuet like a tropical hurricane resembled the London fog. Heat whirled in her center and spiraled out to her limbs, pulsing to a furious beat. The rhythm called to her, pulled her consciousness inward with insistent tugs—until she followed it, sinking deep, deep into the heart of herself.

Here was passion . . . desire . . . wild, untamed emotion.

Here was the enemy of all her hopes and dreams.

And yet—he was the one to retreat.

"Oh." The syllable escaped her lips the instant his pulled away. He stared down at her, so divinely handsome, clearly anticipating her further response. But what more was there to say? She could not reproach him, when any fault was just as much hers as his. A taste lingered on her lips, that warm elixir of brandy and desire. Bel pressed her lips together to savor it a moment longer.

Soon they would have to go back inside. She would piece together her wits and refresh her composure and find herself a husband. A man who would offer her wealth and influence but hold no influence over her. A man who didn't stir her blood with a wink or a smile, who would pose no threat to her principles. A man who tasted of custard, not brandy and fire.

Someone safe.

When she swept back through those doors, Bel would regain control of her emotions and refocus on her goals. But for these few stolen moments, in the arms of this charming devil . . . all rational thought was lost. Her soul belonged to him.

She closed her eyes, to remain in the darkness. If only a moment could last forever.

If only he would kiss her again.

Well, Toby thought, he wouldn't be trying *that* again.

So much for curing her solemnity with a kiss. She still carried the weight of the world on that lovely brow, while he . . . he seemed to have contracted a deathly case of serious. The night felt darker now; vast and humbling. He couldn't have made a joke if he'd tried. And that kiss had left him too breathless to tease.

He'd kissed her. How had that happened? Hadn't he just decided *not* to pursue her?

No. He'd decided not to ruin her as a means of revenge. And somewhere between that moment and this one, he'd decided to kiss her, simply for her. It had been lovely. Damn near magical. He couldn't regret it.

Still, he said, "I think we had better go back inside."

He slid his hand down the slope of her shoulder for one last caress, and her eyes fluttered open.

Blast. Now he'd done it.

Toby recognized the dazzled look in those eyes. He knew it all too well. Charming young ladies was his singular talent, and he'd developed it through years of practice. He knew the precise instant he had them. When they took all their youthful hopes and romantic dreams and shaped them into a tight little ball and tossed it into his hands. *Here,* they said. *Take my heart and break it.*

Normally, Toby was happy to oblige. What was that line in the novel his sister Augusta loved so well? "A girl likes to be crossed in love a little now and then." Truer words were never penned. He took that ball of hopes and dreams, made a little show of juggling it, and handed it back—a bit dented, perhaps, but largely intact. Occasionally, he misjudged and the ball slipped from his grasp to shatter on the floor. But even then, the young ladies recovered quickly enough.

Because they always held something back. This little plaything they tossed him—it held the affections of a girl. Their true womanly hearts, their deepest passion and love, this they guarded, saved for another man. Anyone who labeled Toby a heartbreaker underestimated the shrewdness of feminine intellect. He knew, from years of experience, that young women were a great deal wiser than general opinion would allow.

There was something different about this woman, however—aside from her enchanting accent and strident politics. When he'd kissed her, she'd offered him nothing—but neither had she held anything in reserve. She didn't know how to flirt. None of his compliments or teasing had warmed her a single degree, but in that moment when their lips met . . . she'd simply been *his*. With her, there could be no half-measures.

That kiss had rocked him to his boots.

His blood was still fizzing with her nearness, her scent, her taste. Her skin was so smooth; the edge of temptation, keen. And just when he'd nearly lost himself in those dark, serious eyes, she pursed her delicious lips and whispered . . .

"Whittlesby."

Toby blinked. Had he truly just heard her say—

"Lord Whittlesby." She swallowed. "When we go back inside, will you introduce us?"

"Wh—" The breath rushed out of him in an indefinable question. He released her, cleared his throat, and tried again. "Wh—"

No use. He didn't even know how to complete that syllable. *Who? What? Why? When?*

Yes, that was it—when? *When did my amatory prowess sink to this low, where I might kiss a young lady on a moonlit terrace and the first thought that springs to her mind is . . . "Whittlesby"?*

"Whittlesby?" he finally echoed, somehow hoping he'd misheard her. Twice.

"Yes. You did promise to find me a husband. I've decided he will do."

A burst of shocked laughter escaped him. "No. No, you've misunderstood. Whittlesby will not do at all."

She frowned. "Then you won't introduce me?"

"I'd sooner die." Indeed, some small part of his pride was withering to dust as he spoke. But this was nothing, compared to the agonies he would suffer, surrendering this vibrant, intelligent, beautiful woman to a lump like Whittlesby.

Good God. *Whittlesby?*

"But you promised to find me a husband." She latched a hand over his wrist. "Tonight."

The pressure of her fingers did strange things to his pulse. He teetered on the verge of taking her into his arms and kissing her again—thoroughly, this time. All night long, if need be. Until he kissed away her memory of any man but him.

Honor, he reminded himself sternly. And something about clinging to the few remaining shreds of it. The honorable course, sadly, did not involve kissing those perfect lips all night—but neither did it mean sending her into the arms of a perfect clod. He needed to set this girl straight. Only then, not before, would he let her go.

The first strains of a waltz reached his ears. "Yes, I promised to find you a husband. And so I shall—inside." Where the light of a hundred candles would hold this feral temptation at bay. "Come," he said, tucking her gloved hand into the crook of his arm. "I'm going to give you a lesson about the true nature of influence and the selection of worthy suitors."

She gave him a puzzled look.

He clarified, "We are going to dance."

He led her back inside and had her swept up in the waltz before anyone could notice their return.

She was an inexperienced dancer, he could tell—she couldn't have had much opportunity to practice on that speck of a tropical island. But still, they glided through the room effortlessly, in perfect time with the music. Because Toby was an excellent dancer, and she gave herself over completely to his lead.

"You dance like a dream," he told her. His dream, likely tonight. Perhaps for weeks to come.

"No, I don't," she replied. "I've never been fond of dancing, but . . ."

"But . . . ?"

She released a sigh scented with brandy and resignation. "But I'm enjoying dancing with you."

Well, praise God for small victories.

"Miss Grayson," he said, feigning shock, "don't tell me you're *enjoying* yourself. And at a *ball*?" When she blushed, he murmured, "Don't worry. Your secret is safe with me. But only if you make me a promise."

"What kind of promise?" she asked, giving him a guarded look.

"Promise me you will not marry Whittlesby. Not him, nor anyone like him."

"I'll promise you nothing of the kind. Who are you, to tell me whom I should and should not marry?"

"Who am I?" He laughed. "I'm the gentleman you charged with finding you a suitable husband. Whittlesby and his ilk are categorically unsuitable."

"But you don't understand. I have goals, priorities." She looked to the ceiling. "I wish to become a lady of influence. It's the only way to have any measurable effect on society. If I do not marry above my rank, I may as well remain unmarried."

"If you do not marry your true equal, you will regret it the rest of your life. Listen to me, Isabel."

His use of her Christian name startled her. Good. Now she was paying attention. Plus, he liked saying it.

"Isabel, you are intelligent. You are young and idealistic and brimming with passion. You don't lack for fortune or family. And you're the most intriguing, beautiful woman in the room. That arsenal of persuasion could bring the whole of London to its knees, if judiciously applied. For God's sake, don't chain yourself to some pudding with a title. The power you seek—it already resides within you."

"Please, spare me your nonsensical flattery."

"Why?" he asked. "Because you might start to enjoy it?"

She set her jaw and stared stubbornly over his shoulder.

"I'm not speaking nonsense, Isabel. It's the most rational thing in the world." Toby shook his head. How could he make her see? "It's like this," he said calmly. "Imagine true disaster were to strike. Imagine you found yourself married to me. A lowly, dishonorable, too-handsome sir, unsuitable in every way."

"I never said lowly!"

"I know," he teased. "But you blush so prettily each time you protest. My point is this—if it's influence you seek, there are any number of ways to achieve it. Even by allying yourself with such a hopeless case as me."

He pulled her closer, ostensibly to whisper in her ear. But he could not help but enjoy the rustle of silk against his boots and the swell of her ample bosom brushing his chest. "Don't make a show of looking," he murmured, "but everyone in this room is staring at you. Can you imagine why?"

"Because you are holding me indecently close? Because we have just emerged from an illicit interlude on the verandah?"

"Precisely. We are the latest scandal."

She went rigid in his arms.

"Now don't distress yourself, darling. Sometimes a little scandal is just what you need. Never underestimate the power of rumor and innuendo. At this moment, we are the object of intense speculation—the infamous rake of the scandal sheets, paired with the newly arrived innocent. They're all desperate to know what we're whispering to one another. Tomorrow, they're asking themselves, what will be the headline? Am I ruining you? Or are you reforming me?" Chuckling, he fanned his fingers across the small of her back. "What a story that would be for *The Prattler*. Your name would be on the lips of every gossip in Town."

Finally, her mouth curved a fraction. "Yes, I can imagine it would be."

"Do you see? Isabel, you are free to marry where you choose, without regard to fortune or rank. Even if the unthinkable occurred, and you were wed to a lowly blighter like me"—he silenced her protest with a wink—"you would still be a lady. You would attract a great deal of notice. You would have a husband with prospects in Parliament." Granted, they were prospects Toby had been purposely avoiding for the better part of a decade, but just for the sake of argument . . . He swept her through a turn. "You would not have married a lord at all, but you would be a lady of influence."

She gave him a cautious smile that set his world spinning. "Surely you're not seriously suggesting I marry *you*?"

"No," he said, forcing a self-deprecating laugh. "I would never suggest such a thing."

She couldn't know how these blithe dismissals kept

wounding him. She couldn't know that bruised male pride was a dangerous beast.

Toby lowered his voice to a seductive murmur. "*If* I paid court to you, Isabel, I would make more than suggestions. I would make promises. I would pledge to value your ideals, never stifle or belittle them. I would vow to display your talents to their best advantage, and to guard you from those who wish you ill."

The music stopped, and Toby whirled her to a halt.

"*If* I proposed marriage to you," he said, "I would kneel at your feet. Pledge to you my undying devotion, a share in my worldly possessions, and the protection of my body. I would promise to cherish you all the days of your life, and make your happiness my own. Because that is what you deserve from a husband. No less."

"Oh," she sighed. Her lips fell slightly apart. Shallow breaths lifted her chest.

At last. He had her well and truly enchanted now. Toby supposed he ought to release her. He'd proven his point, hadn't he? He still knew how to dazzle a girl. But something compelled him to go on.

"And *if* I did offer for you," he asked, "would it be so very horrible?"

He hardly knew what murky pit of his soul that question had crawled out from, but he knew it wasn't aimed at this girl. It was meant for Sophia, and Lucy, and every other young lady who'd grown out of loving him and married some other man.

But it was Isabel who must answer for them all. She was here, and she was breathless in his arms, and she had the power to crush or redeem him with a single syllable. Yes, he still knew how to dazzle a girl—he'd practically emerged from the womb with that gift. But deep down, at his core—could he ever find what it took to secure a woman's love?

Give me a word. One word.

"Would it be so unthinkable?" he asked softly, earnestly.

Before she could speak, someone stepped between them and the nearby candelabra, throwing a shadow over them both.

"Excuse the interruption." The voice was a smooth baritone. "But I'd thank you to let the lady go."

Without releasing Isabel, Toby cast a glance toward the speaker. Of course, it was her brother. Sir Benedict Grayson, paragon of valor, miserable dancer, and great hulking brute with murder in his eyes. Worse, behind him stood Jeremy, Lucy, and the woman who'd left him at the altar and fled halfway around the world—Sophia.

Now he needed to hear Isabel's answer more than ever.

Toby said, "I beg your pardon. This is a private conversation."

"Not any longer, it isn't." Grayson folded massive arms over his chest. "The conversation is over." Lowering his voice, he growled, "Get your hands off my sister."

The musicians struck up a new melody, but no one in the room was dancing. All eyes were on their little tableau.

"In a moment," Toby said smoothly, enjoying the upper hand. He refused to let Grayson cow him. The man might be a dockside laborer in gentleman's clothing, but Toby was taller. "I'm still waiting on a word from Miss Grayson. I've asked her a question, and she hasn't yet answered."

He turned back to Isabel, tripping straight into her solemn, remarkable eyes. A strange sense of destiny overcame him. In his gut, Toby knew that the events of the next minute could very well mean the rearrangement of his life, his face, or both. He had a choice. He could release her, from his embrace and his question, surrender a second lady to this thieving bastard, and continue the miserable pastime of searching for his misplaced self-worth at the bottom of brandy decanters.

Or he could hold on to this beautiful, intelligent, passionate woman.

Perhaps forever.

Grayson scowled. "Bel, what the devil is he talking about? You don't have to answer this man anything." He lowered his voice to a gruff whisper. "Do you want me to hit him?"

"No!" she gasped, her gaze flitting around the assembled crowd. "No, nothing of the sort. Sir Toby just asked me—"

"To marry him," Toby interrupted. Loudly and clearly, with a certainty that surprised even him.

An excited murmur swept the crowd.

Leveling a cool gaze at Grayson, he continued, "I've asked your sister to marry me. And now I'm waiting . . ." He glanced over his shoulder. "It would seem we're all waiting . . . to hear her reply."

The excited murmur dissolved into silence. Grayson's face turned a satisfying shade of ash. And suddenly, Toby was having the time of his life. He'd stolen Isabel straight from the scoundrel's arms, and he was not going to give her back. Not without a fight.

He released Isabel's waist and took her soft, delicate hand in both of his. "Was it public notice you wanted? All eyes are on you now, my dear," he said, grinning. "And I must confess, I've always wanted to do this."

She stared at him, mute with shock, as he sank to one knee.

"Miss Isabel Grayson." His voice echoed off the marble tile. "Would you do me the inestimable honor of becoming my wife?"

CHAPTER
FOUR

"I'm engaged." Bel joined her brother and sister-in-law at the breakfast table the next morning. "Can you believe it?"

"No," Gray said tersely, his face hidden behind a newspaper. "I can't."

To be honest, neither could Bel. She'd passed a fitful night, plucking at the lace-edged coverlet and reliving the evening's events again and again in her mind—each time hoping for a different conclusion. By dawn, she'd nearly convinced herself the entire episode was simply a strange, vivid dream. But judging by her brother's ill-humor this morning, it would seem to have been real.

"I'm engaged," she said again. If she said it enough times, she might begin to believe it.

Gray cleared his throat. "For God's sake, Bel, you're not—" He stopped himself and appeared to consider before beginning again, more softly this time. "Your . . . *engagement*"—he ground out the word—"is still a matter of discussion."

"What your brother means to say, is that it happened so quickly," Sophia said. "It's taken us all by surprise."

It had taken no one by surprise more than Bel. She couldn't even recall her thoughts at the moment when her traitorous lips had formed the word "yes." Obviously, there had been no thoughts in her head at all. Only the sight of Sir Toby's devilish grin, and the warmth of his hands grasping hers, and the sound of a hundred pairs of lungs seizing in anticipation of her very next word.

And—God help her—some emotion akin to enjoyment.

Madness, that's what her acceptance had been. A moment of sheer insanity.

Not that she could let anyone suspect it now. No, the only thing worse than impetuously accepting a proposal at her first ball would be callously breaking it the next day. She would appear fickle, immature, prone to wild vacillations of emotion: everything a lady of influence was not. The decision had been made in a moment of madness, but as Sir Toby himself had pointed out, a marriage to him could still further her goals. So long as, from this point forward, she behaved with restraint and acted as though it were all part of her plan.

"Yes," Bel replied. "It did happen quickly, and I'm glad of it." She nibbled at a point of toast. "But why did we have to leave the ball so early? People wanted to congratulate us."

"There's nothing to congratulate, not yet." Gray attacked a slab of ham with knife and fork. "I haven't given my consent."

Bel stared at him. "You don't mean to withhold it? You promised I might marry whomever I choose."

"I should know better than to make promises," her brother grumbled around a bite of ham. "Picked a devil of a year to start keeping them."

Sophia mediated with a soothing tone. "Gray wants to speak with Toby before he gives his formal consent. Joss will want to meet him, too. He may not be your guardian, but he is your brother."

"Where is Joss this morning?" Bel asked.

"He took a tray to the nursery. Little Jacob is cutting teeth and feeling out of sorts."

"What in God's name did that man say to you?" Gray

asked, snapping open a newspaper. "I can't imagine what dastardly lies he must have spun, to persuade you to accept him."

"I'm sure he did not tell me any lies," Bel replied calmly. "We merely had the opportunity to converse, and arrived at the conclusion that we would be well-matched."

"Well-matched," her brother echoed with disbelief. "You say he told you no lies? Well, then I suppose he told you about his history with—"

"*Gray,*" Sophia whispered in a reproving tone. The two exchanged pointed glances over the paper before Gray folded it and laid it aside. Whatever conflict had existed moments ago was evidently resolved now, as evidenced by the affectionate brush of Gray's fingers over his wife's wrist. Bel normally found it sweet, the way they conversed in looks and light touches in place of words.

It was less sweet when they were clearly discussing *her*.

"We need to speak privately," Sophia whispered to Bel, dismissing the servants with an elegant, self-assured flick of her wrist.

Bel sighed inwardly. She loved her new sister, but living with Sophia meant a daily struggle with envy. She was so beautiful, so graceful. And though Bel rejoiced to see her brother happily wed, in moments of weakness she—just the tiniest bit—resented sharing his attention.

But she needn't share Sir Toby's attention with Sophia. He was her betrothed; he belonged to Bel alone. The thought sparked a little fire inside her.

Sophia inched her chair closer to Bel's. "I wasn't certain how much to say last night, but after talking it over with Gray . . ." She cast Gray a cautious look, and he nodded in encouragement. Sophia turned back to Bel. "There is something I must tell you. Before I met your brother, I was betrothed to another man. Bel, I was engaged to Toby."

Bel choked on her toast. "No."

"Yes. We were to have been married last December."

"What happened?"

Sophia worried a crease in the tablecloth. "I lied to him, and to all my friends and family, and then I ran away."

"What dreadful act could Sir Toby have committed, to make you flee your home?"

"No, no," Sophia said. "Toby was a perfect gentleman. The dreadful acts were all mine, I'm afraid. I can't regret making the choices that led me to Gray, but I'm still ashamed of how I treated Toby."

Bel inhaled slowly, absorbing this new information. Sir Toby, once engaged to Sophia! So much for claiming the gentleman's undivided attention.

Gray swore under his breath. "The man's an oily bilge rat. He's angry with me for taking his bride, and now he's just trying to get back at me by—" He bit off the sentence when Sophia threw him a sharp look.

"By marrying me," Bel finished for him. "I see. You assume the only reason Sir Toby would propose to me is to get back at you. He couldn't possibly be interested in *me*. Is that what you're implying?"

"Bel, no." Gray scrubbed his face with his hand. "Of course, any man would be desperate to marry you. But considering past events, and the speed with which he pursued you—"

"But how could he harbor any such scheme?" Bel asked. "Sir Toby didn't even know my name."

They both stared at her.

"Is that true?" Sophia asked. "Are you certain?"

"Yes," Bel insisted. "When we . . . left the ballroom together, he had no idea I was Gray's sister. When I told him my name, he was shocked indeed—and even more surprised that I did not recognize his. He was sure you would have mentioned him to me."

"I should have," Sophia said. "I'm so sorry, I should have told you earlier."

"Don't apologize," Gray told his wife. "How could you have predicted last evening's events? Normally, there's time between introductions and betrothal to discuss such things." He sighed. "Bel, you must admit, this 'proposal' happened with suspicious alacrity."

"That wasn't entirely his fault, either. I'm the one who broached the topic of marriage." Bel pinched the bridge of her nose. "I'm not certain what came over me," she said, too stunned to censor her comments. "One moment, he was a handsome stranger, and the next I was conversing with him as though I'd known him for years. He . . . he put me so at ease. He made me smile."

And he'd kissed her. It wasn't as though she could neglect that bit. She'd lain awake all night, trying to erase the sensation of his lips against hers. Trying to forget the taste of him, so forbidden and sweet.

"Don't worry," Gray said. "When the rat comes calling today, I'll send him scurrying. You're not going to marry him."

"But I must," Bel protested. "Or what will people say?"

"They'll say you've come to your senses, recovered your wits."

They'll know I lost them. They'll see me as another flighty, impressionable girl.

Bel said, "I'm going marry Sir Toby." She turned to Sophia. "What's past is past. I don't see why your prior engagement should affect mine. Say what you will, I cannot suspect him of any malicious intent."

"To be truthful, neither can I," Sophia said.

While Gray harrumphed and made a show of busying himself with his food, Sophia pushed aside her plate to make room for a stack of newspapers tied with twine.

"You ought to see these," she told Bel. "I know you do not read *The Prattler*. I'm not so fond of the scandal sheets as I once was, but Lady Kendall saved these and passed them along to me." She picked open the knot and opened the top paper to the third page. "There," she said, pointing out an illustration with her fingertip. "This appeared in February, a full month before we arrived in London and my marriage to Gray was announced."

Bel took the paper from her sister's hand to examine it more closely. The image was most definitely a likeness of Sir Toby, though his harmonious features were thrown out of balance by the caricaturist's pen. His forehead was too wide; his jaw, unnaturally square. Regardless, he remained breathtakingly handsome, even rendered in unkind strokes.

Bel read the caption aloud. "The Rake Reborn." Then beneath it, a line in smaller print: "London's famed Lothario survives to carouse another day." In the background of the illustration, a group of ladies struck desperate postures, hands to their foreheads and shoulders limp. Ribbons of speech flowed from the ladies' mouths. "It's his golden-haired beauty," one sighed. "No, his silver tongue!" argued another. The third fanned herself and declaimed, "How he gives me the vapors! We must recover by the sea." At the bottom, the caricature was signed, *H. M. Hollyhurst*.

Bel looked up, puzzled. "Recover by the sea? I don't understand."

"When I disappeared, my parents spread the word that I'd taken ill and been sent to the seaside to convalesce. Instead of focusing on the scandal of my disappearance, the gossipmongers—and this Mr. Hollyhurst—took a keen interest in Toby. They labeled him the 'Rake Reborn,' insinuated that he rejoiced in my illness and used it as an opportunity to prolong his debauched bachelor life."

Bel looked at the illustration again, cringing. She'd suspected him to be a rake, but seeing the evidence in print . . . Sir Toby surrounded by fair-haired, slender, classical beauties adorned with plumes and jewels. A dozen Sophias.

She laid aside her toast. "I understand why Sir Toby said he's weary of gossip."

"He must be," Sophia said, riffling the papers, "for he's been in *The Prattler* every day for months. If it's not one of Mr. Hollyhurst's caricatures, it's a notice in the society column. They've cataloged his attendance at every ball, boxing match, opera house, and gaming club. The paper has even gone so far as to tally the number of his paramours, since his near escape."

The number of his paramours? Bel almost asked Sophia to relate the estimate, then stopped herself. "Surely you don't credit any of it? Sir Toby told me himself, one shouldn't believe everything in the newspapers. Do you believe such behavior of him?"

"No," Sophia said. "At least, not to this degree. But I am amazed that he has tolerated such treatment." She lowered her voice. "Do you realize, he could have made an immense scandal when I eloped, or even sued my father for breach of our marriage contract? Yet he said nothing, at least not publicly. He allowed the illusion of my illness to stand and took a drubbing in the papers all the while."

An unhappy realization settled on Bel. "He must have been very much in love with you."

Gray coughed violently.

Sophia pursed her lips. "No, actually. I don't believe he was. But his pride must have incurred deep wounds, even if his heart remained intact. It must have been difficult for him to endure all this"—she indicated the newspapers—"so quietly. I don't know why he did, after the way I used him so ill. But he has borne the brunt of public speculation regarding our broken engagement, and if he had not, I would have been ruined. We should not have been welcome in Society. Your own prospects for marriage would have been destroyed."

"We owe him much, then."

"Yes, we do." Sophia gave her a meaningful look. "We owe him the chance to find happiness. I did not love him as a wife should, but I cared for him—I *care* for him too much to see him trapped in a polite society marriage."

"Trapped?" Bel's teacup met its saucer with a loud crack. "Are you saying Sir Toby shouldn't marry me? Am I not good enough for him?"

"No, that's not it at all," Sophia replied.

"Bel, he's not good enough for you," Gray said.

"I don't mean to say that, either." Sophia took a deep breath before continuing. "Bel, Toby will make some lady a fine husband. And you are everything he could dream of in a wife. Together, I daresay you could be very happy indeed—if you loved one another."

"She's not in love with the man." Gray's knife clattered to his plate. "She only met him last night." He muttered an oath.

Bel cringed. *Love.* It seemed there was no escaping that word lately. Her brothers, Sophia . . . they all exhorted that she must marry for love. As if by saying this, they granted her some grand indulgence, a gift any young lady would be delighted to receive. But to Bel, this insistence on a love match presented an unwelcome obstacle. "I don't wish to marry for love. Not romantic love, at any rate."

"Whyever not?" Sophia asked.

She hedged. It seemed impolite, and most likely ineffective, to decry romantic love to two people so thoroughly steeped in it. Her parents had married for love, as had both of her brothers. Of the three matches, two had ended in desolation and the third—successful as it appeared thus far—was just a few months old. She avoided love for the same reason she eschewed spirits: she'd witnessed, firsthand, the ravages of both.

"I have so many plans, so much work to do," she said. Striving for a diplomatic tone, she added, "And I've noticed love has a way of altering a person's priorities."

"As well it should, if the thing's done right," Gray said.

Sophia touched her wrist. "Of course you could not be in love with Toby so soon. But deep in your heart, if you search, do you detect some inclination to affection? Could you grow to love him, with time?"

I hope not. Bel pushed back from the table and stood. "Sophia, please understand. I am delighted that you and my brother have found one another. I know you mean to be kind. But I do not wish to marry for love; and I would ask you to consider that perhaps Sir Toby feels the same. Otherwise, why did he propose to you?"

Sophia made a subtle wince. Bel's was overt. Those were the most uncharitable words she'd ever spoken to her sister. Perhaps the most uncharitable words she'd spoken to anyone. But here she'd resolved to embrace this engagement with optimism, and Sophia seemed determined to ruin it all—first with her revelations, then her stack of scandal sheets, and now this questioning.

"Please," Bel said, sinking back into her chair, "I know you mean well, but Dolly . . ." She turned to her brother, knowing he was powerless to deny her anything when she employed a soft tone and his pet name from their youth. "Dolly, you promised I might marry whom I choose. I choose to marry Sir Toby."

"For God's sake, why?"

"For . . . several reasons."

Not because she desired him, or because she'd allowed him to kiss her on the terrace.

Truly, that wasn't it at all. It wasn't.

"I want a marriage that will place me in the public notice and make me a lady of influence." She gestured toward the stacked copies of *The Prattler*. "Sir Toby is perfect. All London takes an interest his exploits, he will soon serve in the House of Commons, and by Sophia's own account he is a fine man."

"Toby told you he would be serving in Parliament?" Sophia asked.

"Yes. Did he never mention it to you?"

"No." She looked stunned.

Gray studied Bel for a moment, then put a hand to his temple. "Bel, it's not that I—"

The sound of the doorbell interrupted them.

"That must be him." Bel stood up again. Blood rushed to her head. Goodness, she'd been up and down so many times, she might as well have been in church. "Do I look well enough?" She smoothed her hands over the skirt of her best day dress, a pale blue muslin frock trimmed with ivory lace.

"Bel, you are stunning, as always. You'll take his breath away." Ignoring Gray's harrumph, Sophia took one bite of her toast and then set it aside. "Shall I come with you to greet him?"

"No," Gray said in a tone of finality. "Bel, kindly go up to the nursery and ask Joss to meet me in my study. If Sir Toby Aldridge wants a glimpse of either of the breathtaking beauties in this house, he'll have to get through me."

"Sir Benedict." Upon entering Grayson's study, Toby made a courteous bow.

His gesture was not reciprocated. The brute narrowed his eyes at him. "Let's not waste time pretending to like one another."

Toby straightened and set his jaw. "Fine with me."

"And call me Gray." Gray indicated a chair as he rounded the desk to settle in his own. "Everyone does, even my enemies."

Toby smiled as he smoothed his trousers and took his seat. "Isabel doesn't. She calls you Dolly."

Instantly, the tension in the room leapt to a new plateau. Gray's narrowed eyes became slits. Then he leaned back in his chair and gave Toby a cold smile. "I've been curious to meet you, Sir Toby Aldridge."

"And I, you. *Gray*."

"It's an interesting position I'm in." Gray ran a fingertip along the edge of his blotter. "I wonder if you can appreciate it. Here before me sits the man who let a remarkable, beautiful woman slip through his fingers last December. I revile you for that idiocy; yet I must also thank you for it. Your mistake was my good fortune."

"My discretion is your good fortune."

Their gazes locked.

"Yes," Gray finally said, "I'm aware of that. But just when I am determined that I must push aside my extreme loathing for an otherwise contemptible ass and express some gratitude"—he suddenly shot to his feet and strode to the window—"the contemptible ass manages to seduce my baby sister."

"Now see here," Toby said coolly. "You may have all the contempt for me you wish, but there is only one seducer in this room. You're the blackguard who absconded with my intended bride. At least I'm here offering for Isabel properly. Honorably. Do you seriously expect me to grovel and plead for the dubious pleasure of becoming your brother?"

Gray turned from the window. "I already have a brother. I don't need another."

"Well, then one wonders why you are bringing your

sister out. It would prove difficult to marry Isabel off without acquiring one." Toby ran a hand through his hair. "Can a man get a drink in this house?"

"A drink? Before noon?" Gray crossed to the bar and uncorked a bottle. "Well, there's one point in your favor." He handed Toby a snifter of brandy and started pouring another for himself. "The papers have a lot to say about you."

"They have a lot to say about you, too," Toby said, thinking of the exalted praise England's newest knight had enjoyed over past weeks. "I know better than to believe them. You're quite the hero, Gray. Tell me, while you were braving fire, storm, sharks, and smugglers to rescue that boatload of helpless kittens and schoolgirls . . . was it a two-headed sea serpent you wrestled into submission? Or did it have three heads?"

"Four," Gray said coolly. "Well then, let's get to the heart of the matter, shall we? May I assume you know how I rebuilt my family's fortune and amassed the generous dowry you would waltz away with in the course of an evening?"

"Privateering, I understand."

"Yes, privateering. Sanctioned piracy. I'm a respectable shipping merchant now, but I've years of cheating, stealing, and bloodshed in my past. I don't like violence, but I'm not above it. I sank ships and spilled men's blood, all so my brother might have a profession and Bel could marry well. We may be of different mothers, but we are all Graysons, all family." Gray drained his brandy and sent the glass clattering to his desk. Then he crossed his arms over his chest and fixed Toby with an intense glare. "Family is everything to me. If you hurt my sister, I will gleefully kill you."

Toby paused. He had no doubt in his mind that Gray meant that threat. Not only meant it, but would make good on it, even if doing so sent him to the gallows and they ended up sharing a hackney to hell. "Fortunately for my neck and yours, I've no intention of hurting Isabel," he said smoothly. "I'm going to marry her."

Gray shook his head. "At most, you're engaged to her. Engagements can be broken."

Oh no, he didn't. Not again. Toby would be damned if he'd let this man break up his second betrothal. "Listen, what's done is done. You wanted to make a public scene at Kendall House last night, and you got your wish. Now your sister and I are quite publicly engaged. There's no way to undo it without tarnishing her reputation. Not to mention, disappointing her hopes."

Gray regarded him closely. "Are you certain? You seem rather invested in bachelorhood, by all accounts. You wouldn't be interested in a nice, long holiday on the Continent instead? A thousand pounds can buy a fellow rather warm hospitality."

Toby stared at him. "You're attempting to bribe me. With a bit of gold and a few Parisian *galettes* as inducement. For God's sake, man, I've a vast estate in Surrey and an income of six thousand a year. Your 'offer' insults us both. Does your sister know what a cheap price you place on her happiness?"

"There is no price I would not pay for Bel's happiness. I've made achieving her happiness my life's work."

"Well, now I'll be taking over that job." Toby smiled and relaxed in his chair. He was enjoying watching Gray sweat. He'd been just a youth when his own sisters married, but he'd already been the man of the family—and he remembered well the helpless ire that accompanied surrendering one's sister to a stranger. Gray had his empathy, but not his mercy. "You're clearly not up to the task. If your sister were happy in her current situation, why would she jump to marry the first gentleman to pay her a bit of attention? She was miserable at that ball last night, until I put a smile on her face. I know how to keep a lady happy."

"Really?" Gray smirked. "I don't think my wife would agree."

Oh, now that was a low blow. And a damaging one. Toby's arrogance took a sizeable dent. It still plagued him late at night, the ceaseless speculation. He'd treated Sophia with solicitude, patience, and, of course, copious charm. What could he have done to push her away, and into the arms of this rogue? She had not even received him today, in her own home.

Gray continued, "Bel is not like other young ladies."

"Yes, well. I had noticed that." All thoughts of Sophia were instantly banished. He thought instead of Isabel's exotic beauty and her melodic accent, and the bold innocence of her kiss. The kiss that hummed in his blood, even now . . .

"That's not what I mean." Gray skewered him with a look, as though he read Toby's thoughts. "Bel's grown up sheltered from society, but she's been a witness to misery no lady should ever see. Our father succumbed to drink and her mother to madness, while—"

"Wait just a minute. Her mother went mad?" If he did want an excuse to back out of this, Toby had just been handed one. Few gentlemen sought a bride with a family history of insanity.

"Not how you're thinking. When Bel was a girl, her mother was stricken with a tropical fever. She survived— barely—but her mind was never the same. Bel grew up essentially alone, once my brother and I were out on the sea. Her faith sustained her. She's strong in spirit, but filled with naïve, fragile hopes . . . and very high expectations."

"You don't think I can meet them."

"Damn right, I don't." Gray resumed his seat. "However, for the sake of humoring my sister and preserving her reputation, I've decided to let you try. But I warn you—if at any point during the engagement, Bel seems anything less than enraptured with the prospect of marrying you, I'll call the wedding off immediately."

His words gave Toby pause, as he recalled the lengths he'd gone to just to elicit those few smiles. Now he would have an "enraptured" bride, or no bride at all? He wasn't sure he liked those odds. Isabel Grayson did not seem a lady inclined to romantic raptures—she'd only agreed to marry him for his influence. "If you've such a low opinion of me, why are granting your consent at all?"

"Make no mistake, I think you're an ass, and it eats away at my gut, just to imagine calling you brother. But I'd take no pleasure in seeing you fail at betrothal again." Gray scowled. It was the expression of a man wrestling his own humility. "Bel's been disappointed with London, despite all our efforts to keep her entertained. Nothing amuses her. She's so damned quiet, so serious. I've watched her frowning in silence through a dozen dinner parties and musicales. But when she danced with you— and God, it kills me to say it—she looked happy. And then this morning, she spoke angry words to Sophia in your defense." Gray shook his head. "I've never heard her speak angry words to anyone. Reproachful words, yes. Disappointed words, more often than I care to remember. But never angry ones."

Toby couldn't quite follow the gist of this argument. She was happy last night, angry this morning . . . "What are you saying?"

"I'm saying, I think my sister's built quite a fortress around her emotions. She'd call it morality; I'm inclined to call it fear. But whatever those walls are made of, for some unfathomable reason, you seem able to breach them. I'm saying, you managed to put a smile on her face last night." He pinned Toby with a threatening look. "Keep it there."

"I will," Toby answered, resolute. Indeed, never in his life had he been so determined to succeed at any venture. It was what he did best, keeping ladies smiling. He would find a way to keep Isabel happy, too. There was nothing in the world that could have convinced him to back down from the challenge in Sir Benedict Grayson's eyes. Nothing.

A knock sounded at the door.

"Come in," Gray called, rising to his feet. "That'll be my brother, Joss."

Toby stood, refreshing his grin and readying a bow. Perhaps the younger Grayson brother would be more congenial. Second sons typically had very different personalities.

"Sir Toby Aldridge," Gray said, "allow me to introduce my brother and partner in Grayson Brothers Shipping, Captain Josiah Grayson."

Well, Toby thought, he'd been right. The brothers were certainly different. Gray had told him the Grayson siblings were born of different mothers, but Toby had been expecting a brother who was half-Spanish, like Isabel. Not one who was half-African, like . . . like scarcely anyone he knew, save servants. Certainly like no one to whom he'd ever bowed.

Toby felt himself the object of keen scrutiny as he stared into Joss's face—a darker copy of his brother's. Begrudgingly, he conceded a silent point to Gray. The bastard had certainly played this card well. Or, rather, he'd played the bastard card well. There was no way Toby could register surprise now. Not when he'd just wagered his pride and self-respect against Isabel Grayson's happiness.

"Captain Grayson. A pleasure." Smile frozen in place,

Toby made a smooth bow. There, that hadn't been so difficult.

"Sir Toby." Joss returned the bow. "I'd say the pleasure is mine, but I have an unfortunate habit of honesty, I'm afraid."

Unfortunate indeed. This Grayson brother was not more congenial than the first. He was less. It was plain to see there was a plank-sized chip on Joss's shoulder, balanced by the weight of general ill humor on the other. A right surly fellow, if ever Toby had met one. Just bloody perfect.

"You're really going to allow this?" Joss spoke to Gray, making a dismissive gesture in Toby's direction. "After one evening, you're going to let Bel marry this ass?"

"I'm going to let her remain engaged to this ass," Gray corrected. "For now. We'll see if she still feels the same, come September."

"September?" Toby echoed. "It's barely April. Six weeks is ample time for an engagement. We'll be married in May."

"August."

"June."

"July, or not at all," Gray said. "That's my final concession."

We'll see about that.

Catching Toby's frown, Joss raised an eyebrow. "By all means, press your case further. 'Not at all' is my preference."

Toby kept his indignant retort to himself. What a family. A dandified footpad playing patriarch, seconded by his disagreeable bastard brother. But no matter. Their mutual loathing would only sweeten Toby's triumph. To win Isabel, he could stomach far worse.

And of course, just as he'd formed the thought, along came worse.

"Papa, Papa!"

A tawny-skinned urchin with close-cropped hair barreled into the room, heading straight for the brothers but colliding instead with Toby's leg. The child went sprawling to the carpet, first scuffing the shine on Toby's boot, then attacking the offending boot in retaliation, to the point of sinking his teeth into the fine-grained leather.

"Ah!" Toby struggled for balance, attempting to shake the little demon off his leg. His efforts only resulted in encouraging the boy to cling more tightly, lashing his arms and legs around Toby's ankle until he seemed a more permanent part of the boot than the tassel. The imp even had the nerve to laugh.

God only knew which brother's indiscretion this boy represented. Neither man rushed to claim him, presumably too amused by Toby's predicament to help.

"Jacob, no!" Isabel flew into the room, coming to land at Toby's feet in a flutter of pale-blue muslin and lace. "Oh, I'm so sorry," she said, attempting to disentangle the child from Toby's leg. "I told the nursemaid I'd take him down to the garden, but then he dashed away from me, and I couldn't—"

"It's all right," Toby said, placing a light touch on her shoulder. "I've ten young nieces and nephews. Really, it's all right." She ceased struggling with the boy and looked up at him.

And the grasping child, the insolent brothers, the world around them—simply ceased to exist.

Moonlight did not begin to do her beauty justice, Toby realized. Isabel Grayson was made for the morning sun. Gentle, warm light that was in no rush, that had the entire day ahead of itself, that labored patiently to illuminate each glossy strand of her hair, each golden contour of her features, the petal-soft texture of her lips. And when coupled with the radiance that emanated from within— there was no other word for it.

She glowed.

"Sir Toby," she said, her expression aggrieved. "My nephew . . . I beg your pardon."

"Please, don't distress yourself." He hooked a hand under her elbow to help her to her feet. She really needed to stand. Once he'd finished his appraisal of her beauty above the neck, it was all too easy to let his gaze descend to where her lace-trimmed neckline gaped, offering a view of lush, full breasts and the dark, enticing valley between them. Toby ceased seeing features and began seeing . . . possibilities.

Yes, she truly needed to stand.

"Jacob." The deep command from Joss had the instantaneous effect of loosening the child's grip. A moment later, circulation resumed in Toby's toes.

"Your son?" Toby asked Joss.

Joss nodded in confirmation.

"Delightful child. And did his mother travel with you to London?"

"No, my wife remained on Tortola," Joss said. "In the churchyard."

Right. A surly, illegitimate widower. The man's ill humor began to make sense.

"Come to Auntie Bel, darling." Rescuing them all from the awkwardness of the moment, Isabel scooped the child into her arms, jutting out one hip to make a seat for him, all the while tickling the squirming bundle of mischief. She had the look of an early Renaissance Madonna: dark, radiant, rounded and soft, serene in the face of squalling infants, and beautiful to an unearthly degree.

A strange compulsion gripped Toby. Sank teeth into him. Before him stood this living portrait of divine domesticity, and in some deep corner of his being, he longed to be a part of it. He'd never experienced a need so sudden, so visceral, so strong. He couldn't even put a name to the sensation. It wasn't desire, lust, infatuation, attraction . . . it most certainly wasn't love. But it still distilled to those three simple words:

I want that.

A wife. A child. All the pleasant activities a man enjoyed with his wife in the getting of a child. Months of anticipating the arrival of said child—wondering if the shade of his hair would be black like his mother's or light brown like Toby's or some shade in the spectrum between. New boots fashioned in cured leather, resistant to the impressions of milk teeth. Marriage. Family. A smiling Isabel.

I want that.

And I'm going to have it.

Isabel blushed. "I'm so sorry for the intrusion. We'll leave you to your conversation," she said, dipping in a little curtsy.

"No," Toby blurted out, snapping himself from his reverie. "That is, don't go. After all, it's you I've come to see. I thought perhaps you'd like to go driving." When she looked nonplussed, he added, "It's something betrothed couples do."

"Oh." She gave him a shy smile. "Then I'd like that."

Toby looked to Gray and Joss. "I believe we've finished our business here, gentlemen?" They offered begrudging nods. "Oh," Toby continued, speaking to Isabel, "there was one thing. We were discussing the wedding date. I suggest July. Never mind the unbearable heat in July. The only reason to be married in June is to make a public splash, to have all of Society watching. In July, many of the good families will already be leaving for the countryside, and the guest list will be smaller. Your brother need not incur so much expense. This is my reasoning . . . but naturally, Isabel, your own preference is paramount."

"Why, if the decision is mine, I think I should prefer to

be married in June." Allowing young Jacob to slide to the floor, she turned to her brother. "I'm certain Dolly is not concerned with the expense."

Toby shot Gray a cold smile. "Well, Dolly, are you concerned for the expense?"

"No, of course not. But—"

Toby captured Isabel's hand and tucked it into his arm. "Then I gladly make the concession. June it is."

CHAPTER
FIVE

An hour later, Bel feared she would not live out the day, much less survive to see June.

"Well, then." Sir Toby nestled closer on the phaeton seat. "This is a lovely morning."

Bel managed a slight nod in agreement. It was all the motion she dared venture. With one hand latched to the seat iron, the other gripping her bonnet, and both feet braced against the footboard, she had no free appendage with which to gesture. And as for speaking . . . speaking was out of the question. She kept her jaw clenched, lest her teeth rattle loose from her skull as Sir Toby urged the horses faster over the cobblestones. When they rounded the bend at a perilous tilt, she did manage a little sound. Unfortunately, it was less of a word and more of a scream.

"What's the matter?" Turning to face her, he took the reins in one hand and stretched the other arm along the seat behind her. "Are you well?"

The phaeton bounced over a small rut, tossing Bel off-balance. Before she could catch herself, she had fallen against his side. His arm enfolded her shoulders, drawing her tight against his chest.

Whistling through his teeth, he slowed the horses and pulled the carriage to the side of the street. "Isabel, darling, are you ill?"

"N-no . . ." Bel fought to recover her breath. The carriage had come to a halt, but her world remained in motion. She was dizzy—not only from that terrifying drive, but now from the sensation of his strong body wrapped so protectively around hers. "I'm not ill, it's only . . . I'm unaccustomed to driving like this, that's all. We don't have such fast carriages and fine teams on Tortola. It's a small island." She sat up a bit, placing her hand between them on the seat as a buffer.

"What a dolt I am. I should have realized. And look, you've gone all pale." He removed his hat and began fanning her with it. "Shall I take you back home?"

"No. No, please don't. Truly, I am perfectly well now." Bel readjusted her bonnet.

"Are you certain?"

"Yes, I'm very certain." The concern in Toby's amber-flecked eyes pleased her. Sophia had been right. He would make a kind, solicitous husband. "I don't mean to complain. It's a lovely phaeton." She ran a hand over the tufted, butter-soft leather.

At his soft command, the horses resumed a sedate walk. "We needn't continue driving at all," he said. "Why don't we leave the phaeton with a groom and have a stroll about the shops?"

"The shops? I suppose we could, but I don't have need of anything. Do you?"

He laughed. "Why, that's the very time to visit the shops—when you don't need anything. To be truthful, however, I have been thinking of buying a new walking stick. I've had my eye on a fine ivory-topped one at Brauchts'."

"A walking stick? Do you have some injury, then?" Bel surreptitiously eyed his legs. They looked fit enough to her, his well-formed thighs and calves sheathed in tailored wool. She flushed and quickly averted her eyes. Yes, his legs looked well indeed. "Or perhaps you suffer from the gout?"

"The gout?" He laughed again, louder this time. "No,

I have not lived such an immoderate life as to develop the gout at the age of nine-and-twenty. Nor have I suffered any injury, save that small one to my pride just now."

"Oh. Then why do you need a walking stick, if you are not infirm?"

"Why, no particular reason. They come in handy from time to time—for gesturing toward sights of interest, rapping on doors, signaling the coachman . . ." He shrugged. "And they look fine. It's the fashion."

"I see," she said, frowning. "So this is the way you wish to spend our morning? Shopping for this . . . this embellished stick, which a perfectly healthy gentleman carries around, for no real purpose other than to indicate his wealth?"

His expression sobered. "Well, that and gesturing," he said slowly. "Don't forget gesturing. And rapping on doors. There's that, too."

Bel had no response. Actually, she would have liked to respond that arms and hands generally worked well for her in those regards, but she had no wish to upset him further.

"Right, well." He gave her a tight smile. "We'll do the shops another day, then. Are you fond of art? Shall I take you to an exhibition?"

Bel perked up. Her appreciation for art had increased under Sophia's influence, as her sister-in-law was an accomplished painter. "Thank you, I would like that very much."

"Excellent." He leaned closer and whispered, "I'll arrange a real treat for you. I've a friend who can get us a private showing of the Parthenon marbles."

"The sculptures Lord Elgin brought back from Greece?"

"Yes, the very ones."

"The ones Parliament just purchased on behalf of the English government?"

"Why . . . yes." He looked askance at her, obviously confused by the brittle tone of her remark.

But Bel could not help herself. Useless walking sticks were one thing, but there was no holding her tongue on this matter. "Sir Toby, do you not realize Lord Elgin stole those statues from their rightful owners, the Greeks? And now Parliament has squandered millions of pounds to purchase them, while hardworking English farmers have not the corn to seed their fields, and orphaned children starve in the streets? It is a travesty!"

He pulled the team to a halt. "So . . ." His lips pursed around the drawn out syllable. "You don't wish to see them?"

She couldn't believe he would even ask! *"No."*

An awkward minute passed. Embarrassed by her outburst but unable to apologize for it, Bel faced forward and made a show of straightening her gloves. She could feel Toby's eyes on her all the while. Eventually, the phaeton lurched into motion again.

Oh, he must think her inexcusably rude. Here he had suggested two different amusements, and she had refused them both. And with intemperate scoldings, no less. Bel made up her mind then and there to greet his next suggestion with polite enthusiasm, whatever it might be.

"There's Berkeley Square just up ahead. Can I offer you some refreshment?"

Bel clapped her hands together and forced a bright tone. "Yes, thank you. That would be delightful." Her breakfast had been cut short, after all. A spot of tea would be most welcome.

He maneuvered the carriage into the green in the center of the square, drawing the team to a halt beneath the shade of a large tree. Alighting from the phaeton, he tossed the reins and a coin to an eager boy, then beckoned a waiter from the establishment across the street.

The two men conferred briefly, and then the waiter returned to the tea shop.

Wearing a renewed smile, Toby strolled around to Bel's side of the carriage. "There we are. Give it a moment, he'll have a lovely treat out for you."

"Shouldn't we go inside?"

"Oh, no." He tossed his hat on the phaeton seat. "It's not the done thing. The ladies all take their refreshment out here, in the square, where they can see and be seen."

Bel folded her hands. She knew it would be impossible to become a lady of influence without attracting public notice; and one did not attract public notice without a certain amount of spectacle—whether that spectacle involved sipping tea in a flashy carriage or selecting an infamous rake for a husband. So long as she reminded herself it was all for a purpose, she could justify the indulgence.

Or so she thought.

The waiter appeared, bearing a tray with a glass dish. In the dish sat something that looked like a child's ball— perfectly round, pale yellow in color, and sparkling in the morning sun.

"How lovely," she said, accepting the proffered dish and a small silver spoon. She looked to Toby. "What is it?"

"Why, it's an ice, of course. Gunter's is famous for them. That's a sample of their newest flavor: lemon and lavender."

"An ice," she said wonderingly. The chill of the glass dish nipped at her gloved fingers. "I've never had one. Nothing freezes in the West Indies, you know. Until we arrived in London, I'd never seen ice of any sort, much less one flavored with lemon and lavender." She prodded the treat with her spoon, breaking through a thin, granular crust to discover a softer, creamy texture beneath.

"You'd best eat it quickly. Or it won't be an ice much longer, but only a syrup."

Bel looked up. "Is that how it's sweetened, then? With sugar?"

"Why, yes. It's sweet and cold, and . . ." He gave her a teasing grin. "And you could discover that for yourself, if you'd only have a taste."

Her spoon hovered over the pale yellow ball. Beads of dew formed on the ice's surface and rolled down to pool in the shallow glass bowl. Bel's mouth watered, but she pushed the dish back at him. "I'm so sorry. I can't."

"You can't?"

She shook her head, feeling indescribably ill-mannered for refusing yet another of his gestures. But of all the things for him to suggest, why did he have to suggest this?

"Why not?" He looked her up and down. "Please don't tell me you're concerned for your figure."

Her face burned, and she dropped her eyes. To be sure, he would have noticed her ample figure. She'd learned some years ago that her body drew men's notice, whether she wished it or not. And she did not. Bel was extremely self-conscious about the voluptuous curves she'd inherited from her mother—over-large breasts, wide hips.

Though she had no wish to see those curves increase, they weren't the reason she declined the ice. "I don't eat sugar," she explained. "Not unless it is imported by my brothers' company."

"Why not?"

"Because the sugar my brothers import is grown and harvested by free men." She cast a pointed look at the ice. "*That* is likely the product of slave labor."

Toby studied the growing puddle of lemon. "Darling, that Quaker sugar boycott—it went out with my grandmother's generation. The slave trade was abolished more than a decade ago."

"The slave *trade* was abolished, yes. But slavery itself remains legal and is still the practice in nearly all sugar-producing countries." Bel clutched the seat iron with one hand, trying to keep a grip on her emotions. "You would offer this to me as refreshment? Tell me, what is refreshing about human bondage?"

"I don't know. I suppose . . . That is to say . . ." He shrugged. "It's only an ice."

They stared at one another then, in exquisitely painful silence. Bel started to wonder if she'd made a very grave mistake. Of course, the entire engagement had been a mistake, but she'd hoped it not an irredeemable one. Toby's infamous reputation would be of benefit in her quest to raise public consciousness, she'd reasoned. But rakishness was one thing, and oppression was another. *It's only an ice.*

Of course, she reminded herself—to him, it *was* only an ice. He didn't look at it and see the misery of a thousand souls served up in a chilled glass dish, as she did. He didn't know any of those thousand souls by name, as she did.

Toby lifted an eyebrow. "It's just going to melt, if you don't eat it. It will go to waste."

Bel sighed. He was right, there was no way to undo the injustice committed in the ice's creation. Still, she shook her head. "I couldn't possibly."

"Then you shan't." Toby handed the dish to the young boy tending the horses. "Here, lad. Have at it."

"Truly, sir? You mean for me to eat it?" A dirt-smeared hand closed around the dish.

"Yes, cert—" Before Toby could even make his assurances, the boy had devoured half the dish's contents. Wielding the spoon like a garden trowel, he ate greedily, as if the treat might disappear on its own, if he didn't work fast. The boy's enthusiasm was infectious, and Bel could not suppress a small laugh.

She suddenly realized Toby was watching her closely.

"Now you're smiling. Thank God. I was becoming a bit desperate there."

"I'm so sorry. I know you meant to be kind, but truly— I could not have enjoyed the ice."

"Yet you can enjoy the boy's enjoyment of it."

"Yes," she said slowly, though she didn't know how to explain. Growing up as she had, she'd been acutely aware that every pleasure or convenience she enjoyed—a clean shift, a warm bath, a cool drink—came at the expense of another person's dignity. But viewing someone else's pleasure felt different. Safer. Last night, she'd liked watching the dancers far more than she'd liked dancing. Today, she could not enjoy eating the ice, but she could enjoy the boy's expression of innocent delight.

Bel tried to make sense of it, but the logic knotted in her mind. Biting her lip, she asked, "Does that make me a terrible hypocrite?"

"Not at all." Gently, he unfolded her fingers from the seat iron. She hadn't even realized she was still clutching the metal rail. His eyes warmed as he kissed her gloved fingers. "It makes you a selfless, generous angel. And it makes me wonder how I will ever deserve you."

Oh, and now a sweet, viscous emotion puddled in her belly. So rich, so indulgent, it made her feel a bit ill.

"You've given me an idea," he said.

"I have?"

"Yes. An inspiration, more like." He released her hand, then summoned the teashop waiter with a subtle nod. Bel watched as the two men conferred quietly. Then Toby returned to his side of the phaeton and vaulted into the seat. "I have in mind an amusement, which I am positive will bring you great enjoyment. But it requires us to drive fast. Can you bear it?"

Oh dear. Anticipation gleamed bright in his eyes, and Bel could not bring herself to dim it. She gave a brave nod and once again latched her fingers over the seat iron.

"No, no," he said, glancing at her two-fisted grip as he

gathered the reins. "You'll only feel more jounced about that way. Best to hold onto my arm."

He offered his elbow, and Bel stared at it. "If you insist . . ."

"I do."

She threaded one arm through his, linking her hands around his upper arm. The waiter emerged from the teashop bearing a large hamper, which Toby directed him to secure behind the phaeton seat. Then, with a clipped word from their master, the horses jolted into motion. Bel clutched at Toby's arm as they turned out into the street. His muscles flexed under her fingers, and a thrill shot through her.

"Are you well?" he shouted, urging the horses faster.

"Yes," she managed in a weak voice. When collision with an approaching barouche seemed imminent, Bel suppressed a cry of alarm and clamped her eyes shut.

Oh, this was much better in the dark.

He was right. The jolts of the carriage felt less pronounced now that she gripped his arm rather than the metal frame. Leaning into him, she endeavored to make her body pliant, weightless. Soon she learned how a small flex of his arm or shift of his weight preceded any alteration in course. The easy command he displayed soothed her concern, as did the familiar, sophisticated scent of his cologne. Yet they also stirred her, in some deep, undeniably feminine way. The more she became aware of his strength, the more her own body softened in response. She coasted along with the rocking motions of the carriage, the fear in her belly replaced by a new sensation . . . a dark, sweet hunger that built and built.

"We're here," he announced, drawing the team to a halt.

Surely we're not, thought Bel, feeling a profound sense of interruption. Wherever this wave of sensation was carrying her, she couldn't possibly be more than halfway along.

She opened her eyes. A forbidding brick-and-stone façade rose up before them. "What is this place?"

"It's Dr. David's dispensary for children." He tossed the reins to a groom and slid down from the seat. "Quickly now," he said, hurrying around to help her down.

Puzzled, she watched him beckon a manservant from the dispensary's entrance. Together, the men worked to unstrap the hamper from the back of the carriage.

Toby grabbed her by the wrist, pulling her toward the entrance. "Hurry along. We don't want it to melt."

Bel followed him, mute with confusion, as they entered a cool, ceramic-tiled foyer and made a sharp left. Behind them, the manservant trotted to keep up, bearing the hamper.

"This way, then." Toby led them up a twisting flight of stairs and down a narrow corridor. A variety of unpleasant scents battled for prominence: sickness, laudanum, vinegar. Finally they emerged into a narrow ward lined with small beds on either side. In each bed lay a pale-faced, wide-eyed waif, frozen in an unnatural attitude of innocence. They wore the smug expressions of children interrupted in the midst of an illicit game and quite satisfied with their success at concealing it.

At Toby's direction, the servant began opening the hamper. Toby strode to the center of the room, clapping his hands. "All right, children. Time for medicine."

A chorus of groans rose up from the beds. A thin voice protested, "We already had our medicine!"

"Ah, yes. But this is a different medicine. Especially ordered by your new nurse, Miss Grayson." He turned to Bel and gave her a frown that she immediately recognized as an exaggerated mirror of her own expression. "Don't worry, I know she looks stern. But I promise, she's soft as kittens inside." He went to the hamper and pushed aside a layer of straw, then a sheet of waxed parchment. Inside, rows of pastel ices glistened like jewels. Toby lifted out two frosted glass dishes and held them out to Bel. "Here," he whispered. "Enjoy yourself."

Impossible man. Surely these children had other, more urgent needs he might have addressed, rather than spending money on this extravagant treat: bandages, linens, nourishing food, *real* medicine. But just like the children, he looked so pleased with his own mischief. And so handsome besides. Smiling, she took the ices from his hands.

"There's my girl," he said, giving her a little wink. A correspondingly girlish thrill swept through her. Turning, he called to the room, "Who likes strawberry?"

The resulting clamor persisted for a good quarter hour, as the ices were distributed and demolished by the eager children. Bel seated herself at the bedside of a spindly-limbed boy sporting bandages on both arms, feeding him spoonfuls of apricot-flavored ice. The rapturous expression on his face warmed her heart.

Toby joined her, sitting on the other side of the boy's bed. "Well? Are you enjoying yourself?"

"You know I am. Thank you."

"This ward houses the children who are nearly ready to be released. Perhaps next time we'll visit some of the truly miserable ones. You'll be in perfect ecstasy, I predict."

Bel looked back at the bandaged child. He had fallen asleep, a cherubic smile on his face. "Peter Jeffers, aged nine, ward of Charlesbridge-Crewe Chimney Sweeps," she read from a slate tacked to the boy's headboard. "Aged nine? Why, he looks no more than five or six!"

"Underfed, most likely. Climbing boys have to be thin, or they won't fit up the flues."

"Up the flues? Whatever do you mean, up the flues?"

"I suppose they don't burn coal in the West Indies?"

She shook her head.

"Well, these boys, they climb up the chimneys with brushes to remove the soot. The flues are narrow and often clogged, so it's dangerous work. This one must have suffered some burns."

Bel noted the bandages on the boy's forearms, and on his elbows above them, gnarled calluses with the texture of gravel. Observing the old, yellowed bruise on the child's jaw, she whispered, "Not only burned, but beaten too." She shut her eyes, imagining the horror of being wedged into a soot-clogged chimney two bricks wide. "And when he is healed, he will be released again to his employers? Only to be injured again, or maimed or killed? Can nothing be done?"

"There's a society, with a ridiculously long name, devoted to replacing the climbing boys with modern machinery. My sister Augusta is a member, but thus far I think they have met with little success. Climbing boys are the traditional method of cleaning flues, and we English do cling to our traditions."

"Traditions." Bel spat the word. "Abominations, more like."

"Shhh." Toby tilted his head toward the boy, who stirred in his sleep. "You'll wake him."

Bel pressed her lips together, fuming in silence.

He stared at her for a moment, then leaned toward her across the bed. "Do you know," he whispered, "that you're uncommonly beautiful when you're angry?"

Bel sniffed. What a time for trite compliments. "I'm not angry."

"Ah, but you admit to being beautiful. Very good."

"That's not what I meant!" Cringing, she lowered her voice. "I do not admit to being beautiful, either." Possessed of a provocative figure, perhaps. But not beautiful.

"Come now. If you will not admit to beauty, I must accuse you of dishonesty."

"I am not dis—" She frowned and narrowed her eyes at him. "Are you teasing me?"

"Yes."

"Why?"

"You've gone so serious again. It's as though the misery of the world settles on your shoulders. If I don't tease you, I shall have to kiss you." He flashed her a sly grin. "And we don't want to shock the children."

Bel's pulse raced. It was appalling, that he could even think of kissing in a place like this. Worse, now she was thinking of it too. How his lips had felt against hers last night, the flavor of brandy in his kiss. How would he taste if he kissed her this morning? Not of brandy, surely.

What a man she meant to marry—by turns insufferably vain and appallingly shallow, but so charming through it all. And so attractive . . . She'd been disappointed in his vanity earlier, but now Bel gave thanks for Toby's flawed character. She might be plagued by desire for him, but at least she would be in no danger of falling in love.

"How is it you thought to bring me here?" she asked. "Surely most gentlemen don't make it a habit to visit the children's dispensary."

"To be perfectly honest, it's not at all a habit for me. I'm a governor of the facility by virtue of a ten-guinea donation, but I've only been here twice and I never attend the meetings. It's actually my—"

"What is going on here?"

The double doors of the ward flung open. A hush smothered the room. Somewhere, a spoon clattered to the floor.

Bel looked up to see an elegant matron silhouetted in the door. High cheekbones lifted a face creased from decades of smiles, and her brows were thin, graceful sweeps. Her moss-green gown was exquisitely tailored, yet simple in style and topped by a dark-gray cloak and a mantle of extreme self-possession. Even the swish of her garments bespoke confidence as she strode forward to stand at the foot of the bed.

"Sir Tobias Aldridge," she addressed him sternly. "Would you care to explain yourself?"

"Of course," he said smoothly, rising to his feet. Bel followed suit, shaking out her skirt as she stood. "But first, allow me to make the introductions. May I present Miss Isabel Grayson? Isabel, this is Lydia, Lady Aldridge. My mother."

Numb with surprise, Bel made an inelegant curtsy. His mother! Well, of course she supposed she'd be meeting his family soon, but she'd expected to be prepared for the occasion. Did Lady Aldridge have any idea of their engagement? She didn't seem to, judging by the brief, indifferent glance she spared Bel.

"Mother compensates for my inattention as governor," Toby explained. "She comes here every Thursday, when she is in Town."

Bel looked from mother to son. Had this meeting been his entire design in bringing her here? "I'm delighted to make your acquaintance, Lady Aldridge."

Toby reached across the bed and grasped her hand. "Mother, Isabel and I are engaged. We're going to marry in June."

Around them, the children burst into whistles and applause. Bel looked to Lady Aldridge, steeling herself against an outpouring of displeasure.

Lady Aldridge fixed her son with a look of mock reproach. "Toby. You really are impossible." She turned to Bel, eyeing the empty dish in her hand and the sated child sleeping in the bed. "Very well, I approve." She skirted the bed and grasped Bel lightly by the shoulders before placing a kiss on her cheek. "Come to the house for Sunday dinner, dear." She spoke over her shoulder to Toby.

"She can meet Augusta and Reginald if she comes Sunday. Of course, we'll have to arrange a more lavish occasion than roasted chicken to draw Margaret to Town."

"Of course," Toby replied. "Will Fanny and Edgar make it for the wedding, do you think?"

"In June?" Lady Aldridge pursed her lips. "I should think so. The babe will be six months old by then."

Bel watched this mother-son exchange with wonderment. The way they'd forgotten her almost instantly, just gone on discussing family matters as if she weren't even there—it was remarkable. Her gaze fell to the maltreated urchin in the bed, then rose again to Toby's charming, easy grin . . .

And suddenly, she understood.

He simply couldn't know. Toby could view this miserable waif, feel a small, inconvenient twinge of sympathy, and then go on discussing kisses and weddings as if nothing had happened—because nothing of the sort had ever happened, to him. One had only to observe the easy, loving repartee between Toby and his mother to see it. He could not know how it felt, to be a lonely, friendless child. He would never understand what it was, to receive beatings at the hand of a trusted adult—to fear the same person he most loved in the world.

No, Toby's world was Sunday dinners with Augusta and Reginald, newborn babies with two living parents, and an efficient, gracious mother who smelled of lavender and dispensed warm kisses, never blows.

And neither he nor his mother could realize the small miracle that had just occurred, when they'd invited Bel to join them. To come by the house Sunday and dine on roast chicken, served up with dishes more exotic and tempting than any flavored ice: stability, affection, normalcy.

For the first time, Bel realized marriage meant more than choosing a husband. It meant acquiring a family.

How unexpected. How . . . wonderful.

Toby's hand squeezed hers. "Are you well, darling?"

"Yes, of course." She forced a smile. "Just . . . a bit surprised."

Lady Aldridge patted her cheek, as if she knew how much Bel craved a maternal touch. "Oh, I know we can be overwhelming at first. You'll grow accustomed to it."

"I'm certain I will." Bel cleared her throat. "I'm so gratified to see the good work you do here, at the dispensary. Might I accompany you on your weekly visits?"

"Isabel is devoted to charity," Toby said.

"Well, of course she is." Lady Aldridge gave her son a beatific smile. "She's marrying you."

CHAPTER
SIX

"Will you take more chicken, Isabel?"

Toby gave the nearest footman a significant look. The servant immediately extended a liveried sleeve toward the domed platter.

Isabel warned him off with a little shake of her head. "Thank you, no. I am quite satisfied."

"Are you certain?" Lady Aldridge asked. "You've been having dinner with us for weeks now, and you seem to grow a bit thinner every Sunday." She turned to Toby. "You must be certain she's eating properly. It won't do to have her fainting dead away in the middle of your wedding ceremony."

"No, of course not." His sister Augusta smiled. "Imagine what the papers would say then."

Across the table, her husband laughed. "Yes, our Mr. Hollyhurst would have great sport with that one, after what happened the last time. Betrothal to Toby would be declared a public health concern, on par with smallpox."

"Watch yourself, Reginald," Toby said, giving his brother-in-law a look of limited forbearance.

"Perhaps I will take a bit more." Isabel extended her plate, and the footman served her another helping. "Thank you, Jamison."

As Bel ate, Toby studied his intended bride for any signs of embarrassment. He found none. Amazing, how easily she'd fallen into the pattern of their family life. Most ladies would have been mortified to have their health or eating habits questioned in company, but Isabel never appeared to mind Lady Aldridge's presumptive mothering or Reginald's brash humor. She seemed only eager to become a part of the family madness, teasing and all. She even knew the footmen by name.

No, he noted no flush of humiliation or displeasure. But his mother was right, Isabel did look a trifle pale. Heart-stoppingly beautiful, as always. But pale.

"Perhaps you're overtired," he said, taking the excuse to stroke the underside of her wrist. Her skin was so soft there. "Between the wedding preparations and your weekly visits to the dispensary, and then those meetings with Augusta's Society of the Ridiculously Long Name . . ."

"It's not so long," his older sister protested. "It's the Society for Obviating the Necessity of Climbing Boys."

"Come now, that's not even all of it." Reginald forked a small potato into his mouth. "Toby's right, it goes on and on. It's a wonder you accomplish any business at those meetings. Once the name has been read aloud for the record, it must be time to adjourn. What is it, the Society for Obviating the Necessity of Climbing Boys, By Encouraging a New Method of Sweeping Chimneys and for Improving the Condition of Children, and so on and so on ad infinitum . . ."

Augusta gave her husband a sharp look. "I refuse to be lectured on verbosity by England's most long-winded barrister."

"Whatever the name," Toby interjected, "perhaps Isabel ought to leave off attending the meetings and the dispensary, at least until after the wedding and honeymoon."

"Oh, no." Isabel's fork clattered to her plate. "I couldn't possibly. Those poor children, Toby . . . you don't understand."

"I do understand. I understand that you are a selfless,

generous angel who would put the most pitiful wretch's health above her own. But if you don't look after yourself, I shall be forced to look after you. I will insist."

"Forced? *Insist*?" Augusta gave him an amused glance. "That's a bit barbaric, don't you think?"

"Precisely what is barbaric about expressing concern for my future wife's health?" Toby set down his wineglass, a bit more forcefully than he'd intended.

Everyone's eyes fell to the table. In unison, each person lifted a glass and drank. Slowly.

"Toby is only teasing," Isabel said. "He knows how important my charitable causes are to me."

Yes, Toby sighed. He knew. Those damnable causes were everything to her. For weeks now, Isabel had declined any typical amusement, finding pleasure only in visiting orphans and collecting charitable subscriptions. Even the wedding preparations were a task she suffered through, he suspected. She probably thought of lepers while she looked at samples of lace.

"How are things in Surrey, Mother?" he asked, desperate to change the subject.

"Well, as always." Lady Aldridge motioned for the footmen to clear the table. "Except for one minor annoyance."

Reginald chortled. "Need we guess the annoyance's name?"

Toby asked, "What's Mr. Yorke done this time?"

"Oh, it's the plans for the irrigation canal. He agreed to the placement months ago. Now that the papers have been drawn up he refuses to sign, the impossible man. I know he does these things just to spite me. Toby, you'll have to speak with him."

"Certainly I will."

"He's always liked you. Though I never understood why."

With a self-effacing smile, Toby laid down his fork. "This, from my own mother."

"You know I don't mean it that way, dear," she said. "It's just—that man doesn't like anyone."

Archibald Yorke owned the lands bordering their estate in Surrey. He was a fixture in the neighborhood, known for his dry wit and shrewd bargains, and as the other primary landholder in the borough, he'd taken some pride in his position as the Aldridge family's archnemesis.

Because Toby had assumed the baronetcy in his infancy, for many years, the task of dealing with Mr. Yorke had fallen to his mother. Now their scuffling had simply become a matter of habit, a sport neither party seemed inclined to give up. Despite the history of rancor between the two—or perhaps because of it—Toby had always liked the man immensely. In his youth, he'd been drawn to the prickly old bachelor. They'd spent many an afternoon in Yorke's stables or by the fishing stream. In keeping with his life goal of thwarting Lady Aldridge, Yorke had provided young Toby with sanctuary and a sympathetic ear anytime he fled a punishment or simply chafed on his mother's leading strings.

"Who's Mr. Yorke?" Isabel asked.

"A friend," Toby replied.

At the same instant, Augusta answered, "Mother's enemy."

"He's just a neighbor," their mother said. "And he's not worth further discussion. Let us speak of pleasanter things."

"Oh, Augusta," Isabel said, brightening. As ever, charity absorbed her complete attention. "I have an idea for the Society pamphlets. My sister-in-law, Soph—"

Her voice trailed off. Forks teetered midair.

"Sophia," his mother completed smoothly. "We know Sophia, dear."

"Yes, of course you do," Isabel murmured. She cast a guilty look at Toby.

He forced a smile and a wave of nonchalance. "Go on then, darling," he said, although he hoped she wouldn't.

"Sophia has agreed to sketch a portrait of little Peter Jeffers, to illustrate the pamphlet. We must put a human face to the climbing boys' misery, to stir the hearts of potential donors. Augusta, don't you agree?"

"I think it's a splendid idea," Augusta answered. "Can your sister provide a sample before the next meeting?"

And on and on it went through dessert—which, of course, Isabel did not eat. Toby stabbed at his portion of quince tart. It wasn't that he begrudged Isabel her good deeds—he just wished she'd warm up to *him* a bit. After nearly six weeks, he was still clinging to this betrothal by the skin of his teeth and an arm-long list of absurd promises.

By his own agreement with Gray, he had to keep Isabel smiling. And none of his usual methods—compliments, jests, fawning attention, little gifts—earned even the slightest twitch of her lips. No, there was nothing to make Isabel Grayson smile like an impetuous act of self-denial:

Yes, of course I'll raise funds for the dispensary's new building.

Though I'd just as soon pay for the thing myself.

Certainly, I'll canvass the gentlemen's club for subscriptions.

The day they terminate my membership.

Absolutely, I'll let grimy gutter waifs ride on my shoulders.

Can't I just give them a pony instead?

No, I didn't notice the children had fleas.

Scratch, scratch, scratch . . .

Charity was all well and good, but Isabel's version of it was extreme. If he made it to their wedding before completely impoverishing or debasing himself, it would be a small miracle. Of course, Toby would promise

Isabel damn near anything now. Once they were safely married, he could negotiate different terms. But it bewildered him that even after weeks, none of his romantic overtures swayed her in the least. By what cruel twist of fate had he proposed to the one woman in creation who remained immune to all his practiced charm?

Well, if he was honest with himself, Toby had to admit there were apparently *two* women in creation who were immune to his charms. And the first had already jilted him.

Isabel said, "I long for the day we can disband the Society altogether."

Now that remark piqued Toby's attention. There was a sentiment he could wholeheartedly endorse.

"Yes," Augusta agreed. "If only Parliament would pass meaningful restrictions on child labor, none of these efforts would be necessary."

"Oh dear," Reginald interrupted. "I smell a new charitable venture in the offing. The Society for Obviating the Necessity of the Society for the Obviating the Necessity of Climbing Boys . . ."

Isabel gave a soft laugh. "No, no. There is no need for another Society. Once Toby assumes his place in Parliament, he will take up that cause."

"*Toby,*" Reginald echoed. "In Parliament."

"Yes, of course."

With an unladylike burst of laughter, Augusta turned to him. "Has Mr. Yorke heard of this? Toby, she can't be serious."

"Augusta." Toby inhaled slowly through his nose. "Isabel is always serious."

Of course, the notion of him serving in Parliament was patently absurd, but he couldn't very well admit it. Not when Isabel looked at him with expectation in those dark, solemn eyes.

Promise her anything. Keep her happy. Make her smile.

"And on Isabel's counsel," he said, "I've been giving the matter serious consideration."

Isabel didn't smile. She beamed, and Toby viewed the expression with profound gratitude and just a trace of alarm. God, what wouldn't he promise her, just to earn her approval? It was a good thing less than a month remained before a clergyman declared them man and wife, or she'd have him renouncing all his worldly belongings and taking orders himself.

"Toby in Parliament," Lady Aldridge said in a tone of false innocence. "What an idea."

He gave her a warning look over his wineglass. She'd been hinting at him to challenge Mr. Yorke's seat in Commons for an age now, and he'd been loudly denouncing the idea for an age and a half. Indulging his mother's petty vendetta was an even worse reason to seek office than appeasing his naïve bride.

Now his mother fixed him with the most unnerving gaze, coupled with a serene smile. Just like a mother, to take an unnatural delight in watching her offspring squirm.

"Mother," he said in a conciliatory croon, "you've ten grandchildren now—three of them tearing apart the nursery as we speak. Might I suggest you sharpen that look on one of them?"

"Isabel," she finally said, still directing her smile at Toby, "have we told you how delighted we are to welcome you to the family?"

"What the devil—"

Josiah Grayson bit off the chain of curses uncoiling in his mind. Such language wasn't meant for a child's ears. But then, neither were children meant to be climbing atop their fathers' desks and emptying inkwells onto stacks of crucial correspondence.

Joss lunged for his son, scooping the boy off the polished cherrywood desktop now marred with inky fingerprints. He attempted to pry Jacob's chubby fingers from the inkwell, holding the wriggling urchin at arm's length so as not to spoil his own new topcoat.

Damn Gray. This was all his fault for leaving London so soon. He'd gone to Southampton to survey progress on two ships under construction, taking Sophia with him. Two days he'd been gone, and already everything had gone to hell. Wouldn't the arrogant devil just love to know it, too? First, Jacob's nursemaid quitting her post, then problems with these insurance contracts, and to top it all off, Bel taken ill . . .

"Jacob, give that to Papa. I said, give it to Papa. Jacob, for the love of—"

Suddenly, the boy let go the inkwell. Bereft of resistance, Joss's arm snapped back at the elbow. Ink splattered him from cravat to trousers.

"Blast, bugger, damn, and hell." There was no preventing the improper vocabulary lesson Jacob received then. Mara would have been furious with him for using that language in front of their son.

"Mrs. Prewitt." Joss summoned the housekeeper from the hallway and deposited Jacob in her reluctant embrace. "Clean him up and send him to Cook for a biscuit."

His son temporarily occupied, Joss turned his attention to the ink-spattered contracts covering his desk. God, what a mess. As partner in Grayson Brothers Shipping, Joss was fully empowered to sign the contracts and deal with the matter in Gray's absence. But it chafed him that he didn't truly understand the crux of the problem, had no idea whether he signed the new contract for good or ill. He had only the advice of their solicitor to work from, and Joss didn't trust that toadying prig with tuppence.

Not that Gray would have known any better how to handle the situation. His brother had no education in legal matters, either. This was why Joss was determined to study law. They couldn't build a successful family business unless one of them could look at these piles of legal prattle and make sense of them.

The butler appeared in the entryway. "A caller, sir."

"I'm not at home."

"It's Sir Toby Aldridge, sir."

"Damn," Joss muttered, sifting through a stack of parchment. Just what he needed—the task of entertaining that insufferable ass in addition to everything else. "Didn't he get the message that Bel's taken ill?"

"Yes, he did," a voice said from the corridor. The insufferable ass himself rounded the doorway and entered the study. "All the more reason for me to call."

Joss dismissed the butler with a look. "You'll have to come back another day," he told Toby, sitting down to his desk. "She's feeling too poorly for social calls, and I'm in no humor for them either."

Toby flopped into a chair opposite. "Don't treat me as if I'm some stranger off the street. I'm marrying Isabel in less than a month, for God's sake. Now, what's the nature of her illness? Has a doctor been called? Can I see her?"

"It's just a sore throat," Joss said. "She doesn't want a doctor. And no, you can't see her."

The butler appeared in the doorway again. "The Countess of Kendall and a Miss Osborne, for Miss Grayson."

"Tell them I'll be there momentarily. I'll show them up to Miss Grayson's chambers myself."

"Now see here." Toby rose from his chair. "You just said she's not to receive callers. Why can Lucy and her friend go up, and not me?"

"Because Bel asked to see them. She didn't ask to see you." Joss brushed past Toby and walked down the corridor to the entryway. Toby's footsteps followed him to the foyer, where Lucy waited. Joss bowed to the countess first. "Please excuse my appearance," he said, gesturing toward his ruined attire. "The work of my son, I'm afraid."

Lucy smiled. "Yes, I've heard young Master Jacob is a handful." Her gaze drifted over Joss's shoulder. "Toby, what a pleasant surprise. I didn't think you'd be here."

"Why should it be such a surprise? Wouldn't any gentleman call on his invalid intended?"

Ignoring Toby's complaint, Lucy continued, "Miss Osborne, this is Miss Grayson's brother, Captain Josiah Grayson, and her betrothed, Sir Toby Aldridge. Gentlemen, allow me to introduce my friend, Miss Hetta Osborne."

"Miss Osborne. You are welcome." Joss bowed to the newcomer, a young lady a few years older than Bel, dressed in a simple muslin frock and a curry-colored spencer. He straightened to find her regarding him with intense, unwavering curiosity. Joss suppressed the urge to pull a face, call attention to her rudeness.

"Miss Obsorne's come to stay with me through my confinement. Her father is the doctor at Corbinsdale. When Bel sent word that she'd been taken ill, I immediately thought to bring Hetta with me." Lucy laid a gloved hand on her friend's arm. "Miss Osborne's practically a physician in her own right."

"A female physician?" Now Joss enjoyed his turn to stare. Miss Osborne was a compact, efficiently made sort of woman. In manner and bearing, she had the air of a matron, but girlish freckles dusted her milk-white complexion. Indeed, she stared with all the unabashed curiosity of a child, but intelligence sharpened her eyes—eyes that were a warm shade of hazel.

They gave him pause.

It had been a long time since Joss had noticed the color of a woman's eyes. Lately, a cursory glance was all he spared any new acquaintance before slotting the person into one of two categories: "Tolerate" or "Dismiss."

But he wasn't sure yet how to categorize this woman. He needed a closer look. Thus, he found himself studying her appearance with undue concentration.

He found himself noting that her eyes were a rather appealing shade of hazel, flecked with green.

Behind him, Toby made a sound of derision. "*Practically* a physician? If Isabel is ill, she's going to be seen by a real doctor. I'll send my own personal physician."

Miss Osborne lifted her chin. "The only reason I cannot claim the title 'physician' is my sex. I've received the same benefit of education and experience as any of my male counterparts."

"As any country quack, you mean." Toby turned to Joss. "You can't seriously mean to entrust your sister's health to this . . . this girl."

Lucy grasped her friend's arm. "Hetta, don't be offended. Toby doesn't know what he's saying. He's just upset over Bel's illness."

"Yes, I understand." Miss Osborne fixed Toby with a withering look. "I'm well acquainted with the irrational behaviors gentlemen exhibit when their ladies are ailing."

"Irrational behaviors?" Joss said. "It's irrational for a man to display concern?" Now Miss Osborne was truly becoming a problem. She was making him side with Toby. Much as he begrudged Toby any consideration, Joss understood all too well the agony of watching—at least, *hearing*—a woman suffer. "One would think you'd have some sympathy," he said.

She gave a one-shouldered shrug. "Sympathy would imply understanding, and I've never understood why women are labeled the weaker sex. In my observation, males suffer the condition of helplessness with far less courage than females suffer pain."

Her grip tightened on a small black valise. "As for me, I do not suffer ignorance. I came here to attend Miss Grayson. I assure you, I have the training and experience to provide her with excellent care, despite the efforts of some"—she shot a look at Toby—"to limit me, simply because of physical characteristics given me at birth." Her eyes flashed as she turned to Joss. "One would think *you'd* have some sympathy."

Well.

Joss inhaled slowly, considering. This Miss Osborne was either an impolitic fool or an example of cleverness. A physician, did she call herself? In a minute's time, she'd managed sharp pokes to both of his raw, open wounds—his lingering grief over Mara's death, and his frustration with the restrictions that accompanied his mixed parentage and illegitimacy. For a purported healer, she was a real pain.

Now she had the temerity to suggest he should reward her acid nature, endorse her abilities just because they shared this tenuous link of skirting social convention. As if it made them allies. He could not deny her access to Bel, Miss Osborne's gaze insisted, without impugning his own intelligence.

His alternative, of course, would be to deny her skills as a physician and turn her away—thereby siding with Toby. Joss suppressed a growl of annoyance. It was a devil's bargain, either way.

Miss Osborne knew it, too. As they stared one another down, her thin eyebrows arched with anticipation. Oh, she was clever. The woman was no fool.

"Very well." Joss made a dismissive bow. "Mrs. Prewitt will show you to my sister's chambers." Damned if he'd do it himself.

"Thank you." Lucy smiled, in an obvious effort to dispel the tension. Watching Miss Osborne ascend the stairs, she whispered, "Please don't mind Hetta. She rather delights in being shocking."

"I understand, Lady Kendall." As Lucy followed her friend above-stairs, Joss turned back to his study. Miss

Osborne did not know her good fortune, to be able to choose the occasions on which she gave offense. People found Joss shocking as a matter of course, whether he delighted in it or not.

Toby's smooth voice stopped him halfway down the corridor. "I can't believe you're permitting this."

Joss sighed. Would the man never leave?

Toby continued, "And here I thought you were the intelligent brother."

"And here I thought you were smooth with ladies. You didn't display any of that reputed charm with Miss Osborne. After the way you insulted her, I could scarcely turn her away. Poorly done, Aldridge."

"Oh, leave off." Toby lowered his voice as he closed the distance between them. "If a dead wife entitles you to become a full-time prick, I should think an invalid betrothed earns me a moment of incivility. If Isabel's condition fails to improve—or God forbid, worsens—I will send for my doctor immediately, and you will have hell to pay."

Joss stared at him. He'd never heard that tone from the man before. What a day this was. Mangled contracts, tipped inkwells, female doctors . . . and now this insufferable ass began to demand his respect. Worse, Joss felt compelled to give it. "Agreed."

"Good. Now agree to let me see her."

"I would let you see her. *If—*" Toby was three risers up the stairs before that "if" halted him mid-step. "If she wished it. But she doesn't."

"What do you mean, she doesn't? I'm going to be her husband in three weeks."

"She's not your wife yet. For now, she's just my sister. And my sister doesn't want to see you."

CHAPTER
SEVEN

"There you are. At last."

Bel looked up from her reading. Toby stood at the entrance to her private sitting room, holding a parcel under one arm and stealing the thoughts straight from her mind.

There he was. At last.

She wished she could stand to greet him, but her head was spinning. Throughout her illness, she'd suffered bouts of dizziness. Spying his dashing figure in the doorway only made matters worse. Perhaps she shouldn't have agreed to see him so soon, but she'd been putting him off for more than a week now.

She laid aside the newspaper, forcing her lips into a tight smile. Oh, how she longed for him to turn away, so she might pinch a blush to her cheeks. Maybe she could manage the appearance of better health, if not the corresponding strength.

But she could tell, Toby was having none of it. "How pale you are," he said, placing his parcel on the table and sinking onto the divan next to her. He made an impetuous motion as though he would embrace her, then seemed to think better of it. Bel didn't know whether to be grateful or disappointed.

He asked, "Do you know how sick I've been with worry? I've come by the house every day, you know. Why wouldn't you allow me to see you?"

Warm brown eyes scanned her appearance. Bel felt his

gaze catching on the dark circles beneath her eyes, the sallow tone of her cheeks, the dull texture of her hair. She must be hideous, and of course he looked as suave and handsome as ever.

"How could I have allowed you? It isn't proper." She fidgeted with the handkerchief in her lap, picking at the tatted edge. It wasn't quite a lie; just an incomplete truth. She couldn't very well tell him honestly, *I couldn't let you see me until I felt completely assured of my sanity.* She'd spent days floating in and out of feverish dreams, terrified that, like her mother, she would never fully return from them. Even once the fever left her, she'd lain awake in bed all night, scouring the darkest corners of her mind for any flitting moths of madness.

"If you'd visited, it would only have caused you distress," she said feebly. "Even now, I must look so ill." She put one hand to her temple, shielding her face.

He ducked, peering under it. "Isabel, listen to me. We are to be married in a couple of weeks. I'm going to stand before all London, the Holy Trinity, and even those two boorish brothers of yours and pledge you my undying fidelity and protection. In sickness and in health." He pulled her hand away from her face, folding his fingers around hers. "And with God as my witness, I will vow to you right now—you are the most beautiful sight I've beheld in ten days."

She couldn't decide whether he was teasing her or deceiving her. But then, she didn't really want to know. "I've missed you," she said quietly. That was the simple truth.

"I'm glad of it." He smiled. "Miss Osborne tells me you've made nearly a full recovery."

"Yes, my fever is completely gone. I'm just a bit weak yet."

"But you're not taking enough food, she says."

"It's . . . it's still painful to eat," she said. "My

throat . . ." She feigned a little cough, in lieu of completing the sentence.

"Isabel, you must make an effort to regain your strength. I've just spoken to your brother. He's suggesting we postpone the wedding."

"Oh, he mustn't! I won't let him." Bel gripped his hand. "I'm feeling much improved already." This, too, was the truth. Perhaps she had been wrong to keep him away so long. There was something about the way he looked at her, with that shadow of a smile in his eyes, that made her feel restored. His teasing infuriated her at times, but she was beginning to understand it as a strange sort of compliment to her character. While bullies teased to belittle and hurt, Toby's good-natured jibes had quite the opposite effect. He teased not out of malice, but because he believed she was strong enough to bear it.

And thus far, he had always been right.

She gave his fingers a little squeeze. "The wedding must go on as planned."

Relief was plain in the relaxation of his shoulders. He added his free hand to the tangle of their fingers, surrounding hers with his strong, warm touch. "Good. To that end, I've brought you some medicine." Releasing her, he reached for the parcel he'd brought.

"Medicine? But Miss Osborne has already dosed me with—"

"This is a different sort of medicine. One you're sure to enjoy." A sly gleam stole into his eyes as he opened the package and withdrew a chilled glass dish mounded with a nut-brown ice. "The flavor is chocolate. Blended with hazelnut and, I'm told, a hint of cinnamon."

"Toby, really . . ."

"I insist." He pressed a spoon into her hand. "If it pains you to eat solid food, you must take what you can. An ice is the perfect remedy for a sore throat. The coolness is a balm; the sweetness is a restorative." He gave her a wicked smile. "And everyone knows chocolate to be invigorating."

Bel could already feel her resistance melting. The glistening ice looked so cool, so inviting. Her raw throat worked as she imagined taking just one spoonful of chilled, soothing sweetness. "I . . . I couldn't possibly."

"Is it the sugar that concerns you?"

She nodded, hoping he would take pity on her conscience and quickly pack the dish away.

He pressed it closer, taking the spoon from her hand and scooping up a bite of the ice. "Isabel, don't be concerned. I ordered this ice specially made for you. It's sweetened with honey."

"Honey?"

"Yes, pure English honey, collected from very contented bees. I interviewed the beekeeper myself, and he assured me the drones were treated most fairly, paid an honest wage, and given the Sabbath to rest. And now that they've done their service, I've arranged for the whole hive to be pensioned off to a charming little beech grove in Shropshire, right next to a meadow abundant with clover. So you see," he said, moving the spoon toward her lips, "you may partake of this ice in good conscience."

Bel giggled. For heaven's sake, she *never* giggled. With those smooth arguments and that persuasive grin, he was bound to be a terrific success in Parliament. "You are teasing me. Most shamelessly."

"Yes. And you're enjoying it." Leaning closer, he lifted the spoon to her mouth. "Really, Isabel. You must eat. You must get well, if we are to marry as planned, and . . ." His voice took on a sudden, thrilling intensity. "And I don't wish to delay."

She closed her eyes. If she were truly strong, she would find it in herself to push the temptation away. But she was ill and weak, and though she knew in her conscience she shouldn't give in . . .

She did.

Her lips closed around the chilled spoon, and she drew on it with light suction, pulling the frozen confection into her mouth.

Oh.

Oh, paradise.

At first, the cold burned her lips and tongue, and the ice crystals abraded her palate like small slivers of glass. But then the sharp edges melted to cream, and each tiny excoriation was now soothed, with exquisite coolness and a dark, bittersweet spice.

Swallowing, she opened her eyes to find him offering her a second spoonful. This bite she accepted with eyes wide open, held rapt by his warm, amber-flecked gaze as the oscillation of sharp pain and rich pleasure teased her senses again.

"Do you like it?" he asked, slowly retracting the spoon from between her pursed lips.

Did she? Bel licked her lips, considering. She couldn't describe the sensation as wholly pleasant, but she knew one thing. "I want more."

He gave a hoarse chuckle—a sound more throaty and raw than his usual laugh. As he lifted another bite to her lips, Bel watched his dark pupils widening with anticipation, his full lips parting in unison with hers. He seemed to experience the same sweet torture she did, as the burning cold flooded her mouth. Once again, he dragged the spoon from between her lips. And for some unknown, wicked reason, Bel found herself pursing them tighter in defiance. As if to tease.

She licked her lips again, slowly, taking joy in the way his gaze riveted to her mouth. Yes, she felt strong when he teased her, but teasing him back . . . this was *power*. The sensation rushed through the top of her head, like cold.

When he spoke, his voice was husky. "May I taste?"

"Yes," she blurted out. How thoughtless she'd been, not to offer before he could ask. "Yes, of course."

Instead of dipping the spoon again, however, Toby set the dish aside. And before Bel even knew what was happening, his hands were framing her jaw, angling her face to his. And then his body was flush against hers, his lips covering hers, and his tongue . . . His tongue was *inside* her mouth, teasing hers. Tasting.

Shocked, Bel closed her eyes. This felt so good, it had to be wrong. She ought to push this temptation away. She shouldn't give in.

But she did.

And she discovered that her future husband tasted even better than chocolate.

His mouth moved confidently over hers as his tongue swept between her lips, in and out. The effect was dizzying. Her breath rushed out in a little whimpering sigh. Toby's hands relaxed where they clasped her face, and his lips paused against hers in a deceptively innocent kiss.

He was offering her a chance to resist. An opportunity to pull away. But as with the ice, she wasn't satisfied with one taste of him. Maybe that fever *had* done something to her. She knew it was wrong, but she wanted more.

Her hands flew around his neck, threading into the locks of his hair where it met his cravat. As he renewed the kiss, she allowed her fingers to explore. How long she'd been wanting to touch him like this! His hair felt every bit as sleek as it looked, and the muscles of his neck were delightfully solid. And his skin . . . When she slid one fingertip beneath his starched neckcloth, she discovered his skin to be smooth and hot and just a bit damp with perspiration. A new thrill went through her, to know that beneath his confident exterior, he was simply a man, raw and elemental. And she made him sweat.

"Isabel."

He murmured the name against her mouth, sliding his hands down to her waist and pulling her close. When her breasts met his chest, a little moan escaped them both. But this time, Toby offered her no gentleness, no chance to retreat. No, he had become a true man of purpose, pulling her tighter still and taking her mouth with a possessive hunger. His kiss tasted dark and desperate, and it was undeniably flattering, how much he seemed to want her. That no matter how much she offered him, he took more, and still more. His mouth moved again and again over hers, his tongue thrusting in and out as he clutched her waist with both hands.

And then . . .

Oh, and then.

He began to slide one hand up. So slowly, so stealthily. His thumb lingered over each rib. With every inch his touch crept higher, Bel grew increasingly certain it would soon stop. It *must* stop.

But it didn't stop, this insidious, tantalizing caress that traveled up and up. And within her some forbidden sensation, some *need,* began to mount as well. It was as if all her awareness converged in her belly, following the rippling heat of his touch. Her breath grew shallow, and her fingers tightened around his neck. Somewhere in her mind, a shrill voice clamored for virtue, but she couldn't obey. The unbearable need climbed her from inside and out—his touch, this sensation—up and up . . . and up.

His thumb grazed the underside of her breast.

Oh. Oh, please.

Bel didn't have the slightest idea what she was begging him for. But she was kissing him back now, arching her body and pouring that wordless plea into light motions of her lips and tentative sweeps of her tongue. He growled deep in his throat and rewarded her daring with another gentle caress up the side of her breast.

She clutched his neck tighter, kissed him harder. Telling

him what she could never, ever bring herself to say in words.

Oh, please don't stop. Please do it again.

Her breasts ached. They were heavy, so heavy. She resented them, these useless, corset-straining burdens she'd been carrying around since the age of fourteen. And now, at long last, they seemed awakened to some purpose. Her nipples gathered to tight knots, straining against her bodice. Straining toward him. They hurt.

He could make it better. She knew he could.

Oh please. Oh please oh please oh please.

His hand cupped her breast. She nearly cried out with relief. His thumb found her nipple, and pleasure sang through her veins and curled between her thighs. So intense, she thought she might faint. With confident fingers, he stroked and kneaded, and Bel kissed him with every ounce of gratitude she possessed. They were heavy, so heavy—but now he had taken the weight in his own strong hand, bearing it for her. Soothing the ache.

It was everything wrong. But it was everything she needed. She needed him, and he had come, armed with chocolate and kisses and that teasing, devilish grin.

He was temptation incarnate, and she was giving in.

At last.

At last.

Toby thumbed her hardened nipple again, groaning into her mouth. How long had he been aching to hold these magnificent breasts? Since the evening they met— weeks now, months. An eternity. God, how marvelously she filled his hand, the warm, soft flesh overflowing his cupped fingers. Desire pounded in his blood. He longed to push her back into the upholstery, wrench her free of this thin muslin bodice, and fasten his lips around the taut bud of her nipple. She would taste so good. These mewling, erotic noises she now made into his mouth . . .

she would make them *aloud*. Just the thought of it drove him into a frenzy.

He'd missed her, more than he could have expected. The need gripped him, to join with her—to carve out a home for himself in all that lush, generous femininity and never, ever leave. And though some fragment of reason in his melting brain insisted that there was no damned way he could deflower Isabel right here, right now, on her sitting room settee . . . a distinctly baser portion of him quite desperately wanted to try.

She was his, after all. She was marrying him in a matter of days, no matter what her brother said. *The wedding must go on as planned.* Those had been her words. The surge of triumphant pride only fueled his desire. He kneaded her breast greedily, relishing the way she arched into his touch, denying him nothing. Finally, she was responding to *him*—not his forbearance with beggars or his philanthropic largesse. At last, here was that passion he'd glimpsed at their very first meeting, all that pent-up emotion she buried under selfless good works. She might hide it from the world, even from herself. But she couldn't hide it from him. He had won her. She was *his*.

She would be his wife.

And . . . and damned if he would steal her innocence like a thief. Not when she would soon belong to him, by rights.

With great reluctance, Toby marshaled his will and released her breast. Framing her face in his palms, he gently pulled her away. Her labored breaths raced his. Resting his forehead against her lovely brow, he whispered, "Darling, I'm sorry. We really should stop."

He saw the flush of guilt creeping up her face.

"I know, I know," she said. "It's wrong. I know it, but . . ." She chewed her lip. "You make me want to do things I know I shouldn't."

With a soft laugh, he pressed a kiss to her brow. "Funny,

isn't it? You make me want to do the things I've always known I should."

"Shall we suit one another, do you think?"

"Splendidly." And he meant it. The past few minutes had banished any of his concerns about their compatibility. During that kiss, they had suited one another to the ground. He couldn't resist stealing one more. And then another. Nuzzling her ear, he murmured, "It's a fortunate thing we're getting married soon."

"Oh, yes." She straightened and inched away, putting distance between them. Passion had been put aside, and her typically placid demeanor had returned. "We couldn't possibly wait any longer. I only wish we could marry today. I hope the timing of the wedding won't interfere with your campaign."

Toby blinked. "My . . . my *campaign*."

"What a shame, that we'll have to postpone the honeymoon. But I expect the Lake District will be just as lovely in August as it would have been in July."

"Postpone the honeymoon? What on earth are you talking about?" Brushing a finger across the tip of her nose, he joked, "Isabel, perhaps that fever affected you more seriously than we thought."

She went rigid, instantly. "What are you suggesting?"

"Nothing," he soothed. "Nothing at all." He slid his fingertip along her jaw. "But my word, you're so beautiful when you take offense. I'm the one who's addled, darling. I don't seem to be following you. Take pity on a besotted fool and explain it again, a little more slowly."

Smiling again, she pulled a newspaper from the table beside her and held it out to him. "Haven't you heard? The Prince Regent is expected to dissolve Parliament tomorrow. It's in all the newspapers. Polling will begin within a few weeks."

Toby stared at the newspaper she'd handed him, trying in vain to form a response. She couldn't possibly be serious. Isabel laid a hand on his sleeve, and his gaze jerked up to hers.

"Isn't it perfect?" she said, a smile spreading across her face. "Our grand wedding, followed so closely by your candidacy? We're certain to be the talk of London, if not all England. At last, you'll have your place in the House of Commons, and I'll be . . ." She blushed and dropped her eyes. "I'll be your wife. I'll be Lady Aldridge."

Good God. She *was* serious. She expected him to postpone their honeymoon and run for Parliament in a few weeks. Toby, on the other hand, had no wish to run for Parliament in a few weeks. Nor in a few years, for that matter. Not when he'd successfully invested a decade in avoiding that very task.

"Darling, there's no need to be in a hurry. Governments come and go. Our wedding will only happen once. Let's enjoy our honeymoon, and then I can run for Parliament the next time there's an election called."

"But that will be years from now."

Yes, precisely.

"Besides," he continued, "you've been ill. You need rest, not the strain of a political campaign."

"But the prospect of the campaign is what's made me feel better! As soon as I saw the paper, I knew I must resolve to recover my strength. You will need me, to stand by you and work with you. Oh, Toby," she said, her dark eyes shining. "Think of all the good we will do together."

He swallowed and looked back at the newspaper. So this was what had prompted her swift recovery, her determination to regain her health and marry him as planned—the prospect of an election. Not the prospect of being with *him*. A bitter taste filled his mouth. "I'm sorry, Isabel, but I just don't think this is the time."

Her eyes grew sharp. "What do you mean? I thought you understood when we became engaged, that I sought a match for political and social influence. You told me you would be serving in the House of Commons."

"I know, but—"

She mimicked his baritone. " 'Even I could have a seat in Commons, lowly sir that I am.' Those were your words."

"Yes, I know, but—"

"But what?" She looked near tears.

He touched her cheek. "But I thought . . . there is something between us now. Something real and undeniable, and stronger than any words carelessly uttered on a verandah." He leaned forward to kiss her.

She pulled away. "Desire, you mean?"

Desire? Toby schooled his expression, trying not to look wounded. Certainly, there was desire—on his side, there was a prodigious amount of desire. But during that kiss just now . . . he'd fancied there was some deeper emotion beneath it.

Evidently, the fancies were all on his side.

She shook her head, casting her eyes to her lap. "Other people may marry for desire, but I cannot. Have I not made it clear from our first meeting, I intend to marry for influence and the opportunity to do good? If you will not offer me that, then perhaps—"

"Wait." He put a finger on her lips, shushing her. Dear Lord, the girl was a breath away from crying off. Desperation welled in his gut. This could not happen again. First Sophia had jilted him; now Isabel threatened to do the same. Was there no lady in England who could see her way clear to actually marry him as promised?

Toby gathered what pride remained to him. Perhaps he could talk her out of this madness. "What I mean to say is, it won't work. Unless you mean for me to purchase a rotten borough—"

"Oh, no!" Her eyes widened in horror at the suggestion of corruption. Just as he'd known they would.

"Then I should have to run against Mr. Yorke, you

see. He's served our borough faithfully for years, and what's more, he's an old friend. He's also very popular."

"Popular? But your mother loathes him."

"My mother is a special case."

"I can't believe anyone could be more popular than you. You're the most popular gentleman in Town."

"In Town, perhaps I am. But these aren't society matrons, Isabel, they're farmers. Mr. Yorke understands their needs."

"So will you, once you have an opportunity to listen."

Dear, ridiculous girl, staring up at him with such expectation in her eyes.

He pulled back, startled. No, this was more than expectation. Her eyes held the glimmer of faith. Wholly unearned and completely misapplied, but faith it was. By some miracle, she believed in him. What a novel sensation. He found himself quite rapidly drunk on it.

"You will win their loyalty," she said. "I'm certain I know of no gentleman more persuasive. For heaven's sake, you just convinced me to eat an ice. Not to mention, to . . ." Her pale cheeks flushed with embarrassment. "At any rate, you're very persuasive."

She smiled at him so sweetly, he almost wanted to believe her. As if farmers would respond to the same charm as debutantes. They'd be mad to vote for Toby over Yorke, even if Toby paid out handsome bribes—which Isabel would never allow him to do. This half-witted MP election scheme would be certain to fail.

But then—perhaps that made it perfect.

Even if he agreed to run, he would most assuredly lose. Isabel would have to give him credit for trying, the sweet girl that she was, and Toby would never have to serve in Commons. By the time the next election rolled around, she'd be occupied with her charities and—God willing—a child or two, and she'd forget all about this Parliament foolishness.

He just had to get her to the altar first.

Promise her anything. Keep her happy. Make her smile.

"Very well, then. I'll do it."

Her face lit up. Oh, that look was worth anything.

"You will?" she asked. "You'll run for MP?"

"I'll run," he told her, basking in her palpable excitement. "Mind, I can't guarantee that I'll win."

"Of course you will. I have complete faith in you."

Yes, Isabel. But for how long?

Toby bent his head to steal one last kiss—and found himself being plundered. Within seconds, Isabel was half in his lap, tentatively exploring his mouth with her tongue. Perhaps there was nothing behind her kiss but desire and a glimmer of misplaced faith—but Toby couldn't bring himself to complain. Right now, this felt like more than enough.

And though their wedding was still almost two weeks distant, he made a vow to himself, there and then. Whatever it took—funds, misdirection, outright deceit—he would find a way to make this last.

Forever.

CHAPTER EIGHT

"Can't you wait a few minutes longer?" Toby asked, as the orchestra struck the final chord and they whirled to a halt. "I was hoping we could go speak with your brothers."

"I can't, it's my . . ." Isabel gave him a pained look, then stood on her toes to whisper in his ear. The delicate warmth of her breath sent heat coursing through his veins. "It's my hem. I tripped on it during the quadrille."

Toby smiled. It was adorable, how aggrieved she became, owning up to something so meaningless as a ripped hem. But it warmed his heart that she overcame her distress and gave him the honest truth. He'd heard his fill of enigmatic feminine excuses, and he certainly had no use for them in a wife.

But truly, of late he found everything about her adorable. Toby was well and thoroughly besotted with his future bride. How could he not be? He'd been the recipient of admiring gazes, adoring ones—he could count a half-dozen girls in this ballroom alone who'd once regarded him with nigh-on-idolatrous worship in their eyes. But none of them had Isabel's principles and discernment, and none of them had ever regarded him with such faith.

"Don't worry," he told her. "If your hem is ripped, it's not noticeable in the least."

"But everyone's staring at me."

"Of course they are. Not only is this ball being held in your honor—"

"*Our* honor."

"Very well, *our* honor—but you've committed the unforgivable sin of being the most beautiful lady in the room." He placed a hand on the small of her back. "Just three minutes with your brothers, and I'll escort you to the retiring room myself."

"Why don't I just go while you speak with them? Whatever it is you want to discuss, surely you don't need me."

"Ah, but I'd miss you." With his signature persuasive grin, he steered her toward the corner of the ballroom currently anchored by the broad-shouldered bulk of two Grayson men. Truly, he didn't need her there. But this was a complicated maneuver he'd been planning for weeks, and all of it solely for Isabel's benefit. There was no way he would allow her to miss the crowning moment.

"Reginald," he called, pausing on his way toward Gray and Joss. "May I beg your company for a moment?"

"Yes, of course." With a polite bow to Isabel, his brother-in-law joined their group. "What is it, Toby?"

"Do you remember that I told you Isabel's brother is interested in studying law, as it affects his shipping business?"

"Yes, of course."

"And do you remember promising to take him as a pupil in your offices?"

"Certainly."

Toby nodded toward the corner. "Allow me to introduce him, then."

"But I've already met Gray," Reginald murmured, as they walked in that direction. "The other week, at Lord Fairleigh's dinner party."

Toby's smile widened.

"Good evening," he said smoothly, as they reached the Graysons. "Gray, I know you've been introduced to my brother-in-law, Mr. Reginald Tolliver."

The men traded perfunctory nods.

"Reginald," Toby continued, "allow me to introduce Isabel's other brother, Captain Josiah Grayson. Joss, this is my brother-in-law, one of England's finest barristers. He's agreed to supervise your legal studies."

To his credit, Reginald refused to display the slightest hint of surprise that his new pupil was part African. After all, he hadn't become a top barrister by being easily rattled. He did, however, shoot Toby a look that told him Reginald knew he'd been manipulated, he didn't appreciate it, and it would be his and Augusta's turn to summer in the Brighton cottage, two years running.

"A pleasure to make your acquaintance, Captain Grayson," Reginald said. "I've heard so much about you."

Toby moved to the side, allowing Reginald and Joss the space to discuss particulars. The step brought him closer to Gray, not entirely by accident.

"Thank you," Gray muttered, in a tone that told Toby to expect no further comment. But really, those two words were more than enough. If all the remarks in the world were ranked according to how much pleasure Gray would take in saying them to Toby—Toby suspected the list would be topped with "I only wish I could kill you twice" and end with something like, "Kiss me again." Just a rung or two above that last would be "Thank you."

"You're welcome," Toby replied in a magnanimous tone. It hardly signified that Gray had already left. His chest swelled with victory, until he damn near floated away.

A tug at his sleeve yanked him back to earth.

"Toby?" Isabel's low voice was resonant with emotion.

"Yes, darling?" He turned to her, prepared to receive an outpouring of gratitude and affection.

"May I please go have my hem repaired now?"

Toby stared at her, then gave a little laugh. He'd just

secured England's most unlikely aspiring lawyer the tutelage of England's most successful barrister, and Isabel's opinion of him hadn't altered one bit. She wasn't impressed, or even grateful in the least. Because she wasn't surprised. She simply expected heroics of him. He couldn't decide whether that response was mildly disappointing, or supremely satisfying in some bone-deep, essential way.

One thing was certain. It was intimidating. Not to mention unsettling, the lengths to which he felt prepared to go, to win his lady's favor. He half wished some fire-breathing dragon would crash through the frescoed ceiling, just so he might have the pleasure of slaying it for her.

"Off with you, then," he said, kissing her hand. "But don't be long."

"I don't know how much time it will take," she said ruefully. "Why don't you find another partner for the next set?"

"At a ball held in honor of our engagement? No, no. Until you return, there's no other lady for me."

"But my dear Miss Grayson, surely you don't expect Toby to be faithful to you." Reclining carefully, Lady Violet shucked her slippers and propped her stockinged feet on the arm of the settee.

Hetta Osborne averted her gaze in an attempt to hide her disgust. Between the offense of Lady Violet's remark and the unsightly bunion on the woman's great toe, Hetta's fingers itched for a scalpel.

From the corner of the room, Isabel gave a huff of shock. Lady Violet flicked it away with her gilt-edged fan.

A blunt scalpel, Hetta amended.

"Come now, we are all ladies here," the matron said, baring her teeth in a predatory smile. "Of course we would not speak so frankly in the ballroom, but the retiring room is our feminine sanctuary. Here, we must be honest with one another. And honestly, we all know Toby to be the most incorrigible flirt." She looked around the assembled ladies. "Is there any lady here who could claim she has never fallen under his spell?"

Forbidden to move by the seamstress repairing her hem, Isabel craned her neck, looking from woman to woman. Sophia and Lucy—and every other lady in the room—developed a sudden interest in the plush blue carpet. Well, Lucy was presumably studying the carpet, if she could spy it around her enormously pregnant belly.

"I haven't," Hetta said clearly, and honestly. From a clinical perspective, she could observe that Sir Toby possessed fine features and the aura of good health. But she had never felt any stirrings of attraction.

Not toward *him*, at any rate.

Lady Violet gave a throaty laugh and massaged her bunion-afflicted foot with one hand. "Of course you haven't. You don't count. Sir Toby may be a rake, but I'm sure he is not the sort to dally with the help."

Before Hetta could clear the steam from her mind to fashion her own retort, Lucy jumped to her defense. As much as an enormously pregnant woman could jump.

"Miss Osborne is not 'the help.' She is my friend, and she is here in Town as a guest of the Earl of Kendall. And at this ball, she is a guest of Her Grace, the Duchess of Aldonbury."

Lady Violet gave another dismissive flutter of her fan. "Calm down, my dear."

"Don't tell me to c—" Lucy began.

"Really, Lucy, it's all right," Hetta said, deciding to expend her reserve of patience on Lady Violet's behalf. She was well acquainted with Lucy's explosive temper, and pregnancy had only shortened the fuse. It would not do to make a scene. "I'm certain her ladyship did not mean to disparage me, but rather to praise Sir Toby." In some bizarre, misbegotten way.

"Exactly so," Lady Violet continued. "Toby may not be so low as to forage through the servants' leavings—"

A blunt, rusted scalpel.

"—but he does have a healthy appetite. As all men do."

"That is absurd," Lucy said. "All arguments of honor and fidelity aside, there is no reason a man cannot be wholly satisfied within the confines of his marriage. If he and his wife are well matched, of course." She gave Lady Violet a coy smile. "We ladies have our appetites, too."

Laughter skittered through the room.

In an obvious attempt to escape the conversation, Sophia rose from her chair and made her way to the refreshment table.

"Why, Lady Grayson, do your appetites lead you to stray?" Lady Violet called after her. "I would think that strapping husband of yours would have no trouble satisfying you."

Reaching for a tart, Sophia gave a little smile. "Of course he doesn't. That's why I'm so hungry."

Lucy's eyes lit, and she clapped her hands together. "Sophia, you sly thing. Why didn't you say something before?"

Isabel's brow wrinkled in confusion. "I'm sure I don't know what any of you are talking about."

"I'm sure you don't," Lucy said. "Really, Sophia, you must pass along The Book."

"What book?" Isabel asked.

"None. There is no book. I know nothing about any book." Sophia gave Lucy a quelling look, whispering, "Gray would murder me."

"No, he wouldn't. That's the best thing about our condition—complete immunity from a husband's displeasure."

"What condition? What displeasure? What book?" Isabel stamped her foot. "Will someone please explain to me what is going on?"

Hetta took pity on her. "Your sister-in-law is with child."

"Oh, Sophia!" Isabel exclaimed. She started toward her sister, but the seamstress yanked her to a halt. "How wonderful! But what does that have to do with a book?"

"Nothing," Sophia replied.

"Everything," Lucy said smugly.

Now Hetta was beginning to feel left out. "Why have I never seen this book?"

"Oh, I gave it to Sophia before I even arrived at Corbinsdale," Lucy said. "And now she seems to be hoarding it."

"There is no book," Sophia ground out, tilting her chin toward Isabel.

Isabel whimpered, "I'm so confused." The maid released her hem, and she strode over to join the group. "But on one point I am certain, Lady Violet. No matter how infamous Toby's reputation, I know him to be a most decent and generous man. Why, just today, he has arranged for my brother to study law under his sister's husband, Mr. Tolliver."

"Gray wants to study law?" Lucy asked.

"No, not Gray. Joss."

The name gave Hetta a start, and she coughed into her lemonade.

"Truly?" Sophia asked. "And Toby arranged it? Well, that is something indeed. Gray's been making inquiries for weeks, with no success. Toby's efforts are a great compliment to you, Bel. There is no love lost between him and your brothers."

"Yes, yes." Lady Violet's eyebrows rose. "He is devoted to securing her favor now. But men behave quite differently as suitors than they do as husbands."

"Not my brothers," Isabel protested. "Both were great favorites with the ladies in their bachelorhood, but I know Gray is devoted to Sophia, and Joss is still—"

Hetta rose from her seat and shook out her skirts. "Miss Grayson, perhaps you should listen to Lady Violet's well-intentioned advice on the inconstancy of husbands. I am certain she speaks from her own experience."

With that, she quit the room. She could not bear to remain a moment longer. Perhaps she had an aversion to gossip. Or perhaps she simply did not want to hear the truth. Familiar as she was with the character of long-suffering widowers—most notably, her father—she was in no humor to hear Isabel extol the depths of Joss Grayson's devotion to his late wife.

But now that she'd escaped, where to go?

Even dressed in one of Lucy's gowns, Hetta stood out at this gathering like a tin kettle amongst porcelain. Well before Lady Violet's comments, she'd been deeply conscious that her mannerisms, her accent, and her bearing all declared "interloper." She would not have come at all, if Lucy had not insisted. To refuse would have been rude. There had been the pull of curiosity, too—it was entirely probable that this would be her one and only opportunity to attend a ball with society's elite.

Oh, feathers. Hetta blew out a breath, annoyed with her own prevarication. What did she care about manners or high society?

There was only one true reason she'd come.

"Are you hiding, Miss Osborne?"

Hetta startled, nearly colliding with a potted tree. "No, of course not. I'm not . . ."

Her voice trailed off as she turned to face the man behind her. Of course, she'd known it must be him. She'd recognized the deep timbre of his voice immediately, but she somehow hadn't quite believed he was there until she spun around and came nose-to-button with his gold-threaded waistcoat. Hiking her chin, she prodded her gaze up to his sardonic dark-brown eyes. "I'm not hiding, Captain Grayson."

"Really?" he replied. "I only ask, because it seems an odd vantage from which to view a ball—through this barrier of foliage. Hardly the place for a young lady to stand, should she wish invitations to dance."

The nerve of the man. As if she would receive any invitations to dance. Still, she couldn't allow him to fluster her. Hetta was not a woman who became flustered. But then, she was not a woman who hid behind potted trees, either. Drat.

"I was not hiding," she repeated evenly, determined to give as good as she received. "Are you?"

"Not at all."

"Well, it seems an odd place, here behind the shrubbery, for a gentleman to troll for a dancing partner."

"Why would you say that?" His lips quirked at the corner. It wasn't a smile. "I've found one, haven't I?"

Her heart fluttered in her chest. "You don't mean—"

"What don't I mean?"

Curse the man. He knew. He knew she'd developed this embarrassing, girlish infatuation with him, and now he was teasing her about it, right here in front of everyone. Or rather, right here behind a potted tree. And now she *knew* she would blush—she was fair-skinned and freckled, after all—and that would make everything even worse. Oh, Lord. She was already lurking in the greenery. Where did she run and hide from here?

His hand captured hers. Neither of them wore gloves. His skin was smooth and warm—which made her immediately conscious that her own hand must be cold.

"Come dance with me, Miss Osborne."

"But we can't!"

He raised an eyebrow. "Why can't we?"

Because she was out of place in this elegance. Because

she barely knew how. Because she found it annoyingly hard to breathe in his presence. For a hundred different reasons, all of which swarmed in her stomach like wasps, and none of which she dared let escape. "I just don't think it's a good idea, that's all."

He stared out over the ballroom. "Hm."

What sort of remark was that? Was he agreeing with her? Arguing with her? Dismissing her? Hetta waited for some further, less cryptic response. None came.

"I'm not in the mood for dancing this evening," she said casually, trying to sound as though she turned down offers of this sort every day. There, that ought to put paid to the discussion.

Still, he did not acknowledge her with a reply. Her hand remained in his, however. It warmed, began to grow comfortable there. Traitorous appendage.

"That's all right," he said at last. "I shan't require you to enjoy it."

He pulled her onto the dance floor and within moments had her trapped in his embrace. There was no way to escape without creating a scene. And before Hetta knew it, she was dancing. She, Hetta Osborne, freckled, plain physician's daughter with little romantic inclination and even less grace, was circling a ballroom in the arms of a tall, handsome gentleman. He led with such agile command, she forgot that she scarcely knew the steps. She almost forgot that she had feet. She floated in his arms, and her wits lay scattered behind her on the waxed parquet. Hetta was breathless.

Unfortunate, then, that her partner wished to converse.

"I'm to take up legal studies soon," he said. "With Sir Toby's brother-in-law, Mr. Reginald Tolliver. It was just decided this evening."

"Yes, I heard."

"You did?" He frowned at her, then made a gruff

sound of annoyance. "I should have known. Nothing surprises the unflappable Miss Osborne."

"Did you wish me to be surprised?"

"I suppose not." A few measures passed before he continued, "Have you no reaction to the idea?"

"What reaction should I have?" If he would tell her, she would attempt to oblige. If he would put a bit more space between them, she might be able to devise replies of her own.

"I don't know." Beneath her hand, his shoulder tensed. The slight flex of his muscle sent a dangerous thrill through her. "I thought you would be interested. You're determined to take up medicine, although its practice is barred to you. I am determined to study law, although its practice is barred to me. We have something in common."

"We do?" Hetta tripped slightly as they whirled past the orchestra. She tried—desperately—not to ascribe any deeper meaning to his remark. She struggled mightily against any stirrings of hope. She failed. "And you wish to explore our common interests?" It was the closest to flirting she'd ever come.

"That is the simplest method of beginning conversation, is it not? To remark on common interests?"

Of course. He didn't mean a thing by it. Most definitely, he didn't mean to impress her. Why would he care what she thought of him?

He didn't seem to care what anyone thought of him, and that was what made him so attractive. During Isabel's illness, Hetta had spoken with the man daily and observed him in the company of others. Unlike his rakish half-brother, Joss Grayson wasted no effort on charm and made only passing attempts at civility. He did not disguise the general contempt with which he regarded the world, nor did he hide the constant pain in his eyes. She'd never met anyone like him. The man was one giant, angry, suppurating wound, and he didn't care who saw it. Wounds like that were difficult for most people to look upon. Most people would rather turn away, and Captain Grayson knew it.

But Hetta was not most people. She was a physician, and inured to the sight of blood and the marks of human suffering. She didn't find him difficult to look upon. To the contrary, she found herself hard pressed to look away. He wasn't simply handsome; he was defiantly so. His jaw was permanently set, teeth gritted on some imaginary leather strop—as though he were steeling himself for an incision. And his eyes fascinated her. They were the rich brown shade of mahogany, and twice as hard.

Drat. She was staring at him again.

Was it her turn to speak? She cleared her throat. "So, you asked me to dance so we could talk?"

"No. Had I merely wished to converse with you, I might have invented any of a dozen excuses. But dancing affords me the excuse to touch you."

His fingers fanned over the small of her back, gathering her closer to him. Hetta gasped.

He noted it. "You see? A little noise like that is most gratifying. Next, I mean to make you quiver."

Her pulse thundered in her ears. He couldn't possibly intend to court her, she told herself sternly, or even to seduce her. Surely there was some mistake, some other explanation. But once again, some unreasonable wisp of hope would not be repressed. It floated blithely about her chest, evading all her attempts to squash it flat.

A strange expression overtook his face. One she'd never seen him make before. It was a smile. Not just a smile, but a devastatingly handsome grin. That smile could wreak havoc in an assembly of ladies. It was a fortunate thing he saved it for rare occasions.

She blurted out, "Why are you smiling?" Because she

was dying to know, and asking seemed the most efficient way to find out.

"I'm enjoying your distress."

Not quite the answer she'd been expecting. Not the answer she'd been hoping to hear.

Stop that. No hoping.

"I'm not distressed," she lied.

And now he laughed. Laughed! It was a brittle chuckle, rusty with disuse. "Oh yes, you are distressed. Distressed, blushing . . . dare I say, mortified? And it is most satisfying to view, after weeks of your cool competence. The unfeeling Miss Osborne proves human after all." He swept her through a turn and lowered his voice. His breath teased her ear. "Allow me to give you a word of advice. It is a dangerous thing, for a woman to cultivate such an air of self-possession. It brings out the base insecurities of men. We long to see her unnerved, made helpless, brought low. We take perverse pleasure in inciting such states."

"So you are distressing me on purpose."

"Yes."

"And taking amusement in it."

"Yes."

"I see." To her dismay, she could not keep her voice from heating a degree. What a fool she'd been. She actually *had* believed they shared something in common. That here, at last, was someone who might intuit the reason for her cool demeanor. Someone who might understand that Hetta had to work ten times as hard as any other physician for each scrap of respect she might gather, and that she didn't dare compromise that hard-won reputation for anything so pejoratively feminine as emotional display.

If she could look straight through his hardened, bitter exterior without flinching . . . she'd fancied he might see through hers, too, and glimpse the woman's heart within.

But no. He saw nothing. He called her "cold" and "unfeeling." Well, for a cold, unfeeling stone of a heart, hers was doing a credible impression of breaking.

Oh, Hetta. This is your own fault. You're an intelligent woman. You should have known better than to dream.

"Do you . . ." She swallowed. "Do you despise me, then?"

He pulled back and regarded her with those hard, dark eyes. "A little. Or perhaps I merely envy you and despise myself for it."

"Kindly release me." She squirmed in his embrace. "I don't wish to dance any more."

He tightened his arm around her waist, forbidding her to leave. "Come now, Miss Osborne. We're having a grand time, indeed. Don't you delight in being shocking?"

"What do you mean?"

"Haven't you noticed? Everyone is watching us."

She had not noticed. She'd been entirely focused on him. But now that Hetta surreptitiously viewed the room, she realized how many eyes tracked their progress around the dance floor.

He said dryly, "We must make quite the striking couple."

Hetta contemplated striking *him*.

"But then," he added smoothly, "I'm accustomed to being the object of curiosity. People stare at me a great deal." He gave her a pointed look, steering her toward an empty corner of the ballroom. "*You* stare at me a great deal, Miss Osborne. Why is that? Am I an object of curiosity to you?"

Oh, why did the worst five minutes of her year have to happen all in a row? Hetta planted her feet. He would not dance her a single step further. "Why are you doing this? What have I done to you?"

"You've unsettled me," he said, gripping her wrist until it hurt, "and I thought to repay the favor. So tell me, how do you enjoy being made a public spectacle? How does it feel, to know you'll be the talk of the ladies' retiring room—the milk-and-roses English miss, dancing in the arms of the bastard half-breed?"

What? As if a woman like Lady Violet would care what sort of gentleman Hetta danced with. As if Hetta would care, should Lady Violet deign to object.

"If I am unsettled," she whispered hotly, wresting her arm from his grip, "it has nothing to do with the censure of others, and everything to do with my own sad error in judgment. I am not some 'milk-and-roses miss,' Captain Grayson. I am a woman, with a name and an education and a profession, and even after this humiliating evening, I still lay claim to a shred of dignity. And as for you . . . I had thought *you* were a gentleman."

A strange emotion flashed in his eyes.

Hetta didn't stay long enough to decipher it. She backed away, desperate to flee. The potted trees were no longer an option, but surely somewhere there was a secluded alcove or insect-plagued balcony where she could fall to pieces in private.

"Thank you," she told him, stumbling away. "For showing me the bastard you truly are."

CHAPTER
NINE

Isabel hadn't meant to go looking for The Book.

Really, she hadn't. She came across it almost entirely by accident.

Sophia and Gray were out that evening, attending yet another ball. Bel had stayed home, presumably to rest—but she found herself unable to sleep. The closer her wedding day approached, the more her sense of nervous excitement grew. Ridiculous, really. Weddings were meant to be solemn, quiet affairs between a man, his bride, and their God. The pomp and extravagant display that would accompany the ceremony were for the benefit of drawing public notice, not to swell Bel's own vanity.

Still, when she laid her head on the pillow at night and closed her eyes, she could not stop her imagination from tracing the pearl-seeded trim of her gown, the Belgian lace flounce that would lap at her silk slippers, the posy of hothouse blooms she would carry . . . Fourteen orange blossoms!

No, she couldn't sleep at all.

Reluctant to rouse the maid at this late hour, Bel rose from her bed and crept to Sophia's bedchamber. She knew her sister-in-law had been having similar problems finding sleep, in these early months of her pregnancy, and Miss Osborne had given her some sort of sleeping draught. Although Sophia's insomnia was due to the aftereffects of marriage, not the anticipation thereof, Bel reasoned the draught might be of aid to her as well.

By the light of a single taper, she cautiously searched the drawers of Sophia's vanity. Finding nothing but ear-bobs and hairbrushes, she moved to the small bedside table. The drawer slid open noiselessly, revealing the corked blue bottle of sleeping draught and—

And a book.

The Book.

This must be The Book, the subject of Lucy's insistent hinting and Sophia's equally insistent denial.

Tilting the leather binding until the embossed letters caught the candlelight, she read the title in a whisper. *"The Memoirs of a Wanton Dairymaid."*

Oh my.

Bel recognized that this moment was one of those little tests life presented, from time to time. She held The Book in her hand, and now she must decide what to do with it. The right thing to do with it, she suspected, would be to put it back in the drawer, take the sleeping draught, and return to her bedchamber immediately.

But then, here was one of those little ironies life presented, from time to time. Knowing the right thing to do was far simpler in daylight, with people looking on and all potential regrets fully illuminated. When one was alone at midnight in a candlelit bedchamber, and any future beyond the present moment was as vague as the shadows . . . discerning the right course—or, more to the point, following it—was considerably more difficult.

A very large, very curious part of her wanted to open the book. And that was what she did.

It began innocently enough. There was a printed text, and then there were pen-and-ink illustrations, which looked to have been inserted after the printing. In parallel, both words and images told the story of a courtship between a dairymaid and her gentleman employer. The dairymaid possessed a buxom, rounded figure, which immediately endeared her to Bel. And perhaps she imagined it, but the gentleman suitor bore a passing resemblance to Toby—lean, dashing, classically handsome.

Feeling reassured, Bel fixed her taper in a candlestick and settled herself on the edge of the bed to continue reading.

The beginnings of the lovers' assignations were almost sweet, she thought, despite her general disinclination to romance. A kiss on the hand here, a whispered endearment there . . . She lingered over one depiction of the couple in a lovely pastoral scene, with rolling countryside in the background and gauzy clouds overhead. Those deft, light strokes, the attention to detail—it was the oddest thing, but Bel felt that the style of illustration was somehow familiar to her.

Feeling certain that a proposal of marriage would be imminent, Bel eagerly flipped another page—and nearly dropped the book.

The dairymaid's sweet, meandering romance had taken an abrupt, quite carnal turn down the road to ruin. There she was in the dairy, reclined against the tiled countertop, hiking her skirts to her knees while the gentleman reached for her bared breast. Bel quickly scanned the preceding pages. No, no proposal of marriage therein. She felt more than a bit disappointed in the moral character of this dairymaid, with whom she'd come to identify. But then, considering the word "wanton" in the title, perhaps she ought to have been forewarned. Even the gentleman looked different in this illustration—less refined, more dark and devious.

Still, she turned the page with great curiosity. Not curiosity of a prurient nature, of course. This was purely academic interest. Gentleman's hand on lady's breast—this much Bel had experienced. But she was to be married in less than a week, and everything that filled the pages beyond could prove invaluable education.

Lady Violet's remarks still haunted her. Toby had such

a rakish reputation. Surely he was experienced in what God intended to be the marital act, even though he had not been married. She was keenly afraid of disappointing him in her ignorance and ineptitude. She was even more afraid he might turn to another—adultery being a sin even greater than fornication—should her efforts fail to please.

That was it. She was reading the rest of The Book for the good of Toby's soul. Certainly not to slake her own depraved curiosity.

With fumbling fingers, she leafed through the next several printed pages, barely skimming the text. A strange rustling sound gave her a start—until she realized it to be her own raw-edged breath. Finally she came to the next illustration.

What an education it was. There were all sorts of body parts on display—male, female—but they remained fortunate blurs in Bel's peripheral vision as her gaze trained in on the gentleman's face. She realized, for the first time in several chapters, the illustration offered a full view of the hero's face. A face that had altered, since the first pages of the book.

It now looked a great deal like her brother's.

Oh dear sweet heaven. It *was*. It was *Gray*'s face. And these illustrations were Sophia's artistic hand at work—that was why the style had struck Bel as so familiar.

With a cry of horror, she clapped the book shut and flung it back in the drawer. She rose from the bed, rubbing her hands briskly up and down her arms. Never mind the hour-long soak she'd taken earlier that evening—Bel felt *unclean*. And well she should, for spying through her sister's personal belongings. She ought to have known it was the wrong thing to do.

No wonder Sophia had resisted all of Lucy's hints that she should pass along The Book. How could she, after filling it with illustrations of such . . . such a private nature?

Well, if Bel had been after an education, she'd certainly learned her lesson. She made up her mind then and there that all further instruction in marital relations would come from her husband, and her husband alone. She did not need That Book, nor anything like it.

"Appalling," she muttered, referring to her own behavior. With a resolute shove, she slammed the table drawer shut.

A moment later, she opened it again.

She might not need That Book, but one thing was clear. She now had desperate need of that sleeping draught.

A quarter-hour before his wedding was scheduled to begin, Toby stood in the annex of St. George's of Hanover, wearing a new tailcoat of close-cut superfine and a wide, idiotic grin.

Hundreds of guests representing the first skim of the cream of English society crammed the church pews, all waiting to see the infamous bachelor at long last take a wife. And they would not be disappointed. They would be treated to a spectacle of blossoms and lace and seed pearls the likes of which London had never seen, and a wedding breakfast so richly spiced they'd be tasting it for weeks. And at the center of it all would sparkle an unparalleled, legendary beauty: Isabel.

His Isabel.

Toby smoothed his coat sleeve. He was determined to present a relaxed exterior, but inwardly he hummed with anticipation. This morning, he claimed a public victory. Tonight, in private, he claimed his prize. Barring a last-moment crisis, this was going to be a good day.

When Gray entered the room and shot him an angry glare, Toby's grin only widened. Gray's presence meant Isabel had arrived at the church; the rage in his eyes meant the wedding was still on.

It was going to be a very good day.

"I can't believe I'm going to do this," Gray said, prowling the small room. "I can't believe I'm going to hand my sister over to you."

Toby watched him with satisfaction. "I thought agitated pacing was the groom's duty. Come on, Gray. It's not so bad as all that. You make it sound as though you're leading her to the guillotine."

"It's your head I'd have on a platter." Gray stopped circling the room and drilled him with a threatening look. "I told you months ago—keep her happy, or there will be no wedding."

The bottom dropped out of Toby's stomach. "Is Isabel not happy?"

"No. She's not happy. She's goddamned ecstatic, and I hate you for it."

Toby covered his sigh of relief with a laugh.

Gray continued, "After today, I've no threat to hold over your head. Well, I suppose I could always kill you." He said this with an insulting, nonchalant wave of his hand that suggested dispatching Toby would cost him all the effort of swatting a gnat. "But I'm not eager to make my sister a widow at the tender age of twenty."

"Er . . . Thank you? I guess?"

"Damn it, I'm serious. After today, I can't order you to keep her happy." Gray approached him. "So I'm not threatening you anymore, I'm . . . Bloody hell, I'm begging you. This is my baby sister. My only sister. And this morning, she's happier than I've ever seen her in her life." He jabbed a finger in Toby's chest. "Don't cock it up."

"Good God, man. I think you're going to cry."

Gray bristled. "No, I'm not."

"You are, I swear it. Your eyes are all glittery." Toby raised a finger to the corner of his own eye. "Look, right here . . . a little tear just about to fall—"

"Go to hell." Gray turned on his heel, making a show of raking his hand through his hair before surreptitiously swiping at his eyes.

Toby felt a pang of sympathy for the man. Perhaps it was poor form to gloat, when he'd already won the battle. "Listen," he said. "You've nothing to worry about. No one wants to see Isabel happy more than I do."

Gray threw him a look of utter skepticism.

"No, I mean it," Toby said slowly, just as surprised as anyone to realize he was speaking the truth. "I know you can't credit it. She's been your sister all your life, and here she's been my intended just a matter of months. I don't expect you to believe me, but I tell you quite honestly, there's nothing more important to me than seeing Isabel happy. Nothing."

Gray made a sound of derision.

For both their sakes, Toby decided to lighten the mood. "Look at it this way. You're not losing a sister, you're gaining a brother."

"God. Now I really will weep." Collecting himself, Gray gave Toby a superior smirk. "Well, I'd best be getting back to Sophia. You know, *my* wife."

"Oh, no. That won't work anymore, either. I'm not envious of you. How could I be, seeing how it all turned out?" For the second time in the space of a minute, Toby's impulsive honesty came as a revelation. It was true. Whatever his mixed feelings toward Gray, jealousy no longer had any part in them. "Mind, I still think Sophia's too good for you."

"Of course she is. I'm no fool."

"And I know we can agree Isabel's simply too good for this world." Toby smiled. "There's nothing for it, Gray. I think we'll just have to get along."

Gray's shoulders scrunched together, as if the idea sent chills down his spine.

"Come on," Toby prodded, enjoying the moment thoroughly. "I'm an amiable sort. I'm friends with everyone." He opened his arms and tilted his head to the side. "Brotherly hug?"

"Oh, for Christ's sake. I'd sooner cut off my own bollocks." Gray made for the exit, leaving Toby's arms suspended mid-air. He paused at the door just long enough to repeat those encouraging words: "Don't cock it up."

Don't cock it up, indeed. What an enlightening chat. All this time, Toby had focused on getting even with Gray—only to find they'd emerged as allies. At some point in their betrothal, somewhere in the midst of begging, charming, cajoling, and outright lying to earn her approval—Isabel had crawled straight into his breast pocket and made a home there. To be honest, it could also have had something to do with the point when his fingers crawled into her bodice . . .

At any rate, the game had changed. He didn't want to get even with Gray anymore, or assuage his own wounded pride. He'd grown accustomed to Isabel's lovely smiles and expressions of kindhearted delight. He'd come to live off her sweet faith, the perfect trust in her eyes when she gazed at him. Now he couldn't imagine surviving without it—any more than he could imagine surviving without air, or food. Whether her brother believed it or not, Toby truly wanted, more than anything, to keep his wife happy.

Which meant keeping his promises.

Good Lord.

All his promises. Every blasted one of them.

The door burst open again. Toby looked up, expecting to see Jeremy, prepared to assume his role of best man. Instead, in walked a much older friend—in more ways than one.

"Mr. Yorke," Toby greeted him. "What a pleasant surprise. Come to give me last-minute advice?"

"How's this for advice? Run away. You're making a terrible mistake. Marriage is for virgins and fools."

"And here you've remained a bachelor all these years." Toby chuckled. "Astonishing."

The old man released a heavy sigh. "Didn't think I'd be able to dissuade you. Thought it was worth a try, though—just to witness the fit that woman would have when her son's wedding fell through for the second time." Mr. Yorke withdrew a flask from his breast pocket. "Since you're determined to go through with it, perhaps you need some encouragement of the liquid variety?"

Toby reached for the flask gratefully. "Actually, I believe I do." He leaned against the stone window ledge and motioned for Yorke to join him. "You do realize, it's been a good fifteen years since she took me to task for drinking. I hope you're not expecting to ruffle her feathers with this." He tossed back a mouthful of liquor.

"I only wish. Speaking of that woman—"

"You know, 'that woman' happens to be my mother. Not to mention, a lady."

"*That woman* has just related to me another of her pernicious lies. She says you mean to stand up against me in the election. You mean to contest my seat in Parliament, she says! I know it has to be a falsehood."

"Well . . ." Toby hedged. Here was one of those promises, come back to haunt him. "It's true, I had been planning to—"

"Do you want to know how I know it's a falsehood? Aside from the fact that you'd have no hope of winning, of course." Yorke took back his flask and downed a swallow. "That woman tells me you're running as a Whig."

"That woman speaks the truth, I'm afraid. But I can explain. You see—"

"Gah!" Yorke drained the brandy and sent the flask clattering to the floor. "Honestly. As a Whig, Toby?" He might as well have recited, "*Et tu, Brute?*" "Have I taught you nothing? It would be one thing if you wanted to take up politics on the proper side. I'd take you under my wing, find a borough for you. Hell, I'd nominate you myself. But after all these years—all those times I let you sleep off mischief in my hayloft, poach grouse from my woods—this is how you repay me? By turning Whig?"

"I know, I know. It's a tragedy. I'll have to start frequenting Brooks'." Toby put a hand on Yorke's shoulder, taking quick stock of his friend and their lifelong acquaintance. The old man was right, Toby did owe him better than this. He owed him a great deal. He recalled many a fine afternoon spent angling for trout in the stream between their lands, and he recalled several occasions when his neighbor had fished him out of a scrape.

What he didn't recall was precisely when Yorke had become so ancient. The man's snowy hair had thinned considerably in recent years, and his once-subtle smile lines had deepened to permanent furrows.

"Give me a moment to explain," Toby said. "It's not my mother's idea, it's my lovely bride's. She's a very principled girl; I don't deserve her at all. She has her heart set on seeing me in Parliament, Lord knows why. But I promised her I'd run, in a moment of . . . weakness. Serious weakness."

"Ah," Yorke said meaningfully. "While your wits had gone south on holiday?"

"Something like that," Toby said. His wits began packing their trunks for a return visit, just at the memory. "Of course, I've explained to my bride your long history of service and unparalleled popularity with the electors. She's been well informed that I have no hope of winning, but she is determined to see me try, I'm afraid. And besotted fool that I am, I've decided to indulge her."

"And to inconvenience me."

Toby raised his hands in an exasperated gesture. "What can I say? She's prettier."

Yorke laughed heartily. "She's a rare beauty, is what she is."

"Isn't she, though? And I'm going to marry her in a matter of minutes. I can't go ruining it the first week, by kidnapping her to the Lake District instead of fulfilling my promise to stand up in Surrey."

"Wouldn't be much of a honeymoon, would it? No, I understand."

"I knew you would. Don't worry, I'll not put up any real opposition. After the nominations, I'll stay away from the hustings entirely. Once Isabel understands how capably you represent the borough and what faith the electors have in you, she'll recover from any disappointment. In the meantime, I'll do my best to find other methods of keeping her occupied."

Yorke gave him a merry look. "No doubt."

"See? There's no need for concern."

"Who's concerned?" The old man harrumphed. "It's not as though I've been running unopposed all these years, you know. I know something about beating out upstart candidates."

"Madman Montague doesn't count. Don't throw me in with him."

"And," Yorke continued, undeterred, "it gives me one more opportunity to thwart that woman's machinations. She'll be bitterly disappointed when you lose."

Toby smiled. "Indubitably. Don't you see? I'll keep my promise to run for Parliament, you'll keep your seat. I'll make my bride happy; you'll continue making my mother miserable. It's the perfect solution, all around."

"So long as the women don't catch on, eh?"

Toby gave a self-conscious tug on his ear. It might not be an auspicious beginning to a marriage, plotting to deceive his bride just minutes before the ceremony. But once they were married, he fully intended to go about deserving Isabel's good opinion. On his own terms, by some endeavor of his own choosing. Surely he could find some way to make himself useful that did not involve sooty foundlings or arse-numbing sessions of Parliament. A method that didn't require him to publicly trounce an old, respected friend.

Chuckling, Yorke held out his hand. "I do like the way you think. Very well, then. May the best man win."

"Precisely," Toby said, shaking it.

"Actually," Jeremy said, standing impatient in the doorway, "the best man is here. And he's tired of fending off anxious looks from the priest, the bride's brothers, and the mother of the groom. Can we get this thing underway?" Remembering himself, he added a perfunctory bow toward the older man. "If you'll excuse us, Mr. Yorke."

Toby stood, pulling down the front of his waistcoat.

"This is your last chance to change your mind," Yorke said. "Are you certain you want to do this?"

"Yes," Toby answered, to all the questions implied. "Yes, I am."

CHAPTER
TEN

At the knock on the connecting door, Bel nearly jumped out of her skin. Absurd, to be so surprised by the very event she'd been standing there anticipating. Her heart slammed into her ribs, and her eyes darted wildly about the bedchamber. Should she meet him at the door? Lie down on the bed? Flee to her dressing room and hide?

And here she'd thought the wedding ceremony taxing on her nerves. Parading down the aisle of St. George's under the scrutiny of hundreds? That was nothing, compared to waiting for her new husband to attend her on their wedding night. At least in church, she'd known in which direction to walk.

In the end, she did what she always did when shock rendered her immobile. She stood still.

The door swung open, and Toby struck a casual pose, leaning one shoulder against the doorframe. "Good evening, Lady Aldridge."

He was still dressed in the same pinstriped trousers he'd worn for the wedding, though his topcoat, waistcoat, and cravat had disappeared. Bel tore her gaze from the gaping collar of his shirt to focus on the one permanent fixture of his appearance: that charming, boyish grin.

She attempted a smile in return, instinctively wrapping her arms about her chest and gathering the edges of her lace-trimmed dressing gown. How she envied his easy confidence in every situation. Throughout the ceremony, the wedding breakfast, their installation here at Aldridge House, and even their first dinner as husband and wife—he'd been the epitome of poise. Bel had remained close to his side all day, praying some of his self-assurance might rub off on her. Perhaps, she thought, the same strategy would serve her well this evening.

Perhaps she did know in which direction she should walk. Really, it was the same as in church.

She walked toward him.

His grin widened as she approached. She felt her own smile growing, too.

"Good evening, Sir Toby," she said, stopping just inches from him.

His arm snaked around her waist, and he pulled her tight for a kiss. It was the briefest, most chaste of kisses, but somehow more intimate than any kiss they'd shared before. This was not a suitor's kiss, but a husband's kiss. Comfortable, authoritative . . . and performed in a state of undress.

Before Bel had any chance to catch her breath, he released her waist and strolled past her into the bedchamber. Now she was the one left leaning against the doorframe for support.

"Did I tell you," he asked, taking up the poker and stirring the fire, "how immensely proud you made me today?"

"You did," she said, smiling to herself. "Several times." In the carriage, after the ceremony. Then again, whispering in her ear during the wedding breakfast. Once more, over dinner. "I begin to believe it."

"Well, I'll be certain to tell you several more times, so there can be no misunderstanding." He replaced the poker and met her in the center of the room, grasping her hands in his. "Truly, Isabel. I'm the most fortunate fellow in England. As long as I live, I'll never forget how lovely you looked this morning."

Once again, Bel wished she had his easy way with words. She wanted to compliment him, too, tell him he'd made the most dashing groom imaginable. That he'd stolen her breath with his radiant male beauty. That she'd been aching for his kiss all day, and the slight brush of his lips against hers just now had her whole body humming with desire.

"Toby, I . . ." Oh, how she cursed her clumsy tongue! "I feel fortunate, too." She stared up at him, hoping her eyes conveyed the admiration her words could not.

His fingertip brushed the place between her eyebrows. "Always so serious," he teased. Smiling, he withdrew a small box. "I have a wedding present for you."

Bel took the box and opened it. Cradled on a bed of blue velvet lay a magnificent pendant, set with an iridescent opal as big as her fingernail and ringed with sparkling diamonds. "Oh, Toby. You shouldn't have."

"Of course I should. I know you're not much for extravagant jewels. Little do you need them, beautiful as you are. But you are Lady Aldridge now, and if you're to be a lady of influence, you must look the part." He plucked the necklace from its box and laced the chain through his fingers. Between them, the pendant twirled, flashing in the firelight. "There are several more valuable pieces in the family, of course, and those will be yours as well. But I wanted to select something especially for you. Did I choose well?"

The pendant bobbed just a bit as he dangled it, and Bel caught a flash of anxiety in his eyes. Sweet man. He was genuinely worried that she might not like it. Her heart squeezed. That hint of uncertainty endeared him to her more than any gift could possibly have done. That, more than anything, showed that he cared.

"You chose perfectly. I adore it, thank you."

"May I put it on you?"

"Now?"

"Yes, of course." He circled behind her, undoing the clasp of the necklace with sure fingers. "I'll tell you a secret. This is the real reason a gentleman gives his lady a necklace. For the pleasure of fastening it round her neck."

"Truly?" Bel shuddered as his fingers brushed the sensitive skin above her collarbone.

"Truly. And lucky me, you've even left your hair up."

"I should have let the maid take it down." Bel cringed. Her maid had asked, and she hadn't known what to tell her. Her hair . . . there was so much of it. It had such a habit of getting in the way.

"No, no. It will be my pleasure to do so later. For now, it makes it all the easier for me to do this . . ." The weight of the pendant settled between her breasts as he fastened the clasp. "And this . . ." His touch whispered up to caress the soft place beneath her ear.

"And this . . ." His open mouth pressed against her nape, warm and wet, his breath rushing over her sensitized flesh.

"Oh." Her knees buckled, and she fell back against his chest. But he was there to support her, so tall and strong.

Light kisses feathered down the column of her neck, each one sending a current of pleasure straight to the soles of her feet. And then his tongue . . . oh, his tongue climbed a path straight to her ear, and desire screamed through her. At least, Bel *thought* she might scream—or faint, or plead, or do something else equally mortifying, like melt into a puddle at his feet. She seemed to be melting already, at the juncture of her thighs.

He drew her earlobe into his mouth and suckled it lightly. Oh. Oh. Yes, something unmistakably liquid was happening down there. Ohhh . . . dear. She tensed every muscle in her body, attempting to solidify her will and her person.

He stopped instantly. "Are you all right?"

"Yes," she answered quickly. Too quickly to be credible.

"Forgive me. I'm moving too fast. We have the whole night ahead of us. Perhaps you'd prefer to rest?"

"No. No, I think I'd rather . . ."

"Have it over with?" His soft laugh tickled her ear.

"Yes. I mean . . ." Bel's face burned as she realized how ungracious she sounded. "That is, unless you don't want to."

His voice went dark. "Oh, I want to. I very much want to." His hands slid to her hips, and for the first time Bel noticed something hard and hot pressing into her lower back. She knew it had to be his manhood. "I've wanted you since the first moment I saw you."

Her breath caught. Against her crossed arms, her nipples hardened and ached. And what was the polite response to such an admission? *Thank you? Sir, you flatter me? Please be gentle, and if at all possible, quick?*

At the heart of the matter, Bel wasn't sure how to respond simply because she wasn't sure how she felt about the entire enterprise. Her racing pulse, her quickened breath, the heightened awareness of all her senses—her body was readying for *something*. She just didn't know what. Excitement and terror mingled in her veins, and she couldn't tell whether her instincts were urging her to fly at her husband or simply flee the room.

Of course, the second was not an option at all. She was married now, and conjugal relations were her wifely duty. The thought calmed her. Bel might not know what to make of this unruly sensation, but she understood duty. And she wanted to make Toby happy, she did. Closing her eyes, she resolved to focus on him—on the warm, solid planes of his chest supporting her frame, his confident hands grasping her shoulders, the heat of his breath against her ear. He was her husband, and she could deny him nothing.

And just when she had decided to turn, face him, and brazenly offer herself for his pleasure, he took a step back. Suddenly cold, she hugged herself tight and shivered.

"We'll take things slowly," he said, twining a finger through the loose strands of hair at her temple. "May I take your hair down?"

She nodded. After pausing to take a hairbrush from the dressing table, he guided her to sit at the foot of the bed and then knelt behind her. It made Bel increasingly anxious, how much time he was spending behind her. She couldn't comfort herself by focusing his warm eyes or his easy grin. He was all seductive touch and smooth whispers and masculine heat. She couldn't see him; she could only feel him. Hear him. Breathe the last traces of his expensive cologne as they evaporated into the natural musk of his skin.

"Here." He teased a pearl-studded pin from her hair and held it above her left shoulder. Bel held up her open palm to receive it. Soon another pin joined the first, and another and another—until her hair tumbled free down her back, the blunt ends just brushing the coverlet. She curled her fingers over the clutch of pins, unsure what to do with them.

"Magnificent," he murmured, lifting her hair and allowing it to spill over her shoulders and around her breasts. "Like black silk." He tugged the brush through her hair in a long, slow motion, stroking a wave of delicious pleasure from her scalp to the base of her spine.

Behind her, Toby made a strange sound in his throat. "It's like pulling a brush through water. Do you know I've dreamed of doing this?"

Had he, truly? Dreamed of this? Bel had experienced some rather intimate dreams of her own the past few weeks. None of them so specific as brushing hair. No, her own dreams were restless and vague and shadowy and just never quite *complete*.

With expert care, he worked his way through each

section of her hair. A pleasant languor settled over Bel as he brushed, and the knot of tension in her belly began to uncoil. She closed her eyes, bracing her weight on her right hand and still clutching the handful of hairpins in the left.

"Isabel?"

"Mmm."

"You do understand, don't you? What occurs between a husband and wife?"

"Yes, I—" She winced as the brush snagged on a hidden tangle. "I understand." At least, she comprehended the basic idea. Even without reading That Book, she'd lived too rural a life to grow up completely innocent of mating.

"Did your . . ." Toby cleared his throat, then continued in a tone of false nonchalance. "Did your sister speak with you, tell you what to expect?"

"No, no. That is, Sophia offered." His hand jerked slightly when she said the name. Oh, how unspeakably embarrassing this was! "But as I said, I already understood the general concept, and I told her . . . I told her I would prefer to learn the rest from you."

He set the brush aside. "Did you?"

"Yes, of course." She craned her neck, needing to see his expression. Had she done the right thing? To her relief, he looked pleased. "I trust you will explain to me anything you wish me to know. And if there are things you do *not* wish me to know—well then, it is best they remain unexplained."

A puzzled smile appeared on his face. "Thank you. I think." He swept a heavy lock of hair behind her ear. Their gazes met, and she caught a peculiar glimmer in his eyes. "Your trust humbles me."

"Well, I find myself quite humbled by my ignorance, so perhaps we are well matched in that respect."

He moved to sit beside her at the edge of the bed,

taking her open hand in his. "I believe we are well matched, in many respects."

She blushed and stared down at their interlaced fingers. His thumb stroked idly back and forth across the back of her hand. So gentle, so soothing—even though his uneven breath betrayed his growing passion. Truly, she had the best, most patient of husbands. How could she not give him her trust?

"Besides," she said haltingly, "it's clear you have considerable experience with . . ." She cast a darting glance over her shoulder, toward the vast expanse of mattress. "With this. How could I doubt your ability to guide me?"

"Considerable experience?" He laughed. "Again, I thank you. I think. Darling, my experience—while not negligible—is probably less than you imagine."

"But—" Bel paused, thinking of the scandal sheets tallying his paramours.

"But what? Don't tell me you've been reading *The Prattler*?"

She slanted her gaze to the floor. "Not purposely."

"I've told you, don't believe all you read in the newspapers." He squeezed her hand. "Isabel, I'm not a monk. But though I may flirt with every debutante to flounce in my direction, when it comes to . . ." His eyes darted toward the bed. "To *this*, there haven't been so many as the papers imply. There haven't been any, actually, in some time. Do you understand what I'm telling you?"

"That you are selective and principled?"

He chuckled. "You always give me too much credit. I'm telling you that I'm quite desperate for you." He let go of her hand and caressed her cheek. Then her bottom lip. The smooth charm in his voice gave way to raw need as the distance between them narrowed. "I've been waiting for you, for a very long time."

His lips took hers in a passionate kiss. Bel's fingers curled into fists. The hairpins bit into her left palm. How absurd, that she was still holding them, but what else could she do? Should she break the kiss to say, *Dear, sweet husband, I know you've been waiting for me for a very long time, but can I beg you to wait a moment longer while I dispose of these hairpins?*

No, of course not. She would not ask him to wait, not a moment longer. She would allow him to kiss her, just as deeply as he wished. And she would kiss him back, stroking his tongue with hers—because he made a little growl of approval when she did so, and Bel craved his approval even more than she craved his kiss. He was proud of her, he'd said. And even if he had told her so several times already, she couldn't hear it—or feel it—enough.

His hands moved to the front of her dressing gown, untying the simple ribbon bow and drawing the two sides apart. With deft fingers, he dispatched the row of tiny buttons dividing her nightgown. One, two, three, four . . . Bel lost count when his mouth broke away from hers to trail urgent kisses along her jaw and down her throat. His fingertips brushed her breastbone as he worked the buttons loose, one after another—and that unbearable, heavy ache swelled her breasts.

Bel squeezed her eyes shut as he parted the sides of her nightgown, exposing her bosom. She could feel him staring at her chest, her nipples tightening under his gaze. But she would gladly forgive him a lifetime of lurid glances, if only he would touch them.

And, oh. Oh, at last. He did.

Someone gave a ragged sigh. Bel wasn't sure if it had originated in his chest or hers. She opened her eyes to see his strong, sculpted hands cupping her breasts, lifting them, taking their ponderous weight from her frame. Oh, heaven. It was like bathing in the sea, buoyant and weightless. Her dark, swollen nipples jutted out for attention, and he brushed his thumbs over the straining tips. Twin jolts of pleasure raced to her core.

"So beautiful," he murmured.

Bel resisted the impulse to disagree. Her breasts always looked grotesquely large and indecent to her, but in his hands they looked—not beautiful, exactly. But as though they fit. As though they were just right. The heavy globes were the perfect size for his fingers to hold, to lift, to shape. Her large, dark areolas seemed expressly fashioned to wedge in the crook of his thumb and forefinger as he ever-so-gently squeezed.

Bel gasped as he bent his head and took her taut, aching nipple into his mouth. She was a perfect fit there, too. Wild sensation swirled through her as he licked and sucked. There she went, melting again. Damp heat surged between her thighs, and she clamped them together. Toby transferred his attentions to the other breast, working dark, dangerous magic with his lips and tongue. All the while, his hand groped for the hem of her nightgown. With rough movements, he gathered the fabric up to her knee, and then his hand encircled her bare thigh.

The air in the room grew thin. No matter how her lungs worked, Bel couldn't draw enough of it.

"Isabel." His brow rested on her chest. "Let me touch you there."

How could she refuse? It didn't seem possible to accomplish what she knew they must accomplish without *some* part of him touching her there. But her panic built as his hand crept slowly higher, up the sensitive slope of her inner thigh, knowing that he would most certainly discover—

He groaned as his fingers reached her cleft. "You're so wet."

To her surprise, he didn't sound appalled, but pleased. Approving. His fingers rubbed against her, and Bel gave a sharp cry. She couldn't help it. The sensation was so intense. The hairpins bit into her palm as she struggled for control.

He kissed her, stifling her next unwilling moan. "I knew it would be like this," he said between kisses, his fingers rubbing her more firmly. More quickly. "You're so serious, my darling. Always so serious. But not here, not with me. Here, I knew you would be so passionate. So free."

No, no, she wanted to protest. *I'm a woman of faith and principle. I refuse to be ruled by my passions. That way lies madness.*

But then with a single finger, he parted her folds and slipped inside her. *Inside* her. The feeling was . . . shocking. Glorious. Incompatible with thought, much less conversation.

A hot, restless longing built as he stroked her relentlessly, inside and out. The sensation was not wholly unfamiliar. Sometimes in the night Bel woke with this same dull ache between her legs. And she'd learned years ago that if she rolled over and ground her hips against the bed, first it got a bit worse, but then it got a bit better—until it broke into pieces and mercifully went away.

But it was never like this. Never this bad. Never this good.

Without ceasing his sweet torment, Toby sank to the floor and knelt in front of her, spreading her legs. It seemed wrong, in so many ways: him kneeling before her, her thighs splayed in this lewd posture, the manner in which her most intimate places were revealed to his gaze, to his touch . . .

To his mouth.

Oh. Oh. Oh.

Never this bad. Never this good. It was too much, too much.

"Toby." She wriggled away from him, but his hand

tightened over her thigh. "Toby, please. Don't you want to take your pleasure now?"

"Your pleasure is my pleasure." He licked her over and over, so very lightly. And sensation detonated in her each time, destroying her presence of mind. She understood why her mother had gone mad from passion. With each tender caress, he pushed her closer to some terrible brink of sanity. She would shatter apart. She would never be whole again.

"Toby, please." She forced the words out. "You must . . . must stop."

"What must I stop?" he asked, his voice joking. "This?" He licked. "This?" He stroked. "Or this?" He pursed his lips and did something ineffably wicked.

Another little cry escaped her. "You're teasing me."

"Yes, I am. Because I know how you love it."

She did. She did love it. In this insane moment she nearly believed she loved him *for* it. Because she trusted him so completely. She knew that when he teased her, it meant she was strong enough to bear it.

Proving the point, he took pity on her unease, kissing his way back up her belly. His hand resumed stroking her, inside and out, as he fastened his lips around her nipple. Pleasure built, rolling through her body, making her quiver and writhe helplessly. Bel tensed again. She didn't like feeling helpless. This all felt so wrong. She'd been fully prepared for Toby to take pleasure from her, but she didn't know how to handle receiving it from him.

"Let go," he murmured, kissing his way from one breast to the other. "Don't fight it. You'll make it better for me, if you just let go."

Let go. You'll make it better for me. His words freed her. She could do this—even this—for him. With a rough gasp, she bucked against his hand.

"Yes," he sighed, stroking her faster. "That's it."

She clutched his shoulder with her right hand, and her left unfurled. The hairpins fell to the floor in a cascade of metallic pings. His hand and lips made wet sounds of suction as they worked her moist flesh. But the crashing roar of her pulse overpowered all; the pleasure overtook all.

And she let go.

CHAPTER ELEVEN

Toby held her tight.

In all his life, he thought he would never hear a sound more arousing than Isabel's hoarse cry of passion. As her climax subsided she slumped against him, spent and breathless. Her intimate muscles were still clenching around his sheathed finger, but Toby's restraint had reached its limit.

"Forgive me," he said, withdrawing his hand and lifting her onto the bed. "But I must have you. And it must be now."

She gave him a groggy nod and a murmured, "Yes."

Toby scrambled to unbutton his fall before his erection burst right through his trousers. God, he was still almost fully clothed. But then, so was she—and he had no intention of slowing down for even the few seconds it would take to rectify the situation. In fact, he loved her this way. The contrast of her glossy black hair and olive skin against that virginal white lace took him from aroused to fair frenzied with desire.

He worked his trousers down over his hips and positioned himself at her entrance, gathering his control just long enough for one last murmured apology: "I'm so sorry. The pain lasts only a moment, darling."

He eased into her, a bit. Then a bit more.

She winced. He held still, offering her body time to adjust even though every cell in his own body urged him to drive home. "Better?" He grated out the word.

She gave a little nod, and he advanced again—this time sheathing himself in one long, gliding thrust that seemed interminable in all the best and worst ways. When at last he was fully seated, he stretched his body over hers, guarding her between his arms. "Isabel," he whispered, closing his eyes and reveling in the blissful sensation of her warm, wet body gripping him, holding him.

Her body made a home for his, her legs spreading a bit wider to cradle his hips, her soft breasts cushioning his chest. When he felt her relax, and every muscle in his own body tensed, only then did he start to thrust. Slowly, at first. As gently as he could. And then, bracing himself on his elbows, he drove a bit harder, a bit faster. Which was a mistake, because as he drove harder and faster, she began to make little sensual noises with each thrust. And those magnificent breasts began to dance to his tempo. Which aroused him further, pushed him harder and faster—until he knew he was striking a most inconsiderate pace, for a gentleman bedding his lovely, innocent virgin bride.

But damn if she didn't give everything he asked, and then more. Her body yielded to his, *moved* with his in ways that made his mind go blank. She felt so good. He was on the verge of abandoning gentleness in favor of brevity and making a desperate surge toward climax, when he looked down to find those solemn, dark eyes staring up at him.

"What should I do?" she asked. "Tell me what to do."

And that was when Toby changed his mind. For this, he would take his time.

"Tell me what to do," she repeated. "I . . . I want to please you."

Just the words shot a thrill down his spine. His jaw clenched. "You could touch me."

Her eyes skipped over his body. "Where?"

"Wherever you like."

She frowned, and stayed still.

"My chest," he said hoarsely, making the decision for her. "Help me remove my shirt."

She grasped the hem of his shirt and gathered it toward his shoulders, and together they worked his arms free before she pulled it over his head. Then, slowly, she reached for him with both hands, until her fingertips rested against his chest. "Like this?"

"Yes. God, yes."

Her touch feathered toward his shoulders, tentative and achingly sweet. He allowed himself to move again, just the slightest of nudges into her intimate embrace. Then her thumbs brushed his nipples, and he had to freeze again, to keep from spilling his seed that instant. That would have been a tragedy, because this was too good to rush.

Using just the pads of her fingers, she cautiously skimmed every contour of his chest, his shoulders, his upper arms. Such light caresses, so devastating in their tenderness. His every nerve, every capillary pressed to the surface of his skin, eager to meet her seeking fingertips. He felt alive, in ways he'd never felt before.

Her fingers skimmed up his neck, pausing against his throbbing pulse.

"Kiss me there," he said, realizing too late that his tone was a bit brusque. To be ordering his wife about on their wedding night, without so much as a "please" . . . he'd always prided himself on being a patient, solicitous lover. But Toby was several inches deep in paradise, and his hands were full of Isabel's generous curves, and charm was simply not within his grasp.

She didn't seem to mind. Without so much as a blink, she craned her neck and pressed her lips to his pulse—once, then again. His low moan of pleasure earned him a third.

"Like that?" she asked, her breath tickling his throat.

"Yes. More."

She trailed light kisses over his neck and chest, and the torture of her velvet-soft lips was even more exquisite than that of her fingers. Impatient with need, his hips drove home of their own accord. Startled, Isabel fell back against the pillow, her swollen lips parted in invitation.

And Toby was never one to refuse an invitation.

He kissed her hungrily as he began to thrust again, relishing the sensation of pressing himself into her two ways at once. Her lovely, fresh scent wreaked its familiar havoc on his senses, but now that hint of verbena mingled with the heady aroma of arousal—his, hers. Theirs.

Oh, this was good. So good. Better than he could have dreamed.

And still he wanted more.

"Isabel."

"Yes."

"Wrap your legs around my waist." She obeyed. Another terse command, another accommodating response. It drove him wild, to know that she would comply with his every wish, willingly. Even eagerly. It seemed the more curtly he spoke, the more aroused she became. Those serious eyes were now heavy-lidded, drugged with desire, and her breath was a shallow tide in her chest, lifting her bosom as it ebbed and flowed.

He growled, "Hold tight to me now."

Yes, she loved it. She ground against him, her mounting desire evident as she laced her fingers behind his neck.

What more would she do for him, if he only asked? A thousand erotic possibilities overflowed his mind, forcing all awareness down to his groin. They would all have to wait. His body clamored for release—*now*. He took her hard and fast, raising up on his arms for better leverage, and she clung to him tightly. Just as he'd told her to.

Rebalancing his weight, he worked one hand between

them. He found that small, sensitive nub at the crest of her sex and covered it with his thumb, circling lightly.

Her eyes flew open. Her neck rotated back and forth, as if she were shaking her head no.

"Yes," he insisted through gritted teeth. "Yes. Come for me again."

And she did. Just as he'd told her to. Crying out and convulsing around him in hot, satin waves, pulling him deeper. Pulling him closer.

Toby clenched his jaw tight, silencing his own passion. The only words that came to mind now were unspeakable, coarse and profane. And then there were no words at all—just a harsh, primal growl of release as the pleasure ripped through him.

It had never been like this. Not ever.

He collapsed onto her, panting into her silken hair. He felt wrung out, exhausted. He felt blissful and blessed. He felt like starting from the beginning and doing it all again. And again.

But most of all, he felt inexpressibly fortunate in his choice of a wife. Or more accurately, in his wife's choice of him.

"Isabel, my darling." He kissed her brow, damp with perspiration. "Thank you."

She made a muffled squeak in response, and Toby realized his weight was crushing her into the mattress. God, what a boor he was. He quickly withdrew from her body and rolled aside, smoothing her hair away from her face and murmuring apologies.

"Please don't distress yourself," she said, her tone one of strained formality. "I'm sure there is no need for apology, or gratitude."

No need for gratitude? "Isabel—"

"No, please don't thank me." She rose up on an elbow, pushing her nightgown back down her legs. "I haven't even given you your wedding gift yet."

And she was up out of bed, before Toby could argue that she'd already given him the greatest gift he could possibly imagine. While she disappeared into the adjoining room, he took the opportunity to straighten his trousers and run a hand through his hair.

He sat on the edge of the bed when she emerged, her dressing gown now wrapped tightly around her body. Her hands were behind her back, and her eyes were downcast.

"It's really nothing," she began. "I didn't have any idea what to get you. You're . . . you're very difficult to shop for, you know."

Toby smiled. Her anxiety was adorable. Combined with her disheveled hair and flushed complexion—the effect was utterly enchanting. She could have pulled a lump of coal from behind her back, and he would have treasured it.

But it wasn't a lump of coal she withdrew. It was a walking stick, topped with carved ivory and inlaid with gold leaf.

"Is it the style you wanted?" she asked, holding it out to him.

"Yes, the very one." He took it from her hand and laid it horizontally across his palm, testing its balance. "I can't believe you remembered. I thought you held walking sticks in the highest contempt." He lifted an eyebrow at her. "An embellished stick, which a perfectly healthy gentleman carries about for no other purpose than to indicate his wealth . . . ?"

She gave him a sly smile. "Well, and don't forget gesturing. And rapping on doors. Truthfully, I still don't understand the idea—but it was the only thing I could think of to buy you. And I must admit, it does suit you." She gave him an appraising look, and he struck a cocky, bare-chested pose that made her blush most satisfactorily. She asked, "Do you like it?"

"I adore it." He held one end out to her, as though

urging her to take it. When she grasped the polished wood, however, he gave a swift tug, pulling her to him. "But I adore you more."

He meant it to be a tender kiss. A kiss of thanks and appreciation. A kiss that made no demands. But one taste of her, and his body formed quite different intentions. Within seconds, he was as hard as a walking stick. Harder.

"Isabel." He nipped her ear. "I want you again. Can you bear it, so soon?"

"Of course." She pulled back and studied him, that boundless trust shining in her eyes. "You would not ask it of me, if I could not."

And right then, Toby knew. He knew he was doomed.

He could run for Parliament. He could win. He could become bloody Prime Minister and the Prince Regent's closest adviser. He could travel to Ceylon and back just to bring her a cup of tea, converting a thousand heathens along the way—and he would still never live up to that look in her eyes. No man could. Someday, somehow, he would hurt her—and it would mean the end of everything. Oh, she would forgive him, generous soul that she was. They would still share a cordial affection. But she would never look at him like this again, as if . . . as if he *deserved* her faith in him. One day, they would both know he did not.

But for now—and for as long as he could keep it so— it remained Toby's secret.

He slid his hands around her waist. "Darling girl. Come back to bed."

CHAPTER TWELVE

"Just a few miles more." Toby peered out the carriage window, watching the familiar landscape roll past. He turned his attention to his obviously uncomfortable wife, whose clear, honey-colored complexion was tinged with green. "You're miserable, aren't you? Too much jouncing about?"

"I'm enjoying the lovely countryside. But I must admit, I'm not accustomed to lengthy carriage rides." Again, she twisted her hips to find a slightly different position on the tufted seat.

He winced. She must be sore. No, she was not accustomed to lengthy carriage rides, nor to lengthy nights of being ridden like a carriage horse. Not for the first time since their wedding, he felt a stab of guilt. He knew he'd been using his wife as if he were a sailor on shore leave—but damned if he could help it. He wanted her, all the time. And she obliged him, whenever he asked.

Even now, the sight of those luscious breasts bouncing in time to the horses' clopping hooves . . .

He said casually, "Perhaps you'd feel the ruts less if you came over here and sat in my lap."

She gave him that typically Isabel look—serious and searching. He could practically see the thoughts turning over in her mind. Could her husband possibly be so wicked, she was wondering, as to suggest what her recently expanded imagination supposed?

No, she decided mutely—and incorrectly—with a little

shake of her head. "It is kind of you to offer, I'm sure. But I would not wish to wrinkle you."

Just like her, to give him far more credit than his due. If Toby had his way, her light-blue traveling habit would meet with a fate far worse than wrinkling. She had so much misplaced faith in him—he only hoped a shred of it might survive his electoral defeat.

"Will it be a large crowd, there at the hustings?" she asked.

"Oh, undoubtedly. Hundreds, most likely."

"But I understood the number of electors to be rather small. Only those freemen who hold land, your mother told me."

"Yes, but it's rather a holiday, you see. It's the spectacle that draws people from miles around, whether or not they can cast a vote. Little enough excitement to be had in a sleepy borough like ours. Any excuse for a day spent gawking and lifting pints of ale will serve. And this is just the announcement of candidacy—wait until the polling begins in earnest. That's when the real debauchery starts."

"And how long will the polling last?"

"Until there is a clear winner—as many as fifteen days, not counting Sundays." It wasn't likely to last five, Toby thought to himself. By all reasoning, Yorke ought to take a commanding lead from the first and end the thing swiftly.

"As many as fifteen days of drunken debauchery?" Isabel's eyebrows rose. "No wonder people anticipate an election."

"It could be worse. Ours is a sedate little corner of England. We could be in one of those counties up north, where the polling always ends in riots. Or worse," he added, jerking his head toward the window, "just a ways back, in Garret."

"What takes place in Garret?"

"Oh, they have a sort of sham election, every Parliament. People from all around come to see it—outlandish costumes, coarse humor, barrels and barrels of ale. You see, a man needn't be a landowner to vote there."

"No?"

"No." He gave her a teasing grin. "There is only one qualification to vote in Garret. A man must have enjoyed a woman in the open air, somewhere within that district."

The green cast of her complexion turned to pink. "You're joking."

"Not at all." Unable to resist, Toby rose from his seat opposite and crossed the gap, settling down next to her. "In fact," he continued, leaning into her and directing her gaze out the window, "I believe we may still be traveling through that district now. You did remark on the lovely countryside. And I think a breath of open air may be just the remedy you need. Shall we venture out and find an obliging little haystack or hillock to enjoy, hm?"

She blushed deeper. "You are an outrageous tease."

"I'm not teasing at all. I'd have a far better chance of winning in Garret than in my own borough. There's just that small matter of eligibility." He snaked an arm behind her waist and cupped her lush, rounded hip in his palm. With his other hand, he reached for his walking stick. "I'll halt the carriage right now, if you like." He stretched his arm, extending the knob of ivory toward the coach's side, as though he would rap to signal the driver.

"You wouldn't!" Twisting her body, she stretched out a hand to stay his arm.

"Oh, yes, I would," he said, reaching out again.

"Toby!" she exclaimed, wrestling his arm with both hands now and wriggling herself straight into his lap. Just where he'd been wanting her.

He said quietly, "I would." Then he paused, waiting

for that beautiful face to turn toward his. "I would, but only if you asked it."

Her frown melted to an inviting, "Oh."

Lowering his arm, he cast aside the walking stick. He needed two hands on her delicious body—one simply wasn't enough. "There now. Isn't it better, sitting like this?"

She nodded breathlessly, her eyes never leaving his.

"You don't feel ill anymore?"

She gave a barely perceptible shake of her head.

"Very good," he whispered, lowering his mouth to hers.

And when their lips met, the world stopped. God, he loved kissing her, nearly as much as he loved bedding her. Toby had never thought himself an especially fanciful fellow, but damned if there wasn't something magical in the brush of her mouth against his. Not in the sense of fairy-story pixie dust or cauldrons bubbling with superstitious claptrap. Magic of the ancient, primeval sort. The unleashing of an elemental force. When they kissed, a vast realm of passion opened between them, wild and uncharted. And they explored it together, feeling their way through the dark with questing lips and seeking tongues and bold, wandering fingers.

He could have held his wife in his lap and kissed her all the way to Devonshire. But as luck—and geography—would have it, they reached his borough in Surrey first.

"*Toby.*"

"Mmm?"

"Is this the town?"

Preoccupied with tasting every inch of her delicate throat, he spared only the briefest of glances out the window. "Probably."

With a little yelp, she squirmed out of his lap and flung herself to the opposite seat.

He followed her. "We've a few minutes yet."

"Toby, no!" She evaded his grasp, volleying back to her original seat.

This time, he let her escape. "It's all right, darling. No one can see in. Unless they're trying."

"Of course they'll be trying! And look at us, all mussed and wrinkled." Her hands fluttered over her gown, and she threw him a grieved look. "Toby, please. Make yourself presentable."

"What? Is my cravat askew?"

"No, no. It's not your cravat that's askew, it's your . . ." She flicked a glance at his lap.

Toby looked down, then laughed. "Well, my wife, unless you intend to come over here and relieve the condition—"

Her eyes narrowed.

"Right. Then the only other remedy would be time."

"Did you know," she asked in a matter-of-fact tone, "that mechanical brushes can clean a flue in one-third the time of a climbing boy, and with twice the efficiency? You might mention that in your speech today."

Time, or talk of chimney sweeps.

"Isabel," he said, making discreet adjustments to his fall, "these are country cottagers. They don't employ chimney sweeps."

"But they are humans, and Christians, and must therefore respond to the plight of those pitiable children. An injustice perpetrated against the most meek of souls is an injustice against us all."

Toby held his tongue. It was becoming a bit of a pattern, he'd noticed. Isabel was a willing, and even enthusiastic, partner in lovemaking. But the moment their physical pleasure was concluded, her charitable zeal returned in double force. Just last night, while he'd been struggling for breath in the aftermath of an explosive coupling, Isabel had popped straight from bed and fished the tinderbox and candle from the drawer of his writing desk. Her reason? It had been imperative, at two in the morning, to pen a note to Augusta regarding some alteration in the text of their Society leaflet.

For his part, Toby had gone to sleep.

Well, he supposed, different women had differing reactions following the coital act. Some found languor and sleep, while others experienced a burst of energy. And no matter what task Isabel rose from their bed to complete, in time she always came back. Toby could understand the habit, on a rational level, and he hardly knew how to object. But he still felt a small surge of resentment, each time he lazily stretched to embrace his wife and grasped nothing but air.

The coach rolled to a halt in the town square.

"Here we are, then," Toby said, leaning forward in his seat. He took his wife's hand. "Shall I have the driver take you on to Wynterhall? Our trunks have likely arrived by now, and the house staff will be expecting you."

"What do you mean? I don't want to go on to the house, not alone. I want to stay here with you, and watch the proceedings."

"Isabel, it's only the nomination of candidates . . . a trifling matter of procedure and an excuse to tap a few kegs of ale. Not a referendum on the human condition. Besides, the hustings can become disorderly. This isn't a scene for a lady."

She peered out the carriage window. "But there are several ladies in the crowd already. Please, let me stay. If you like, I'll sit in the carriage and watch from here. I want to witness the birth of your political career." With a little smile, she added, "And I'd so looked forward to hearing your speech."

"Had you?" Toby asked, suddenly wishing he'd prepared one.

*   *   *

Isabel asked the coachman to retract the landau top so she might enjoy the open air. From her vantage point at the edge of the square, she watched the crowd churn with anticipation. The taverns bordering the green were doing a brisk business, and the dry-goods merchants as well. Wandering piemen and orange-sellers hawked their wares in colorful song. Above all, a string of bright banners fluttered in the breeze. Bel had never attended a country fair, but in her imagination, they looked much like this.

A man wearing an outmoded jonquil-yellow topcoat mounted the hustings platform and called out to the throng. His voice was every bit as loud as his coat. Bel could tell from his proud bearing, he took his duties very seriously.

"All right, then," he called. "We all know how this goes. As your returning officer, empowered by the sheriff to oversee this election, I've summat to read aloud." He withdrew a folded sheaf of parchment from his pocket.

"Can't we skip over that part?" a voice whined from the crowd.

"No, we can't skip over that part," the yellow-clad man mimicked back. He shook his clutch of papers and fortified his booming voice. "It's procedure, you idiot. It's government. It's this paper what separates us from the heathens."

Another bystander called out, "It's that paper what makes you a pompous arse."

"No, it ain't," a third shouted. "It's that bloody coat."

"Trust me, gents, it's neither." This came from a round-cheeked woman draped over the sill of a second-story window. "He's a pompous arse, wearing nothing at all."

The crowd roared with laughter, and the yellow-clad man's face turned a violent shade of red.

"I only wish he'd read me that paper some night," she continued. "Couldn't be any more boring than his—"

Bel couldn't make out the remainder of her remark. A fresh storm of laughter drowned it out. Still, she blushed as her mind filled in the blank.

"Enough!" the man in the yellow coat berated the crowd. "Drink your ale, you uncivilized idiots. And you, woman"—he waved a finger at the cackling figure in the window—"I'll paddle your meddling arse six shades of red this evening."

"Oh, Colin," she sang out, fluttering her eyelashes. "Do you promise?"

When the crowd finally settled—several minutes later—the man in the yellow coat began to read. Bel understood why the crowd had protested the idea. First there was the writ calling for a new Parliament, and then the act against bribery. Then another man came forward, to administer the officer's oath against bribery. And as the gears of government creaked along, the sun inched higher in the sky, baking the square with soporific heat. Soon the horses were stamping and whickering with impatience. The coachman's head slumped to the side, and even Bel was swallowing back a yawn.

Finally, the yellow-clad returning officer put out the call for nominations.

"Montague!" the crowd roared as one. They repeated the name until it became a three-syllable chant: "Mon-ta-gue! Mon-ta-gue!"

Montague? Who was Montague, and why had Bel not heard of him if he possessed such a loyal following? She'd thought Mr. Yorke posed Toby's only opposition.

A bent, decrepit man mounted the platform, helped up the stairs by a man half his age and twice his size. He wore a faded Army redcoat with tarnished buttons and cuffs worn white at the edge. The crowd's chanting increased in volume until he doddered to the center of the stage and snapped a military salute.

To a man, the assembled electors came to attention and saluted in return.

"All hail Madman Montague!" a man cried out from the throng.

The hulking man at the candidate's elbow made a threatening gesture with his fist. "Don't you be disrespecting the colonel."

"Aw, come on. Ain't as though he can hear me."

The man in the yellow coat regained control of the stage. "Colonel Geoffrey Montague is hereby a candidate for the office of Member of Parliament."

A general cheer rose up again. The old man saluted with even greater vigor, sending the epaulette of his uniform askew.

Bel understood it now. The crowd took amusement at this old man's expense. He must present himself as a candidate in every election, with no serious hopes of winning, and the people of the borough took from him a hearty laugh. It was pathetic, really. Poor thing.

"Others?" the man in the yellow coat called out.

"I nominate our esteemed incumbent, local freeholder and my friend, Mr. Archibald Yorke." It was Toby's voice. Wasn't that a bit odd, Bel thought, for a man to nominate his own opponent? But perhaps it was a show of good sportsmanship on Toby's part.

Mr. Yorke mounted the platform, accepting the crowd's generous applause with a gracious nod. He spied Bel in her carriage and tipped his hat, his silvered hair glinting white in the sun. A twinge of conscience pinched her, to think that Toby would usurp not only this old man's seat in Parliament, but this accompanying measure of public respect. How sad for Mr. Yorke. But then she remembered Lady Aldridge's dislike of the man. Bel trusted her mother-in-law's judgment. Besides, Mr. Yorke was a *Tory*, which meant he sat in opposition to nearly every cause she intended to champion.

Mr. Yorke has had his time. It's Toby's turn now.

"All right, then that's done," the returning officer said. "Any others?" he asked, in a tone that said he expected none.

Mr. Yorke tapped him on one yellow-covered shoulder. "I have a nomination to make."

The crowd quieted, seemingly as confused as Bel by this statement from the incumbent MP.

"But you're already nominated," the officer replied.

"I know, but I'd like to nominate someone else."

"Someone else? Well, I don't know that you can." The officer riffled through his sheaf of papers. "Seeing as you're already a candidate . . ."

"I'm a freeholder in this district, aren't I?" Mr. Yorke asked gruffly. "Well then, I can nominate a candidate."

"Er . . . all right."

"I nominate Sir Tobias Aldridge."

The crowd reacted with silence. Men looked from one to another, seemingly uncertain whether to laugh or applaud.

Bel decided to pity their indecision. As Toby mounted the platform, she clapped heartily, and soon a wave of polite applause built, sweeping toward the stage. Toby removed his hat and made an agile bow. The interest level of the ladies scattered through the assembly increased appreciably. They did not merely look; they gawped.

And who could blame them? Oh, he looked so handsome. The golden highlights of his hair caught the sunlight and reflected it to dazzling effect. The white gleam of teeth in his charming, boyish grin was visible even from here, at the edge of the square. Had he not been attired in such elegant clothes and so animated with youth and vitality, one could have mistaken him for a purloined Greek sculpture. A possessive sense of pride swelled her heart, to think that this tall, dashing figure of a man commanding the admiration of hundreds—he belonged to *her*.

"Well, this is interesting," the man in the yellow coat said, scratching the back of his neck. "Seems we may actually need to count votes this year. We haven't done that in a generation."

"Speeches!" someone called from the crowd.

The request was quickly seconded, and soon the whole assembly clamored for oration. "Speeches! Speeches!"

"All right, all right." The yellow-clad man indicated Mr. Yorke. "We'll hear from the incumbent first, if you please."

Bel had not heard many political speeches in her life. In fact, this one counted as her first. Still, Mr. Yorke's address from the hustings struck her as very odd. For one thing, it was short—barely a few minutes in duration. For another, he spoke not a word on any matter of legislative importance. He merely reminded the electors of his years of service in the House of Commons, cobbled together a few phrases about service and progress, and promptly ceded the floor.

Bel was almost offended on Toby's behalf. Did Mr. Yorke think so little of Toby's threat to his candidacy that he would first nominate Toby himself, then make only the slightest attempt to woo the electorate? While the crowd rewarded Mr. Yorke with a smattering of polite applause, she sniffed and busied herself arranging the folds of her skirts across the carriage seat. Well, perhaps she should be grateful for Mr. Yorke's overconfidence and underestimation of her husband. Once Toby took the platform, he would charm the votes right out of the old man's pocket.

A roar of excitement rose up from the milling throng. Bel looked up to see the ancient Colonel Montague shuffling to the center of the stage. Merciful heavens, why did they have to put the old man through such humiliation, just for a bit of entertainment? Did so little of interest happen in this borough?

The crowd hushed as Montague snapped another open-palmed salute.

"Duty!" The word creaked from the old man's throat.

"Duty!" the assembly echoed, at a volume magnified one thousandfold.

"Honor!" Montague called.

"Honor!" came the unified roar. Fists pumped in the air.

The aged colonel raised both arms as high as he could. Which ended up being barely shoulder-level. "Vigilance!"

"Vigilance!" the crowd returned, overlapping the colonel's own cry. It was clear this was a familiar litany to everyone in attendance.

Everyone but Bel, that was. She looked around the square. Hadn't Toby called this a sedate borough, not prone to rioting? Over the waving arms of the crowd, she managed to catch her husband's eye. He gave her a carefree shrug and a cheeky wink, apparently unconcerned. She could not say the same for the team of horses, who stamped and whickered with each rousing cry.

"My friends and neighbors," Montague addressed the crowd, "our noble country faces a threat. An enemy more pernicious than any Moorish infidel or encroaching barbarian."

Who on earth did he refer to? Surely not Napoleon. The Battle of Waterloo was three years ago now.

"No, our enemy attacks not from without," the old man continued, "but from within." His voice trembled, as did his raised fist. "Yes, I speak of traitors. Those vile betrayers who would raise arms against their own king."

Now Bel was thoroughly confused. At the moment, England wasn't even under the rule of a king. No one in the crowd seemed especially concerned about infidels or traitors, however. The general mood remained one of amusement.

"We must quell the rebellion," Montague went on. "It

is the moral imperative of every Englishman to stamp out the uprising, seek out the treasonous brigands, and bring them to justice. Secure England's rule and God's dominion, before the traitors come after *you*." He leveled one bony finger at the assembly and swept it in an arc, pivoting to stare down individual members of the crowd.

For a moment, his bent finger and wild-eyed gaze rested on Bel, and she shifted nervously on the carriage seat. She began to understand the large turnout for these proceedings. This was high drama indeed. How the carriage driver could sleep through it all was beyond her.

"Attack is imminent," the old man warned, his voice cracking as its pitch soared. "The peril is real." With a shaking hand, he withdrew an old-fashioned pistol from his coat and waved it in the same arc his finger had just traced. The general mood of the onlookers went from amusement to concern. Apparently, this was not part of the script. A nervous murmur rippled through the square, and the horses danced with unease.

"I call on every able-bodied man to join us. To take up arms with the Montague Militia. To secure our home county by answering the call: Duty! Honor! Vigilance!"

Montague pointed the pistol heavenward and called out, "Make ready!"

From behind her came a chorus of loud clicks. Bel pivoted in her seat to see a half-dozen men lining the rear edge of the square. One of them was the burly fellow who'd helped Colonel Montague onto the platform. In unison, the men lifted muskets to their shoulders, pointing the barrels high into the air above the assembly. Accordingly, the people in the assembly threw themselves to the ground. Somewhere a woman screamed. Bel wasn't certain, but it might have been her.

"Aim!" the colonel ordered, tightening his own bony finger over the trigger of his pistol. "Fire!"

A salvo of shots fractured the silence, and then panic

poured through the cracks. Deafened by the booming shots and smothered in acrid smoke, Bel could scarcely tell her boots from her bonnet. All around her, people swarmed and shouted. The pair of carriage horses reared and whinnied, and the landau rocked on its wheels before lurching forward into the crowd.

And now there was no doubt about it. Bel really did scream.

The carriage driver, finally startled awake, hauled on the reins. "Ho, there! Ho!"

But the horses' panic would not be quelled. They charged forward, dragging the carriage on a wild, serpentine course through the square. Before them, people leapt and dove, scrambling out of the way. Bel clung to the door sash and prayed, expecting at any moment the carriage wheel would meet with a human obstacle and leave a maimed or lifeless body in its wake.

Instead, the carriage wheel met with an inanimate obstacle—the stone border of the sidewalk—and for a heart-stopping moment, the landau teetered on its two left wheels. Bel was thrown against the side of the cab, and the driver—

Oh, God. The driver was thrown completely. The landau righted itself with a bouncing jolt, and Bel looked up to see the driver's box empty and the reins dangling. Then the reins, too, slipped from view.

With them went her last shred of hope. There was no way she could stop this carriage. Even if she could somehow leap the gap to the driver's seat; even if she could somehow retrieve the reins—if an experienced coachman could not slow these horses, Bel had no hope of doing so herself. In their panic, the horses would drag her on until one of them stumbled or the carriage overturned. In all likelihood, she was going to die. It was only a matter of how many human and equine lives went with her.

Her impulse was to shrink low in the carriage and

simply close her eyes until it was all over. But she couldn't even bring herself to move that far. Instead, she remained frozen, clutching the seatback and door sash in white-knuckled grips as the horses continued their frenzied rampage through the square.

Between the threats of musket fire and an out-of-control carriage, much of the crowd had already dispersed, the people squeezing into any available building or doorway. The remaining onlookers huddled around the hustings platform itself—on it, under it, clinging to its girders.

And, having careened off the sidewalk and altered their course, now the horses were headed straight for them.

No.

No, no, no. Not all those people.

"Run!" she cried. And the people obeyed, fleeing the spurious safety of the wooden platform for the edges of the square. They scattered in different directions, but wise souls that they were, they all ran away.

Except for one. One man was running straight at *her*.

Toby.

CHAPTER
THIRTEEN

Bel's pounding heart rate kicked into a gallop.

Dear God, no, she prayed. *Not Toby.*

While everyone else in the square had spent the past thirty seconds fearing for his life, Toby had apparently used the time to shuck his topcoat. His arms were blurs of white linen as he leapt from the hustings platform and dashed out to meet the stampeding team.

"Toby, no!" she screamed. *"Muévete!"*

Madre de Dios. She needed to warn off her English husband, and suddenly her tongue could only work in Spanish. He was going to die, and it would be all her fault.

Even now, the horses were gaining speed, bearing down on him. Any moment, he would be trampled, dragged under the carriage. She only prayed God would be merciful enough to take her with him.

As if he'd come to his senses, Toby drew to a halt. Just in the perfect place for the horses to brush past him and the carriage wheels to grind him up.

But it never came to that.

As one horse came abreast of him, Toby changed course, now running alongside the panicked beast. He grabbed its mane with both hands and jumped, vaulting onto the horse's back. Bel looked on in disbelief as Toby grabbed the reins near the bit and tugged with one hand, pulling the horse's head to the side. The team and carriage followed, turning in a tight spiral.

Flung against the side of the cab once again, Bel

muttered incoherent prayers and imprecations in her mother's tongue. All the while, Toby soothed the horses, and her, with his deep, steady baritone.

"Ho, there," he told them. "Easy now."

Holding the reins firmly, he kept the team turning in a circle, murmuring succinct commands and words of assurance. Gradually, the hoofbeats slowed. Bel's thundering pulse slowed, too.

Toby eased up on the bit, steering the team off the green and onto a side road. They ambled on for several minutes thus—Toby droning on in a hypnotic monologue, holding tight to the reins, never turning his attention from the horses. As they moved away from the center of town, the dwellings they passed grew smaller, further apart. The cobblestones paving their path gave way to dirt, muffling the horses' hoofbeats. The world felt very quiet.

Finally, Toby drew the team to a halt where a wooden stile marked the boundary between town road and country lane. Sliding down from the horse's back, he lavished pats and verbal praise on the mare as he looped the reins around the stile.

Then—at last—he turned to Bel.

"Softly now," he said, approaching the carriage door and unlatching it with a gentle click. "We don't want to startle them again." He held out a hand to her.

Bel stared at it. She'd been clutching onto the carriage with both hands for so long, she couldn't muster the courage to release them.

"It's all right now," he said, in the same deep, soothing tone in which he'd spoken to the mare. "Give me your hand."

That tone worked on her, too. She gave him her trembling hand, and he helped her down from the landau—slowly, cautiously—supporting her with one arm about her waist. There were no people milling about the nearby cottage; presumably its occupants had assembled at the square. Wordlessly, he led her over to a low wall of stone, beyond which farmland spread like a rumpled quilt.

Lifting her effortlessly, he set her on the wall and stood back a step. His eyes scanned her from head to toe as he assessed her condition. "Are you well?" he asked, frowning with concern. With sure fingers, he untied her bonnet and set it aside. He lifted one of her arms, then the other, running his hand along each to test the soundness of her bones and joints. "You're not injured? You took such a blow with that turn, I'm concerned for your ribs." He placed his hands flat against her torso, framing her ribcage.

"Toby," she said quietly.

He did not lift his head. "Are you hurt here at all? Any difficulty drawing a breath? Do you feel any pain when I—"

"*Toby.*" Bel raised a hand to his lips, damming the stream of anxious speech. Then she slid her palm along his smooth-shaven jaw.

Exhaling slowly, Toby closed his eyes.

"I'm fine," she told him. "I'm unharmed, thanks to you."

His hands slid around her waist, and he gathered her to him tightly. Tightly enough that, had she truly suffered a broken rib, there would have been no denying it.

"My God," he said, sighing into her hair and gently rocking her in his arms. "My God."

Bel buried her face in the linen of his shirt, now softened with heat and the scents of both man and horse. And then she began to weep.

"Yes, darling," he murmured, stroking her back. "Go ahead, cry. The danger is over and you are unharmed, and for that you may weep just as long as you wish. Shed tears enough for us both, if you'd be so good."

"Oh, Toby." After a time, she sniffed against his waistcoat. "I've never been so frightened in all my life."

"That makes two of us, then."

"Does it?" She lifted her face to his.

"No," he said, his brown eyes growing thoughtful. "No, I think it makes us one. Doesn't it?"

Bel nodded as he lowered his lips to hers. Yes, she understood perfectly. Nearly a week ago, they'd been married. She'd lost count of the times they'd engaged in the marital act since. But only now, in this moment, did she feel truly *wed* to him. As though they shared one future, one life. For better or worse, in safety and in peril. He'd risked his life to save hers, and now—now there was no more "his life" or "hers." This was *their* life now.

And their life began with a sweet, tender kiss.

The kiss didn't stay sweet or tender for long.

Toby tried to hold back. He really did. But one stroke of her tongue against his, and the reins of his passion slid straight out of his grip.

So he filled his hands with Isabel instead.

With artless greed, he clutched at her hips, her breasts, her bottom, her thighs. He wound the fingers of one hand into her hair and cinched it so tight, she gasped.

"I'm sorry," he murmured against her throat. "I'm so sorry. But Isabel . . . Christ, I need this."

"I know," she said, tugging at his cravat. "I need it, too."

He needed to feel her. All of her. Every living, unharmed inch of her body. For a terrifying moment, she'd been lost to him. She'd been safely returned, thank heaven, but it wasn't enough to simply see her alive and hear her say she was well. He needed to feel it. To verify with his hands, lips, tongue that each glossy strand of hair and silky curve of her flesh remained exactly the same.

"Isabel." He groaned as she worked her hands under his collar and her fingernails raked against his bare flesh. "You have to stop me. God knows, I can't stop myself."

"Don't. Don't stop."

Three more arousing syllables were never spoken.

He had so much energy coursing through him—the fuel of resolve and desperation and vein-chilling fear. And now that there was nothing to fear, no desperate crisis . . . all that energy simmered inside him, building, rising, needing release. He wanted nothing more than to get inside her and let it all explode. Right here, on this stone wall—which seemed to be just the perfect height, God bless the world.

And God bless his wife, she pulled up her skirts so he could nestle his hips between her thighs and test that theory.

Yes. A low moan escaped them both as he pressed the hard ridge of his erection against her feminine core. Just exactly the perfect height. Now it was only a matter of removing these bothersome layers of fabric . . .

He snaked one hand under her petticoat. Her thigh went rigid beneath his palm.

"Toby, someone's coming."

He rested his brow on her shoulder and cursed. *Someone's coming.* Oh, why, why, why, why couldn't it be him?

"It's the coachman," she said. "Oh, I'm glad he's alive."

"So am I," Toby said. Stepping back, he released her thigh and rearranged her skirts with sullen tugs. "Now I can kill him."

Here came that gently reproving Isabel look, and the matching patient tone. "Toby—"

"No, no. I know you're right. I'll sack him. Without a reference. And then I'll kill him."

"It wasn't his fault."

No, it was mine, Toby thought ruefully. He should never have let her stay. He should have anticipated the melee. He should never have agreed to run for office in this blighted borough in the first place. "Are you well enough to drive home?" he asked.

She paled. "Must we?"

"Well—"

"Please, Toby. I can't get back in that carriage right now, not with those horses. Not today. I just can't." Tears welled in her eyes, catching on the ebony fringe of her lashes.

"No, of course not. I understand, darling." He cast a glance over her shoulder, out at the countryside. "Wynterhall is only about two miles' distance, if we cut across the fields. Would you prefer to walk?"

"Oh, yes." Her face brightened. "I would prefer it. In fact, I suspect I'd enjoy it."

Toby suspected he would, too. There were any number of stone borders between here and his estate. Haystacks, too, and smooth-barked trees. Yes, walking could prove a very enjoyable alternative to traveling by carriage.

He exchanged a few words with the driver and then vaulted the wall before swinging Isabel around and helping her down the other side. She laughed. It was a giddy, girlish sort of laugh that he didn't recall ever hearing from her before. He liked it.

He took her hand, and together they started off across the field.

For some time, they did not talk. It seemed too soon to speak about what had happened in the square, but also too soon to think of anything else. So they simply walked in silence. They walked like children, letting their linked hands swing between them as they made large, purposeful strides past the knee-high grain. First fast, then slow, then quickly again as they gathered momentum coming down a slope.

When they reached the opposite edge of the field, Toby helped her squeeze through a gap in the hawthorn hedgerow.

"Just a moment," he said, once they'd both made it through. "You've a bit of bramble in your hair." He disentangled the offending twig and held it up for her inspection before tossing it aside.

"Thank you." She blushed, popping up on her toes to kiss him.

It was lovely, that kiss. Petal-soft, and innocent. And it told Toby instantly that he would not be tumbling his wife against a tree, somewhere along the journey home. All that sensual urgency between them earlier—they'd lost it somewhere in that barley field. Now it was comfort that warmed the place where his fingers grazed her wrist. Comfort, and companionship, and a general sense of all being well with the world. Toby couldn't honestly say it was better than sexual release. But neither could he say it was worse.

It was different. Different from anything he'd known with a woman before.

He was still pondering it minutes later, when Isabel gasped and drew to a halt in the center of a pasture.

"Good Lord, what is it?"

"Your speech!" She clapped her free hand over her mouth and turned to him, smothering a burst of giddy laughter with her palm. Lowering her hand, she continued, "Oh, Toby. You never made your speech."

"Never you mind." Chuckling, he squeezed her hand as they continued walking. "It's not as though anyone would have listened after that uproar, now is it?"

"But . . . but what happened? That Colonel Montague and his strange speech, the musket fire . . . I still don't understand it."

"Colonel Montague is our local war hero. He stands for every election and has done for decades. Always runs on a platform of subduing treasonous rebellion in the American colonies."

Isabel slanted a look at him. "Haven't the American colonies been independent for—"

"Thirty-five years? Yes. He's not called Madman

Montague for nothing. The old soldier's a bit touched in the head, in case you hadn't noticed."

"I had. And I thought it was horrid, how his illness was exploited for the public's amusement. The poor man."

Toby refrained from noting that the "poor man" had very nearly got her killed today. Just like his sweet wife, to look back on the afternoon's horror and feel nothing but sympathy for the decrepit sot. "It's not so mean-spirited as you might think. The old fellow enjoys the attention; the crowd enjoys his enthusiasm. He never gets any votes that don't come from those oafish nephews of his; but one could say he achieves his goal just the same."

She gave him a skeptical look.

"He rallies the borough," Toby explained. "For an entirely fictional cause, to be sure, but the unity he engenders is real. It can't be a completely bad thing, for the townspeople to gather every few years and answer the call of duty, honor, vigilance." He recited the words with gusto and gave her a wide grin.

She was not amused. "I take it the musket salute is not usually part of the routine."

"No, no. That part was a surprise, I assure you. And I'm certain this will have been Montague's last candidacy. Wild-eyed speeches are one thing, but he'll not be permitted to pull a stunt like that again." Toby shook his head. "Don't know what the old fool will live for now. It's a bit tragic, really."

Isabel replied hotly, "What's tragic is a man stripped of his dignity. If he's touched in the head, as you say, he should be pitied and protected. Not paraded before the town every few years as a laughingstock." Her accent grew increasingly pronounced as she spoke; her strides became clipped. "Madness is a serious condition, not a joke."

Toby couldn't recall ever seeing her so agitated. Was this some misdirected reaction to the day's distressing events? The way she defended Montague so vigorously, one would think she had a personal reason to take offense.

Bloody hell. She did. Toby silently cursed his thoughtlessness.

"Isabel, I'm so sorry," he said. "I'd forgotten your mother's illness." Her fingers slipped in his grasp, but Toby tightened his grip. She wouldn't get away from him that easily. "Forgive me, I didn't mean—"

"How do you know about my mother's illness?"

"Gray told me. Before we were married."

"Truly?"

He nodded.

"And it didn't disturb you at all?" she asked.

"Why should it disturb me, that your mother contracted brain fever?"

She gave him an incredulous look, as though the answer ought to be obvious. "Because she went mad. No one wants to marry into a family with a history of insanity." Her eyes fell to the carpet of grasses and wildflowers. "I should have told you myself, but I was afraid you . . ."

"Afraid I would change my mind?"

She nodded.

Toby pulled her close and wrapped an arm about her waist. He wasn't certain how to reassure her. He could tell her that of all the potentially objectionable things about her family—their precarious social standing, her connections in trade, her bastard half-brother Joss, her other half-brother Gray, who was his own brand of bastard . . . not to mention the fact that her sister-in-law was the woman who'd jilted him not one year ago—the information that her mother had narrowly survived a tropical fever would hardly have tipped the scales.

But he suspected that little speech wouldn't help.

"Darling, I can assure you—your mother's condition never gave me a moment's pause. Everyone's family has some sort of madness in it. If you think there's none in my own . . . well, you simply haven't spent enough time around my sister Fanny yet."

She smiled. It wasn't quite the girlish laugh he'd been trying for, but it was an improvement. Soon she grew thoughtful again. "Sometimes I wonder if my mother truly was touched in the head, as you call it. Perhaps she was simply heartbroken and angry. She loved my father, and he . . ."

Her voice trailed off. Curious as he was to hear the end of that sentence, Toby suspected prompting would not result in its completion. They covered a good bit of ground before she finally continued.

"Anyway, my mother disagreed with the doctors. She did not believe she was mad. Not from a fever, at any rate."

"But mad people never know they're mad. That's part of their illness. Do you think Colonel Montague believes he's mad?"

"I suppose not." She frowned.

"Of course he doesn't. He wouldn't stand for election if he did. That's the paradox of it—if you're aware that you're mad, then you're not mad."

"But that's nonsensical."

"Precisely." He gave her a reassuring squeeze. "Montague's nephews don't accept the extent of his illness, either, or they wouldn't have put on that display today. It's only natural, for people to believe the best of their loved ones. Their affection blinds them to the truth. Love is its own form of madness."

"Yes. My mother said that, too."

She fell into a ponderous silence. They walked on together, joined at the hip.

"What will happen now?" she asked, as they entered a copse of beech trees. "With the election?"

"Colin Brooks—" He kicked a stone out of their path. "He's the returning officer . . ."

"The one in the horrid yellow coat?"

"God, yes." Toby laughed. "He'll set a date for the polling to begin, probably a few days hence. There'll be speeches at the hustings every day, and the accumulated votes tallied each afternoon. When one candidate has a clear majority, they'll close the polls."

"I don't want to go back there," she said, shuddering.

"I wouldn't allow you to return, if you did. Even I don't have to attend. Some candidates stay away from the hustings entirely, and let their supporters speak for them."

"Oh, but you must attend! How else will you persuade the electors to give you their votes? You never had a chance to address them today." She looked up at him through her lashes. "Though if your heroics with the horses did not convince them of your suitability, I don't know what will. The way you leapt onto that moving horse . . ."

"Really, it was nothing," Toby said, in a tone of false humility that he knew would draw him even more praise. Isabel's admiration was perhaps a bit more than he deserved, but he wasn't about to spurn it.

"It was wonderful. And terrifying. Oh, Toby. I was so certain you would be trampled."

She nestled close to him, and he let his hand wander down the curve of her hip. Really—shouldn't a daring rescue like that entitle a man to a few liberties? Here he'd been wanting to slay a dragon for her, and Toby supposed subduing a panicked carriage horse was as close as he'd ever get.

"Thank you," she murmured, resting her head on his shoulder.

"Really, the trick of it's all in the timing. And it's Mr. Yorke you ought to thank," Toby replied, breathing in the delicious scent of her hair. "I'd never have learned that maneuver if not for him."

"Truly?"

"My mother forbade me to practice that vault, you see. Told me I'd break my neck. So naturally, Yorke encouraged me just to spite her. I spent most of my fourteenth summer in his eastern pasture, practicing. Took me weeks, and I took my share of nasty spills, but I finally mastered the way of it."

"I can understand why your mother objected. It sounds horribly dangerous." She raised her head and looked up at him. "Why on earth did you want to learn?"

"I had my heart set on joining the cavalry. Though deep down, I knew I never could. With my father gone, it was too great a risk. If I died without an heir, my mother and sisters would be left alone. Still, at fourteen I had my dreams. Pictured myself charging around French battlefields, spilling Bonapartist blood."

Toby laughed a little. Ah, to be young and spend hours spinning detailed, grandiose fantasies of changing the world. Isabel certainly wasn't a girl any longer, but she'd somehow retained that youthful idealism he'd long outgrown. He didn't always understand her zeal, but he did admire it. At times, he envied it. Honor, Justice, Charity . . . the way she pronounced those terms, he could hear the capital letters implied. They were words she spoke often, but never lightly. And she took the same earnest tone when she spoke of being a Lady, with a capital L.

Toby hadn't thought much of being a Sir since he was a boy, envisioning himself the hero of a lost Arthurian legend: Sir Toby the Valiant. Isabel made him feel that there could be something to this whole notion of nobility, aside from assuming his place in the throng of bored aristocrats—men with nothing better to do of an afternoon than sit at the club swilling brandy. Perhaps he could make his title something more than just the fading gleam on a centuries-old suit-of-armor.

Or perhaps Isabel could.

"Cavalry or no, that vault turned out to be a useful trick." He squeezed her hand and donned a devilish grin. "Soon I came to appreciate its other application."

"What's that?"

"Why, impressing the young ladies, of course." He brushed a light kiss on her lips. "Did it work?"

She nodded, blushing.

"Very good. Let's see if I can impress you further." He thrust his free arm under her hips and swept her off her feet.

She squeaked with surprise. "Toby!"

"Oh, I like that noise," he said, holding her in his arms as he crossed the shallow stream. "Can you make that one again?" he asked, lowering her to her feet. "Later tonight?"

She dismissed his teasing with a little wave of her hand and walked on ahead.

"That's rather bold of you," he said, grinning at the enticing sway of her hips as she marched away. "How do you know you're not walking the wrong direction?"

"Am I?" she asked, without pausing to look back.

"No."

"Well, then."

He watched her walk a few paces more before starting after her. Following her path at a leisurely pace, he twisted a length of ivy from a nearby branch and worked it with both hands.

"Wait," he called. "Hold right there."

She paused, framed between two trees—standing in the doorway between this small, shaded grove and the sunlit world beyond. A corona of golden light surrounded her, caressing every lush curve of her silhouette.

"What is it?" she asked.

Toby couldn't even answer. He just stood there, blinking, awestruck by the vision of loveliness before him. Swallowing the lump in his throat, he slowly approached his wife.

One by one, he pulled the pins from her hair as she looked up at him, adorably befuddled. At last her dark tresses tumbled free, and she arranged them about her shoulders with an unconscious toss of her head.

"There, that's better." Grinning like a fool, Toby adorned her gleaming ebony crown with the ivy wreath he'd fashioned, then framed her bewildered smile in his hands. "Isabel, I know I've told you this a hundred times or more. And now I regret not saving the words for this moment. For that matter, I regret ever speaking them to anyone else, because now the words seem too paltry, too common. Completely inadequate. But I promise you, I've never meant them more honestly than I do right here, right now. You are . . . beautiful. Truly, you take my breath away."

Her eyes widened. "Oh, my. Now that was impressive indeed."

"Was it?"

"Yes," she laughed. "Even I'm breathless, and I'm not romantic by nature. I can't imagine what that little speech must have done to your young, impressionable ladies."

Toby felt his grin fading. He'd never made that speech to anyone else. The crown of ivy nonsense, countless times—but never that speech. Those words were for her alone.

"You do realize I've already married you?" she asked. "And here you are pulling out all your best tricks. Why is that?"

"I don't know," he said honestly. What an astute question she posed. Why, indeed? Out of habit? Simply for sport?

No. No, it was because he knew—they both knew—

he might have stolen her away from Gray, wedded and bedded her, even rescued her from certain peril, but he hadn't yet engaged her heart. He, who had female hearts flung at him with all the frequency, and velocity, of cricket balls—hadn't secured the adoration of his own wife.

And she was his *wife*. For whatever shallow reasons he'd begun this courtship—for the first time in his life, Toby was out of his depth. Isabel was a woman of strong principles and simmering passions. It would take more than adolescent flirtation to touch her heart. But her heart was the only one that mattered. He had to win it before he lost the election, or he might never have a chance again.

She looked out at the sloping hillside beyond the woods. "I think we must be nearing your estate."

"That stream was the property line, as a matter of fact. How could you tell?"

"Your whole manner has changed," she said, placing her hands on his chest. "You're . . . boyish. Carefree. Full of mischief." She smoothed his waistcoat with her palms. Toby knew it wasn't wrinkled. She simply wanted to touch him.

And God, did he want to touch her. It was all coming back now, the rush of desperate need.

"Full of mischief, I'll grant you." Sliding his hands to her backside, he backed her up a step, so that she stood braced against the trunk of a tree. "But boyish?" He ground his hips against hers, eliciting her small gasp. "I have to disagree with you there."

"Toby," she said, her voice tight. Her open palms pressed against his chest. "We really should keep moving."

"Oh. Very well."

He released her, but stayed close—denying her the space to walk away. Heart pounding with lust and brain churning with confusion, he stared down at his wife's flushed countenance. She wouldn't even meet his eyes. Something was wrong, but damned if he knew how to name it. He couldn't understand why one minute she could be so passionate, even flirtatious, drawing him near—and the next, pushing him away. As she said, they were already married. And today he'd used all his most impressive tricks, and invented a few new ones in the bargain.

"Someday," he said, "I'll take you back to visit Tortola."

"Why would you do that?"

"It's your home. Don't you miss it?"

"Not today." She tried to wiggle past him, but he had her boxed in.

"I'd like to see your childhood home. I wonder, would I see the girlish Isabel there? Carefree, full of mischief?"

"I don't know." Her tone was light. Falsely so. "I don't know that I was ever full of mischief."

Nor carefree, he supposed. A hint of sadness pulled at the corner of her mouth, and Toby found himself wishing he could perform the truly impossible—reach back in time to slay the dragons haunting her past.

She toyed with the end of his cravat where it hung loose about his neck, then looked off into the distance for a moment. A heartbeat later, those wide, dark eyes flashed up at him again. "Perhaps you're seeing her now."

With that, she plucked the cravat from his neck, ducked under his arm and ran off—charging up the hill, scattering laughter on the breeze behind her. Toby gave chase. Despite her head start, he gained on her quickly. He caught up to her at the crest of the hill, where she'd stopped in her tracks with her back still to him. The cravat fluttered in her dangling hand.

"I've caught you now." He whipped one arm around her chest and reached for the cravat with the other. "Give it here, you minx."

He encountered no resistance as he yanked the neck cloth from her grasp. She didn't even turn to look at him. Instead, she simply reclined against his chest and stared down at the valley below.

"Oh, Toby," she said in a tone of breathless awe. "What is it?"

Smiling through his labored breaths, he hugged her tight. He'd been wrong. He did have one last trick up his sleeve, and this the most impressive one yet.

"Why, that's our home."

CHAPTER
FOURTEEN

Isabel had always been a grateful sort. She had always been aware that her life situation was one of great wealth and comfort, relatively speaking. But if she had felt one source of deprivation in her girlhood, it was that she had grown up in a house with very few books.

Very few books of interest to a young girl, at any rate. Still, she read any volume she could, several times over. There had been a book of fairy stories she could probably recite by heart even now, if she tried. And the frontispiece of that book was permanently engraved upon her memory. It depicted a castle. A smallish one, though stout. Fortified with a turret and moat, but made friendly by the ivy clinging to its stone face and the manicured gardens in its shadow. As a girl, Isabel had stared at that etching for more hours than she could count, imagining the homelands of her parents, dreaming of centuries long past, missing her brother when he was at Oxford, and sometimes simply wishing to be anywhere far, far away.

And now—here it was. Her castle. Moat, turret, ivy, gardens . . . it was an exact rendition of her girlhood dream, washed in brilliant color. Real.

"How can it be?" she asked.

Toby's arms tightened around her waist. "I told you we'd be here soon enough. It isn't a long walk."

"No, I mean . . . I've seen this place before. This very house, in a book."

"Really?" She felt him shrug. "I don't doubt it. More

than one artist has painted this prospect. When my great-great uncle had it built, he was excessively proud of the place. Invited just about everyone in England to come visit."

"You mean it hasn't been here for centuries?"

"Oh, no. Not even one. It's only built in the medieval style, but it's quite modern inside. The old man had a rather romantic imagination, wouldn't you say?"

Twisting her neck, Isabel looked up at him. "I would say he shared the family talent for impressing young ladies." She looked back down at the fairy-tale vista. "And you truly live here?"

"*We* truly live here. And you, my dear, are the lady of the keep." He released her waist and stepped to her side, kissing her hand gallantly before tucking it into his elbow. "I'm near famished. Shall we go home?"

Together they picked their way down the gentle slope and through the hedge-rimmed gardens. As they approached the castle, Isabel was surprised to discover how much smaller it was than she'd first thought. The proportions had been carefully designed to give a grand appearance from a distance. Up close, however, the house had a human scale that made it welcoming, rather than imposing. The moat was a clear, shallow pool dotted with lily-pads, and Toby was able to open the arched wooden door with one hand.

"Welcome to Wynterhall," he said. "Hope you don't find it too fanciful for your tastes."

"It's . . . it's enchanting." Truly, there was no other word. Bel stood gaping at the grand hall into which they had entered. It was oval-shaped, and capped with an oval skylight that, with the blue sky shining through, gave the appearance of a cabochon sapphire set in gold. The floor was tiled in an intricate pattern of black and white marble.

Toby led her toward a narrow stone staircase. "Our chambers are upstairs."

As they ascended the steps, Bel was conscious of how their footfalls echoed through the silence. "Is there no one else here? Have you no servants?"

"*We* have an army of servants," he replied as they reached the top of the staircase. He led her down a wide, carpeted hallway. "They are led by Mrs. Tremaine, the housekeeper, a woman of unflagging good spirits and infinite energy. I'm sure she's prepared a completely overwhelming display to welcome you—food, décor, music, every comfort you could imagine. It wouldn't surprise me if she's taught the parlormaids and footmen some sort of song and dance routine in your honor. That's why I sent word with the driver that they were to clear out for the afternoon. You've had a trying day, and I thought a bit of restful quiet was in order. Meeting the servants, touring the estate—all that can wait."

Bel breathed a sigh of relief. He was right, she didn't feel up to a grand welcome just now.

"And"—Toby pushed open one half of a set of double doors—"I directed them to bring your things here for the time being, to my suite." Ushering her inside with a rakish smile, he added, "After all, it's not as though we're going to sleep apart."

"We aren't?"

"Well, I—" He paused. "That is, unless you wish to, in which case I'll—"

"No," she interrupted, sorry to have caused him doubt. "No, this is fine." She wished she hadn't blurted the question out, but it was something that had already been on her mind. They'd slept in the same bed every night of their marriage thus far, but Bel had been uncertain whether it was merely a honeymoon arrangement or a habit in the making.

The latter, she hoped. She liked having him nearby. Heavens, what a wanton she was becoming! She would have thought her desire for him might have waned, now that the elements of curiosity and novelty had been removed.

But no. Not waning at all. Waxing by the day.

"At any rate," she said, "it looks as though four or five of us could fit in that." She gestured toward the bed—an enormous, ancient four-poster affair with golden velvet draperies and a jewel-toned coverlet. It was a bed fit for a king . . . and a queen. And a handful of courtiers besides.

"Ah, yes. The ancestral bed." Toby walked over to it and sat, bouncing on the high mattress. "Now this bed truly is centuries old, even if Wynterhall is not. I think my great-great uncle must have built the entire house around it." He patted the space next to him, and Bel accepted the invitation to sit. "Yes, this bed has served its purpose well. Generations of Aldridge heirs have been conceived under this canopy."

Taking her hand in his, he flopped on his back, leaving her no choice but to do the same. She could hear the devilish grin in his voice as he said, "I shall do my best to make you pregnant in this bed."

Bel's cheeks burned as she stared up at the embroidered canopy. "What a thing to say." She refrained from adding, if the past week had not constituted his best attempts at making her pregnant, she was quite uncertain what more to expect.

"But first," Toby said, releasing her hand and struggling up on his elbows, "we really must have something to eat. I did give instructions . . . Ah, there it is. I knew she would not disappoint." He rose from the bed. Bel turned on her side in preparation to follow, but he stilled her with a gesture. "No, stay right there. I'll just bring the tray."

"Are we to have a picnic, then?" Bel rose to a sitting position, kicking off her slippers and folding her legs under her skirts. She unbuttoned the restrictive spencer of her traveling habit and laid it aside, leaving her dressed in a chemisette and skirt.

"Just so." Toby returned, balancing a covered tray on one hand. Bel drank in the sight of him. When this marvelous castle had come into view, she'd lost eyes for anything but Wynterhall. But now, Toby recaptured her full attention. With his untied cravat slung loose around his neck, his hair mussed, his skin aglow with sun and exertion . . . she could have told him to skip the picnic and proceed straight to dessert.

But that just wasn't something Bel could say. She was a bit shocked at herself for even thinking it.

"Mrs. Tremaine will have my head," he said, uncovering the tray and setting it in the center of the bed. "She's likely prepared a ten-course feast downstairs, and here I'm serving you cold chicken and bread as your first meal at Wynterhall."

"Oh, it's perfect." Bel broke off a piece of bread and bit into it gratefully. She reached for a leg of chicken. Until he'd placed the food before her, she hadn't realized how hungry she was.

"Good," he said, chuckling. "Good. Eat up, darling. This is why I requested simple fare. I knew you'd not eat a morsel if it was accompanied by too much pomp and display." He sliced into a small wheel of cheese and held out a wedge to her. Her hands occupied with bread and chicken, she accepted the bite with her teeth.

Absurdly, her eyes misted as she chewed that little bit of cheese. Such an intimate, caring, husbandly gesture. He was right, she would never have accepted a bite of food from his fingers, had they been seated at table in an opulent dining room. Toby had known just the way to make her feel immediately comfortable in his home. She had simply grown comfortable with *him*.

After they ate, Toby cleared the tray and returned to the bed. "Now," he said. "How are you feeling? Are you certain you are unharmed after the . . . after the incident earlier?"

"Yes, quite certain."

"Shall I ring for your maid? Perhaps you'd like to undress, bathe, sleep . . . ?"

"All three, eventually—but I'm in no rush."

He cocked his head. "Are you still feeling frightened? Do you need me to hold you?"

She smiled. "I'm not frightened anymore." *But oh, how I need you to hold me.*

"That's fortunate. Because I'm still a bit rattled, truthfully, and I think I need to be held." Reclining, he laid his head in her lap. "There, that's much better."

She smoothed the hair from his forehead.

He closed his eyes and sighed. "Yes. Much, much better."

She combed his golden-brown hair with her fingers, massaging his temples and scalp with light pressure and enjoying the little groan of pleasure that ensued. After a few minutes, his breathing steadied. He seemed on the verge of falling asleep.

Bel didn't want him to fall asleep.

"Perhaps . . ." she whispered.

"Perhaps what?" he mumbled back.

She lost her courage. Instead of the amorous suggestion she'd intended, a flood of nonsense came forth. "Perhaps we should ring for a maid to remove the tray. There's still so much food there; it would be a shame to let it spoil. Perhaps there's a servant who could take it home to his family."

He chuckled. "You are always so good, always thinking of others."

"No. I'm not, really."

"Yes, you are. It's so refreshing. Do you know how few ladies of your rank would think of sending leftover chicken home with the servants?"

Bel shook her head. If only he could divine the true nature of her thoughts right now, he would understand just how selfish they were—and how common, among ladies of every rank who chanced to look on this beautiful man. She ran her fingers through his hair again, and he nestled deeper into her lap. Her heartbeat raced, and a sweet, hollow ache built in her womb. Really, she was becoming quite desperate for him.

He murmured, "Isabel, you are too good to be true. Tell me honestly, are your motives always so pure? Don't you ever want to do something that you know is just wrong?"

She laughed dryly. "Oh, Toby. Only every time I look at you."

"What?" His eyes flew open and locked with hers. "What do you mean?"

"I mean . . ." Bel's face heated. She'd meant it as a joke. He was supposed to laugh. But instead, his expression had gone completely serious. That would teach her to attempt humor. "Surely you must know what I mean."

He rose from her lap and sat up, facing her. "Are you saying you desire me?"

"Are you going to force me to say it?"

"You desire me," he repeated. "And you think this is wrong."

Bel didn't know what to say. This was terrible. She'd meant to compliment her husband, in the same way he always showered her with praise. And somehow she'd managed to offend him.

He took her hand. "We're married, Isabel. I'm your husband. There's nothing at all wrong with desiring me."

"Yes, well." She chewed her lip. She'd come this far; there could be no prevarication now. "To be truthful, it started long before we were married."

"How long before?"

"I suppose . . . from the first time I saw you."

"And I wanted you from the first, as well. All the more reason for us to have wed." He inched closer to her on the bed. "And still, we did wait. We did everything properly, and believe me I know—because doing it the proper way damn near killed me. But still, you think it's wrong. Why is that? Does it . . ." He lowered his voice. "Does the act feel unpleasant?"

"Oh, no!" Bel bounced on the mattress with the force of her disavowal. "It feels very pleasant indeed. Too pleasant, I fear. Anything that feels so good must be a little bit wrong."

He stared at her, obviously dismayed. "So this is why you're always so eager to leave our bed," he said. "Afterward. You feel guilty, having experienced pleasure, and you feel compelled to atone for it with some good deed."

She shrugged. He was correct, in part. There was more to it than that, but Bel didn't know how to explain. How to tell him, that in those moments of physical release, she lost all other cares, all other motives, all thoughts of good or charity or even her husband? She lost her *self*. How could she tell him, that every time she slipped into that blissful nothingness, she was a little bit afraid that she would never find her way back?

"Isabel," he said. "I won't have you feeling that way about making love to me."

Fear gripped her heart. Did he mean they wouldn't make love anymore? She didn't want *that*. As conflicted as desire made her feel, she could not bring herself to reject it.

Toby's eyes grew dark. With anger, she feared—or perhaps, simply with determination. With his free hand, he slowly removed the cravat hanging loose round his neck. "You trust me. Don't you, Isabel?"

"Yes, of course," she assured him, squeezing his fingers. "It isn't that at all."

"And you know . . ." he said, sliding his hand up to circle her wrist. "After today, you must know—I would give my life before I let you come to harm."

"Yes," she whispered, her mouth going dry. "Yes, I know." She pictured him rushing straight for those panicked horses, risking death to save her. The memory quickened her pulse, until it throbbed against the pressure of his fingertips. And the way he stared at her now—so intently, so possessively . . . She'd never been so aroused in her life.

Her heartbeat only pounded more furiously as he wrapped the cravat about her wrist, winding it tight. What did he mean to do?

"I do trust you," she assured him quickly. "With my life, with my body."

"Hm. Yes, but not with your heart."

Bel had no answer to that. She had no more words in her head. She stared at the long swath of linen as he knotted it securely around her wrist.

"You will," he said, hoarsely. "I swear it. You are my wife, and I mean to have all of you. I shall win you one piece at a time, if I must. Give me your other hand."

She could not refuse him. She could not have refused him anything at this moment. Her desire only grew as he bound her wrists together, slowly winding the smooth fabric over her galloping pulse, then cinching it tight. Between her legs, she softened and ached.

"Lie down," he told her. "Flat on your back."

She obeyed him willingly, allowing him to position her body as he wished. He arranged her diagonally on the bed, then lifted her arms, stretching her bound wrists over her head. She felt a series of sharp tugs as he tied the loose end of the cravat to the upper left bedpost.

"Is it painful at all?" he asked, testing the knot.

She shook her head.

"I would never hurt you."

"I know."

Bel could not pretend to understand why her husband was lashing her wrists to the bedpost, nor why her body quivered with excitement as he did so. But whatever his intended purpose, she knew he would not hurt her. Of that, she had no doubt.

He placed a pillow beneath her head, and she looked down at her body, still clad in her sensible, light-blue traveling habit. With her arms positioned thus, her breasts thrust upward, straining her buttons of her high-necked chemisette.

Toby's fingers went to the row of overworked buttons, freeing them with a series of swift, deft flicks of his fingers. Once all were undone, he pushed the sides of the garment aside to reveal her stays and light summer shift. He undid the small closures of her skirt and tugged the garment down over her hips, knees, stockinged feet.

"There now," he murmured. "Isn't that more comfortable?"

Comfortable? Was he teasing her again? She was tied to a bedpost. And any relief that normally accompanied the shedding of clothing was more than offset by the sweet tension coiling in her belly. Her breath rolled in her chest, shallow and quick, lifting her bosom in rhythmic waves.

He slid one hand up her thigh to untie her garter, then slowly rolled the stocking down her right leg. His fingertips brushed her sensitive inner thigh, caressed the vulnerable hollow of her knee, then swept down to the tingling arch of her foot. She shuddered with pleasure, twisting on the bed.

He grasped her ankle firmly. "Now, Isabel. Can I trust you to remain still? Or must I use your stockings to bind your legs?"

"I . . ." Her voice faltered, and she swallowed hard. "I will be still."

"Good girl. Spread your legs a bit wider, then." His voice was dark and brusque—a tone she'd come to know well, from their nightly encounters. A tone she'd come to welcome, even adore. It thrilled her, to hear the impatient need in his voice. To know that he'd passed the threshold of tender solicitude and gone over to raw, masculine want. And it gave her so much pleasure, to obey his terse directives. When he spoke to her thus, he absolved her of the burden of choice. She could not feel conflicted over her own feelings of desire, not with her husband demanding her willing compliance. It was simply her duty to please him, and to accept the pleasure he offered her, and she delighted in doing precisely as he bid.

Only later—only afterward, did shame and regret creep out from the shadows.

He removed her other stocking, putting her through the same slow, sweet torture as he drew the fine silk down her left leg and eased it over her foot. Sliding his hands back up to her waist, he undid the ties of her petticoat and whisked it down and away. He would not look her in the eye, but concentrated on his task as he placed his hands around her ribcage and rolled her slightly onto her side.

As his fingers yanked at the laces of her stays, a rush of air entered her lungs. Bel went dizzy with euphoria. The cravat chafed her wrists as she wriggled to help him remove the corset entirely. She was intoxicated with the delicious irony of it—how he was binding her and freeing her at the same time.

And now she lay naked, except for her simple, unadorned shift. The thin muslin was damp with her perspiration and clung to her skin, growing increasingly translucent. Toby repositioned her on her back and knelt between her outstretched legs, just inches from the place where she throbbed and ached for him. She could clearly see the outline of his arousal, so large and male, pressing against the fall of his trousers. Her body bowed as her hips arched toward him in an instinctive invitation. She was desperate for him to possess her body, to take his pleasure from her.

But that wasn't what he had in mind.

"No," he said gruffly, smoothing his palms over her waist and pulling her chemise tight against her breasts. Her nipples hardened with the tantalizing friction. "Not yet. I have bound you, Isabel—not for my own pleasure, but for yours. And I shall not release you until you have reached your peak—"

"Toby—"

"Three times."

Three times? He couldn't be serious. She wrestled her bindings and drew one knee up, planting her foot on the mattress. "But—"

He grasped her thigh and pushed her leg back down, gently but firmly. "I thought you promised to remain still. Must I retrieve the stockings?"

"No." *Yes.* "No," she said again, willing her body to relax. "But Toby, don't you want—"

"Oh, I want," he said, his voice regaining a bit of that devilish charm. "Believe me, I want."

Framing her between his arms, he leaned forward and drew her nipple into his mouth, licking and teasing it through the muslin of her shift. Her hips jerked upward as the pleasure lanced through her, and her mound brushed against his erection. He moaned around her nipple, then gave it a gentle bite. "Be still," he murmured.

Bel obeyed him, as best she could. She lay perfectly, miserably still as he leisurely suckled one breast, then the other. All the while, a terrible need built in the cleft of her legs. She felt her flesh swelling there, growing moist and ready. So ready.

She was far past ready and well into desperate when at last his hand slid down the length of her body, lingering over her breast, her hip, her thigh, and finally gathering to a fist around the hem of her shift. He drew the fabric up over her waist, then eased his palm up the slope of her inner thigh. As he approached her center, Bel panted with anticipation.

So close. Closer. Closer still, but just not quite—

There.

His hand cupped her sex, and Bel couldn't lie still. She rocked against the heel of his hand—once, twice. And then she came, in a bright explosion of bliss and relief.

With a throaty chuckle, Toby raised his head from her breast. "My, that was fast. Almost too fast. I shall have to take care, or this will all be over too soon."

It couldn't be over soon enough for Bel. The climax had merely blunted the edge of her desire. She still ached for him, but now she felt a strange sense of remorse . . . and guilt, that he was denying himself because of her.

"Toby, please," she said, lifting her head with great effort. "Release me now."

"Oh, no." He shook his head. "No, my darling. I know this is the moment where you long to pop out of bed and pen charity leaflets, or roll bandages for the dispensary. But I shan't let you. I'll not allow you to do penance for something that isn't wrong. The desire between us—it is nothing but what God intended for a husband and a wife."

Sitting back on his haunches, he drew her shift up and up, until her breasts were bared and the thin muslin bunched under her arms. "Look how beautiful you are," he said, lightly stroking his hands over her nude, trembling body. "You are everything perfect and right."

Bel looked down at her full, rounded figure, illuminated by unforgiving sunlight. Lucidity pierced the fog of her brain. Heavens, it was only the middle of the day, and he had her tied nude to the bedpost . . . She hoped he'd been serious when he'd told her all the servants had been dismissed for the afternoon.

"So lovely," he murmured, gently spreading her legs.

Dear Lord. Must he examine her *there*? She closed her eyes, shivering with pleasure as his fingers explored her tender, sensitized flesh. Her bound hands curled into fists. "Toby, please stop."

His hand stilled, and he looked up. "Why? Am I hurting you?"

"No, but you're making me uncomfortable."

"By touching you?"

"By looking at me."

"Why should you be uncomfortable? I'm simply admiring my beautiful wife." Dropping his eyes again, he resumed stroking her, tenderly parting the folds of her sex.

Bel squirmed. "Couldn't you admire a different part of me?"

"I admire every part of you." He withdrew his hand. He crawled up her body on hands and knees, surrounding her. Covering her, like a blanket. "I admire this glorious dark hair . . ." He pressed a kiss to the crown of her head. "This stern, serious brow . . ." His lips brushed the place between her eyebrows. "This exquisite nose . . . these luscious lips . . . the adorable turn of your chin . . ." He trailed soft, sensual kisses from her nose, to her mouth, to her jaw.

She wished she could thread her fingers into his hair, pull his mouth back up to hers for a deep, lingering kiss. But her hands remained bound above her, and Toby continued along his downward path.

"The delicious curve of this neck . . ."

He kissed his way down her center, pausing to rest his chin on her breastbone, plump her breasts with his hands, and give her a cheeky grin. "And I think you know how much I admire the view of this happy valley."

His mouth dipped lower. "Your navel tastes of apricots," he murmured, tickling her with his tongue.

"It does not."

"How would you know?" he teased. "And here . . ." He settled between her thighs and lowered his mouth to her core. "Here, you taste of paradise."

Bel whimpered with pleasure as his lips and tongue caressed her most intimate place. She'd grown more accustomed to this form of . . . attention, since their wedding night. He brought her to climax this way nearly every time they made love—and clever devil that he was, he'd learned how to bring her there quickly.

He'd also learned—clever devil that he was—how to take his time.

He teased her mercilessly with his mouth and hands, until she was molten with desire. As he slid a finger inside her, she bit her lip so hard it bled.

"Cry out," he told her. "Don't fight it. I live for those passionate noises you make."

"Toby."

"Ah, that was almost it. The one from earlier, you know—when I carried you across the river? Let's try once again." He pressed another finger into her.

"Toby!" she scolded, her voice tweaking.

"Yes, yes. That's the one."

Growling with frustration, she arched against his hand. Finally he took pity on her and put that teasing mouth to better use. Within seconds, he had her crying out in exquisite pleasure.

The second climax left her shuddering and weak. Her whole body sang with bliss, but she still ached for more. She needed him inside her, needed to feel that sense of completion when their bodies joined.

He stroked her thigh. "What do you want, Isabel? Tell me. Ask me anything."

"Release me."

"Anything but that. I'll unbind your wrists in time, but I mean to free your passion first."

"I don't—"

"You do. You're the most passionate woman I've ever known. You're so passionate, you're frightened of it. Don't be." He gently caressed her between her legs. "God, you are so wet, so ready. You're wet for *me*. Ready for *me*. Don't deny it. Don't deny me. Tell me what you want."

"I want . . ."

I want you inside me.

She just couldn't say it, not like that. Not with him staring down at her in the full sunlight, while she lay bound to the bed. He had all the power in this situation, and while that had excited her earlier . . . now she found herself needing to even the balance.

"I want you to disrobe," she said. If he would not loose her restraints, at least she could force him to remove his clothes. They would be equal in nakedness, at least.

"Gladly." With a roguish grin, he unbuttoned his waistcoat and cast it aside, before making short work of his cuffs. In a matter of moments, he'd gathered his shirt and pulled it over his head. Then he sat up to remove his boots, offering Bel a splendid view of his bare-chested form. She admired the lean, sculpted tone of his muscles; the masculine grace of his movements. She had to remind herself again that this paragon of male beauty was her husband—*hers*.

His boots removed, Toby unfastened his trousers and smallclothes and slid them down over his hips. And then there he sat, gloriously naked and proud. He hadn't a tremor of self-consciousness in his whole body, and Bel envied that strength and confidence almost as much as she desired to feel it, covering her. Inside her.

"And . . . ?" he prompted. "Tell me what now."

Come make love to me. Join with me.

But she couldn't say it, not yet. He still had her at his mercy, and she did not want to beg.

"Come kiss me," she whispered.

"With pleasure." Cautiously, he stretched his naked body over hers. Tenderly, he touched her lips with his. Those lips that had so recently tasted every inch of her body, so that it was almost as though Bel were kissing herself. How curious. She did taste of apricots.

They kissed slowly, and then deeply. And then quite urgently.

His arousal pulsed against her thigh, and her own body throbbed and ached for him.

"Tell me you want it," he whispered against her neck. "God, tell me soon, or I swear I shall die. I've wanted you all day, every moment. So fiercely I thought I'd explode with it. Say the words, Isabel. Let me in."

Bel felt a wide, giddy smile stretching her face. At last. He might have her bound by the wrists and panting with pleasure, but she had him naked and desperate and utterly tied in knots. And now, all the power was hers.

She hooked one leg over his and ground against him in invitation.

"*Isabel,*" he groaned. "Tell me what you want."

"You know what I want."

"You have to say it," he demanded, in that curt, arousing voice.

She laughed. He lifted his head, and their eyes locked.

"No, I don't," she said, giving him a coy smile.

His amber-flecked eyes warmed with understanding. "You tease," he accused, a grin spreading across his face. And then, taking her mouth, "That's my girl."

He kissed her passionately, moaning against her mouth as he lifted her hips and—merciful heaven—*finally* slid into her.

Oh, it felt so perfect. So right.

Holding steady deep within her, he reached over her head to untie the cravat. Once her hands were free, they flew straight to him. He took her in strong, deep strokes, and she explored his body boldly with her fingers, caressing him in places she'd never dared to touch before: the taut swell of his buttock, the downy slope of his thigh. She felt free now, free to possess all of him. Locking her ankles behind his back, she reached under them, to touch where their bodies joined—his hard, thick shaft sliding in and out of her body, the soft, vulnerable sac beneath.

He swore. "I can't—"

She squeezed gently, and he groaned.

"I—God, I can't stop it."

"Don't try." She raised both hands to his shoulders and clung to him tight. "Just let go."

Grasping her hips, he took her hard and fast, driving her back toward the edge of that blissful nothingness.

And in that last moment of delicious tension before she cried out in release, Bel thought to herself—if she never returned from it, she would not mind.

CHAPTER
FIFTEEN

The next morning, Bel knew she must have gone mad sometime during the night. Surely she must be seeing things.

Lambs.

Honestly, *lambs*. White, fluffy, innocent lambs frolicking on a sloping green. They even made adorable little bleating noises to one another.

As if Wynterhall weren't idyllic enough already—as if Bel hadn't just spent the morning touring what was now her very own enchanted castle and made the acquaintance of a benevolent house staff surely taken from the pages of some fairy story—now Toby had swept her out onto the terrace to see the well-tended gardens.

And greet the lambs.

Really. Even for her, this was a bit much. And it felt so incongruously innocent, after the torrid night of passion they'd shared. She could scarcely look at Toby this morning without blushing.

"Are they pets?" she asked, as one of the bleating creatures nosed her skirts. "Some sort of pastoral decoration, like park deer?"

Toby chuckled. "No, they're a nuisance. We're overrun with the creatures. Our steward increased the flock last autumn—with the new stocking factory down the river, wool is a good investment. And then it was a particularly fruitful spring for lambing, I gather. Now we're drowning in the things."

Together they walked across the green. The grass was still damp with the last touch of morning dew.

"They were meant to have the north fields for pasture," Toby continued. "But those plans met with a bit of a snag when the north fields flooded last month, and now . . . now, they're rather everywhere. It's positively biblical, isn't it?" He tugged sharply on her hand. "Watch your step, darling. Their leavings are everywhere, too."

"Oh!" Bel hopped, narrowly missing the offense to her slippers.

Toby gave her a sheepish grin. "This is rural life, I'm afraid."

"Don't be concerned on my account. I grew up on a plantation. I spent my childhood tossing grain to the chickens and gathering eggs."

"Truly? You were made to tend chickens?"

"Oh, no one made me. I wanted to do it." Bel bit back a laugh. "I'll tell you a secret, if you like."

"I would like."

"I used to redistribute their eggs, depending on how well I liked the hens. My favorites, I tallied as good layers—whether or not it was the truth. If one pecked my fingers, however, she would be . . ." Bel shrugged.

"Dinner." He gave her an exaggerated look of reproach. "You scheming thing, you. I tell you, my entire opinion of you has changed. I'll never look at you the same again."

Bel made a show of laughing, because she knew him to be in jest. She knew it in her mind, but still, some anxious twist of her belly argued otherwise.

"What confessions you make," he said. "I shall make you wait years to hear mine, until you are old and feeble and mostly deaf. Even then, I'll have to surround you with pillows in the event you fall over with shock."

"I think I'd just as soon never know."

"Yes, that's probably best." They had crossed the green now and entered a wooded glen. Toby turned them onto a narrow, root-scored path. "This is the way to Yorke Manor."

"Then why would we wish to follow it?" she asked.

"Why, to visit Mr. Yorke."

"Truly? But you're opponents." Wouldn't it be awkward for the two of them to meet, socially? Bel would find it awkward, at any rate.

"Yes, we're opponents since yesterday. But we've been friends for years, and neighbors since I was born. None of that is negated by the election."

"You're right, of course." Bel sighed. It hadn't been very gracious of her to object. She felt so on edge with Toby this morning, as though he would disapprove of her every remark. Perhaps it was the pressure of entering this grand estate as its mistress.

No, of course not. She knew her anxieties stemmed from their lovemaking yesterday. And last night. And very early this morning.

By all evidence, Toby had been well pleased with their use of the ancestral bed—as had she—but Bel worried that he would regard her differently, now that she'd been so bold with him. Had any of his respect for her survived the night?

"Do you know, your little chickens tale started me thinking."

"Really?"

"Yes, really. Me, thinking." He gave her a self-effacing look. "Hard to credit, I know."

"Oh, that's not what I meant."

"I know it." Smiling, he took her hand in his. "But I was thinking, about what a supremely fortunate fellow I am. I get along with most everyone, Isabel. There are many people I like, many people I call friend—but in all my life, I've met few individuals I can honestly say I admire. Do you know what I mean?"

"Perhaps," she answered carefully, worried about where she now fell in that divide. "But we each have a measure of goodness. Surely one can find *something*—some act or personal quality—to admire in any person."

"Surely *you* can do so—but you are better than me. No, I can count only a small number of my acquaintances that I deem worthy of unequivocal admiration. Can you guess who they might be?"

"Your mother?" That was an easy guess. Isabel admired her mother-in-law, too, for her sharp wit and easy grace.

"Yes, for one. Mr. Yorke is another." He laughed a little. "And if I ever wanted to start an interesting scene, I should gather them both in the same room and tell them so." With his free hand, he picked up a fallen branch and swung it idly, swatting at the bushes and vines as they went. "Don't you see? If there are only a handful of people I can admire in the world, how lucky am I? I was born to one of them, grew up a stone's throw from another . . ." He brought her hand to his lips and kissed it. "And now I've managed to marry a third."

Bel's heart warmed. How did he do it? How did he always intuit just exactly what she needed to hear and then speak the words so convincingly? It was beyond charm, it was . . . She didn't even know what to call it. "Toby, that's very . . ." *Romantic? Generous? Undeserved?* ". . . sweet."

"Sweet?" He hurried forward a step, then swung around to face her, halting her progress. Suddenly, his tone wasn't teasing anymore—simply husky and soft. "It's nothing to do with being sweet. I'm being honest."

"Truly?"

"Truly."

"You wouldn't lie to me?"

"Lie to you?" Pausing, he gave her a little smile. "Never."

And how could she doubt him, when he looked at her thus—with those amber-flecked eyes warm with admiration, wide enough to reflect all her hopes and dreams?

"I honestly meant what I told you yesterday," he told her, skipping his finger from the crown of her head, to her brow, to the tip of her nose, to her chin. "I admire every part of you, inside and out. And I'm . . . I'm simply so very grateful."

"Grateful?" she breathed. "For what?"

"For the fact you're not wearing a bonnet this morning." He cupped her face in his hands and kissed her.

She almost laughed into his kiss, for in that moment Bel was grateful, too—and for an equally absurd reason. Not because she'd married a man who could turn her insides to jelly with a smile, or because he'd made her mistress of her very own lovely, lamb-plagued castle. Not even because she trusted him so implicitly, so completely that she could accept not only kisses, but pleasure and praise from these lips.

No, in that moment she was overwhelmed with a most vain sort of gratitude—for the fact that Toby was tall. Taller than she, when so many men weren't. She would always have to reach for his kiss—stretch her neck, arch her feet—and feel just a bit girlish and uncertain and excited as she did. This kiss would never lose its thrill.

A giddy bubble of infatuation rose in her belly. By sheer force of will, she tamped it down. She may have lost the struggle against desire, but she was doubly resolved to guard her heart. Desire would inevitably fade—but love?

Love had a way of altering one's priorities. And Bel needed to keep hers intact.

She pulled away, and he growled deep in his throat.

"Yes, that's enough of that," he said, planting one last firm kiss on her lips before releasing her. "Else we'll never make it to Yorke's this morning."

"Why is it we're going there at all?"

"Just a matter of estate concern. It's this business with the irrigation canal."

"Ah, yes." Isabel remembered her mother-in-law's complaint. "Mr. Yorke went back on his agreement, simply to vex your mother?"

"I'm certain there's more to it than that. Mother has a way of exaggerating when it comes to Yorke. You'd think him the three-eyed ogre under the bridge, rather than the neighbor living across it." Their boots made hollow clunking noises as he led her over the graying planks that bridged a small rill. "I hope you don't mind the walk," he said. "I didn't think you'd feel up to the carriage just yet."

"No," Bel agreed, her pulse accelerating at the mere mention of yesterday's calamity. She'd be just as happy never to ride in a carriage again.

"And I suppose I could have left you at home and allowed you to rest," he continued, winking at her. "But I'm too selfish for that. This is our honeymoon, after all, and I mean to keep you close."

They edged a wheat field in silence, walking arm in arm, and Isabel tilted her face to the warm June sunshine. If God had ever created a more beautiful morning, Isabel would still prefer this one. She didn't think her heart could withstand a day that came any closer to perfection. If the breeze teasing the grain were just a degree warmer, if this sky were just a slightly deeper shade of blue . . . if her husband, the handsomest thing under the sun, winked at her just one more time—true disaster could strike.

She could fall in love.

"We have a problem."

Toby frowned as Mr. Yorke tugged him closer to the garden hedge. Behind them, Isabel marveled over a clump of late-blooming strawberries, gathering the tiny red fruits in one palm. Imagine, the dear girl had never seen strawberry plants. There were so many things he could show her, so many delights she'd never experienced.

"We have a serious problem," Yorke whispered again. "This little plan of yours is off to an inauspicious start."

"How so?" Toby asked.

"Let me give you a hint. If you don't want the populace to support your candidacy, you shouldn't go performing dashing heroics in front of the crowd. You're the talk of the borough, after that little trick-riding stunt."

Toby winced. He'd imagined that wouldn't help his cause. "Well, I couldn't have done differently. Should I have simply stood back and waited for disaster?"

"No, of course not." Yorke looked over his shoulder at Isabel. "And even I have to applaud you. It was well done, Toby. For a moment there, even I was certain you'd break your neck. But you should know, much as it pains my pride to admit it—now you may have to make a real effort to lose."

"It's only a bit of excitement and chatter. Don't worry. I'll be completely absent from the hustings; I'll send no one to speak in my stead. You're still a sure bet for re-election, I'm sure of it."

"Perhaps. But it is a problem."

"What's a problem?" Isabel asked, surprising them both with her sudden nearness. She extended her hand to Toby. "Have some strawberries?"

He declined with a slight shake of his head. It was all the movement he could manage, what with his heart thudding against his ribs. Surely she hadn't heard them. She didn't have the look of a trusting newlywed bride who just discovered she'd been betrayed by her husband, less than one week into her marriage.

Toby cleared his throat. "We're just discussing the irrigation canal. Mr. Yorke was about to tell me what his problem is."

"I don't have any problem."

"Then why are you suddenly refusing to proceed? I need that canal, Yorke. Ever since they built that factory downriver, the north fields are flooding every spring. Meanwhile, our lands to the west are under-watered. The canal remedies both conditions."

"Ah, but those are *your* problems. Not mine. Why should I allow you to dig a trench through my land, let alone share the costs of the labor to dig it?"

"Because the canal will water your western fields, too. Hadn't you complained of the low yield last harvest?"

"I had," Yorke said. "But I've since realized, it's not for lack of water. The land's merely overworked. I've decided to let it lie fallow this season, and therefore, I'll reap no benefit from your canal. Neither do I have the extra income to pay for it. It'll have to wait until next year."

"Oh, but the lambs!" Isabel said. "Think of the lambs."

"The lambs?" Yorke echoed.

"Yes, the lambs," Toby groaned. "They're overrunning Wynterhall. And they're reasonably compact and adorable now, but by next year they'll simply be sheep. Great, woolly, malodorous sheep. I need those north fields drained for pasture, *this* year."

"So build the canal. Just keep it on your lands."

"You know very well that would double the length and the cost. Come on, man. Be a friend."

"Be a friend?" Yorke gave a chortling laugh. "What sort of negotiation is that? If you want your canal, you'll have to make it worth my while."

Toby narrowed his eyes at the old man. For the first time in his life, he was growing truly impatient with Yorke. "Crafty old devil. You want this canal, too. You're just trying to get out of paying for it."

Yorke puffed his chest. "Now you're starting to sound like that woman."

"Leave that woman—" Toby bit off that sentence and began again. "Leave my mother out of this. We're the landholders, and this is between you and me. Now, if we can't begin work on that canal directly, I shall have to spend much more time in Surrey this summer. I may have to go talking with the farmers in the neighborhood. Perhaps even perform another display of horsemanship."

He stared hard at Yorke, letting the implications of his words sink in. The old man looked a bit shocked. Toby was a bit shocked, too, truth be told. He had no idea where it had come from, the gall to threaten his friend's seat in Parliament simply to see a trench dug in the dirt. But much as he appreciated Yorke's friendship over the years, he wasn't going to let the man take advantage of it.

"Be careful, my boy," Yorke said in a low, warning tone. The old man's watery gaze flicked toward Isabel. "I don't think that's a bluff you want me to call."

Oh, no. He wouldn't dare. A knot formed in Toby's gut. Surely Yorke wouldn't betray their secret. If Isabel learned about their gentlemen's agreement to fix the election, she'd never forgive him. He'd spend the rest of his life sleeping with the sheep.

Mr. Yorke smiled at Isabel. "May I, Lady Aldridge?" he asked, plucking a strawberry from her palm.

"But of course," she replied, returning his smile. So sweet, so innocent. So completely unaware of what a deceitful cad she called husband.

"A word to the wise, Toby," Yorke said, popping the strawberry into his mouth. "Never gamble with something you're not prepared to lose."

Toby exhaled with frustration. He knew he was beaten. Yorke knew it too, damn his eyes. The old man could demand to plow a canal straight through Wynterhall's gardens, and now Toby would be forced to agree.

"Surely some compromise can be reached." Isabel raised another strawberry to her juice-stained lips. "Take pity on the lambs, Mr. Yorke," she said, her eyes twinkling. "Don't God's little lambs deserve a home?"

"Is that the newlywed love talking?" Yorke directed his question at Toby. "Or is she always like this?"

"Oh, I'm always like this," she said. "Aren't I, Toby?"

"Yes." Toby smiled despite himself. Only Isabel could insult him so sweetly.

She continued, "I'm not a romantic, Mr. Yorke. Fairness, justice, honesty—these are the qualities that move my heart."

"Is that so?" Yorke gave Toby a chastening look.

Toby shrugged and studied the oak standing sentinel atop a distant hill. He imagined he saw his own noose hanging there, twisting in the breeze. *Yes, old man. There you have it. I'm sunk.*

"Very well," Yorke said gruffly. "In the interests of fairness, we'll proceed with the canal as agreed, *if*"—he stayed Isabel's thanks with a curt gesture—"if you lease my western fields for the summer."

"But you just said you plan to let them lie fallow!"

"I do. You can use them as—"

"As pasture," Toby said, shaking his head as the obvious dawned. "Of course. And the land will be the richer for it, in time for winter planting." He had to hand it to Yorke; the man really was shrewd. No wonder he'd been so successful in Parliament all these years. What mad whim had led Toby to consider making a serious challenge? "This was your plan all along, wasn't it?"

"No, it wasn't," Yorke said, slapping him on the back. "Really, Toby. You were supposed to be clever enough to think of it yourself. It's a fortunate thing you married this one," he said, nodding at Isabel. "At least she knows God's little lambs need a home."

CHAPTER
SIXTEEN

A primal scream greeted them as Toby and Isabel crossed the threshold of Grayson House.

"Dear heavens." Isabel clutched at his arm, drawing her body into his. Her instinctive response gave Toby a deeply male sense of satisfaction. His wife trusted him. To protect her, to pleasure her. Surely it could not be long before she surrendered her heart. When this absurd election was over, Isabel would put aside her disappointment, and Toby had every hope that their relationship could continue to deepen and grow. In short, life was good.

A savage growl shook the walls.

Or not so good.

Sophia rushed toward them, her cheeks flushed and hair in disarray. "Thank God you're here."

"What the devil is going on?" Toby handed his hat and gloves to a footman. "Are they murdering cats above-stairs?"

"It's Lucy," Sophia said. "She's gone into labor."

"Here?" Isabel asked. A moan rumbled through the plastered ceiling, and she tilted her head toward its source. "Now?"

"Yes." Sophia ushered them toward the salon, drawing them aside for a private conference just before they entered. She lowered her voice to a whisper. "She and Jeremy had some kind of row, and Lucy left in a fit of temper. She drove here in the phaeton, and by the time she arrived her pains had already begun. Miss Osborne says it's not safe to move her. She must deliver the child here."

Toby exchanged a quick glance with his wife. "We really should leave."

Isabel nodded. "Yes, of course." When another muffled cry floated down the corridor, she turned to Sophia. "We'll come for the Society leaflet another time."

"No!" Sophia reached for them, grasping Toby's arm in one hand and Isabel's wrist in the other. "Don't leave, I beg you."

Toby said, "Surely Miss Osborne has matters in hand. Or would you like me to summon another physician?"

Sophia shook her head. "It's not Lucy I'm concerned for. Hetta says her labor is progressing well, if a bit slowly. That's normal with first babes, she says. No, it's Jeremy who needs looking after."

"Jem?" Toby flicked a glance toward the salon. "He's already here?"

"Yes. Gray and Joss are there with him, but I think he'd be glad for the company of a friend. He's not taking this well, I'm afraid."

A long, piercing scream interrupted their conversation. All eyes rolled ceiling-ward.

"No," Toby said finally, staring at the stamped plaster. "I can imagine Jem wouldn't be taking this well at all."

"Did you say Joss is with them?" Isabel asked. Sophia nodded, and a speaking glance passed between the ladies. "Oh, dear. This must be torture for him."

Toby thought it rather sounded like Lucy was the one being tortured. He himself wasn't overly concerned, seeing as how his three sisters had survived ten noisy births, collectively, and he knew Lucy to be hardier than any of them.

But then—he took the briefest moment to imagine

these were Isabel's cries of pain. He immediately shared Jeremy's unease. Now each small moan and whimper had him wincing like a kick to the gut. How much worse for Joss, who had lost a wife in childbirth?

Sophia squeezed his arm. "Please, just sit with them." Imploring him with watery blue eyes, she tilted her head toward the salon. "Try to convince Jeremy that all will be well. Keep his mind occupied with other things. Just . . . Toby, just be yourself. More than anyone I know, you have a gift for putting people at ease."

Words failed him for a moment. Of all the people he hadn't expected to hear praising his character, the woman who'd run away rather than marry him was at the top of the list.

At length, he gave a mute nod of assent.

Releasing his arm, Sophia turned to his wife. "Bel, would you come upstairs and help me? I'm gathering fresh linens and supplies."

"Yes, certainly."

Toby watched them disappear up the stairs, hand in hand. Remarkable. He wished now were the time to really talk to Sophia. To ask her why—if he put everyone so at ease—she'd fled halfway across the world rather than speak to him about ending their engagement.

But now wasn't the time. At the moment, he had a friend in need.

Mustering all the blithe, irreverent charm he could find, Toby donned a carefree smile and sauntered into the salon. "Good afternoon. Gray, Joss . . . Jem. No, don't get up." He crossed to the bar and began pouring himself a brandy. After filling his own glass, he took the decanter over to Jeremy and topped off his friend's drink, noting the pale, drawn mask of worry on his face. "Well, Jem," he said lightly. "I understand congratulations are in order."

Jeremy stared into his glass. "Prayers are in order.

This shouldn't be happening. It's too soon. And it's all my fault. We argued, and . . ." He scrubbed his face with one hand, leaving his eyes heavy and laced with red. "I should send an express to Waltham Manor."

"Let me do it," Gray said, sitting down to a writing desk. "She's at my house, after all. Shall I address it to her father or her mother?"

"To her brother, Henry. Lucy hasn't any parents living." When another growling moan sounded from above, Jeremy dropped his head in his hands. "Oh, God. I can't endure this."

Toby sat down next to him. "It's perfectly normal, Jem. All my sisters sounded the same in labor, or worse. And babies arrive in their own time—a few weeks early, a few weeks late. Everything comes out fine."

"Except when it doesn't." Joss rose from his chair and strode to the window. Toby glared at him, and Joss stared back with hollow eyes.

"Don't, Joss." Gray gave his brother a warning look.

"Don't what?" Joss asked defensively. "Don't prepare a man for all possibilities? There's no benefit in denying the truth. We all know women die in childbirth. It happens."

Jeremy groaned into his hands.

"Yes," Toby said in a matter-of-fact tone, "it happens." He refused to let his annoyance with Joss taint his efforts at reassurance. "But this is not some random woman we're discussing." Lowering his voice, he spoke to Jeremy. "They don't know Lucy like we do, Jem. Listen to me. I've a mother and three older sisters, all of whom eat adversity for breakfast. I'm married to the most principled lady on earth. But when it comes to strength of will, Lucy bests them all. She's healthy, she's young, and she's determined to give you a beautiful child. And when Lucy's determined to do something, she does it."

"Jeremy!" Lucy's pained cry clawed through the ceiling.

"If you hear me down there, I want you to know . . . You are never. Coming near me. Again."

Toby and Jeremy looked at one another.

The voice became more of a growl. "Never. Ever. Again."

"You see?" Toby remarked at length. "That's determination for you."

When Jeremy made no response, Toby decided it was time to speak of other things. Diversion, that's what this group needed. "How are the legal studies progressing, Joss?"

Joss stared out the window. "Fine."

Several moments' silence followed. Well, so much for that vein of conversation.

"I met with Felix in the park the other day," Toby began again. "Jem, really—one of us needs to ward him off whenever he mentions Tattersalls. Or accompany him, at the least. He laid down an outrageous sum for a team of bays last week, more than double their worth. They're not evenly matched at all, and his carriage pulled left so egregiously, I found him spinning in circles in the midst of Rotten Row." Toby chuckled. "Not that driving has ever been Felix's forte. He really ought to leave it to coachmen, instead of—"

"Toby." Lifting his head from his hands, Jeremy gave him that insufferable autocratic Look. There really was no disobeying that Look. He would make a formidable father, indeed.

"Yes?"

"Shut it."

Toby raised his eyebrows. "Very well."

Jeremy lowered his head again, and quiet reigned. Gray sipped his drink. Joss stared out the window. Toby tugged at his neck cloth. The midsummer heat choked the room, oppressive and mute.

A scream tore through the tense silence.

Every man froze.

"Toby," Jeremy said, his fingers white-knuckled webs against his black hair.

"Yes?"

"Keep talking."

So he did. For hours. Afternoon faded toward evening, brandy dwindled in its decanter, and coats and cravats peeled away from restless, perspiring men. Through it all, Toby kept talking. He talked of foxhounds and boxing and every inane, meaningless topic he could dredge from his imagination. Mundane, everyday concerns that he hoped would serve as a reminder that beyond this day, beyond Lucy's labor, mundane, everyday life would continue.

As the sinking sun painted the salon carpet in shades of plum and crimson, Toby was just embarking on a detailed description of the new writing desk he'd ordered for his study. By this point, he was growing hoarse, and boring even himself. But until Jeremy told him to stop, he was going to keep talking. "I ordered dark-blue felt to line the drawers," he said, yawning. "And the handles are carved in the shape of—"

Miss Osborne saved them all, thank God, when she flung open the salon doors.

Jeremy shot to his feet. Toby, Gray, and Joss followed suit, with lumbering movements.

"No babe yet," Miss Osborne said.

Four chests deflated in unison. Jeremy sank back into his chair with a muttered oath. "Oh, God. She's going to die."

"She is not going to die," Miss Osborne said firmly. "There is no cause for concern. Everything is progressing as it should. First labors are always lengthy, and Lucy is weathering the pains well. I expect it will be a few hours more."

"Can I see her?" Jeremy asked.

She paused. "No, my lord."

At the words "my lord," Jeremy seemed to recall his position of authority. Toby watched the decision to pull rank travel up his face, starting with the firming of his jaw and ending with his ice-blue eyes and heavy brow as they flexed the Look.

"I'm going to see her," he said, standing again and drawing to his full height.

"No, you're not."

Toby had to salute Miss Osborne. There weren't many women—there weren't many *people*—who would have stood their ground against Jeremy in full Earl-of-Kendall arrogance.

"You can't keep him away from her," Joss objected. "She's his wife."

Gray joined the effort to argue Jeremy's case. "Miss Osborne, surely you can permit him a few minutes with Lucy."

The young woman shook her head. "It's not a matter of me granting my permission, it's a matter of Lucy granting hers." Her sharp gaze landed on Jeremy. "And she doesn't want to see you, my lord. She expressly told me so, and I will heed my patient's wishes above even the demands of an earl."

Jeremy swore again.

When Joss echoed him, Miss Osborne threw him a strange look.

"I came to inform you of Lucy's condition," she continued. "Now that I've done so, I must return upstairs."

She turned to leave, but Jeremy darted forward to catch her arm.

"Hetta, please." His voice cracked. Toby thought he had never seen his friend look so vulnerable. "I know Lucy's angry with me. We did not part well earlier. But you must let me see her, give me a chance to put things right."

"You will have a chance, my lord. After the babe is born, but not before."

"You mean to keep me from her?" Jeremy loomed over the young woman. Her face blanched, throwing her freckles into sharp relief. "If I decide to see my wife, ten men couldn't keep me from her."

"Jem." Toby stepped between them, placing a hand on Jeremy's shoulder and guiding his friend back with a light yet firm touch. "I know it's difficult, but you must respect Lucy's wishes. As Miss Osborne says, you'll have ample time to make up later."

"Listen to your friend, my lord." With that, Miss Osborne dropped a perfunctory curtsy and left the room.

Frustrated, impotent silence resumed. Jeremy paced the carpet. Gray moved to uncork a fresh bottle of liquor. With a vicious oath, Joss quit the room. The door slammed shut behind him.

Toby supposed he ought to start prattling again, provide more distraction. But he didn't really feel like talking. What he felt like doing was charging upstairs, finding Isabel, gathering her into his arms and burying his face in her sweet-scented hair. He didn't want to kiss her, or lie with her, or even speak to her. He just wanted to be near her. Desperately. The yearning hit him like a fist, leaving a dull ache in his chest. And with it came a realization that left him without words.

He was deeply, irretrievably in love with his wife.

"What the devil do you think you're doing?"

Miss Osborne froze on the first riser of the staircase, hand on the banister. She didn't turn around.

"If a man wants to see his wife, who are you to stop him?" Joss demanded, stepping closer. Staring into the fine wisps of auburn hair where they curled against her pale neck. So delicate and soft. So completely unlike her.

"If a woman does not wish to see her husband," she

said calmly, pivoting to face him, "who am I to force her?" Miss Osborne was a small woman, but with the benefit of one step's height, she stood nearly eye-to-eye with him.

"Do you know what it does to a man, listening to his wife in such agony, knowing he is powerless to help her? Knowing she could die? It is the most acute form of torture imaginable. Any devoted husband would swallow hot coals to spare his wife a moment's suffering." He jabbed a finger toward the closed salon door. "That man is sick with worry, and your heartless remarks only multiply his distress."

"If Lord Kendall is sick with anything, it's guilt. He regrets their argument, and well he should, from Lucy's report of it. But his apologies will have to wait. I'm here to deliver an infant, not coddle a grown man's conscience."

Her impersonal tone only added fuel to Joss's anger. It was clear from her prim carriage, the proud jut of her chin—she meant to deny his presence had any effect on her. But he knew it did.

He stepped closer, knowing she would not back down. Though she stood perfectly still, her pupils widened a fraction, and her auburn lashes quivered as she blinked. Good. He wanted to unsettle her. He wanted to crack open the ice encasing this woman and discover the warm, beating heart that instinct told him must lie somewhere within. "Miss Osborne," he whispered. "*Hetta.* Can you truly be so cold, so devoid of sympathy?"

"I'm not cold, I'm competent. I'm a physician."

"A physician treats *people,* not merely injuries and illnesses. You would be a better doctor if you gave some consideration to your patients' feelings. And you would be a better person if you allowed yourself to feel."

She laughed bitterly. "*You* would encourage me to feel. Of course—by your accounting, one cannot claim true suffering without a proportional measure of public grief. Not all of us have the luxury of indulging our emotions, Captain Grayson. Don't you know Lucy is my dearest friend? I do not enjoy watching her in pain, any more than Lord Kendall does. Should I come join you gentlemen, then? Spend the evening cursing into my brandy? Perhaps that would give you sufficient proof of my sympathy, but it would not help Lucy deliver her child."

"Miss Osborne, you're the most educated woman I know. Surely you're more clever than that argument implies." Joss inhaled slowly, tempering his frustration. Why did this woman affect him so? Every time he was in her presence, he felt compelled to defend his behavior, explain himself in ways he shouldn't need to explain himself to anyone. He didn't know why it should matter what she thought of him, but somehow it did. It mattered a great deal. "You needn't choose between the two," he said. "Can't you be both a physician and a human? Both Lady Kendall's doctor and her friend?"

She stood silent for a long moment. Joss waited for her to speak.

"My mother," she began at last, "was ill, bedridden for more than a year. My father personally saw to her treatment. He consulted specialists, spent long nights scouring medical journals for new treatments. Not once—not even toward the end, when she forgot our names—did my father indulge in a moment's self-pity. Not once did he allow her to see his distress. And the day she died, did he sit by her bedside and weep useless tears, just to prove his love for her? No, he went to tend victims of a mining explosion the next county over. Because he was the doctor, and they needed his help." The sparks of green flashed in her hazel eyes. "Everyone has wounds, Captain Grayson. Some of us do our bleeding on the inside."

Suddenly, she raised a hand to her temple and closed her eyes. Her posture softened, and Joss finally glimpsed what he'd been waiting to see since the day of their introduction. At that moment, she wasn't a doctor. She wasn't efficient or headstrong or abrasive or cold. She was simply a woman—and an exhausted one, at that. The long hours of work weighed heavy on her shoulders. Eyes still shut, she swayed slightly on her feet. She desperately needed a rest.

More than that, she needed to be held.

He could hold her. He had two strong arms, and her slender frame would fit quite neatly in their circumference. On another day, she might be strong enough to hold him in return.

But it couldn't be that easy. Nothing was ever that easy. There were questions and enmity and ghosts between them. And Joss knew from experience that taking a woman in his arms was a great deal simpler than letting her go.

"I'm sorry." He rested a hand on the banister, sliding it slowly higher until it rested an inch from hers. "I realize this day has been a trial for you as well. It's just that I know what a living hell it is to be in Lord Kendall's place. In many ways, his misery is my own. If you cannot have a care for his feelings, perhaps you could have a care for mine."

"You would ask me to care," she said, eyes still shut. "Care for you."

"Yes, damn it. Do I not deserve as much? Am I not just as human as Lord Kendall, as any man?"

"Lord. You are just as much a fool, as any man."

Her eyes opened and looked to his. There was something there. Not the respect he'd been seeking, but something better and worse at once. Emotion, raw and intense. She did care for his feelings. She cared a great deal. Good Lord, the girl was half in love with him, the devil knew why. For weeks now, he'd been searching for her weakness, and the truth had been staring him in the mirror all the while. *He* was her weakness. And now that they both knew it, she trembled.

"Oh," he said softly. "Forgive me. I didn't realize."

She made a choked sound, rather like a swallowed sob.

Some tender, protective impulse uncoiled in his heart. Leaning forward, he slid his hand along the banister until his thumb rested in the crook of hers. A warm pulse fluttered there, where her skin was chafed and cracked from frequent scrubbing. He soothed the spot with his thumb, at every moment expecting her to pull away. She didn't.

"Could you, Hetta?" he asked quietly. "Could you care for me?" He hadn't known, until that moment, how much he'd been wanting to ask her exactly that. Neither had he realized how much of his rudeness had been aimed at avoiding the answer.

"Captain Grayson . . ."

"Joss," he corrected, raising his other hand to cradle her smooth, flushed cheek. Closing her eyes, she leaned ever so slightly into his palm. "My name is Joss."

Then a low moan sounded above them. Hetta bristled away from his touch. Joss dropped his hand from her face, but he kept the other twined with hers. They stared into one another's eyes for a few seconds more, and in that remarkable shade of hazel, Joss read possibilities and questions and fears. And then—he saw the moment of her decision.

He released her before she could pull away.

"I can't care for you," she whispered. "Grief, bitterness . . . those are wounds I don't know how to cure."

"Hetta, wait. I didn't mean—"

"I have work to do." Crossing her arms, she retreated up the staircase. "Go back to your brandy and be at ease. No one is going to die here today."

*   *   *

"I'm going to murder him."

Bel exchanged a worried glance with Sophia. Her sister-in-law stood at the other side of the bed, fanning Lucy industriously. For her part, Bel placed a fresh damp cloth against Lucy's brow.

Their efforts did nothing to cool the laboring woman's temper.

"I'm going to murder Jeremy for doing this to me," Lucy said, panting for breath between contractions. "Does he know how much this hurts?"

"You've been making enough noise to give him a fair idea." Miss Osborne swept back into the room, bearing an armload of towels in one hand and dabbing at her eyes with the other.

"Good," Lucy growled, curling in on herself. Her face contorted in pain as another spasm gripped her.

Bel noted Sophia's bleached countenance. She'd probably never witnessed a woman in the worst pains of labor. Bel herself was no midwife, but she'd been present at a handful of births—most notably, and most tragically, that of her nephew, Jacob.

She knew enough to realize something was wrong.

Skirting the edge of the bed, she approached Hetta at the washstand.

"Did you tell Lord Kendall?" Bel murmured, making a show of folding and refolding the towels as Hetta scrubbed her hands with the cake of soap.

"No. What purpose would it serve? He's already worried sick."

"Do you intend to tell Lucy?"

"No. There's no benefit in distressing her." Hetta flicked a glance over her shoulder at Sophia. "And your sister-in-law looks ready to faint as it is."

"She's just anxious for her friend, and for herself. It will be her turn, come the winter. Right now, she is imagining herself enduring the same ordeal. Perhaps you could explain to her, afterward . . . why it is likely to go easier for her."

"But it might not." Hetta rinsed her hands, and Bel offered her a towel. "One never knows. I can't make your sister any promises. A physician never makes promises."

"But you have attended births like this before? Where the babe is turned backward?"

"Yes, several. Most of them with perfectly healthy outcomes for both mother and infant."

"Most." Bel's stomach knotted. "But not all."

"No, not all." Hetta turned to her and looked her square in the eye. "Lucy and her child will be fine. I've made a promise, and I mean to keep it. No one is going to die here today."

"I thought you just said a physician doesn't make promises."

"I know." Wilting against the washstand, Hetta put a wrist to her brow. "A physician doesn't. That promise was made by a stupid, fanciful girl." Shrugging back into her mantle of brisk professionalism, she added, "But the physician means to keep it."

Hetta returned to her position at the foot of the bed, lifting the bedsheets to examine Lucy's progress. Bel returned to Lucy's side, replacing the warmed cloth on her forehead with yet another, freshly doused. There was little she could do, except make Lucy as comfortable as possible. And pray.

Silently, she resumed the litany she'd been reciting all afternoon. Now she expanded her petitions, applying not just to Father, Son, and Holy Spirit, but to the Virgin Mary, too. Normally, Bel avoided anything that smacked of papist beliefs. She avoided following her mother's example in general—be the passions holy or profane. But sometimes it comforted her, to put faith in a divine mother. One who embodied all the serenity and grace her own had lacked.

God knew, the women in this room could stand to borrow some grace and serenity.

Another scream forced its way through Lucy's gritted teeth.

Sophia looked as though she would be ill. Typically Bel envied her sister-in-law's elegant self-possession. At times, she'd even resented her for it and longed to see Sophia—just once—the tiniest bit ill at ease. But watching her come unraveled like this . . . it brought none of the satisfaction Bel had imagined. And finding herself the voice of composure between them, well—that rather flipped her world on its ear.

When the contraction subsided, Hetta pushed the bedsheets to Lucy's waist. "Lucy, listen to me. The hard work is about to start."

"To *start*?" Lucy shouted. "What the devil do you mean, to *start*? I know you did not just tell me, after I've been laboring in this bed for six hours, that we are just about to *start*."

"You are going to start to push. It's time to deliver your child. With the next pains, I want you to grasp your knees and bear down."

Following Hetta's instructions, Bel and Sophia helped raise Lucy to a half-sitting position. They all stood frozen, waiting, until Lucy's low growl began again.

"All right now," Hetta directed. "Push."

Lucy pushed. And she pushed Bel's eardrums together, with the splitting scream that accompanied her effort.

"No more screaming," Hetta said, once the pains had passed and Lucy sagged limp in Bel and Sophia's arms. "Every scream is effort wasted. You need to save your strength."

"How long will this take?" Sophia asked weakly.

"Impossible to tell," Hetta answered her. "Hours, perhaps."

"Oh, God," Lucy moaned. "Hours? I can't do this for hours!"

"Yes, you can," Bel told her.

"No, I can't," Lucy said hysterically. "I really can't. I've changed my mind. Go tell Jeremy I've changed my mind. It's all his fault this child won't come out. What was I thinking, marrying a great, stubborn brute? I should have married the vicar's son. He'd have given me runtish, compliant babies. Babies that wouldn't take *hours* to—" Her rant gave way to another pained cry.

"Push, Lucy," Hetta ordered. "Push as hard as you can."

"One day," Lucy panted, once the contraction had ebbed, "it will be you in labor, Hetta, and I'm going to stand by the bedside and repay you tenfold for all this heartless tyranny."

"And you'll be welcome to do so, Lucy, should that day ever come."

For an instant, pain shimmered in Hetta's eyes. She quickly blinked it away, but not before Bel saw it. Saw it, and felt it twisting in her heart. While the three of them fell to pieces, this one woman was holding them all together—and she was doing it all on her own. Alone. At the end of this day, Hetta was the only one of them who would not know the comforting embrace of a husband.

Bel closed her eyes. Behind her eyelids floated the image of Toby's reassuring smile. On the heels of reassurance, however, trod confusion. Somewhere in the past hour, she'd stopped pleading with deities and started picturing her husband. Where were her priorities?

Her eyes flew open when someone clutched at her shoulder.

It was Sophia, reaching across from Lucy's other side. Her eyes were wide, and she trembled. She mouthed, *"I want to leave."*

Bel shook her head. *"You can't."*

"I'm scared," Sophia whispered.

"I heard that," said Lucy, through clenched teeth. "If I have to stay, so do you."

"Lucy, you're doing beautifully," Bel said, smoothing the damp hair from Lucy's brow. "Just think, soon you'll be holding your baby. It won't be much longer now. It can't be."

CHAPTER
SEVENTEEN

But it was.

After more than an hour of pushing, Lucy was pale and soaked with perspiration. "I can't do it," she moaned through cracked lips.

"Here, take a bit of tea." Bel raised the cup to her lips.

"No, no." Lucy shook her head. "I don't want tea. I want this to stop. I want out. I can't do this, really I can't."

"All right then," Hetta said, stepping back. "Perhaps you can't."

"What?" Sophia cried. "But how will—"

"She doesn't mean that," Bel soothed. "Lucy's doing beautifully." Meanwhile, panic fluttered in her stomach. If even Hetta was losing confidence, they were really in trouble.

They all watched as Hetta untied the apron from around her waist and went to rinse her hands at the washstand. Then she made for the door.

"Where do you think you're going?" Lucy demanded, craning her neck to see her friend.

Hetta stopped at the door. "I'm going downstairs, to tell Lord Kendall you can't do it."

"May I go with you?" Sophia asked, ignoring Bel's attempts to shush her.

"What's Jeremy going to do about it?" Lucy asked. "It's not as though he can come up here and birth the child hims—aah!" She curled around another contraction. Bel supported Lucy's shoulders as she pushed, murmuring words of encouragement in her ear.

"No, he can't do anything about it," Hetta said, speaking over Lucy's cries of pain. "But perhaps he'd like to say good-bye."

"*Good-bye?*" Bel and Sophia exclaimed in unison. If Lucy could have spoken through her pains, Bel was sure she would have made their duet a trio.

Arms crossed over her chest, Hetta strode back to the bedside. "Lucy, listen to me. Your child is breech. The chances of—"

Bel grabbed Hetta's arm. "Don't. Please." They couldn't give up hope, not yet. There were still a few saints she hadn't petitioned.

"I know what I'm doing," Hetta murmured. "I know Lucy."

The contraction over, Lucy flopped back against the pillows and glared up at her friend with flashing green eyes. "Don't you dare. I've no intention of saying good-bye to Jeremy. I'm still too vexed with him over this morning."

Hetta sat on the edge of the bed and took Lucy's hand. "Then listen to me. The babe is breech, not headfirst as it should be. That's the reason you're having such difficulty."

"Good Lord." Lucy blew a wisp of hair from her mouth. "He's an incorrigible brat already."

"Yes. Clearly he takes after his mother."

"Am I going to die? Tell me honestly."

"You know I would never lie. There is danger, for both you and the child. But when has a bit of danger prevented you from doing anything?" Hetta squeezed Lucy's hand. "Lucy, you're the most stubborn, foolhardy woman I know. Your friends love you despite it. Your husband loves you *for* it. Lord Kendall believes you can do anything. Don't make me go down there and tell him otherwise. Don't let him suspect you've given up, or you know as well as I, you'll never know the end of it. If he's overprotective now . . ."

"You wouldn't dare." Lucy's eyes narrowed. "You're a cold woman, Hetta Osborne."

"He'll place more restrictions on you than ever," Hetta threatened. "He'll treat you like a plate of glass. He'll be so afraid of getting you with child, he'll—"

"Never touch me again?" Lucy scoffed. "Not likely. If he were *that* strong-willed, we'd have never married in the first place." She sighed up at the ceiling. "But he might hold out for a year, or two."

"Exactly," Hetta replied. "Lucy, you *can* do this. If you concentrate and work hard, and most difficult of all, follow directions, both you and your baby will survive. But if I go down to Lord Kendall right now, your pride will never recover."

Lucy closed her eyes and lay still, breathing steadily in and out through her nose. Her dry, pale lips thinned to a line, then curled into a grimace.

"It's all right, Lucy," Sophia said. "We're all here to help."

"You can't help me," Lucy bit out. "No one can."

Hetta released her hand. "Very well, then. I'm going downstairs."

"Over my dead body." Lucy struggled to her elbows and gritted her teeth. "No one can help me, but I'll do it myself. I'm going to push this baby out, if it kills me."

The supper trays went untouched. As the evening wore on, Lucy's cries grew louder. And then fainter. The poor girl must be exhausted, Toby reckoned. He certainly was, and he hadn't done a damn thing beyond sitting in this salon all day, talking himself into a stupor and watching his best friend in agony. He envied Isabel her manual tasks. Why couldn't he have been put to work boiling linens?

Gray apparently shared his feelings. He prowled the room like a caged animal. "God. How much longer can this go on? I can't take much more of this."

Still holding down the same armchair he'd occupied all evening, Jeremy raised his head. "You think it's difficult for you? Imagine how I feel."

"Oh, he is imagining it," Toby said to Jeremy. "That's precisely why he's so agitated. It'll be his turn soon enough." He raised his head and called to Gray. "When's Sophia expecting? Late November, I'd guess."

"December." Gray stared at him. "How did you know? Unless . . . Surely she didn't tell you?"

"No, she didn't have to," Toby said. "I've three older sisters, with ten nieces and nephews between them. I can just tell. Congratulations."

"Can we please speak of something besides breeding?" Joss asked, propping his boots up on the side table. He leveled a gaze at Toby. "Surely there is some topic left untouched in that prodigious lexicon of yours. Think of it as practice for your career in Parliament."

"There's a topic. Let's hear about the campaign," Gray said. "How is it progressing?"

"It's . . . progressing." Toby shifted in his chair.

"Last I heard, the polls were running dead even between you and Yorke."

"They are. But most of the electors have yet to cast their votes. They're waiting, I expect."

"For what?" Joss asked.

"For bribes." Gray flicked a glance at Toby. "They want to see which candidate will pay the highest price. Am I right?"

Toby scratched his neck. "Perhaps. But they'll wait in vain. Mr. Yorke is unlikely to engage in bribery, and you know as well as I how Isabel would react to the idea of my buying votes."

Gray and Joss chuckled.

"Exactly," Toby said.

Some topic of shipping or tariffs took the Grayson brothers on a separate branch of conversation.

Jeremy rose from his chair and went to the window. Toby followed him.

Lowering his voice, he said, "Can I ask your advice on something, Jem?"

Jeremy grunted in assent.

"You're in the House of Lords, obviously," Toby continued. "Tell me, with regards to this election . . . what do you think is the surest way to lose?"

"To lose? Don't you want to win?"

"No, not especially. I mean, Yorke's served our borough for years. Parliament is his life. Doesn't seem right to take that away from him. The man's a friend."

"Then why are you running in the first place?"

"Because I promised Isabel, before we were married." Toby sighed. "She's got this idea that if I'm an MP, she'll have more influence in society."

Jeremy gave a half shrug. "She likely will. And from what I hear, Yorke's influence is waning. He's ready to retire. Seems like a beneficial arrangement all around."

"Yes, for everyone but me."

Jeremy gave him a questioning look.

"I can't help it, Jem. I don't want to be an MP. I know, it sounds disgustingly self-serving. It's just . . ." Toby ran a hand through his hair. "It seems like running for Parliament is something I ought to be doing for my own reasons, you know? Because I want to do it. Not just because it's what Isabel wants me to do."

This was all coming out wrong. Toby honestly did yearn to find some goal, some larger purpose to his life beyond tending an estate that hardly needed tending and waltzing girls onto verandahs. He realized now, watching Isabel's principles in action, he'd been craving just that for years. But, selfishly enough, Toby wanted to find that purpose or goal for himself—not be handed it by someone else. Not even her.

"My Lord. Can you hear yourself?" More ungodly noises filtered down from upstairs, and Jeremy winced. His eyes rolled toward the ceiling. "Someday that's going to be *your* wife up there, screaming. Going through hell just to bring your child into the world. At this moment, there is nothing—*nothing*—I would not give for Lucy, up to and including my own life. And here you're complaining about the prospect of sitting through a few boring committee meetings and assuming your long-shirked duty as a gentleman of privilege. You want me to advise you how to *lose*."

Toby cringed. Well, when he put it that way . . . For a plan that was supposed to keep everyone happy, this election scheme was making him feel a downright cad.

"I'll tell you how to lose," Jeremy continued, his voice a raw whisper. "Start an argument with your very pregnant wife. Shout hateful, unforgivable things at her. Send her tearing off in a fury so she'll go into labor a month too soon. Endanger her health and the life of your unborn child. Make her so bloody angry with you that she won't even allow you at her bedside while she's suffering. That is how to lose . . . everything."

Toby hurt for his friend. He knew Jeremy was prone to bouts of dark humor, but this was extreme pessimism, even for him.

"Jem." He leaned closer, forcing Jeremy to meet his eyes. Keeping his voice firm and level, he said, "Lucy's going to be fine, and the babe as well. You'll see. Whatever row the two of you had, it will all be forgiven when you're cooing over your newborn child."

Jeremy shook his head. "How can she forgive me? I will never forgive myself."

"What happened, precisely? I can't imagine any argument so horrible as you're implying."

Jeremy blew out a slow breath. "I came home early, around noon. I suspected I'd find Lucy in the new nursery. Lately she spends the whole day in there, arranging and rearranging it. Imagine, I'm rounding the door, eager to surprise my wife by coming home for luncheon—only to find her standing atop a tiny three-legged table, adjusting the netting that goes round the cradle." He ran a hand through his hair. "Of course I startled her, and with her being so awkward and round, perched on that spindly table . . ."

Toby's heart stalled. "Did she fall?"

"No. Thank God."

"Then what happened?"

"I raced to her side and bodily hauled her down from the table. I may have uttered some rather coarse words in the process."

Toby fought the urge to chuckle, imagining that scene. "And how did Lucy take that?"

"How do you think?" Jeremy raised an eyebrow. "Of course she took offense, started berating me for my interference. But damn it, she could have fallen at any moment. What was the woman thinking? We have no shortage of servants to fuss with netting, if that was what she desired. No, Lucy had to do it herself—never mind her own safety, or that of the baby."

"They all get like that, when the time is close." Toby sipped his drink. "Toward the end of my sister Fanny's last pregnancy, her husband found her down on her hands and knees, using a hairpin to clean the grooves between the kitchen floorboards."

Jeremy shook his head. "It wasn't the fact that I pulled her down, it was everything that came afterward. We argued, like we haven't argued since the first weeks of our marriage. I was so damned scared, and then I was so damned angry. The things I said to her, Toby . . . Lucy will never forgive me. That's why she's refusing to see me now. She knows I pushed her away, pushed her into labor before her time. She wants to punish me, and God knows I deserve it." He made a fist and pressed it against the window sash. "Right now, I scarcely care about the baby, that's what a fiend I am. I just want Lucy to be all right. I don't know what I'd do if I lost her."

"You won't lose her." Toby put a hand on his friend's shoulder. "Jem, I hate to put it this way, but Lucy knew well before this morning what an overbearing tyrant you are."

"An addle-brained brute." Jeremy grimaced. "That's what she calls me when she's cross."

"Very well. She knows you're an addle-brained brute, then. But she also knows you love her. And she loves you. You're not the only one with protective impulses. If she's keeping you away, I doubt it's from some desire to punish you. If I know Lucy, she's the one shielding you. As your little row this morning proves, you can't bear to see her in distress. She knows that, and she doesn't want this to be any harder for you than it already is."

"You're wrong." Jeremy rubbed his temples. "But I wish to God you were right."

"When it comes to women, I'm always right."

With that, Toby lost his grip on the conversation. Joss and Gray had long ago ceased talking, and the room tumbled into a well of silence. Eerie, lifeless silence. No screaming Lucy. No wailing infant. Just silence.

"It's gone quiet up there," Gray finally said. "Or had you noticed?"

Toby cursed inwardly. Of course he'd noticed. He'd been trying not to speculate on what it meant.

Jeremy returned to his armchair and sank into it. With a low moan, he buried his face in his hands.

"She's fine," Joss said. "She won't die, not today."

Jeremy made a sound of derision. "Suddenly you're the voice of optimism? How do you know she'll be fine?"

"I just know."

Before there was any time to elucidate that pronouncement, Miss Osborne entered the salon. The young woman's apron was rumpled and stained, but her cool self-possession was intact. Her placid expression revealed no hint of emotion, neither sorrow nor joy. "Lord Kendall," she said, "Lucy's asking for you now."

"Oh God," Jeremy groaned. "She's dying, isn't she? That's the only reason she'd want to see me. She wouldn't ask for me unless she was dying."

"She's not dying," Miss Osborne said.

Jeremy paused. "The child?"

The young lady sighed. "My lord, I think you should go upstairs and see for yourself."

Jeremy swore under his breath. "That doesn't sound good. Are you certain Lucy wants to see me?"

"I'm certain. She asked for you, in no uncertain terms."

Jeremy rose to his feet. "Tell me what she said. I want to know her exact words."

"Very well." Miss Osborne crossed her arms over her chest. "I believe they were something like this: 'Tell my addle-brained brute of a husband that his son is in need of a name.'"

Toby added his voice to the masculine chorus of congratulations. "You see, I told you all would be well. You've gained a son, and you haven't lost Lucy."

"Haven't I?" Jeremy's face remained impassive. "You heard her words. She can't forgive me."

"You didn't allow me to finish, my lord." The faintest hint of a smile played on Miss Osborne's lips. "She said, tell my addle-brained brute of a husband that his son is in need of a name, *and* . . ."

"And?"

"And his wife is in need of a kiss."

Toby imagined that a rare smile cracked Jeremy's stern expression as he bolted from the room—but he didn't really notice his friend's exit. His attention was occupied with the arrival of Sophia. She brushed past Miss Osborne and flew straight to Gray's embrace, burying her face in his chest. As she wept, Gray exhaled with obvious relief, releasing a string of colorful oaths befitting a seaman. Toby would never have uttered such words in a lady's presence—hell, he'd never even heard a few of them before—but Sophia didn't seem to mind. Her shoulders shook with laughter along with the tears.

Then he noticed Joss and Miss Osborne exchanging peculiar glances. The two stared at one another, not speaking—Miss Osborne still frozen in the doorway and Joss still reclined on the settee, arms propped behind his head. Toby could not quite name the emotions conveyed in their eyes, but he could tell they were of a private nature. No gentleman—not even one as ill-mannered as Joss—greeted a lady in that posture unless some intimacy existed between them.

Well, this was a day of surprises. Of all the unlikely couples in the world . . .

Feeling a voyeur, Toby turned to stare out the window. A profound sense of envy welled inside him. It wasn't jealousy. No longer did he hate Gray for stealing Sophia. Clearly the two belonged together, and without their marriage, Toby would never have found Isabel. No, he envied Gray—and Jeremy, and perhaps now Joss, too—for a different reason altogether. They were loved, unreservedly. Unconditionally. Not just for their strengths, but for their weaknesses, as well. Jeremy could rant and roar at his wife by morning, and find forgiveness before nightfall. Sophia was devoted to her husband, whether he was a fêted knight or a coarse sea captain.

Toby knew Isabel cared for him. So long as he lived up to all her ideals, he felt secure in her esteem. But just how long would that be? He was only human, after all. Even if he managed to come through this election business unscathed . . . he'd always known, from the day of their wedding onward, that he would inevitably falter in her estimation. When Isabel did see him at his most callow, self-serving worst, he would have no loving reprieve. It would be over.

What a fool he was. He'd been working so hard to win his wife's heart, he'd neglected to guard his own. Now it beat for her, yearned for her, and the stakes were higher than ever. If he lost her regard now . . .

"Toby."

A light touch warmed his hand. Isabel had entered so quietly, he hadn't even heard her. But here she was—solemn, graceful, and so damned beautiful his heart ached. Only the shadows pooling under her eyes betrayed her fatigue. He pulled her into his arms, settling her weight against his chest. "Oh, my dear girl. How hard you've worked today."

"He's a beautiful baby," she murmured, nestling into his body.

"Of course he is." He pressed a kiss to the crown of her head, inhaling the familiar verbena essence of her hair. He loved this scent, so fresh and comforting. He loved this woman. Someday he would tell her so—and then stand there with his heart lodged in his throat, waiting to hear if she felt the same.

But not today. Today, he was all out of words.

CHAPTER
EIGHTEEN

"Really, Toby. Are you certain it's proper?" Isabel frowned up at the gilded, curlicued sign: *Mme. Pample-mousse, Modiste.* A young couple jostled past, causing her feet to shuffle on the Bond Street pavement. "Do gentlemen truly accompany their wives to such a place?"

"No," he said, holding open the door for her. "Gentlemen usually accompany their mistresses to such a place."

Bel halted, one slipper balanced on the threshold.

"Don't look so anxious," he teased, prodding her inside and up the narrow staircase. "I wasn't referring to me. If I'd brought a mistress to this establishment, I wouldn't bring my wife around now, would I?"

"Sir Toby!" As they reached the top, an unseen woman called from the interior. Her voice blended silk and smoke. "*Mon dieu.* We thought you'd never return."

"Wouldn't you?" Bel asked, eyeing her husband warily as she stepped inside.

A dazzling sight waited within. Bolts of fabric in every color of the rainbow, lining both walls in perfect, parallel symmetry. After blinking a few times, she realized the fabric actually lined one wall, and mirrors covered the other, creating the illusion. Spools of ribbon and lace filled any available gap between the bolts, and toward the window, a glass case held a glittering array of plumes and brilliants. The crowded, colorful space gave the appearance of disarray, but the floorboards beneath Bel's slippers gleamed. The corners were the cleanest parts of the room, free of cobwebs or collected dust.

"We heard you had married." A silver-haired matron clad in violet silk swished forward to greet them, her broad hips trading the rustling weight of her skirts back and forth. As the woman took Toby's arm, her thin, dark eyebrows rose. "We did not want to believe it. We were so delighted when you escaped that little pale thing, that Sophie. She had an eye for color, that one, but I always knew she would have played you false." She turned to Bel. "But I see your taste has improved. This one, she is not English?"

"Only half," Bel told her.

"Ah," Madame said, looking Bel up, then down. "One hopes it is the correct half."

Bel gaped at Toby. He gave her a sly grin. "Isabel, allow me to introduce Madame. She's designed every one of my sister Margaret's gowns, since her debut Season. I was Margaret's unwilling escort for many a fitting."

"Unwilling?" The Frenchwoman pursed her lips in a rouge-red moue. "This does not match with Mirette's account."

"Mirette?" Bel bit her lip. Had she said that aloud?

Madame Pamplemousse grasped Bel's arm. "My niece and apprentice seamstress, come from Paris to learn our trade. Sir Toby corrupted her most horribly."

"I corrupted *her*?" Toby laughed. "I was a tender fifteen years old. That niece of yours had three years on me, and a half-dozen beaux on her chatelaine. It was all I could do to wheedle a kiss."

The modiste made a very French sound of skepticism. "What of Josephine?"

"Pray, let us not speak of Josephine."

"Marie-Claire?"

"Let us not speak of Marie-Claire either." Toby pressed

a hand to his lapel and made a dramatic face. "Do you know, this shop made a pincushion of my adolescent heart. Sent me down the path toward waste and ruin. Forget good intentions. I tell you, the road to hell is paved with toile. But—" His hand caught Bel's waist. "I have here to protect me my very own angel, who is determined to redeem my corrupted soul."

Madame Pamplemousse turned her kohl-rimmed gaze on Bel. Her lips curved in a feline smile. "An angel? I do not think so. Not even half." She slowly circled Bel, running her palms over the contours of her shoulders, her arms. Then her hips. Bel stiffened.

"Arms to the side, *ma chère*." With two well-placed jabs to the ribcage, Madame forced Bel's arms out. Then, grasping her by the hips, the modiste pivoted her body until they faced the wall of mirrors. Bel felt rather like a marionette.

"To be a true angel," the modiste said, sliding her hands up Bel's corseted torso, "you must offer men a glimpse of heaven." With that, she cupped Bel's bosom in her palms and thrust upward, until olive skin overflowed her muslin bodice in two generous scoops.

Mortified, Bel worked her throat. No sounds came out. Most likely, the woman had cut off her supply of air. Fortunately, Toby had bent over the display case and was not watching.

"Yes, much better," Madame said, scrutinizing Bel's reflection. "Lady Aldridge, we will make you a proper corset. One that will have these"—she plumped the handfuls of flesh again—"floating like clouds."

The modiste dropped her hands, and Bel's breasts fell back into her stays with a nearly audible plunk. Immediately, she crossed her arms over her chest to ward off any further assault. She must be nearing her courses. Her bosom was already heavy and achy today, and Madame's liberties hadn't helped matters any.

"She needs a gown," Toby said, turning from his study of plumes. "Suitable for the opera, ready three days hence."

"The opera?" Bel echoed. "But we can't!"

"Three days?" Madame clucked her tongue. "Impossible."

"Certainly we can," Toby said, striding forward and meeting Bel's gaze in the mirrored reflection. Turning to Madame, he continued, "And it is possible. I have seen you work miracles before. Don't tell me those nimble fingers are losing their touch, Maxime."

"What would you know of my nimble fingers?" She threw him a coquettish glance as she retrieved a measuring tape from a drawer. "You should not have wasted your time with those girls, *mon lapin*. I would have corrupted you beyond all hope of redemption."

"Promises, promises," said Toby, catching the Frenchwoman's hand and kissing her fingers playfully. Then he murmured something in French. Something that sounded exceedingly ribald—but then, in French, nearly everything sounded ribald.

From behind the draperies at the back of the room came a chorus of feminine giggles. Ribald it must have been.

Bel sighed. She wondered if she would ever grow accustomed to watching Toby flirt with other women. The envy nipping at her elbows was absurd, she knew. Like Madame, most of his partners in this sort of repartee were not even especially young or attractive. They were simply women Toby sought to amuse or flatter, for one reason or another. She doubted he was even aware of it, this constant trade in compliments, any more than he tracked the pennies that entered and left his pocket. He gave the ladies what was, in essence, a glittering token: a fleeting moment of feeling desired by the most attractive man in London. In return, they gave him . . .

pretty much whatever he wished. And as she was well aware of her husband's desirability, Bel could not argue that it was an unfair trade.

At least he did not treat her the same way. He gave Bel more than moments, she reminded herself. He gave her whole nights of tender affection and asked nothing in return. And it wasn't as though she expected his wholehearted devotion. It wasn't as though she wanted his *love*. Therefore, she should not be jealous. In fact, she ought to encourage his use of charm—the same talent, albeit differently employed, would ensure his political success.

But still. Those giggles grated on her nerves, to an alarming degree.

She really must be nearing her courses.

Growing even more tetchy at that thought, she protested, "We can't go to the opera this week. You can't expect the polls to close early again." He'd surprised her that afternoon, arriving home shortly after luncheon due to some unexpected event. "What was the reason, again? The returning officer's wife took ill?"

If he heard her question, he did not acknowledge it. "On the day of the opera, I'll simply leave early. A few hours' absence from the hustings won't damage my campaign. It may hurt the tavern keeper's profits, but that can't be helped."

"This way, my lady." The modiste beckoned her toward the rear of the shop. "We will take measurements."

Bel ignored her. "Well, even if your schedule will accommodate frivolity, mine will not. The Society is planning our demonstration of chimney-sweeping machinery on Friday. There are leaflets to be printed, invitations to be delivered. I must speak with Cook about the refreshments, and—"

"Isabel." He placed a hand on her shoulder. It was a weighty, authoritative gesture, and it made Bel keenly aware of how childish she sounded. "It's an opera," he said calmly. "Not a bacchanal. Why does the idea distress you so?"

"I . . . I don't know." And she honestly didn't. But it did distress her, greatly. She didn't like being in this shop, perfumed as it was with Toby's amatory past. She wished they could just leave. "I don't need a new gown," she tried again. "I have a closet full of gowns at home."

Toby dismissed them all with a shake of his head. "Debutante gowns. Virginal, modest, pretty. You're a married lady of wealth and influence, and you ought to look it. Worldly, bold, exquisite."

Bel frowned. None of those words described her in the least.

Madame Pamplemousse tugged at her again. "Come then, my lady."

"Just a moment," Toby told the modiste. "Isabel, tell me about your demonstration. What is its purpose?"

Had she not told him a dozen times? Didn't he listen to her at all? Her voice clipped and impatient, she answered, "To demonstrate the modern advances in flue-cleaning machinery. To convince the influential ladies of society that climbing boys are inefficient and obsolete. To keep poor children from suffocating to death in chimneys."

"Yes. And worthy goals, all. But do you really think the machinery's efficiency will be the persuasive factor? No, of course not. Perhaps if you were inviting housekeepers it would be, but the ladies of the *ton* care little for function. They care for fashion. To persuade them to take notice of automated brushes, you must make those brushes appear beautiful, desirable, and au courant. More to the point, *you* must appear beautiful, desirable, and au courant—and therefore, worthy of emulation. The first two qualities, God has already provided. Let us entrust Madame with the third, hm?"

Bel gave up. It seemed ridiculous, the idea that her purchasing an opulent gown would somehow save the lives of miserable waifs. But the argument was so tangled now, she didn't know how to unravel it.

Toby spoke to the Frenchwoman. "She needs rich color, and sparkle, and the most stylish cut."

"Yes, yes," Madame tutted, herding Bel toward the room's fabric partition.

"I want her shining like the jewel she is," Toby called after them as they ducked behind the velvet drapery.

"First I was an angel," Bel muttered as two young maids beset her, prying apart hooks and unlacing tapes. "Now I'm a jewel?"

"My lady," the modiste said in a lilting whisper, "be happy your husband admires you so and wants others to admire you, too. Take care you do not drive him to call you unpleasant names. Take care you do not drive him into another's arms."

One of the maids made a comment in French. Bel couldn't understand the exact words, but she gathered the general implication: The girl's own arms would be open and available, should Bel fail to heed Madame's advice.

More giggling.

Bel growled.

"What's that giggling about?" Toby called in a teasing voice. "Must I come back there and supervise?"

The maids tittered at the suggestion.

"No," Bel answered sharply. "All is well." Except for this unreasoned, bitter jealousy in her heart. She flung her arms wide to aid the young women in removing her clothes. "Let's do this quickly, please?"

Madame Pamplemousse lifted her voice. "Sir Toby, be seated. There are newspapers behind the counter, should you require diversion."

"Are there?" The sounds of his footfalls and rustling

paper filtered through the draperies. His tone became one of amused discovery. "Yes, indeed there are. Including the most diverting publication of all . . . *The Prattler*. What are they saying about me today, I wonder?"

Bel winced. "Toby, don't. Don't torture yourself. It doesn't matter what they say. No one reads that horrid thing anyway."

"But of course they do," Madame Pamplemousse said. "Everyone in London reads *The Prattler*."

"Not just everyone in London," Toby added. "Since polling began, it's the best-selling paper in Surrey, according to Colin Brooks. Perhaps I ought to deliver copies when I ride out there each morning."

"You wouldn't," Bel said.

"No, I wouldn't," he replied. "Because—according to today's edition—I'm not riding to Surrey at all."

"What?"

"It says right here, I've been completely absent from the hustings. My entire candidacy is a sham."

"What? But that's absurd!"

"Is it?" Toby's slow footfalls crossed the room.

"Yes, of course it is. You've been gone from dawn to dusk every day. Where else would you have been spending your time?"

He paused. "Do you really wish to know?"

Bel considered. *Did she?* His serious tone boded ill, but in the end her curiosity won out. "Yes. Yes, read me whatever scandalous falsehood they're peddling now."

He heaved a dramatic sigh. "Well, according to this distinguished publication, I've been spending my days here in London, at the Hidden Pearl. There's a charming illustration provided by Mr. Hollyhurst. Would you care to see?"

"*No.*" Bel closed her eyes. "Dare I guess the nature of this establishment, the Hidden Pearl? I don't suppose it's a shop that sells jewels."

"Well . . . I wouldn't call them jewels. Cheap trinkets, more like."

"Toby!" Bel's teeth ground together. How he found this amusing was beyond her comprehension. "But—" She jostled on one leg as a maid peeled the muslin gown from her torso. "But that's a preposterous assertion!"

"Completely," Toby agreed. His voice sounded nearer now, just on the other side of the drapery. "I haven't gone near the Hidden Pearl in weeks."

Bel gasped with indignation.

"Very well, months."

She pulled the drape to the side and craned her neck around it to glare at him.

He grinned at her over the paper. "Years?"

Insufferable tease. "It's not a laughing matter, Toby!"

"Of course it is. As you say, it's a preposterous assertion. The only thing for it is to laugh."

"We know it to be preposterous, but what of everyone else? What if people read that paper and believe that you . . . that you . . ."

"Have a penchant for trinkets?" His eyebrow quirked. "Don't tell me you're jealous. Have you so little faith in me?"

Bel gripped the curtain to her chest and blinked away an unshed tear. "I'm sorry. I don't know why I'm so out of sorts today."

But she did know. *Stupid girl,* she chided herself. She'd been well aware of Toby's reputation before she married him. Her husband was an infamous rake. What had she thought, that public speculation would miraculously cease on their wedding day? That the women of London would stop batting their lashes in his direction? That *The Prattler* would plaster his image on a broadsheet as a sterling example of morality—"The Rake Reformed"?

Stupid, stupid girl.

Toby's gaze flitted back and forth between her face

and the velvet drape wrapped around her chest. "That's a lovely color on you," he said thoughtfully. "Yes, that will serve very well."

She sniffed.

"Come with me to the opera, darling." Tossing aside the newspaper, he framed her face in his warm, confident hands. His brown eyes held her, made her strong. "Let me dress you up and devastate London with your beauty. I promise you, no newspaper will dare accuse me of dallying again—because no one would ever believe it. They'll know, no painted bauble at the Hidden Pearl could ever compare with the radiant, elegant woman I married. One look at us together, and they will know the truth." His thumb stroked her cheek. "There's no other lady for me."

Bel's lips pressed together. The rest of her fell apart. Oh, how she wished he would kiss her. Right here in the modiste's fitting room, while she stood wrapped in her shift and a velvet curtain, in front of all these preening French coquettes.

He did.

And this time, she did not mind the giggling.

Toby held that kiss just as long as he dared. While he kissed her, her lips couldn't form questions. While he kissed her, his lips couldn't lie.

There's no other lady for me.

That much was the truth. The simple, soul-baring truth, and he poured it all into this chaste, sweet kiss, hoping his wife could feel and believe it.

Lord knew, she wasn't too quick to recognize truth when it was spoken aloud.

His heart still pounded in his chest, after that close scrape just now with *The Prattler.* He'd come a heartbeat from simply confessing everything. But once again, she'd displayed such complete faith in him, he just couldn't bring himself to destroy it. Confession was out of the question.

No, Toby had a different plan.

"Now, then," he whispered, breaking the kiss. "Be a good girl and have your measurements. Allow me to discuss the style with Madame. I'll make certain you're happy."

And he would, he vowed silently, dropping a final kiss between her eyebrows. He would make her happy. Underneath all those angelic ideals and heavenly curves beat a heart that was simply human. Simply woman. And though he might have no head for philanthropy or politics, Toby understood women.

He had this one week. For God knew what reason, he and Yorke remained close in the polls, but the numbers were certain to turn at the end. In a handful of days, the polling would close and Colin Brooks would certify his defeat. Somehow, in that short window of time, he had to replace Isabel's naïve faith in him with deeper emotions, ones he could sustain.

It was time to step up his campaign, and it all began with the opera. She was so wary of life's little amusements—ices, jewels, beautiful gowns. Pleasure distressed her, for some unfathomable reason, but he could help her overcome that distress. Surely his success in the bedchamber could be repeated in other settings. He could teach her to enjoy herself, and to enjoy being with him. He would make her feel perfect and adored and deserving of every indulgence the world had to offer.

And then, she would surrender her political dreams and embrace a future of domestic bliss. He didn't have to destroy her faith in him, just give it a new foundation. Love.

That was the plan.

And if he got her with child in the process . . . call it insurance.

"Oh, Madame?" he called, holding up the edge of the velvet drape. *"Ce couleur, s'il vous plaît."*

"Bon choix, monsieur."

He traded instructions with the modiste in French, so that Isabel would be unable to understand, and therefore unable to object. Aside from the gown for Tuesday, he ordered three more evening gowns and five day dresses, as well as a full complement of petticoats and the like. His wife would have protested the expenditure with every word in her bilingual vocabulary—but Toby knew her to be worth every penny, and more.

An hour later, they emerged from the shop.

"Fancy a drive in the park?" he asked.

Isabel shook her head violently. "Oh, no."

Toby cursed inwardly. Stupid suggestion, that. Ever since that incident in Surrey, she suffered carriage rides with all the enjoyment of a kitten receiving a bath.

"Is there anything else you need to buy?" He tucked her hand in his arm. "Or shall we find a teashop and take some refreshment?"

"I'm not hungry, thank you. But if there is a draper's nearby, the children's dispensary is in need of new bed linens."

"Very well." He turned them left, and together they ambled down the street. "While we're at it, let's choose some for ourselves."

"Oh, we couldn't."

"Why couldn't we? Don't we deserve new linens, just as much as sickly foundlings do?"

"It isn't that," she hissed, in a voice that communicated her wish for him to lower his own. "It's not proper, for a husband and wife to go shopping for bed linens together."

"Whyever not? Seems the most proper thing in the world, to me. But if we are to be shocking, why stop at linen? Let's order five sets of sheets in aubergine satin."

She did not even reply to that, aside from turning a shade that hinted toward aubergine, herself.

He murmured in her ear, "Have you ever experienced that sensation, Isabel? The feel of satin against bare skin? *All* your bare skin?"

She squirmed. "Toby, stop."

"No? It's like gliding through water, darling. Cool and smooth at first. And then the heat of your flesh makes it warm and slick, like—"

"Toby," she growled, drawing to a halt. "You must stop. Now."

"Like oil," he finished, bending low to whisper in her ear. "Oil, perfumed with the musk of your skin and—"

Her bright voice interrupted him. "Good afternoon, Mr. Yorke."

Toby froze, his lips poised less than an inch from his wife's ear. Fortunate thing he hadn't followed the impulse to lick it. As if sensing itself in danger, Isabel's ear dipped out of reach. Right. She was curtsying.

Following his wife's example, Toby greeted his silver-haired friend with a polite bow. "Yorke. Hadn't expected to meet with you in Town." *In other words, why the devil aren't you at the hustings, in Surrey?*

The old man regarded him with a bemused expression. "Hadn't expected to meet with you, either."

Isabel said, "Yes, so unfortunate isn't it? The returning officer's wife, taken ill."

Yorke looked to Toby. "Mrs. Brooks took ill?"
Damn.

"Surely you heard?" Isabel asked. "Weren't you there when they closed the polls earlier?" She looked to Toby. "But perhaps I misunderstood."

Toby glared at the old man until he startled, realizing his mistake.

"Oh, yes," Yorke said hastily. "Yes, of course. She

took ill. What was her ailment . . . ?" He snapped his fingers. "Rheumatism."

This would have been a perfectly acceptable answer, had Toby not chosen the exact same moment to blurt out, "The grippe."

Isabel's brow creased as she looked from Toby to Yorke, and then back.

"Well, she's achy, you know. And generally out of sorts. Bit of a fever, some stiffness. It's a medical mystery, really. She has the doctor quite flummoxed." The words streamed from Toby's mouth at record speed. If he spoke quickly and incoherently enough, he might squeak through this muddle. He hoped. "But last I heard, she's on the mend. I'm certain the polls will reopen Monday."

"Right," Yorke said. "I suppose I'll see you on Monday, then?"

"Oh, yes. Monday." Toby said, absorbing Mr. Yorke's strange look. A look that said the crafty old fellow would be nowhere near Surrey on Monday.

"If you're staying in town, perhaps we'll meet at church tomorrow," Isabel said.

"Perhaps, Lady Aldridge." With a smile and a tip of his hat, Mr. Yorke went on his way.

Toby stared after him. What the hell was going on? Toby hadn't been in Surrey today, but apparently neither had Yorke. Was it possible the old man wasn't even campaigning? It would explain why the polls remained so close, and the turnout of electors so low.

He found himself wanting to chase after Yorke, take him to the club for some quality liquor and one of their honest discussions. The man was hiding something, and Toby was, too. And he didn't know where that left them, but he knew it was a great deal further apart than they'd been before. That was a damned shame.

Scenarios tumbled together in his mind. There was no

way to explain it, except to assume Yorke wasn't making much effort at reelection. And if that was the case, the unthinkable could happen.

Toby could actually win.

"Toby?" Isabel pulled on his arm. "The bed linens?"

"Right," he said, gathering his wits and flashing her a carefree smile. "Aubergine satin."

What was he thinking? He had no chance of victory. Yorke knew that too, that's why he wasn't even bothering to make an effort. And really, which was a better use of Toby's time? Trolling the farmlands of Surrey for votes, or waging a campaign of sensual persuasion to win the heart of his beautiful wife?

No contest there.

Winning the election would be a mere temporary victory—a stay of execution, until Isabel next put him to the test. No, to ensure their lasting happiness, he had to win *her*. And he would. He had a new weapon in his arsenal now: Love. He loved her, and that had to count for something.

He only hoped it would count for enough.

CHAPTER NINETEEN

"Toby, it is indecent."

"*It* is merely a well-cut and finely-sewn piece of silk, with no moral code to speak of. And you, my dear wife, are ravishing."

Isabel tugged at the bodice of her gown, trying to coax it higher. She turned slightly, eyeing the effect in her mirrored reflection. Perhaps she could tuck a fichu under the neckline? Oh, what was the use? A mortifying amount of cleavage would still be on display. It would be like trimming a haunch of mutton with paper frills, and hoping they discouraged the appetite.

"Trust me," Toby said, his reflected image sidling up behind hers, "the style is not so brazen as you think. It's practically prudish by French standards."

"But we are not in France." And never would they travel there, if Bel had anything to say about it. It wasn't only the cut of the gown that shocked her. The deep wine-red hue was the color of sin itself, and the crystals sewn into the bodice flashed like little beacons designed to draw prurient attention. But Toby had ordered the gown made thus, and judging by his expression in the mirror, Bel assumed he was well pleased with the result. "I just feel so exposed. But if it pleases you . . ."

"It does please me, and that is why. Because you are exposed. That's what the opera is about—seeing and being seen."

"I thought the opera was about Don Juan."

Chuckling, Toby placed his hands on her nearly-bare shoulders. Tracing lazy circles with his thumbs, he leaned over to brush a kiss below her ear. "I love your hair like this, upswept." His lips trailed down her neck and over her nape. "So tightly coiled and expertly bound." The words sent excitement rippling down her spine. "It makes me think of the exquisite joy I will have, freeing it later tonight." His tongue flicked against her ear.

As he drew his fingertips down the sensitive flesh of her arms, Bel's knees dissolved. At this rate, they would never leave the house. She could not say that she would mind. Their planned outing made her uncomfortable, in any number of ways.

"You are beautiful," he crooned, resting his chin on her shoulder and wrapping his arms around her. Together they stared at their entwined reflections. "We are beautiful together."

She had to concede they did make a striking couple. People commented on it so often, she was growing accustomed to hearing it.

"I think I'll make love to you like this," he whispered. "Right here, in front of the mirror."

Comments like that, on the other hand, she had not grown accustomed to hearing. At all. Not that they were unpleasant to her ear. She loved hearing how badly he wanted her—loved feeling the evidence of it pulsing against her back. Her cheeks went crimson in the mirror.

"Would you like that?" he asked, his voice an insidious rumble against her nape. "Would you like me to strip you bare and kiss you all over until you watch yourself cry out in ecstasy?"

Just the suggestion had her moist and aching between her legs. She swallowed hard. Her voice came out as a squeak. "Now?"

His smiling brown eyes caught hers in the mirror. "No. Not now. Later. For now, it is enough to know you desire me." His voice grew rough, and his hands moved down, roving over her silk-sheathed hips. "*Isabel*. I want you to want me, the way that I want you. All the time. Always. Tonight your beauty may be on display for all London to see, but underneath this gown, you belong to me. All evening long, in your darkest, most secret places, I want you hot and wet and yearning for me. And when we come home, I intend to claim what's mine. Do you understand?"

She nodded, entranced by the commanding desire in his eyes and aroused beyond all reason. Her nipples peaked, and she turned in his arms, rubbing her breasts against his strong, solid chest to ease the ache. If only he would make love to her now, strip her free of this indecent gown and make her tremble with pleasure.

She pressed her lips to his throat. "Toby."

"No. Not yet. It's too soon." Grasping her by the elbows, he pulled away. His eyes bored into hers. "Isabel. I want you to want me, the way that I want you. And that is not the work of a few minutes. No, to make you truly comprehend, I shall require hours, darling. Hours."

Hours? He meant to make her wait for hours?

"How—" She knew he would laugh the moment she asked. But she couldn't help it. "How many hours?"

To his credit, he did not laugh too loudly. He tucked her arm in his and steered her toward the door. "Well, the performance itself is nigh on four. Then we have the carriage rides to and fro, the intermission . . ." His free hand cupped her bottom as he guided her into the corridor.

They nearly collided with a footman, and Bel gasped. Toby quickly donned his usual grin—that charming expression of equal parts innocence and devilry. "I should say above five hours, Lady Aldridge. Why ever do you ask?"

*   *   *

Five hours. How many had passed? Not even one yet, by Bel's estimation. And here she was practically a puddle of wax on the floor of their theater box. How would she survive the night?

It was a private box, of course. Perfectly chosen for this war of seduction her husband seemed so intent on waging. Seduction was not even the right word—that would imply he sought her surrender. No, this was a campaign of subtle, sensual teasing with no end in sight. It was not battle, but torture.

It was exquisite.

In the carriage, he'd stared blankly out the small window in an attitude of perfect nonchalance. All the while, his gloved fingers were working their way beneath her voluminous skirts, caressing her calf, her knee, her thigh.

When they joined the crush of opera attendees, he held her close at his side, guiding her through the crowd with an authoritative touch. With an insouciant smile pasted on his face, he kept up a steady stream of suggestive whispers in her ear. To the casual onlooker, it probably looked as though he were relating the latest *on-dit*, or perhaps discussing the weather. But the only humidity of note was the perspiration collecting between her breasts, not to mention the veritable storm of arousal gathering at the apex of her thighs.

And now they were seated in their box, surrounded by ornate, gilded majesty and cascades of heavy blue velvet, listening to the discordant hum of the orchestra tuning their instruments.

Toby pressed a glass of champagne into her hand.

Bel stared at it, entranced by the small bubbles soaring to the glassy, amber surface. "Oh, I couldn't. You know I don't—"

"Tonight, you do. This is the opera, my dear. It's about excess, spectacle, sensation, and opulence. It's about pleasure. We've been working so hard, between the charities and the campaign. You've earned the right to enjoy yourself tonight. Have I not earned the right to spoil you?"

She smiled. He was right, they had both been working tirelessly over the past week. Every day, Toby rode out to the hustings in Surrey while Bel went about her charitable endeavors. In the evenings, they reunited just in time for dinner and bed, where a bout of lovemaking—sometimes tender, sometimes wild—sent them into an exhausted sleep. There was no doubt in Bel's mind that her husband had been laboring tirelessly to satisfy her, in every way. How could she deny him this one evening of amusement?

She took a small sip of the champagne. The tart-sweet taste exploded on her tongue, fizzing through her whole body.

"Do you like it?" he asked.

"It's so strange." She sipped again, holding the potent liquid in her mouth. Bubbles teased her nose, and she swallowed, giggling. "But delicious."

She sipped again and closed her eyes. When she opened them, the world stayed dark. It took her a moment to realize they had dimmed the gaslights to signal the beginning of the performance. Her brain felt misty. The air was cottony around her, warm and soft to the touch.

"May I taste?" Toby asked.

"Yes, of course." She offered him the glass, but that wasn't what he wanted. She realized her mistake the instant before his mouth captured hers. As their lips met, some champagne-soaked shred of her conscience trilled in alarm. Here they were kissing in *public*. In full view, for anyone to see.

It was marvelous.

She leaned into the kiss, caressing his tongue with hers, sipping lightly at his lower lip. She couldn't get enough of him, and she wanted all London to see. Perhaps it was the champagne, or the rich surroundings, or the arousal he'd so cleverly been stoking all night. But at that moment, Bel wanted the world to know how much her husband desired her, how much she desired him. How beautiful they were together, how young and alive.

Then the orchestra struck a chord, and she jumped in her seat. The kiss broke apart. Champagne splattered the exposed tops of her breasts and the bodice of her indecent, extravagant gown—and she didn't even care. Because the music was beginning, and the music . . . it was *everything*.

The orchestra launched into the overture, and Bel felt certain the power of the music would lift the roof from the opera house. She felt it reverberating in her bones. She breathed it into her lungs. It had colors, and flavors—and that was when Bel realized she must be a bit drunk, to believe she could taste a piece of music. But she sipped her champagne again, wanting to stay drunk forever. Wanting to drown in this sea of glorious sound.

Then the curtain opened to reveal a fantastic garden and costumed performers who shortly began to sing. With voices surely stolen from angels, they sang. And the whole world fell away. Bel forgot even Toby. The champagne went flat in her glass. She was swept into the grandeur of *Don Giovanni,* and if she had not known it to be impossible, she would have later sworn she did not breathe or blink once during the whole of the first act.

As the curtain closed for intermission, Toby's hand covered hers. "Are you enjoying yourself?"

She clutched his hand. "Oh, Toby. It's wonderful. I never dreamed . . ." The amber fog of the gas lamps slowly diffused, and she looked up into his handsome face. "Thank you."

"Don't thank me yet." He grinned. "The best is yet to come."

Oh, no. The unthinkable reality struck with orchestral power. An ominous, thundering chord of truth.

She loved him.

What a fool she'd been. It wasn't the music that made her feel everything so acutely. It wasn't the champagne that laid waste to her inhibitions. No, it was this man sitting next to her, who'd wreaked havoc on her senses and stoked her passions since the moment they met. It was Toby, all Toby.

And she loved him.

A dark, sweet melody played in her heart, and her pulse beat a fierce, insistent percussion. She loved him. Loved him, loved him, and it terrified her.

Worry creased his brow. "Are you well? Shall I fetch you another glass of champagne?"

She shook her head. "Perhaps some water."

"Certainly." He kissed her hand before releasing it. "I'll be back in a trice."

Then he was gone, giving Bel a few precious moments to collect her thoughts and reevaluate her life. She'd fallen in love with her husband, and now everything was ruined. Wasn't it? How could she fully devote herself to service and charity, with this loud, symphonic love suffusing her body, drowning out all her best intentions? She tried to recall her schedule for tomorrow. She was certain she had some appointment, some visit scheduled . . . perhaps a meeting with the house staff about the upcoming demonstration of flue-sweeping machinery? But for the life of her—for the love of Toby—she couldn't remember.

The champagne's effect had faded now. Bel saw clearly what she needed to do. She must choose. This love had infected her unawares, but perhaps she still had hope for a cure. It was not too late to deny this passion, to push her husband away and refocus on her work. She'd been in London society long enough to understand the polite, affectionless arrangements that characterized most marriages. She could insist upon the same.

Or she could love. Freely, deeply—embracing both

passion and terror at once. She could place her soul in the keeping of a man well known to be a suave, charming rake.

Really, there was no choice at all.

"Here we are." Toby slid back into the box, a dewy glass of water in his hand.

Bel took it, tipping the glass and downing the water gratefully. Slowly. So long as she was drinking, she need not speak. Soon the lights dimmed again, and Toby pulled his chair close to hers. Close enough that she felt his warmth, even in the dark.

"Are you able to understand the opera?" he asked in a low voice. "I don't suppose you have any Italian?"

"No," she whispered back, setting the water glass aside. "But I learned Spanish from my mother. It's similar enough that I can follow the story." And what a story it was—the dashing, infamous lothario and the besotted women who would follow him anywhere, even to his grave. Out of blind, unrequited love.

Yes, she'd learned this story from her mother in more ways than one. If her father had had fewer lovers than Don Giovanni's thousands—it surely was only because their island was so small. And yet, despite the man's faithless philandering, her mother had loved him with a fierce, loyal passion—even beyond the boundaries of reason and health. The doctors said her mother's madness was a lingering effect of her brain fever, but her mother had believed otherwise.

She insisted she'd gone mad with love. *El amor es locura,* she'd said. Love is madness. An all-consuming, feverish passion that robs the mind of sense, that spins a soul toward darkness and despair.

Bel would be a fool to follow that example. Her gloved hands fisted in her lap. She must resist this love. She must break free of the bond he'd somehow tied around her heart.

Then the woman on stage began to sing, Toby's hand covered hers, and she knew. She didn't truly want to be freed.

"Have you seen this opera before?" she asked.

"Yes."

"How does it end?" She turned to him. "I need to know how it ends. Happily?"

"No, darling." He chuckled. "Our hero dies, alone and unrepentant, and the devil takes his soul to hell."

Oh, God help her.

As she listened to the haunting aria, the hairs rose on Bel's neck and a familiar, terrible heaviness formed in her chest. She wanted to cry, but the tears wouldn't come. Until a few weeks ago, she'd believed this to be the sort of tension a woman could only resolve by weeping. Now, thanks to her talented husband, she knew there to be another cure. Her body cried out for the pleasurable release only he could give.

"Remarkable, isn't she?" Toby's whispered question mingled with the fading applause.

"Yes," she whispered back. "The way the note hangs in the air, even after she ceases to sing . . . I know I'm not actually hearing it any longer, but I feel it, resonating in the air. In me."

He was silent. Bel's cheeks heated. She must sound ridiculous and naïve.

"I understand perfectly," he finally said. His voice held no trace of amusement—only warmth and tenderness. "I think I feel that way sometimes, when I'm parted from you. Even when you're not with me, it's like . . . there's an echo of you that settles in my chest." He lifted her hand from her lap and brought it to his lips, then pressed it to his solar plexus. "Here. I feel you here, always. Sometimes it hurts."

Bel swallowed hard. "Toby?"

"Yes, love?"

"Would you take me home? I want to go home."

"Are you certain?" His eyes searched hers in the near dark. "The second act has only just started. Don't worry about the ending. It's a comedy, you know."

"I want to go home. Immediately." Bel squeezed her eyes shut to gather her strength, then opened them again. "I want *you*," she said meaningfully, lifting her free hand to cup his strong, handsome jaw, "to take me home."

He said nothing. Only sat motionless in the dark, like the chiseled marble likeness of a Roman god. But as she inched closer, Bel thrilled to the evidence that he was very much alive. His breaths came thick and ragged, and his pulse hammered against her hand.

Scooting closer, almost into his lap, she craned her neck to kiss him. "I want you," she murmured against his lips, kissing him again to silence her moan as his free arm lashed about her waist. Oh, how she needed his hands on her. Needed it more than she needed air. She was mad for him, and she didn't care what price she would pay tomorrow, or for the rest of her life and beyond. Tonight, she just wanted him.

"I want you to take me home," she whispered, licking lightly against his ear. "Take me home and make love to me, Toby."

A few minutes later, they were in the carriage.

It really was a remarkable feat. Toby doubted Isabel could appreciate the amount of strategy, charm, and discreetly exchanged silver required to collapse what was normally a twenty-minute process to less than five. Amazing, what a man could accomplish when his lady lit a fire under him.

Lit a fire *within* him, more like.

Toby was burning for her like he had burned for no woman in his life. The air in the carriage was arid with heat. All his plans for hours of slow, sensual teasing? Evaporated. He wanted her, as soon as he could possibly have her.

And apparently—miraculously—she felt the same.

She gripped his arm, pressing her body to his as the coach lurched into motion. The soft swell of her breast against his biceps was pure, sweet torture.

"How long will it take us to get home?" The throaty pitch of her voice sank straight to his groin.

Toby cleared his throat. "Ten minutes . . . perhaps fifteen."

She fell silent, still clutching his arm. He clenched his hands at his sides to keep from mauling her. She had asked him to take her home, after all. Take her home and make love to her properly. Not sweep her off for a crude, sweaty tup in the coach.

Suddenly, she launched herself into his lap, hiking up her red silk skirts to straddle his hips. The sound of fabric ripping registered in his brain just an instant before his wife's husky whisper: "I can't wait that long."

Oh, thank God.

Toby scarcely recognized the woman tugging impatiently at his cravat, thrusting her tongue into his mouth, scraping her teeth along his jaw. Was this truly his solemn, saintly wife? She was frenzied with passion and desire. She wanted him, just as desperately as he wanted her.

They were fighting to get closer, kiss deeper, expose more skin to press against hot, damp skin. They ceased the tussle just long enough to unite against the common enemy of her skirts, hiking yards of silk and petticoats up to her waist until the fabric settled around them in a shimmering cloud. He grasped her hips and pulled her feminine core flush against his aching erection. A fierce groan rose from his chest. Straightening her spine, Isabel rode him eagerly, rocking her hips against his hard length again and again. Even through the layers of his smalls and trousers, she felt warm and soft and absolutely amazing.

So. Damn. Good.

She leaned forward, grasping the seatback behind him for leverage. And now her breasts were thrust in his face with each rolling tilt of her hips. Yes, this passionate, lustful woman was indeed his wife. Toby would know these magnificent breasts anywhere. He pressed his face into her cleavage, inhaling deeply, then stroked over their exposed tops with his tongue.

"Delicious," he murmured. "You taste of champagne."

"Yes," she gasped, straightening in his lap and pulling her bosom out of his tongue's reach. His disappointment was short-lived, however, for she grasped her bodice in both hands and eased it downward, aiding the process with erotic, wriggling motions of her shoulders. "Yes, taste them. Touch them."

Her breasts finally sprang free, in all their bounteous, dark-tipped glory, and Toby thought he would spill in his trousers for the first time since the age of fifteen. He gratefully caressed, lifted, suckled, and she rode him faster, grinding her hips against his in a frantic rhythm.

She gave a little cry, and he knew by the timbre of it that her peak was near. It was tempting to slide a hand between them and stroke her over the edge. Better yet, wrench open his fall and slide into her just at the moment she came. But instead he held back. This time, he didn't want to bring her to pleasure. He wanted to observe her as she pleasured herself. There was nothing more arousing than the feel of her riding him, the acceleration of her breath against his ear. He allowed her to set her own pace, learn the rhythm and pressure and precise angle that would send her into bliss.

She did it all on her own, his passionate lover, his beautiful wife. But as her climax rocked her, it was *his* name she called.

And that was when Toby knew himself to be the luckiest man on earth.

Isabel was still quivering in his lap and breathing hard against his neck, when the carriage rolled to a halt. He helped her adjust her bodice and skirts as best she could, offering his coat for her modesty as they alighted from the coach. She ducked her head as they entered the house, avoiding the curious gaze of the servants. Toby sent them away with a pointed glance.

"Look at me," she whispered as they entered the foyer, indicating the wine-stained, bedraggled condition of her gown. "What a state I'm in. Perhaps I should clean up, before . . ."

"Before?" he prompted, a grin spreading across his face.

"You know what I mean." She blushed.

Toby thought about telling her that he rather liked her mussed and soiled, and whatever repairs she made to her appearance were likely to be undone in seconds . . . but he supposed he could rein in his desire for a few more minutes, to indulge her feminine sensibilities. A very few.

He pulled her close, thrusting the hard ridge of his arousal into her hip. "How long?" he asked gruffly. "How long before you'll be ready for me?"

She pulled away and gave him a coy, seductive smile. Good Lord, but he'd done himself no favors, teaching this woman to tease.

"Ten minutes," she said, fluttering her jet-black lashes. "Perhaps fifteen."

"Minx." Toby lifted her into his arms and swept her into the nearest room with a door, which happened to be the blue parlor. "You know I can't wait that long."

He kicked the door shut and pressed her against it, using one hand to lift her leg over his hip and working his way under her skirts with the other. The moment his fingertips found the slick warmth of her sex, there was no more coy conversation. There was only need—mindless and intense. He needed to get inside her, and he needed to come. Ideally in that order.

With shaking fingers, he unbuttoned his fall and freed his straining erection. She helped him, hooking her legs around his waist and tilting her hips to ease his way. He positioned himself and thrust, sinking straight into her moist heat with no resistance. His body came alive with bliss. Lifting her backside with both hands, he pistoned his hips, pounding her against the door again and again. He thrust fast and hard, shamelessly using her snug, willing body. Pursuing his own release just as selfishly as she'd chased hers in the coach.

And she loved it. She writhed and moaned in his arms, urging him on. Taking him deeper. Pulling him closer . . . closer . . .

There.

A hoarse cry ripped from his throat as he came. He sagged against her, spent and weakened. But far from sated.

He rested his brow against her bare collarbone. Her skin was slick with perspiration—his, hers. Theirs.

"I'm not finished with you," he told her, digging his fingers into her hips. "You do know that, don't you? I'm going to take you upstairs and strip you of every last stitch of clothing and have you in as many different ways as I please. In crude, animal ways that will turn you pale with shock and then pink with pleasure. And tomorrow, the beggars and foundlings of London will just have to fend for themselves, because my wife will be too exhausted to move." He raised his head and stared straight into her dark, almond-shaped eyes. "What say you to that?"

She smiled. "How long will it take us to get upstairs?"

Laughing softly, Toby nuzzled the curve of her neck.

"I love you. My God, how I love you." He couldn't help but say it. He couldn't hold it in a second longer.

Her fingers stilled in his hair. "Oh, Toby. I—"

"Hush. Don't speak, I beg you."

She blinked at him.

Toby's heart pounded in his chest. This night had been so perfect. If she didn't love him in return, he didn't want to know. Not tonight. Heartbreak like that could wait for tomorrow . . . but tonight, he would embrace ignorance. If he wanted her to love him, the way that he loved her—it seemed logical that he should first let her know how very much that was.

"I . . ." He smoothed her cheek. "I've never said those words before, to any woman. I've never felt this before, for any woman. You're so rich with love, my darling. You give of yourself so freely to even the most undeserving wretches, and I include myself in that group. When it comes to love, I'm but a pauper next to you, but even we paupers have our pride. Perhaps I have just this one coin to give, but I should like to watch it glitter a bit, before you go burying it under ten-pound notes like the generous angel you are. So for tonight, just . . . just listen. All right?"

She nodded, biting her lip.

"Isabel, my heart. My own." He kissed her tenderly. "I love you."

Her fingers laced behind his neck. "Toby, take me to bed."

CHAPTER
TWENTY

As it turned out, Bel did find enough strength to move the following day. Eventually.

Long after Toby had left for the hustings, she dragged herself from their rumpled bed. As she stretched, her body protested with pain. It was the sort of mild, dull ache one typically experienced the day following some strenuous exertion—the muscles clinging to their memories of flexing, stretching, drawing taut. The ache ensured she would think of him and their passion, all day. It was not at all unpleasant.

She examined herself in the mirror, finding other ways in which he'd marked her. Her fingers lingered over a berry-stain bruise at the crest of her right breast. No daring necklines for her today.

She found another small purpling mark, just below her nipple, and she remained there for several minutes, transfixed by its reflection.

It had been a long time since Bel had stood before a mirror thus, contemplating wounds inflicted by love. Not since she was a child. Bruises, scratches . . . bite marks, on occasion—her mother had given her all these, and more.

El amor es locura. Love is madness.

There had been so many good days. So many lovely hours spent in that quiet, sunlit room. Her mother would brush and plait her hair, all the while humming pleasant melodies and murmuring words of love and praise.

It took only an instant for everything to change. It didn't matter how good she was, or how carefully she followed the rules. And Isabel knew, because she had tried hard—so very hard—to be good. In the space of a heartbeat, the spit of a curse, the smack of a silver brush—the madness would take hold. The madness would clutch at anything within reach: clothing, hair, flesh.

Then it would release its grip, just as quickly. So quickly, Bel could have imagined the whole feverish, violent episode to be only a dream, were there no bruises or marks to bear witness.

But they hadn't been a dream, all those years of love twining inexorably with hurt. And last night hadn't been a dream, either. It had been a revelation.

Toby had wounded her, here—her fingers drifted to her other breast—and here. And this morning, she looked upon those marks without a trace of shame or self-loathing or fear. In fact, she found them thrilling.

Yes, he had marked her in a moment of wild, mindless passion, just as her mother had done. But these marks were different, so different. Everything was different. He'd changed her life, this dear, sweet man who would never lie to her, never let her come to harm, who would risk his life to guard hers. With Toby, at last she felt safe.

Not only safe, but loved.

He loved her. How many times had he told her so, the night before? She'd stopped counting at four. She might have—now that she thought about it—briefly lost consciousness at four. At any rate, it was clear that he'd been wishing to say it for some time, and now she could expect to hear it quite often.

He loved her, and she loved him. And shouldn't life be wonderful now?

Perhaps it was the first whisper of madness speaking, but as Bel bathed and dressed, she began to believe it could be. Surely her heart was strong enough, surely her love was sufficiently deep. She could devote herself to both Toby and charity. Passion by night, good works by day.

Why couldn't she have it all?

She found herself humming a theme from *Don Giovanni* as the carriage conveyed her to the printer's shop, where she retrieved two stacks of Society leaflets bound with twine. Bel scanned one with satisfaction. Augusta's clear prose described the plight of the climbing boys and articulated the argument in favor of replacing horrific child labor with grown men and modern machinery. And while Augusta's text appealed to the reader's reason, Sophia's deft illustrations pulled at the heart. Now it fell to her, as a lady of increasing social influence, to convert sympathy into action. That was the purpose of the demonstration Friday.

And Bel's mission today, as befitted a lady of influence, was to issue personal invitations. It was time to pay a call on Aunt Camille. Otherwise known as Her Grace, the Duchess of Aldonbury.

The Duchess of Aldonbury was, as duchesses went, a rather minor one. She was not a royal duchess. Nevertheless, Aunt Camille held her own version of court. She hosted a ladies' card party on the third Wednesday of every month, and she guarded the invitations with every ounce of supercilious zeal her aristocratic rank allowed. Add to this the talent of a renowned French-trained pastry chef, and each third Wednesday afternoon saw London's most elite and influential ladies converging on Her Grace's residence. To merit an invitation, one must bring a purse bursting with coin to wager and a quiver of witty rejoinders to amuse. Bel didn't meet either qualification, but she was family and therefore exempt.

When she entered the Roman-styled parlor, there were already nearly two dozen ladies in attendance, arranged in neat clusters of four. Sophia was seated at a table of whist players near the hearth. Bel exchanged a warm smile with her sister-in-law as she moved to greet her aunt.

"Your Grace." Bel dipped in a graceful curtsy, and followed it with a warm kiss to the matron's rouged cheek. "How are you, Aunt Camille?"

"I am well, child." Aunt Camille waved Bel to a seat and then promptly forgot her. Which suited Bel's purpose, because she was here to speak with everyone except Aunt Camille. Armed with a small clutch of leaflets, she approached a knot of ladies chatting by the tea service.

"Lady Violet, Mrs. Breckinridge," she greeted them brightly. The ladies turned to her with expressions of benign amusement. "I'm so delighted to see you. Did you receive my invitation to breakfast at Aldridge House, this Friday?"

"Yes, and I thought surely it was a joke," Lady Violet replied. "Breakfast, at half-eight in the morning? Why, I'm scarcely abed by five."

"It's not only a breakfast," Bel said. "The meal will be followed by a demonstration, of an exciting innovation in household management. This is the reason for the early hour, you see."

"Oh." Lady Violet gave her friend a speaking look. "An innovation."

"And an exciting one," Mrs. Breckinridge said with a smile. "It must be thrilling indeed, my dear. You're positively aglow. I should like to learn your secret."

The ladies tittered, and Bel's confidence wavered. Then she thought of Toby and lifted her chin. "I do find it exciting," she said. "There is a grave transgression being perpetrated on the helpless children of London, and we have the power to stop it."

"Through innovations in household management?" Lady Violet looked dubious.

"Yes." Bel passed each of them one of her leaflets. "As a member of the Society for Obviating the Necessity of Climbing Boys, I—"

"What an absurdly long name," opined Mrs. Breckinridge. "Why, it hardly fits on the leaflet."

Bel resisted the urge to roll her eyes. "As a member of the Society, I invite you to attend our demonstration this Friday. The practice of forcing small children to remove soot from flues is not only barbaric, but inefficient. As our demonstration will show, the proper cleaning of chimneys is a task that can only be performed satisfactorily by a grown man."

"A grown man." Lady Violet's eyes went wide. "Did I hear you correctly? Only the services of a grown man are satisfactory?"

"Yes. Well, not any grown man . . . he must have the proper equipment, of course."

Mrs. Breckinridge looked on the verge of losing her mouthful of tea. She swallowed with apparent difficulty. "But of course. Tell me, Lady Aldridge, will your husband be a party to this demonstration? I think all the ladies of the *ton* have been curious regarding the state of Sir Toby's equipment. One has only to look at you to see his services are quite satisfactory."

Now Lady Violet choked on her biscuit.

Bel frowned, trying to imagine why these women would think Toby would be cleaning his own flues. "Why, my husband is currently occupied with the polling in Surrey. But if the election concludes early, perhaps he will attend. The demonstration itself will be performed by a chimney sweep."

"Ah," Lady Violet murmured to her friend. "She has turned to the help already. And a chimney sweep, no less. Worse than a footman."

"This is not a demonstration for gentlemen," Bel went on, ignoring the cryptic comment. "The power to change this deplorable situation rests within the female sex." She continued speaking over their giggles. Why did this strike them as so amusing? "It is a true mark of our modern age, when we, the ladies of English society, find ourselves in a position to exert influence over our husbands and effect social change."

Lady Violet struggled to compose her expression. "And what position would that be, Lady Aldridge? For exerting influence over one's husband? Not supine, one supposes?"

"No, indeed not. This is precisely my point. We must not take this injustice lying down."

The ladies collapsed into laughter. Bel wanted to growl with frustration. Why could she not make these women see? Were they purposefully misunderstanding her, or merely that obtuse? And was it her passion-addled imagination, or did all of their barbs have a distinctly carnal implication?

"Yes, well," she muttered, rising to her feet. Perhaps she would find a more sympathetic audience with the Countess of Vinterre across the parlor. "I do hope you will be able to attend."

"Oh, we shall," Lady Violet said. "We wouldn't miss it for the world, Lady Aldridge. Friday promises the best amusement of the season."

It is not meant for your amusement, Bel longed to retort. *It is for your edification, you silly, thoughtless wench.*

Oh, heavens. Had that thought truly originated in her brain? She felt so queer, so out of sorts. She would have liked to blame her odd behavior on fatigue from the night before, but she suspected the lingering passion had more to do with it. Even staring at the illustration of poor, maltreated climbing boys, she could not muster her usual zeal. Instead, as she surveyed the assortment of wan ladies decorating the richly hued salon, all she could think was that she wanted to return home, return to bed. Return to Toby.

And worse, it was as though everyone in the room could sense it. Lady Violet's comments were only the beginning. From every corner of the room, the ladies stared at her, whispering to one another across the card table and laughing into their tea.

"Bel." Sophia touched her elbow. "The air in here is so close, and with the baby"—she laid a hand over her abdomen in a universal gesture of incipient motherhood— "Will you take a turn with me, outside?"

Bel nodded and followed her sister-in-law out the door and into the garden. The moment they rounded the corner of a hedge, Sophia turned to her. "You haven't seen it?"

"Seen what?"

"This morning's *Prattler*."

Bel shook her head. She avoided the rancid tabloid on principle, only bothering to glance at it when Toby needed soothing over another assault on his character. Why that paper had such a vendetta against her husband, she could not comprehend.

Sophia withdrew a scrap of rolled newsprint from her reticule and extended it to Bel with one hand, taking the stack of leaflets in her other. "I am so sorry to be the one to show you this. But after Lady Violet's comments inside . . . I really thought you must be made aware. People will be talking."

Bel's stomach plummeted as she took the bit of paper and unrolled it cautiously. Had they linked Toby with another woman? She knew now that *The Prattler* grossly overstated his rakish exploits, and she believed that no rumor of infidelity would have a mite of truth. But still—it wounded her, to hear the gossip suggest he had already strayed.

And as she took her first glance at the caricature, she

thought indeed that was what the illustration implied. It depicted Toby with a loose woman on his arm, her clothing agape and one sleeve sliding from her shoulder. Her exaggerated breasts squeezed to the top of her bodice, overflowing her gown as she leaned against Toby's frame. The two figures were depicted in the dark of night, tripping down the stairs of a grand stone edifice. Bel peered closer. Why, it was the opera house!

She read the caption aloud. "The Rake Unrepentant. Is Sir Toby London's own Don Giovanni?"

"Oh, Bel," Sophia said. "I'm so sorry."

Dread stirred in Bel's chest as she looked again at the loose woman draped over Toby's dashing form. For the first time she examined the face, instead of the voluptuous figure indecently spilling across the page. Black hair. Wide, dark eyes.

"Oh, dear Lord."

It was her. *She* was the woman on Toby's arm, slavering over her own husband like a glassy-eyed prostitute. Now Bel noticed the ribbons of speech attributed to these disgusting renditions of her and Toby. From his mouth: "Did you really think to reform me?" From her: "La! I never knew ruin was so sweet."

Behind them, in the shadows of the opera house, Mr. Hollyhurst had drawn a pair of underfed children, their hands out in an attitude of begging. Their pleas went unheeded.

"Thank you," Bel said numbly, rolling the paper again. "Thank you for showing me. It explains a great deal." No wonder the ladies inside had greeted her overtures with amusement, doubted her charitable intentions, taken all of her words as innuendo. This was their opinion of her: a lust-mad female, incited to depravity by her husband's rakish charm and dissolute example.

And the worst of it was—Bel worried that they were right. Mr. Hollyhurst, Lady Violet, Mrs. Breckinridge.

Why would anyone draw such an image, or give credit to its implications, if it did not contain truth at its core? She thought of leaving the opera house last night, flushed and frenzied with desire—too desperate even to wait until they returned home. Good heavens, she'd thrown herself on him in the carriage! A respectable lady of influence didn't behave in such a manner. And had there truly been hungry children, huddling in the shadows in need of help, whom she had ignored in her passion-blinded state?

There could have been.

Who would look to such a woman for their moral direction? How could such a woman be the wife of an influential MP?

"Don't make overmuch of it," Sophia said. "As scandals go, desire for one's own husband is not much of one. Never mind Lady Violet—she's just an old, embittered dragon. She can't help but breathe fire. She'll tire of teasing you quickly enough, if you refuse to give her the satisfaction of showing distress."

"It's not just Lady Violet. All London reads *The Prattler*."

"Yes, and there is a new issue printed each morning. Within a few days, people will find a new topic of gossip, and this will all have been forgotten."

"I'm sure you're right." But in a few days, the election would be over—the demonstration, as well. And all of it could be ruined, because of her. Because she had allowed passion to overrule her principles. "I . . ." She choked back a wave of bile. "I feel suddenly ill. I think I'll slip out by the garden path and make my way home. Please make my excuses to our aunt."

"Yes, of course." Sophia stroked Bel's arm soothingly. "If there's anything I can do—"

"No, no." Bel forced a little smile. "Really, this is nothing. I'm just fatigued. I need to rest, that's all."

After bidding Sophia good-bye, Bel made her way to the front of the residence. To make her failure complete, she ordered the carriage to simply return her home. She knew Toby would still be out, campaigning in Surrey. Perhaps she ought to complete her visits to distribute leaflets, or take supplies to the children's dispensary. But she didn't want to be near ladies or orphans right now. She wanted to be near Toby, in whatever way she could. She would cast off this fine, French-striped day dress and beribboned bonnet, put on one of her old, plain muslin shifts, and creep into the bed that might still be warm from their night of passion—that might still retain some comforting hint of his scent. And then she might weep, or fitfully dream the day away, until he came home to hold her and love her.

Oh, she was weak indeed.

When she entered Aldridge House, she heard low, masculine voices down the hall. Her heart leapt. Was Toby home? Perhaps he'd been laughed off the hustings in Surrey, if today's *Prattler* had reached the borough already. To her surprise, Bel didn't even care—so long as he was here, with her.

On light feet, she hurried down the corridor. The voices seemed to be coming from Toby's library. Nearing the door, she recognized the warm timbre of her husband's voice. It *was* him. Thank heaven. Toby would make everything better. Toby loved her. He would never let her come to harm. With him, she was safe.

As she put a hand to the door handle, it dimly registered in her mind that Toby was not just speaking, but shouting. Bellowing, really, as she'd never heard him raise his voice to anyone.

"You had clear instructions," he thundered. "She was never to be a part of this."

A milder tenor answered. Bel had to press her ear to the door to make out the words. Her conscience pricked her for eavesdropping, but how else was she to discern if it was safe to interrupt?

"Yes, but it wasn't working," the milder voice argued back. "You told me to be more severe, do my worst."

"Your worst at me, not her," Toby answered. "There's no excuse for—"

"And didn't you tell me you wanted to lose, at any cost?"

"Yes, but—"

"Then it had to be her. There's nothing left to insinuate about you. That's how I reasoned it, at least."

A loud crack reverberated through the door, startling Bel. Her stomach plummeted with the weight of dread. Perhaps she should summon a footman.

Toby's voice again. "Damn you, Hollyhurst, you're not paid to reason. You're paid to draw."

Hollyhurst? Was that vile man here, in Toby's study?

Bel didn't recall making the decision to open the door. The next thing she knew, she was standing in the center of the Aldridge crest stamped in gold on the blood-red carpet. The men stared at her; Toby from behind his desk, and—could this truly be *the* H. M. Hollyhurst, reclining in the chair opposite? He wasn't at all the grizzled, pointy-eared troll she'd imagined him to be. He was barely older than she, Bel judged—smooth-faced and handsome.

Pale with shock, the young man rose to his feet. "Bollocks," he muttered.

"Toby?" Bel's voice shook. "What is going on?"

CHAPTER
TWENTY-ONE

Toby knew precisely what was going on. This ill-fated day was gathering to its horrific climax. The jig was up. This was the moment he'd been dreading ever since the day they married. And yet, there came with it an odd sense of relief.

"Isabel, may I introduce Mr. Hiram Hollyhurst?" The anemic twit bowed clumsily. Toby added with a pointed look, "He's leaving."

Hollyhurst was not so obtuse that he missed that hint. Isabel stood frozen in the center of the carpet, staring at Toby in disbelief for long moments after the door had been closed and they were alone.

"I—" Her jaw worked. "Toby, I don't understand."

Of course she didn't, the sweet girl. She could never understand the motivations behind such callous behavior. It simply wasn't in her to comprehend. "Will you sit down?" he asked.

"Thank you, no." She clasped and unclasped her hands, as though unsure how to begin. "So that was Mr. Hollyhurst."

It wasn't a question. Which was fortunate, because Toby really did not want to answer. What he wanted to do was hold her. After all that had happened this morning, the news he had just received—how cruel, that he should destroy his marriage on this, the day he most needed the comfort of a wife.

"*The* Mr. Hollyhurst," she continued. "The same man

who has vilified you in *The Prattler* all these months by drawing those horrid caricatures."

"Yes," he said finally. "We're . . . friends."

"Friends?" she cried. "But how can that be? However could you become friends with a man like that?"

"He's the son of a former steward, and . . . and it's not important how we met." Toby paused. "I've been paying him, Isabel. All those caricatures, the assaults on my character—they were all created at my behest."

She made an inarticulate noise in her throat. Her eyes then slid toward the ceiling, as though some explanation for his behavior might be found in the scrolls of the brass chandelier. A silent "why" formed on her pursed lips, but she seemed to lack the breath to dislodge it.

"Really, please sit down." Toby moved toward her and laid a hand on her arm.

She shook it off. "Thank you, no." Still, she could not form the question.

He sighed. He would not force her to ask. "It began last year, after Sophia disappeared and her parents spread the falsehood about her illness. It was winter, and people had little enough to talk about. The gossips would out the truth inevitably, I feared—unless I gave them something else to discuss. I came to London and tracked down Hollyhurst. Hiram and I devised this 'Rake Reborn' nonsense."

Toby moved toward the bar. God, he needed a drink. "At first, I simply meant to deflect suspicion, absorb the brunt of the scandal," he continued, pouring whiskey into a glass. "Should Sophia miraculously return and still wish to marry me, her reputation would be intact. Later, when it became clear she wasn't returning . . . then I suppose it became a matter of pride. I didn't want anyone to know why she'd truly jilted me. Hell, even I didn't know why she'd truly jilted me. Far preferable to let people suppose my dissolute behavior drove her to cry off."

At last, Isabel found her voice. "But why continue it, even after we became engaged? After we married?"

Toby took a slow draught of whiskey, allowing her time to piece the reasons together. He knew she would. She was a clever girl.

When he lowered his glass, she was frowning down at her hands. See? Hadn't taken her but seconds.

She said, "Mr. Hollyhurst mentioned a plan, to lose. Was he referring to the election?"

"Yes."

"You've been trying to lose?"

Toby felt like telling her it was more that he'd been trying not to win—but that would be mincing words. Anyway, it scarcely mattered, given the morning's events. "Yes."

"But the campaigning, the hustings—you've been going to Surrey every day."

Toby shook his head slowly.

"Dear Lord. You haven't?"

A look of revulsion formed on her face, and it nearly killed him to view it. But he wouldn't allow himself to turn away.

"If you haven't been going to Surrey," she asked, "where have you been spending your days? Not . . . Oh, heavens. Not at the Hidden Pearl?"

"No," he said firmly. "Never there, nor anywhere like it. I went . . . different places. The park, the club. Much of the time, I was simply here in my study. I half-expected—half-hoped, I think—you'd one day discover me, and the ruse would be over. But you're always so occupied with your charitable efforts, your society meetings . . ." He shrugged. "You never noticed I was here."

"Of course I didn't notice you! Why would I go searching the house for my husband, when he's supposedly off in Surrey? I believed in you. I trusted you. I thought you wanted this, as much as I did. Even before our wedding, from the first night we met, you—"

"Come now, Isabel. Be honest. You know I never truly wanted to run for MP."

"Yes, but I thought you wanted me!" She brought a hand to her throat, as if astounded by the volume of her own anger. "Even if politics wasn't your inclination, you knew I sought a husband with influence in Parliament. And before we were married, you promised to run. You *promised* me, Toby."

"I promised you many things, darling. The promises came to me easily then, when I had no real intention of keeping them." Toby took a deep breath and put down his glass. There was no going back now. Half-confessions served no purpose. It was time to lay the truth out before her, and let her do with it what she would.

"When we first became engaged," he continued in an even tone, "I would have told you anything you wanted to hear—tales, fancies, lies. I simply had to make you mine, by any means."

"But why?"

"Pride," he said in a matter-of-fact tone. "And some juvenile form of retribution. I wanted to take you from Gray the way he'd taken Sophia from me."

"Sophia?" Her hand dropped from her throat to her stomach, and she looked as though she might be sick. "All this time, it was about her? You never wanted me."

"No, that's not true." Toby rushed forward, catching her in his arms. She tried to pull away, but he held her firmly. "Isabel, I wanted you from the first, before I even learned your name. And once I knew you for the intelligent, principled, passionate woman you are, I fell in love with you, body and soul. By the time we married, I wanted nothing more than to keep you happy. But by then I'd made you so many absurd promises, and you had this naïve, idealized impression of my character. At first, I wanted to earn that good opinion. I wanted to deserve you. And I thought maybe, if I just tried hard enough—"

"At first." She refused to look at him, staring instead at his lapel. "At first, you wanted to earn my good opinion. But not anymore."

"Because I can't." Toby's mouth went dry. "I just don't have it in me. To be truthful, I'm not sure any man would. Your expectations are so high. I knew I'd inevitably disappoint you—if it wasn't by losing this election, it would be by losing the next, or by failing to gain the level of influence you desired . . . Sooner or later, I knew you'd learn the truth. I'm not the man you'd wish me to be."

"But you *could* be that man. With a bit more time, if you only made the effort. You have so much potential. Such warmth, such compassion, a natural gift for—"

"Stop. Just stop." Toby released her and raised a hand to his temple. "Don't tell me what I could be, with just a bit of improvement. I'm not one of your blasted charity projects, I'm your husband. And you're right, it's not enough for me anymore, to earn your good opinion. I want your love, whether I deserve it or not."

She choked back a sob. "You *lied* to me. The campaign, the opera, Mr. Hollyhurst . . . and now *this*." Fumbling with the pursestring, she opened her reticule and withdrew a scrap of paper. "Look at this. Just look at it."

She waved the caricature under his nose. Toby didn't need to look at it—the horrid image was burned into his memory.

Mimicking his voice, she continued, " 'Let me take you to the opera,' you said. 'Let me spoil you,' you said. 'If you want to be a lady of influence, you must appear beautiful, desirable, au courant.' And look at me in this horrid drawing—depraved, disgusting, mad with lust. Who would listen to that woman, I ask you? What kind of influence can I have now?" She balled the paper in her hands and threw it at him. "You've made me a public joke. You've ruined everything. If you really loved me, how could you do this? You . . . you *liar*!"

"Isabel—"

With an open palm, she buffeted his shoulder. "You told me you would never hurt me. You said you would die before you let me come to harm." She hit him again. "You made me trust you, you . . ."

She unleashed a series of epithets in Spanish. From the tenor of them, Toby was glad he could not understand their meaning. She punctuated each insult with a blow to his shoulder.

"Isabel, please."

"*Bastardo!*" she cried, striking him again.

That one, he understood. And accepted as his due.

"Liar!" she cried again, pulling back her arm.

He caught her wrist before she could land another blow. "*Isabel.*"

Breathing hard, she stared at her hand with disbelief. The anger in her eyes cooled to shock. Finally she whispered, "I struck you."

"Yes."

A tear rolled down her cheek. "I've never struck anyone in my life."

"I wish I could tell you it didn't hurt."

Gentling his grip, he folded both her hands in his and held them tight. Almost the same way they'd stood as they'd recited holy vows. Together they paused there, just breathing. Holding disaster at bay for a few moments more. Her bottom lip trembled. It gutted him, that he didn't feel he had the right to kiss it.

"I went to my aunt's card party this morning," she said quietly, staring at their hands. "The ladies there . . . they were all laughing at me, whispering about me in the corners. And then Sophia showed me that picture of me, crazed and disheveled. Just like my poor mother. No one listened to her, either. You can't know how long I've worked, how hard I've tried to never be that woman. *This* woman." Her voice cracked, and Toby's heart cracked with it. "I wanted their respect, and they all laughed."

"Darling, I'm sorry. So sorry. But every lady in England could laugh at you, and I would love you still. And I'd gladly endure the derision of the world, if you could feel the same for me."

It was true. All his life, Toby had been happy to be every man's friend. But it wasn't enough anymore, to be that fellow everyone liked. He wanted to be the man one woman loved, beyond reason.

"Isabel, this is who I am. I'm a flawed, self-absorbed aristocrat of middling consequence. I enjoy my life, my friends, and my family. I like to have a good time, and I like to surround myself with nice things. Much as I admire your zeal for charity, I doubt I'll ever match it. I have no interest in Parliament and accordingly little talent for politics. I am deeply, deeply sorry to have hurt you, but I'll spend a lifetime making it right if only you'll give me the opportunity."

She struggled against his grip. "You would—"

"Isabel, please." Desperation frayed his voice. "Give me one moment. Afterward, I promise you, you may strike, insult, and berate me as much as you wish. I know I deserve it. But for just this one moment, pretend with me that this morning never happened. Pretend the lies were never spoken. Look at me."

He waited until she did.

"Look at me," he repeated slowly, "for just this moment, and see me for the man I truly am. And know that I love you, more than I can express. More than I can comprehend. Can that be enough for you?" His heart climbed into his throat, and he swallowed hard around it. He needed to ask. "Isabel, can *I* be enough for you?"

Tears slid down her cheeks. Impossible to say whether

despair or joy propelled them. Blast those enigmatic female tears.

She said, "You don't know what you ask of me."

He slid his hands to her face and cupped it roughly. "Yes, I do. I'm asking you to love me, the way that I love you." He kissed her lips, needing to taste her. More tears escaped her trembling eyelids. "Completely," he said, kissing her cheek, then her jaw, her ear. "Unreservedly, passionately, madly . . ."

Her body went rigid in his arms, and she made a strange sound in her throat. Planting her hands on his chest, she pushed away. "I'm sorry, Toby. Last night, I thought perhaps I . . . but now you've . . ." She shook her head and turned away. "I'm sorry."

And there it was. The verdict he'd been dreading. She didn't love him. At least, not the way he loved her. Perhaps she loved him in some dutiful, selfless, Christian way. But she did not live and breathe and burn for him, the way he lived and breathed and burned for her.

Very well, then. Now he knew.

And look, the world even kept turning.

"I'm sorry," she repeated weakly.

"Stop apologizing. The fault is entirely mine. I understand."

Awkward silence blanketed the room.

"Well, I won't keep you," he said, clearing his throat and stepping back around the desk. As he walked, his step faltered slightly. He felt off-balance, as though he were learning to walk with a javelin skewering his chest. "I know you're busy. You must have some kind of meeting or appointment to keep. But before you go, I have something to tell you." He picked up the urgent message he'd received that morning, fingered the broken wax seal. How odd, to think he'd read it just hours ago.

"Mr. Yorke died last night," he said. "Or perhaps early this morning. I'm not sure. At any rate, he was here in

Town, and he has no close family . . ." Toby made a fist
and propped it on the chair's back. "*Had* no close family. My mother and I will accompany his body back to
Surrey, for the burial."

"Oh, Toby."

She came toward him, and he turned to look out the
window. It was a revoltingly sunny day.

Isabel stopped a few paces away. "Toby, I'm so sorry.
I know how fond you were of him."

"Do you, really?" He stared hard at the wavy pane of
glass. "Because I don't think I ever truly did, until today.
It wasn't until today that I realized . . . Yorke was the
closest thing to a father I ever had."

She made a soft, soothing noise and reached for his
hand.

He pulled it away, folding his arms over his chest. Of
course, *now* she would comfort him. She could shower
him in sweet, generous affection *now*, when he was down
and plainly hurting and as wretched as some leper in a
parable. Isabel had no shortage of pity to offer him. It was
only the deep, abiding passion that he was denied.

"You'll have everything you wanted now," he told her.
"I'll be the MP. You'll be Lady Aldridge, the influential
MP's wife. This house is yours, to host as many demon-
strations and Society meetings and social functions as
you please. Turn it into a home for foundlings, if you
wish. I really don't care. I'll be in Surrey for the foresee-
able future."

"You're . . . you're just leaving me here?"

Her tone was wounded.

Good. Petty though it might be, he wanted to hurt her.
To inflict just a fraction of the pain she'd caused him.

"Did you have some better plan?" Toby walked
around her, crossing to the doorway. "Forgive me, but I
really must be off to Yorke's townhouse. There's a sort
of gathering, and I promised my mother—"

"Oh, your poor mother." Suddenly she flew across the carpet to stand before him, latching one hand over his arm. "Toby, let me come with you."

"To Surrey?"

"Well, I meant to the townhouse." Her brow wrinkled. "I mean, I do have the demonstration Friday. The invitations have already gone out. I must be here in Town for that, I couldn't possibly cancel it now."

"No, of course," he said bitterly. "You couldn't possibly. I understand you perfectly, Isabel. You're under no obligation to come with me to Yorke's house, nor to Surrey . . ." He gave her what he hoped was a cold, unfeeling look. "I'm certain we'll see one another soon enough." He turned to leave.

She dodged around him, blocking the door. "Toby, please. I can see how you're hurting. I want to help. Let me go with you."

"No."

She winced. "But—"

"No," he repeated firmly, walking past her to exit the room. "You're not welcome. This is a family matter, not a charity event."

CHAPTER
TWENTY-TWO

Toby had been an infant when his father died. He had no memory of the man, nor any recollection of his mother in her year of mourning. When she referred to Sir James Aldridge she did so in respectful, dispassionate tones—and always in past tense. By all appearances, the dowager Lady Aldridge maintained a cordial relationship with her late husband's memory.

"Cordial" had never described her relationship with Mr. Yorke. The two had argued over one thing or another—and yet another—for as long as Toby could remember. They made cutting remarks to one another's faces and said worse behind each other's backs. By all appearances, they were equally matched in only one respect—mutual dislike.

And never, until this day, had Toby realized the obvious.

They had been in love.

How had he missed it? Toby prided himself on his keen understanding of women, but as it turned out, he had a blind spot of mother-sized proportions. But then, she'd never been "a woman" to him, because she was his mother and he'd never looked for her vulnerabilities. He hadn't wanted to see them. She was his only parent, the rock of their family, the strongest person he knew.

But not today. Today, she was a pale, teary shambles.

"Mother, why did you never tell me?" Toby sat at her side, holding one of her hands while she pressed a handkerchief to her eyes with the other. The two of them were tucked away in the corner of Mr. Yorke's parlor. The room was filled with visitors, come to pay their respects before his body was taken to Surrey. People came and went, seemingly at a loss as to where to direct their condolences, considering the deceased's lack of immediate family.

His mother wiped her eyes and whispered, "Should I have told you about my lover? Really, Toby, I know we are close. But there are some conversations a mother does not wish to have with her son."

She had a point there. "How long had you been . . ."

"A very long time."

"Years, then?"

"Decades."

Decades. Toby frowned at the carpet, trying to decide whether he wished to know how many.

"Not for that long," she said, reading his thoughts. "I was never unfaithful to your father."

"I've no memory of my father," he said. He glanced up, toward the bedchamber above-stairs where Yorke's body lay. "All my memories are of him."

"He loved you, Toby. He told me he would have left his estate to you, were it not entailed. I know he thought of you as the son he never had."

"Why not the son he did have? Why did the two of you never marry?"

His mother shook her head. "We would have killed each other, had we lived under the same roof. No, I was accustomed to my independence, and we were both simply too stubborn." She released Toby's hand and blew her nose. "His health had been failing for some time. The doctors told him to slow down. For years, I begged him to resign his seat in Parliament, but the mule-headed man wouldn't hear of it."

"That's why you've been after me to run against him?"

She nodded.

"Mother, you should have just told me the truth. I would have—" Toby clapped his mouth shut. There was no way to complete that sentence without indicting himself as a complete and total fraud. *I would have kept the spirit of my promises. I would have accepted the duty that accompanies my fortunate birth. I would have put someone else's needs above my own, for a change.* All things he should have done, regardless.

"Perhaps I should have told you," his mother said. "But again, there's that uncomfortable matter of discussing one's lover with one's son. At any rate, he came around in the end. He told me just last week, he'd decided to let you win. You were ready now, he said. He thought you and Isabel made a good team . . . something about lambs."

Toby felt a pinch in his chest. So that was why the polls remained so close, and why Yorke had been in Town the other day. Toby had been right—the old man hadn't been campaigning at all.

Just then, Jeremy entered the room, accompanied by Miss Osborne. Toby stood to greet them. "Jem, Miss Osborne. Good of you to come."

"We just received the news," Jeremy said. "Lucy wanted to join us, but—"

"No, of course she couldn't," Toby replied. "Not with a week-old infant at home. How is little Thomas Henry Trescott, the fifth Viscount Warrington?"

"Living up to his aristocratic lineage," Miss Osborne answered. "He has the whole household at his beck and call already."

"I can't claim to be surprised," Toby said with a smile. He indicated chairs nearby and invited them to sit. "You'll remember my mother."

"Had Mr. Yorke no family?" Miss Osborne asked, scanning the room, presumably for black armbands or mourning gowns.

"No," Toby replied. "No close family, at any rate. There are some cousins, I believe, but—"

"He had us. We're his family," Toby's mother interrupted, beginning to cry anew. "Don't make it sound as though he was alone."

"No, of course he wasn't." Toby grasped her hand again. To Jeremy and Miss Osborne, he explained, "Our families have always been close. He and mother were . . . good friends."

"We were lovers," she said, impatiently wiping her tears. When the other three simply stared at her, she said to Toby, "I'm an old woman, and now he's dead. It doesn't matter who knows. We were lovers."

And now Jeremy and Miss Osborne stared anywhere *but* at her.

His mother's outburst, however, would not be subdued. Whatever dam she'd built to restrain her grief had cracked, and a tide of emotion flowed forth.

"You were right, Toby. I should have married him. He asked me, you know. So many times, but I always refused. And now"—her speech caught on a sob—"now I've no right to claim him. I've no right to wear mourning for him, no right to be buried next to him. No right to go upstairs and make certain his valet dresses him in his green striped waistcoat, not that horrid blue."

"Mother, please don't cry," Toby said. "I . . . I'll speak to his valet."

Good Lord. Of all the lame attempts at comfort. His mother was falling to pieces before his eyes, and Toby hadn't the slightest clue how to hold her together. Normally, this was his forte, making women feel better. Ladies crossed ballrooms, streets, even lines of propriety just to exchange a few words with him, because they all knew: a girl could always depend on Sir Toby Aldridge to put a smile on her face.

Suddenly, he'd lost the gift. Because now *he* knew: A girl shouldn't depend on Sir Toby Aldridge for anything. Any trust his wife had in him had vanished the moment she saw him for his true self. His own mother had been keeping secrets from him for decades. He wanted to soothe her, make her feel better, but he didn't know how anymore. It was a talent built on a cornerstone of arrogance, and this wretched day had knocked the foundation straight out from under him.

He spied Reginald entering the room. Behind him trailed Joss. Toby rose to his feet again, whispering, "Mother, Reginald is here."

"Oh, let him know, too," his mother said, wringing her handkerchief. "It doesn't matter anymore. Yorke's dead, and nothing matters anymore." She broke into tears, listing sideways until her head came to rest on Miss Osborne's shoulder.

The young woman's eyes widened in alarm. "What do I do?" she asked Toby, gesturing discreetly toward the matron wetting her sleeve with tears.

Toby had no advice to offer her, only a helpless shrug. He'd never seen his mother in such a state. Ever.

Having picked his way through the crowd, Reginald finally reached Toby's side. "Augusta sent a note to my offices. Yorke, gone. What a damned shame." He cast a glance toward Toby's mother. "Taking it hard, is she?"

"Apparently they were close," said Toby.

"We were lovers," his mother cried, pressing her face further into Miss Osborne's shoulder.

Raising his eyebrows, Reginald whistled quietly through his teeth. "Well."

It was the greatest display of shock Toby had ever seen him make.

Miss Osborne raised a hand to the older woman's shoulder and gave her an awkward pat. "There, there."

"Hullo, Joss." Toby nodded at his brother-in-law, who stood a pace behind Reginald, looking every bit as uncomfortable as Toby felt.

"I'm sorry to intrude," Joss replied. "I was at Mr. Tolliver's offices when the notice arrived, and I thought to pay my respects." He looked toward the women huddled on the divan. "I didn't realize . . ."

"Don't be sorry," Toby said. "No one realized. It was good of you to come."

His mother began to sob. Miss Osborne stiffened.

"Is that Montcrief at the door?" Jeremy asked hopefully. "I've been meaning to speak with him."

"No," Toby snapped, cutting off his friend's path of retreat. Not that he could blame Jeremy for trying. He'd escape the scene, too, if he could. It was hell, sitting here, feeling the loss of his friend and his wife in one morning, watching the pillar of strength who'd supported his home, his family, his life, dissolving in abject grief. Knowing he could have—should have—prevented it all. In all his life as a pampered child, a directionless youth, a pleasure-seeking gentleman of leisure—Toby had never felt so utterly worthless.

"I don't even know how he died," his mother cried, her words muffled by the fabric of Miss Osborne's sleeve. Reginald offered her a fresh handkerchief, which she accepted blindly. "They say some kind of apoplexy, but the doctor won't talk to me. Was it painful? Did he suffer? I can't bear it, the thought of him dying here alone, in his bed . . ." She sobbed again. "It's too horrible to contemplate."

"If it was apoplexy," Miss Osborne said quietly, "and it happened in his sleep . . . he likely suffered no pain."

"That's kind of you to say, dear. But if you'll forgive me for saying so, I would feel more assured if that came from his physician."

"She *is* a physician," Joss said.

"What Captain Grayson means to say," Miss Osborne explained, sparing Joss only the briefest of glances, "is that I've received a great deal of medical training and experience by virtue of being a doctor's daughter. But what I tell you now, I learned as a child. My mother suffered an apoplexy when I was a girl—a severe one. She survived, but the attack left her paralyzed and bedridden, unable to walk or speak. Over the next year, she suffered many spells." She swallowed hard before continuing. "I always sat with her, you see, while my father was working. I would read aloud, work my lessons, spoon her tea and broth. Her fits were difficult to even recognize at first. It almost looked as though she were asleep, in the midst of a dream. She would tremble a bit. Her breathing went agitated, and her eyelids fluttered against her cheeks. Afterward, she would be weakened and perhaps a bit scared, but not in pain. Never in pain."

No one spoke. Toby was certain it was because they were all thinking the same, unspeakable thing. Thank God Mr. Yorke had gone quickly and not remained clinging to life in a useless, wasting shell. What a tragedy that would have been—not just for Yorke to live through, but for his mother to witness. To imagine a young girl, forced to become caretaker to her own parent . . .

No, no one had much to say to that.

"He didn't suffer, then?" Lady Aldridge asked weakly. "You're certain?"

"Yes," Miss Osborne answered, her voice growing warm and soft. "I was there with my mother, when she died. She went peacefully."

"I am glad of it, for her sake. And yours."

"Mother." A voice from the periphery pierced their bubble of silence. "Mother, I'm here."

Heads lifted. Augusta had arrived, bringing with her a fresh reserve of womanly efficiency. Toby absorbed the accompanying wave of relief. He gratefully moved aside, offering his sister the seat beside their mother.

"Oh, Augusta." The older woman slid from Miss Osborne's shoulder to meet the waiting embrace of her daughter. "Augusta, I loved him."

Augusta soothed her, with soft touches and soft words. Mumbling some excuse, Miss Osborne bolted from the room. A heartbeat later, Joss followed her, leaving Reginald and Jeremy to make strained conversation amongst themselves.

And Toby just stood there, alone.

Hetta lurched from the room, pausing in the foyer to borrow strength from the carved walnut banister. Clinging to it with both hands, she bowed her head to her sleeve and wept. Noisily.

She wished she could have made it a bit further away before breaking down, rather than dissolving in tears six feet from the parlor door. She wished the emotion tearing her to pieces were a more altruistic empathy for Lady Aldridge in her time of mourning, or grief for her own long-dead mother—but it wasn't. It was envy, mixed with fear. Envy for anyone who knew the comfort of lasting affection. Fear that she would live her whole life and grow into an old woman with no one to mourn.

And no one to mourn her.

Strong hands gripped her shoulders. Every muscle in her body tensed.

"Go away," she choked out, without lifting her head from her sleeve. She didn't need to look up. She knew who it was.

"No," came the predictably contrarian reply. "No, you need to be held. I'm going to hold you."

There was no fight left in her, no more pride in the way. A word, an embrace—whatever scrap of affection he offered her, she would gratefully accept. The strong hands turned her away from the banister, and then strong arms folded her into his chest.

She burrowed her face into his coat and sobbed. "Oh, Joss."

"Shhh. It's all right."

His hand went to her hair, stroking and soothing. As no one had soothed her in a very long time, since before her mother took ill. He released her name as a deep, soulful sigh, and his whole body relaxed, making a soft place for her. She breathed deeply, too, inhaling the comforting scents of clean linen and masculine spice.

He murmured comforting words as she wept, and Hetta tried desperately to stem the flow of her tears, so she might hear them.

"What you said to Lady Aldridge . . . it was brave of you, Hetta. I know it wasn't easy, but you gave her some peace."

She sobbed again, and he held her tight.

"What an ass I've been," he said. "I've treated you so ill. Can you ever forgive me? I know I don't deserve to be forgiven."

"No, you were right," she said, wiping at her eyes. She was only too glad to share the blame for their arguments. Perhaps now they could be friends. "I know I should be more feeling with my patients, with their families, but . . ." She made an impatient gesture with her hands, indicating her red, swollen eyes. "But it's difficult. Just look at me."

"I am looking at you."

He thrust a finger under her chin and tilted her face to his. Oh, how unfair that he should be so composed and handsome when she was a teary disgrace.

"I am looking at you," he repeated, "and I can scarcely understand—how can this tiny, delicate woman possess so much strength, so much intelligence and courage?" His hand lifted to her cheek, brushing away a tear. "All this, and such lovely eyes."

No. Surely he wouldn't be so cruel as to tease her again.

His hand caught her chin. "No, don't dare look away now. Do you know how those eyes have haunted me?"

Hetta shook her head, suddenly afraid to blink.

The corner of his mouth curved. "At first they annoyed me, no end. They were always staring at me, asking me questions I didn't want to answer. Then I found myself wanting to stare back, ask questions of my own, and that irritated me even more. Then Bel recovered, and suddenly you weren't coming around anymore, and I found myself"—he sighed heavily—"missing them. Intensely. That made me angriest of all."

"Because you felt disloyal to her."

"God, no." His arm tightened around her waist. "Because I felt alive. Suddenly, painfully alive, when I'd invested so much time and effort, making myself dead to the world. Because I began to yearn for things I swore I'd never seek again. You can't know how I resented you for it."

She choked on a laugh. "I think I have some idea."

"I'm sure you do, to my shame."

"I never thought you a curiosity," she told him, needing him to understand. "I tried not to stare at you, really I did. But you're so handsome and attractive and . . . and I just couldn't help it."

He cocked his head to the side. "Hm."

Hetta held her breath, waiting. Then she said, "I hate it when you say that, with that smug, enigmatic expression! I don't know what it means, and—"

"Shh." His thumb covered her lips, then brushed over them in a tender caress. "It means I'm going to kiss you now. All right?"

"All right."

And he did. He kissed her gently, sweetly—and then Hetta kissed him back, with every ounce of passion she possessed. She felt uncertain and vulnerable and suspected she was doing everything wrong—but since she'd reached the age of three-and-twenty before receiving her first kiss, and since her first kiss stood an excellent chance of also being her last, she wasn't about to hold anything back.

When his hand fisted in the back of her gown and a little growl rumbled through his chest, she hoped it meant she'd done something right.

And then it was over, and he held her in his arms again.

"You're trembling," he said.

"Yes. I'm afraid."

He squeezed her tight. "Don't be. I mean to marry you, Hetta."

"That's what I'm afraid of."

"Why? Don't tell me you're worried what people will say. I know it wouldn't be easy, but we're both of us accustomed to—"

"No. No, of course it's not that." Pulling away, she met his questioning gaze. "You're very kind, Joss, but you don't have to offer. I'm not expecting—"

"I'm not kind in the least. I know I don't *have* to. I *want* to."

"But . . ." Tears pricked at her eyes again. "But you can't possibly want to marry me. I've no money, for one thing. I'm prickly and preoccupied, for another. I won't give up medicine. I'd make a terrible wife. And you have a child . . ." She shook her head. "I've no idea what to do with a child, once the cord is cut. I'd make a horrid mother."

He laughed.

"Why is it you only laugh when you're laughing at me?"

"I don't know," he said, "but you'd better marry me,

Hetta. Or I may never laugh again." He planted a quick kiss on her lips. "First, I couldn't give two straws whether you have a dowry. I'd never ask you to give up medicine, or anything that meant so much to you. And I'm certain you *would* make a terrible housekeeper, and a perfectly horrid nursemaid. But I don't need either of those. My son needs a mother who believes he can do anything, who won't accept the restrictions society will place on him. And as for me . . . I hardly know how to put words to what I need, but I know I'm holding it here in my arms. I need not just a wife, but a partner. A strong, intelligent woman who expects no less of me than I expect of myself. I need to laugh, and often. And you need all those things, too."

Hetta stared numbly at his cravat.

"I need to love," he said quietly, gathering her to his chest. His heartbeat pounded against her cheek. "And be loved. Do you think you could love me, Hetta?"

"I think I already do."

"Very good, then." His chin settled on her head. "And now for the trickier part. Can you allow me to love you?"

She closed her eyes. "I think so. Yes."

He pressed a kiss to the crown of her head, and she felt his wide smile. "There now," he teased. "Was that so hard?"

"Yes. It was terrifying."

He held her tight. "I know, my dear. I know."

CHAPTER
TWENTY-THREE

It was nearly dark by the time Toby left Yorke's town-house. After seeing his mother into the keeping of Augusta and Reginald, playing impromptu host to a parade of mourners, and speaking with Yorke's valet—about the waistcoat, among other arrangements—he finally made his way to the carriage.

"We're for Wynterhall," he told the driver before climbing in. It didn't matter that it was late, or that he hadn't any of his belongings packed. He'd send for them tomorrow. Perhaps he was a coward, but he just hadn't the heart to go home and face Isabel again.

Toby settled onto the seat of the gloomy carriage and immediately turned his gaze to the small window. He couldn't abide the darkness right now, and he certainly couldn't sleep. Every time he closed his eyes, he saw her tear-streaked face, her pale expression of betrayal. That image would haunt him forever—as would the knowledge that he'd caused it.

Staring out the carriage window thus, with his mind so filled with sorrow and regrets, it took him some moments to realize he was not alone. Not until the shadows across from him shifted in a stealthy, sinister way, drawing his eye. Toby's heart began to pound in his chest. He held his breath.

And then . . . the shadows spoke.

"Bel sent me a note."

Toby jumped in his seat. "Jesus," he said, pressing a

hand over his racing heart. He leaned forward, blinking to make out his companion's form. "Sophia? Is that you?"

"Of course it is," she said.

"Good Lord." He exhaled loudly. "For a moment there, I thought you were Gray, come to kill me."

She gave a disbelieving laugh. "Why would Gray want to kill you?"

Well, if that answer wasn't obvious to her . . .

Toby cleared his throat. "Just what did Bel's note say?"

"That Mr. Yorke had died, of course. And that you'd be leaving for Surrey. Gray's away on business today, but I wanted to come pay my respects." She leaned forward and placed a hand on his arm. "I know he meant a great deal to you, Toby. I'm so sorry he's gone."

"Thank you." He stared at her hand on his sleeve, until she withdrew it. "Why didn't you come inside?"

"It didn't seem right," she said. "I knew your whole family was there, and considering our history . . . I didn't want to be a distraction."

The carriage wheels rattled over cobblestones as they rounded a turn.

"Why did you do it?"

He had to ask. He had to know, no matter how much it hurt to hear it, just what it was that made him so patently undesirable as a husband. And she was the only one who could tell him. "Why did you run?"

She faded back into the shadows and fell silent.

"Why did you jilt me?" he continued, growing agitated. "Why did you leave without saying a word? Was it something I did? Something I didn't do? Was the prospect of marriage to me so revolting that you simply had to remove yourself to the other side of the globe?"

"Toby, I—"

He punched the seat cushion. "I said nothing. When

you disappeared without so much as an adieu, I said nothing. When you returned from your little honeymoon cruise and all London was toasting Gray . . . I said nothing, to anyone. I could have ruined you both, made you the center of speculation and scandal. But I didn't. And still, even now—we're practically family, and yet you're barely civil to me. Damn it, you owe me some answers."

"I do," she said hurriedly. "I know I do. And I know I owe you far more than that. I've simply been so ashamed, so sorry for how I treated you. I didn't know how to face you again."

"Well, if you're so ashamed of your behavior, why did you behave that way in the first place? Did you have so little regard for my feelings?"

"No, of course not. I cared for you, Toby, a great deal. I . . . I suppose I cared for you too much to marry you."

He laughed bitterly. "What a sentiment. Truly, it warms the heart."

"I cared for you, but we didn't love one another," she said. "And I thought we both deserved to find love."

He snorted. Oh, yes. He had gotten what he deserved all right.

She spoke slowly now. Gently. "I know the way I fled our wedding was wrongheaded and thoughtless, and you can't know how sorry I am for causing you pain. But would you have me regret it? Would you wish I hadn't left?"

Now it was Toby's turn to evade answering. "I think you shouldn't ask me that today."

"What's happened?" she asked. "Did you and Bel have some sort of row?"

He dismissed her question with a shake of his head. There was no way he was going to explain Hollyhurst to her. Instead, he tapped his knuckles against the coach side to signal the driver. It took several smart raps before he caught the man's attention and could direct him to the Grayson residence. If he'd only had his walking stick, he would have had an easier time of it.

"No real purpose, my eye," he grumbled.

"What?" Sophia asked.

"Nothing." He heaved an exasperated sigh. "No, there is something. I don't want to ask it. I don't want to hear the answer. But I simply have to know."

"Yes?"

Toby crossed his legs, then uncrossed them. There was no way to say it but to say it. "Why couldn't you have loved me? What does Gray have that I haven't?"

"Oh, Toby. Please understand. It wasn't like that at all." She crossed the carriage to sit beside him. "This may not be what you want to hear, but it's the truth. My leaving had very little to do with you, and everything to do with me."

"Good Lord. I can't believe you're giving *me* that line. Have you forgotten to whom you're speaking?" He adopted a patronizing tone. " 'It's not you, darling, it's me.' I've used that excuse a hundred times if I've used it once. It's never the truth."

"I know . . ." She wrung her hands in her lap. "I'm trying my best to explain it."

"Try harder." Toby didn't even attempt to mask the bitterness in his voice. He was hurting. No, it wasn't entirely her fault, or even mostly her fault, but she was the one nearby. Even though he had no hope of saving his marriage to Isabel, for some self-punishing reason he needed to understand why the first one had failed before it had even begun.

"Toby, I knew you admired my good qualities. My genteel accomplishments, my beauty . . . my considerable dowry."

"I wasn't some impoverished fortune-hunter," he objected. "I didn't need to marry for money."

"Can you tell me honestly it wasn't an inducement?"

Toby sighed. He couldn't. It wasn't so much the dowry itself, but simply the suitability of the match. With her fortune and accomplishment and beauty, Sophia had seemed the sort of lady he *ought* to marry. The sort of lady who *ought* to want to marry him.

She continued, "I never felt like you truly knew me. At first, your praise was flattering. You were so charming, and you said all the things a girl most wants to hear. But after a while, those little compliments made me feel like a fraud. You always treated me as though I were perfect—and I wasn't. No one is. I feared I'd be living a lie for the rest of my life—that if you knew my true nature, any regard you had for me would disappear." She looked up at him. "Can you understand? I had no shortage of people to admire my best qualities. What I needed was a man who understood me, and loved me even at my worst. Gray is that man."

"I understand," he told her. "I understand perfectly." Some help this conversation had been. She hadn't shed any light on Isabel's feelings, just made him even more acutely aware of his own. That was all he wanted, to be loved at his worst. And he'd married a woman who just couldn't do it.

Bollocks.

The carriage rolled to a halt at the Grayson house. "It's late," he said. "I'm anxious to be getting on to Surrey. Will you be offended if I don't see you in?"

"Not at all." The carriage door swung open, and Sophia reached for the footman's hand.

At the last moment, she stopped. She said, "I know I don't have to tell you, Bel is very invested in goodness. If I was anxious about revealing my worst to a husband, I can only imagine her fear. It must be ten times what mine was."

Silly woman, talking about Isabel as though she had

something to fear from him. He loved that woman, body and soul. He'd told her so, time and again. She was the one rejecting him.

"Sophia, my wife has nothing to worry about. Isabel doesn't have a worst. She's a selfless, perfect angel."

"Toby." Sophia's blue eyes flashed at him in the dimming twilight. "Do you honestly want to know what drove me to jilt you?"

He nodded mutely.

"Statements like that."

CHAPTER TWENTY-FOUR

On Friday morning, Bel waited for her guests in the Rose Parlor.

Except, it wasn't a rose parlor this morning. It was white—all white. In preparation for the chimney-sweeping demonstration, the curtains had been removed and the carpets rolled away. The bric-a-brac had been boxed up, and each painting or stick of furniture had been carefully draped with a muslin dustcover.

In its austerity and simplicity, the space reminded Bel very strongly of her girlhood, and the hours spent in her mother's bedchamber. That room, too, had been stripped of drapery and ornament, for her mother's safety. After that horrific incident with the bedcurtains—and then, a year or two later, the hearthrug catching fire . . . Simple décor had seemed best.

Yes, Bel thought, twisting her hands in her lap—this morning, the Rose Parlor bore a striking resemblance to that spare, sunlit bedchamber in Tortola. All it lacked was the madwoman.

Or . . . perhaps it didn't.

El amor es locura.

Folding over her lap, Bel buried her face in her hands. She did not cry. In the two days since Toby had left, she'd simply exhausted her supply of tears. Still, her shoulders quivered with the echoes of sobs. So many emotions cycled through her, faster and faster with each hour since he'd left—anger, despair, fear, loneliness, heartbreak.

One moment, she missed Toby so fiercely she began packing for Surrey; the next, she would remember the artistic stylings of one Mr. Hollyhurst and resolve never to see his patron again.

She didn't know what to think anymore. Except that she must be going mad.

She ought to be grateful, that Toby had gone away. It had saved her the task of removing herself, or even more difficult—creating false distance between them while they lived under the same roof. Because she had to distance herself, for both their sakes. After the way she'd flown at him, cursed him, *struck* him . . .

No, she couldn't allow that scene to ever recur. She had to stay away from him. By leaving, he'd spared her the trouble.

Not that they would stay apart forever, of course. They were married, after all. Eventually, she and Toby would have to cross paths. But by then, their anger with each other would have cooled, and their passion as well. With clear heads and mended hearts, they could begin again— and have the same kind of cordial marriage so many of their peers enjoyed. The sort of marriage Bel had always intended to have.

She knew Toby would have no difficulty finding physical pleasure in the arms of another; or *others*—and Bel would not deny him that. She wanted him to be happy, and his warm, personable nature would not lend itself to solitude.

No, that part would be Bel's. She would put her emotions aside. She would rededicate her heart and mind to charity. She would save miserable waifs from suffocating in chimneys.

Love and passion were not for her.

The room gradually filled with ladies, all attired in shades of gray and black, in accordance with the invitation. The women arranged their dark skirts over the muslin-draped furniture, until the entire tableau began to resemble not a snowdrift, but rather a flea's-eye vantage of a spotted hound.

And here came the flea.

"Lady Violet Morehouse," the butler intoned. The matron swept into the room, dressed head to toe in a repellent shade of puce.

"Lady Aldridge, my dear." She curtsied and flashed a smile so brittle and false, it threatened to slide right off her powdered face and shatter on the floor.

Bel yearned to help it along.

"I apologize for not adhering to the dress requirements," she said, indicating her plumed, blood-red gown. "But while your morning may be beginning, my own evening is just coming to its close. I have not yet been home."

"No matter," Bel said, forcing a generous curtsy. "I'm simply delighted that you could find time to join us."

Lady Violet cleared her throat and placed a hand to her temple. "I don't suppose you have a spot of tea to offer? I imagine wine is out of the question. I feel as though I've wandered into a Quaker meeting."

The ladies tittered with laughter.

Bel tamped down the irritation rising in her breast. *Charity.* She was living for charity now, and Lady Violet needed a great deal of it. "To be sure, I can offer you tea." She turned to address the room. "Or coffee, or chocolate. Ladies, shall we go in to breakfast?"

As the ladies filed down the corridor, someone clutched at Bel's elbow. She wheeled about.

"Sophia! Oh, I'm so glad you've arrived." She wrapped her sister in a warm embrace. "I was beginning to worry you wouldn't come. Augusta's in Surrey, of course, and I'm on my own this morning."

"Certainly I came. Do you think I'd leave you to face these dragons alone?" Sophia's blue eyes twinkled. "But before I forget," she whispered, "I have a gift for you."

She placed a small, flat package in Bel's hands, wrapped in brown paper and knotted with twine. "It's a book," she explained in a low voice. "But don't open it now."

"Not *the* book. The one Lucy kept hinting about?"

"Yes. Well, not that exact volume. I had to send a manservant to locate a fresh copy." The corner of her mouth pulled in a grimace. "What an errand that was. Anyway, you really ought to have it. These things are meant to be passed on."

With a regretful look, Bel pushed the parcel back at her. "I don't know how to tell you this . . . but I've already seen it. Your copy, I mean."

Sophia clapped a hand over her burst of laughter. "You didn't."

"It was by accident, I assure you. I was looking for a sleeping draught and—" Bel nudged her sister down the corridor, where they could speak without drawing notice. "I scarcely looked at the pictures, I promise. Once I realized . . . what I realized, I quickly put it away. But truly, I read enough to know I'm not interested in reading the rest. You can take it back."

"You didn't read all of it?"

"Heavens, no." Bel pressed the package toward Sophia again, but her sister would not take it.

"Then you absolutely must have this one."

Bel shook her head. "I don't want it. Come now, *The Memoirs of a Wanton Dairymaid*? It's ridiculous."

"Precisely," Sophia said. "It's a ridiculous book, filled with wicked fantasies and silly notions and improbable romance. But you ought to read the rest, just the same."

"Why?"

Sophia smiled. "Because it has a happy ending."

Too disheartened to argue further, Bel accepted the book and laid it on a side table. With a weak smile, she said, "This morning will end unhappily indeed if I keep my guests waiting any longer."

Crumpets dusted with powdered sugar, iced cakes, jam tarts, and macaroons . . . all these and more weighed down the sideboard in the breakfast room. Bel had been planning this menu for weeks. She held her breath as Mrs. Framingham plucked a glacéed apricot from the apex of an artfully arranged pyramid. When the tower of fruit refused to topple, Bel heaved a sigh of relief.

"I must say," Sophia murmured, biting into a crumpet, "as social gatherings go, I've never seen its like. A ladies' breakfast party with requisite mourning attire, rife with potential for scandal and innuendo? Remarkable."

"Are they really here for the potential of scandal and innuendo?"

"They're not here for chimney sweeping, I'll tell you that much."

Bel wilted in her chair. With Toby away and in mourning, she thought surely Mr. Hollyhurst's last caricature would have faded from public memory. If they had wished to see a lust-crazed Bel slavering over her rakish husband, they ought to have known it would not happen today.

It would not happen, ever again.

"But they are here," Sophia continued, "and you'll see, good will come of it. Sometimes a little scandal is just what you need."

"Yes, Toby once told me the same."

Toby had told her many things, so very few of them true.

"Lady Aldridge," Mrs. Breckinridge called, her mouth full of cake. "You must tell me how your cook gets this icing so creamy, so perfectly white. Is it a special recipe?"

"Oh, it's sweetened with love," Lady Violet said smugly. "That's the secret ingredient. This is a honeymoon house, you know."

"No," Bel blurted out. She bit her lip. "I mean, it isn't the recipe. It's the superior quality of the sugar. We use only the most refined sugar, imported by my brothers' shipping company. It's farmed on Tortola, on a freedmen's cooperative." She perked with inspiration. "If you like, I can give you a list of the merchants who stock it."

"Please do," Mrs. Breckinridge mumbled, taking another bite of cake. "This is divine."

Immediately, several other ladies expressed an interest in receiving the same list.

"You see," Sophia murmured, giving Bel a smile. "I told you good would come of it. And we haven't even had the demonstration yet."

"Speaking of the demonstration, I had better make certain the equipment has been readied." Bel ducked into the corridor and made her way back toward the Rose Parlor. Then she stopped short.

A tall, familiar masculine silhouette filled the foyer. Bel's heart leapt.

"Joss!" she exclaimed, hurrying to greet him. "How good to see you. I'm so glad you're here. I need a list of the merchants who stock sugar from the cooperative. The ladies are . . ."

Her voice trailed off as she noticed something odd about her brother's appearance. He was smiling. Grinning, really. Almost idiotically so. She hadn't seen him wear an expression like that in nearly two years, not since before Mara's death.

"Forgive me," she said. "You obviously have something to say, and here I'm blathering on. What is it?"

"I need to ask you to help look after Jacob. I'll be away for a month or so."

"But of course I will. Are you going to sea?"

"No, no. This is a land journey." He took her hands in his. "Bel, I'm getting married."

Her mouth fell open. The breath whistled in and out of her a few times before she could convince her lips to form words. "Married? But to whom?"

"To Miss Osborne."

"To *Hetta*?"

He nodded, grinning wider still.

"Married. To Hetta." Bel shook her head wonderingly. "I can't believe it. I thought you—"

"Despised her?"

"Something like that, yes."

"I thought I did, too. Fortunately, Hetta's a great deal more clever than I." His eyes lit with pride. "We'll be traveling north, to see her father and be married from her home. Lord Kendall has generously offered us Corbinsdale for our honeymoon." He bent his head, seeking her gaze. "Bel, are you all right? You've gone pale."

Bel put a hand to her brow. "I'm sorry, I don't mean to act so shocked. I adore Hetta, and I'm happy for you both. It's just such a surprise. After Mara, I didn't think you'd—"

"I know." He squeezed her hand. "I didn't think I would, either. But I've never been so happy to be proven wrong."

"But marriage, Joss? And so quickly? Aren't you . . ." She chewed her lip. "Aren't you frightened at all?"

"Of course I am," he said, chuckling. "I'm scared witless. That's how I know I'm in love."

The mellow tones of his laughter warmed Bel, deep inside. She hadn't seen him like this in so long. How cruel life could be. She was getting her brother back and losing him again, all in the space of one morning. "That would explain why I'm terrified for you," she said. "It must be because I love you so much."

His demeanor turned serious. "I'll never forget Mara," he told her. "I loved her. I know you loved her, too. And I'll never forget how devastating it was to lose her. But I can't let fear keep me from living, from loving. Not anymore. I've survived some of the worst life can throw at a man, but I'm not going to let that keep me from enjoying the best."

She blinked back a tear. "When do you leave?"

"Tonight, on the mail coach. Sophia and Gray are there with Jacob, of course, and his nursemaid. But I know he'd enjoy frequent visits from his Auntie Bel."

"Then he shall have them."

"Bel?" Sophia called from down the corridor. "I think the ladies are nearly finished with breakfast."

"I'll be right there," Bel said, sniffing. She gave Joss an apologetic smile. "I must go. I have guests."

"I should be going, too." He bent to kiss her cheek. "Offer my congratulations to Toby, when you see him next."

"Congratulations? On what?"

"On his election, naturally. The polls close today. I heard it from Gray, just this morning. Not that the outcome is in any doubt." Joss grimaced. "It's a shame. I'm certain Toby would rather have won under different circumstances."

"Yes," Bel said, not wishing to make any contrary statement she would then be forced to explain. She was sure Toby would rather have not won at all. He'd gone to such lengths to ensure his defeat. The image of that appalling caricature appeared in her mind, and she felt the stab of his betrayal anew. This, from the man who claimed to love her.

Well, she was accustomed to receiving gestures of love and hurt from the same hands. She was a fool to have ever dropped her guard with Toby. And she most certainly should never have entertained notions of loving him in return. Bel knew how to survive the wounds of love, but she couldn't live with herself for inflicting them. He'd made her feel safe, but it had all been a lie. No one could protect her from herself.

Meeting Joss's concerned gaze, she willed a smile to

her face. Truly, she had no reason for complaint. Toby had been right—now she'd gotten exactly what she wanted. A polite, advantageous marriage to a man with a seat in Parliament, and the funds and opportunity to work tirelessly for the causes of good.

This was her happy ending.

"Please give my best wishes to Hetta, as well," she said brightly. "She's won herself the best of husbands. Here—" She snatched the paper-wrapped book from where she'd left it earlier, on the side table. Pressing it into Joss's hand, she said, "An engagement gift for your bride."

Having bid her brother good-bye, Bel returned to the breakfast room and invited the ladies to join her in the parlor for their demonstration.

"Now," said Lady Violet, settling into the wingbacked chair nearest the hearth, "where is this strapping chimney sweep with his marvelously efficient equipment?"

Laughter rippled through the assembled ladies.

"The equipment is here," Bel said, waving her hand toward a slender, jointed rod topped with an arrangement of stiff wire brushes. "But there is no chimney sweep. No man, at any rate. I will be the one to demonstrate the machinery."

The ladies all stared at her in shock, but Bel ignored them as she threaded her wrists through the armholes of an apron. After the scene at Aunt Camille's card party the other day, she was not about to bring a man into this assembly to be the target of carnal jibes, or worse—the supposed object of Bel's lust. Besides, how better to demonstrate the brushes' efficiency than to show that even a lady could use them?

Her apron donned, Bel lifted the brushes for the ladies' inspection. "You see, the wires are arranged like a parasol. They remain collapsed as the machine is inserted into the flue." She flipped the brushes over. "As they are withdrawn, the bristles expand to scrub the walls clean. Unlike a climbing boy, who has but two arms and one small brush, this machine reaches every corner of the flue at once."

Bel knelt at the hearth to insert the brushes through the fireplace. Unfolding the jointed rod and locking the sections into place, she advanced the contraption higher and higher. It wasn't quite as easy as she'd imagined it would be. The flue was clogged with a winter's worth of soot, and it took a great deal of effort to push the brushes through the narrow passageway. Small trickles of ash filtered down periodically, dusting her hair and clothes.

As she worked, she sensed the ladies in the room growing restless. She surreptitiously wiped her brow on her sleeve.

"Is your husband not at home, Lady Aldridge?" Of course, it was Lady Violet's smug voice.

"No," Bel clipped, forcing the brushes upward with a vicious shove. "He is away."

"Pity," Lady Violet said. "He is so amusing with the ladies. One can always count on Sir Toby to enliven a dreary party."

"I beg your pardon," Bel said, her movements growing more agitated. "This isn't a party. If it's amusement you seek, you may wish to go elsewhere."

A hush cloaked the room. The scrapings of brush against flue were the only sounds.

"As for my husband," Bel continued, "he is not amusing any ladies this morning. He is in Surrey."

"Oh, but surely there are ladies in Surrey," the matron said significantly. "Ladies eager to be amused, no less. But from what I read in *The Prattler,* Sir Toby's corner of Surrey has a most interesting geography. I understand it quite closely resembles an establishment known as the Hidden Pearl."

"I'm sure I don't know what you mean."

"I'm sure you don't, dear girl." Lady Violet gave her a cruel smile. "That's probably why he's there."

Bel's every muscle tensed. Anger heated her blood, but she could not let it boil over. She'd worked so long and so hard to make this demonstration a success, and the lives of children could very well hang in the balance. Even though she was annoyed with Lady Violet for making such crude insinuations, and even more ir-ritated with Toby for the caricatures that spawned them . . . she would not be a slave to unpredictable passions.

Patience, she admonished herself. *Goodness. Charity. Miserable waifs.*

"The brushes are fully inserted now." She addressed the room calmly, rising to her feet and clapping the dust from her hands. "And now, I give a small twist on the handle to expand the bristles, and as I retract the device, the soot will be removed." She gave Lady Violet an innocent smile. "You may wish to retreat now, my lady. To the back of the room, perhaps. Or further. This may get dirty."

"Oh, I think I shall remain. I'm enjoying my front-row view immensely. What an enlightening morning this is proving to be."

"Very well." Bel knelt again and began retracting the brush with rough yanks, twisting and turning the rod as she did. With each motion, a shower of soot rained down the chimney, settling around her skirts.

"Now, typically this method is not so untidy," Bel ex-plained as she worked. "Sweeps who use this machinery also have a set of curtains that they arrange before the hearth, so as not to—" She stopped short as her brush caught on an obstacle. "So as not to soil the—" A rougher tug gained her nothing. She braced one boot on the grate and pulled hard with both hands.

No progress.

"I believe it's stuck, dear," Lady Violet said helpfully.

"Yes, it's stuck," Bel snapped, releasing the rod and scrambling to her feet. Her breathing was quick and shallow. "Just as these young children get stuck in flues with alarming frequency. Imagine, Lady Violet, that you're the one wedged into that flue two bricks wide. Imagine that you're the one stuck, unable to move, suffocating in a cloud of soot, frightened beyond belief. Imagine that your cruel master below is jabbing pins into your flesh to convince you to move—or, if that fails to work, lighting straws on fire and using them to toast the soles of your feet. Imagine, Lady Violet, that you are a miserable, impoverished, friendless child about to die. To be sacrificed on the altar of English tradition simply because a lady of the *ton* could not be bothered to instruct her house keeper to embrace modern improvements." Bel sniffed and pushed a stray wisp of hair from her eyes. "Are you enjoying that image, Lady Violet?"

"No," the matron said smugly. "But I think you are."

Bel gasped. Lady Violet was right. She *was* enjoying the image of a cramped, choked, soot-covered Lady Violet. She was enjoying it far too much. What was wrong with her? This was meant to be a charity function, not an exercise in hostility. But she had so much emotion churning inside her—she felt like a volcano, preparing to erupt. The worst of it was, she couldn't very well flee the danger, when it resided in herself.

She could do this, she told herself, taking a deep breath and releasing it slowly. She could conquer her simmering passions and complete this demonstration with dignity and grace. She would not explode.

Sophia moved toward her. "Bel, you've been working so hard. Perhaps you need a rest."

Bel warned her off with a shake of her head and bent down to take up the rod again. "What I need is a bit of assistance. Let us work in harmony, Lady Violet. May I ask you to lend a hand?"

The matron cast her a withering look. "Surely you're joking, Lady Aldridge. As if—"

"Not strong enough, then?"

"It isn't that, I assure you—"

"Afraid of a little soot?"

"No." Lady Violet's mouth thinned to a slim red gash in her face. She rose from her chair and placed her hands on the rod above Bel's. "Anything to get me out of this madhouse," she muttered to Bel. To the room at large, she sang, "What a lark this is, Lady Aldridge. It's giving me all sorts of ideas for my next party. I think I shall distribute aprons at the door and invite all the ladies to take turns at scullery maid. After tea, each guest must wash her own cup and saucer."

The ladies giggled. Bel seethed inside, but she forced herself to remain outwardly calm. "On three, then?" she asked through gritted teeth.

"On three," Lady Violet agreed. "Oh, but wait! I've just had a brilliant idea for my autumn house party. We'll all play at dairymaid!"

Bel ignored the laughter and began counting. "One . . ."

And somehow—in that brief, fleeting moment—a strange thing happened in Bel's mind. Grasping that wooden rod in her hand, listening to the mocking laughter of her peers, feeling the anger bubble and rise inside her . . . she faced down the specter of madness.

"Two . . ."

She felt it keenly, the temptation to just give in. To go into a rage, scold Lady Violet, cast these insufferable women out of her home, and smash a few ceramic figurines, just to complete the dramatic effect. It would be so easy, to fly off the handle.

But Bel chose not to. Instead, she made a very calm, very rational decision.

To let it go.

"Three."

Bel released her grip and stepped back. She stood watching a few paces distant as—

Whoosh.

Lady Violet's full-strength tug released a deluge of ashes and soot. A plume of black vapor swallowed her puce-clad form.

Turning away from the cloud of ash, Bel clapped her hands over her face.

Oh, there was no more laughter now. The room was so silent, she could hear the coal dust settling to the floor. Slowly, she lowered her hands, uncovering only her eyes, and turned back to face the hearth.

Lady Violet stood before her, coated with coal dust from crown to toe, sputtering and fuming like a snuffed candlewick. Around them, a dozen ladies stood stock-still, handkerchiefs pressed to their mouths in horror.

Bel kept her own hands clamped over her mouth, to no avail. No matter how hard she pressed her fingers against her lips, she couldn't prevent it.

She laughed.

It started with a few inane giggles, then quickly progressed to full-throated peals of laughter. She couldn't help it. This demonstration was a travesty and her marriage was a disaster and she was very likely going insane—and there was just nothing for it but to laugh. Laugh loudly and long. Really, where was the benefit in being a madwoman, if it didn't entitle one to bursts of wild laughter?

Bel laughed until her sides ached and she was wiping away sooty tears with her handkerchief. Then she met Lady Violet's shocked blue eyes, staring out at her from an ash-powdered face. The matron stood frozen in place, hands raised in surrender, and before Bel even knew what she was doing, she embraced the woman. She caught Lady Violet in an unabashed, exuberant hug and laughed harder still.

"I wish I could say I'm sorry for your gown," Bel said at length, stepping back. "But really, the invitation did explicitly call for black."

She removed her own soot-matted apron and cast it aside. "Well," she said to the gawping ladies, who had now most certainly witnessed the scandal they came for, "this concludes the demonstration. Lady Grayson will pass round the list of professional chimney sweeps who use machinery in place of climbing boys. I do hope you will employ their services in your households. Unless, of course, Lady Violet is taking on clients." She giggled again as she headed for the door.

Sophia rushed to her side. "Bel, where are you going? Are you well?"

"I don't know that I'm well. But I'm going to Surrey." Craning her neck, she glanced at the clock in the corridor. "And I have to make haste, or I'll be too late."

"Too late for what?" Sophia asked.

Ignoring her, Bel turned to the ladies. "Please excuse me, but I've just remembered an urgent appointment and I need to . . ." Her laughter turned to nausea as she realized what her plan entailed.

Oh, blast.

But she'd made the decision now. Just as Joss had said, she couldn't let fear hold her back. She finished weakly, "I need to order the carriage."

CHAPTER
TWENTY-FIVE

Toby stood at the foot of the hustings platform, waiting for Colin Brooks to wrestle into that abominable yellow topcoat and come make his victory official. As he waited, he paced back and forth, every so often tossing his walking stick into a fresh grip and resisting the urge to do something truly ridiculous, like fondle the ivory knob.

Really, what a sentimental fool he'd become. He had a full set of clothing at Wynterhall—more than enough to see him through Yorke's funeral and the election—yet he'd sent two servants to Town with directions to pack up half his wardrobe. All that effort, simply an excuse to retrieve this useless walking stick.

Certainly, if he could have done so without looking a complete ass, he would have requested even more embarrassing mementos. A lock of jet-black hair, a verbena-scented pillow, a swatch of that red silk gown . . . But this walking stick was the only thing of *her* that belonged unequivocally to *him*—and as a consequence, he was making rather a fetish of it.

"What's keeping Brooks?" he asked the sheriff's deputy.

The man gave him a mumbled "dunno" and picked his teeth.

Toby paced away again, swinging the stick with impatience. The sooner Brooks arrived, the sooner the election results could be made official—and the sooner Toby could be on his way back to London. To her.

What an idiot he'd been. Sophia's words had shown

him the error of his ways even before he'd left the Town limits. Well, truthfully, he'd sulked most of the way to Surrey, but he'd come to his senses sometime before the carriage drew up to Wynterhall's moat.

All he'd wanted was for Isabel to see him at his worst, and love him. And stupid blighter that he was, he'd failed his own test. He'd professed his undying love for her, and the moment she'd become (quite rightfully, he might add) angry with him, he'd deserted her.

God, what a struggle he'd had over the past two days, fighting the urge to ride back to her and simply fall at her feet, beg her forgiveness. But there were things he needed to do here in Surrey—not just because they needed doing, but because Toby needed to do them, to prove his own worth. He needed to see his friend buried with honor, he needed to lend support to his grieving mother . . . and now he needed to secure this seat in Parliament.

Really, it was all she'd ever asked of him. Such a small thing. Why the devil had he ever resisted? He could have so easily secured her regard, if not her love.

Now he'd lost any chance for either.

He could only try his best to put things right and hope her anger would fade with time. Perhaps he'd never earn her love, but Toby could live with being allowed to love her. He'd have to learn to live with that much, because he certainly couldn't survive without her. The past two days had taught him that.

"Toby."

He ceased pacing. His eyes snapped up, and he spied a familiar figure coming toward him.

Make that two familiar figures.

"Gray. Jem." Toby nodded at his brother-in-law, then his friend. "What the hell are you doing here?"

"I'm financing your campaign," Gray said, patting the pocket of his coat.

"What, with bribes?" Toby asked.

"If it comes to that. So far, pints of ale are doing well enough."

Toby turned to Jeremy. "What are *you* doing here?"

"Honestly?" Jeremy shrugged. "I have no idea. Gray made me come."

"I bring the gold," Gray said, gesturing toward Jeremy, "and he brings the class. Figured it couldn't hurt to have an earl backing you."

Toby scratched the back of his neck. "Gray, you do realize that, of the two opposing candidates, one has died—"

Gray nodded.

"And the other is the local bedlamite."

"Aye."

"And nearly all the votes have been cast and tallied, and I have an insurmountable lead. Yet you still seem to think I need bribes and aristocratic backers to scrape out a victory?" Toby shook his head. "Your faith in me . . . What to say? It's so inspiring."

"I'm not here for you," Gray said testily. "I'm here for Bel."

"I'm here for Bel, too," Toby said. "Jem, are you here for Bel?"

Jeremy heaved an exasperated sigh. "I have no idea why I'm here. I really wish I weren't."

"Good," Toby said. "Then go home, the both of you."

Gray narrowed his eyes. "Now see here. I'm not taking any chances with—"

"No, you see here." Toby leveled his walking stick at his brother-in-law. "Isabel is my wife. She asked me to run for Parliament, not you." He turned to Jeremy. "And she hasn't asked you for anything."

"I know," Jeremy said, raising his hands in defense. "I told you, I don't know why I'm here. He told me we were going to the club."

Toby continued, "When I win this election, it may be

no great victory—but it will be *my* victory. Mine alone to lay at Isabel's feet. I refuse to share whatever thimbleful of glory I earn with either of you. So go home. You don't get to be the heroes today."

"Actually," a gravelly voice announced from behind, "none of you do."

The barrel of a musket forced its way into their triangle, sending Toby's walking stick clattering to the ground. All three men took a quick step back—

Only to freeze in unison when they heard a chorus of ominous clicks—the unmistakable sound of several guns being cocked.

"Bloody hell," Toby whispered, raising his hands. He swiveled his head to either side. Colonel Montague's oafish nephews surrounded them, each training a gun on Toby's person. "What the devil is going on?" he asked the nephew who'd spoken. The largest one, he noted with dismay.

"Now Sir Toby," he said, "we don't think you really want to be a candidate for MP."

"Yes," Toby said. "I assure you, I do."

The oaf prodded Toby's chest with his gun. "No, you don't. A London toff like you? You never cared spit about this borough before. Going on thirty years, the colonel's been standing up as a candidate. The old man's getting weaker every winter. He won't likely have another chance. And now that Yorke's dead, he can finally win. So you're going to let him."

"Let him?" Toby echoed, incredulous. "Even if I wished to, I couldn't. The polling is closed. Colin Brooks will be out here any moment to make the result official."

"Colin Brooks is currently having a little chat with my cousin," the oaf said. "I have it on good authority, he won't make it out here until after you've withdrawn your candidacy."

At that moment, Gray took a step to the left. The

red-faced oaf swung around, training his gun on him. Gray froze.

"Don't anyone try anything funny," Montague's nephew said.

Toby sighed. "For God's sake, man. Do you honestly think you're going to shoot us? I may be just a baronet, but Jem there is an earl. Murdering a peer of the realm is a certain ticket to the gallows. And you're surrounded by witnesses." He gestured broadly at the spectators pressing in around them, all of whom had gone stone quiet. "Not to mention, the Colonel's election would never stick. Someone would have him declared incompetent and removed from office, and where would that leave the poor old fool?"

"Well, then he'd have been an MP, wouldn't he? Even if only for a while. The poor old fool would die happy."

"This is pointless," Toby said, shaking his head. "It doesn't matter what you say. I won't do it."

The gun swung back to point at him. "You really think you've earned this seat in Parliament? You think you want it as badly as the Colonel does?"

"No, and no," Toby answered. "But my wife wants me to have it with a righteous passion. And I love my wife more than I love the Colonel."

The crowd erupted in laughter, and Montague's nephew's face turned an impressive shade of purple.

"I'm sorry," Toby said, lifting his hands and flashing a disarming grin, "but it's the truth. She's prettier." He slowly extended one hand toward the man. "Come on, now. Let's not do things this way. I have great respect for your uncle, I do. So does everyone here. We can work out some other way to honor him—declare him the borough's sergeant-at-arms, perhaps. Tell your cousins to lower their guns. Let's all head into the tavern for a pint, and we'll discuss this like civilized folk."

And just when Toby was sure he had him—just when

the man's face faded to a pinkish hue, and the barrel of the musket lowered a fraction—it all went to hell.

From the back of the crowd, a panicked cry went up. The sounds of hoofbeats on stone and horses whinnying quickly followed. Spectators began to scatter, though the armed men surrounding them held their ground. Madman Montague had trained them well.

"Oh, no," Toby whispered. "No, no, no." His heart plummeted to his boots. He couldn't possibly be reliving this nightmare.

But evidently he was.

The crowd parted, just as it had that day. And here was the carriage bearing down on them, the horses driving at breakneck speed.

And there, perched on the tufted leather, clutching the irons for dear life, her face a pale mask of terror—was Isabel.

"You can stop now," Bel called.

The driver hauled on the reins, drawing the horses to an abrupt halt in the center of the village square. Bel didn't even wait for someone to help her down. She leapt from the open carriage as soon as its wheels slowed and raced toward her husband.

"Toby," she said, gulping air. "Toby, I need to talk to you."

He stared at her, keeping his hands raised near his shoulders, as if he was afraid to touch her. Well, and really—who wouldn't be? Bel's hands flew to her face. Heavens, she must look a sight. What bits of her that hadn't already been covered in soot were now dusty from the road, and her hair was blown every which way. And of course, Toby was turned out in magnificent splendor, every inch the tall, dashing gentleman.

"You look marvelous," she told him, just because she could.

"Thank you," he said slowly, taking in her appearance. "You look . . . rather singed. But I'm very glad to see you, despite the fact that you nearly scared me into an early grave just now."

"I'm sorry," she said, shaking out her skirts. "I told him to drive like the devil was on our heels. And I am a bit crisped at the edges, aren't I?" She laughed. "It's to be expected, I suppose. I spent my morning dueling a dragon. They haven't called the election yet, have they?"

He shook his head no.

"Oh, good. Truly, I apologize for scaring you. I just had to speak with you right away."

"Yes," he said, still holding his hands up. "You, and several other people."

He twisted his head from side to side, and for the first time since she'd driven into the square, Bel looked at something other than her husband.

Oh, my.

Here was her brother. And Lord Kendall. And a half-dozen men surrounding them all with guns. She took a startled step back, tripping over something that felt like a stick—not that she was going to look down to verify it.

"Toby?" she asked in a cautious voice. "What's going on?"

"Well, you see—"

A big red-faced man poked Toby in the chest with the barrel of a musket. "What's going on is that we have guns. And you'll listen to us."

"I don't think so," Bel said, turning to stare up at the man. "I've just traveled three hours by carriage at a thundering clip"—she turned to her husband—"and Toby, you know how I hate traveling by carriage."

"Yes," he said, flashing a gorgeous smile. "I know."

She turned back to the man with a gun. "Anyhow, I've suffered through three hours of torment just to speak with my husband, and guns or no guns, he's going to listen to *me*."

"Bel," Gray said in a low voice, "perhaps you should—"

"Dolly, please don't take this the wrong way. But why are you even here?"

"I've been asking him the same thing," Toby said.

"As have I," Lord Kendall said dryly. "Perhaps we'd have received a more satisfactory answer if we called him Dolly."

"Dolly?" A few of the men with guns began to snicker.

Bel clenched her hands into fists and dropped her gaze to the ground. Why was it that whenever she had something important to say, the people around her couldn't stop laughing? Her eyes caught on Toby's walking stick, where it lay at her feet. That must have been what she'd tripped over earlier.

"Enough," the red-faced man shouted.

The laughter ceased.

The man continued, "Beggin' pardon, my lady, but Sir Toby doesn't have time to listen to you just now. Sir Toby is going to make his way onto that hustings platform and make a little announcement. Or else."

"Or else what?" Bel asked.

"Isn't it obvious? Or else I'll shoot him," the man ground out, jabbing Toby again with the gun.

"Oh, please," Bel said, rolling her eyes. "You're not going to shoot anyone."

"My lady," he snarled, his face reddening further, "I suggest you go back to your—"

She never did hear that suggestion in its entirety. Bel crouched, grabbed Toby's walking stick, and came up swinging. She smacked the oaf in the head with its blunt ivory knob, and he slumped to the ground with a thud, unconscious.

Bel yelled at him anyway. "I'm speaking to my husband,

you . . . you . . . Oh, you're not worth it." She held the stick aloft and turned to Toby. "You were right. It does come in handy."

"Yes." A burst of laughter escaped him. "Yes, it does."

She looked around at the other armed men, who had all lowered their weapons, seemingly bereft at the loss of their leader. Then she looked back down at the unconscious brute. "Did I truly just do that?"

"Yes, you did," Toby said, coming forward wearing a smile handsome enough for the devil. "And it was magnificent." He took the walking stick from her hand and let it fall to the ground before folding her into his arms. "My God, Isabel, I—"

"No, wait!" She pushed away from him. "Toby, I came here to talk to you."

"By all means," he said, still smiling. "I'm listening."

"I came here to say that I . . ."

He nodded encouragingly. "That you . . . ?"

"That I'm so angry at you!"

His face shuttered. "Oh." He shifted his weight, flicking a self-conscious gaze sideways. "That's what you've come all this way to say? That you're angry at me?"

"Yes," she said, her hands balling into fists. "Yes. You need to know. You need to see me for who I truly am. I"—she jabbed a finger in her chest—"am a woman who gets angry."

"I see."

"No, you don't. How could you? I didn't see it until just today. I'm not selfless, Toby. I'm certainly no angel. And I can't be mad. Didn't you tell me, if you're aware that you're mad, you're not mad?"

He nodded.

"Then I can't be insane. What I am is angry. I get angry, all the time, in the most useless ways. I get angry at things I can't hope to correct, like injustice and violence and oppression. I get angry at things years in the past—at my brothers for leaving me to grow up alone, at my poor dead father for being an intemperate lecher, and at my poor dead mother just for going mad. I get angry when people make fun of the old and infirm. I go positively livid when I see a maltreated child."

"I understand," he said, stepping toward her.

"No, you don't," she insisted, tears stinging her eyes. "You couldn't possibly understand. You've always been happy, always been so loved. You can't know what it's like, to see people in pain and feel that suffering, all tangled up with your own. To need some way to channel all that anger into something good . . . or you'll simply go mad with it."

He stretched out a hand. "Darling, please. Let me—"

"And you," she said, ignoring his hand and leveling a finger at him. "When women flirt with you, I get so angry I could stick them with pins. When men point guns at you, I get so angry I'll club them with sticks."

The oaf at her feet began to moan and stir.

"Be quiet," she told him, "or I'll do it again." To Toby she asked, "What did he want, anyway?"

Toby tilted his head and regarded the crumpled figure. "He wanted me to withdraw my candidacy."

"Oh!" A wild giggle bubbled up from her chest. "That's what I meant to ask of you, too." She tapped the man's shoulder with the toe of her boot. "So sorry."

"I can't withdraw my candidacy," Toby said, frowning, "or Colonel Montague will win."

"So?" Bel asked.

"So . . . he's ancient, deaf, and insane." Toby crossed his arms. "I can't allow it to happen, in good conscience. Besides, isn't this what you wanted? You wanted a husband in Parliament."

"I wanted you," she blurted out. Her hand went to her throat. "I wanted you, from the very first moment I saw you. I've been pushing you into all these political and charitable roles ever since, so I could pretend I had some nobler cause in mind. But I didn't. I just wanted you."

"Isabel . . ." He came toward her again, arms open.

"No." She stayed him with an open palm. "I'm not done being angry yet."

"Oh." His arms fell. "All right. I'll just . . . wait for you to do the embracing, then."

"That would be best." She sniffed. "Toby, of all the things and people I'm angry at, I'm most angry at you. I trusted you, and you lied to me. And I understand why you did it, and I can even forgive you . . . but that doesn't make it hurt any less. So I'm angry at you for lying, but I'm angrier still at how deeply you've made me care." Tears leaked from the corners of her eyes, and she dabbed at them impatiently. "You made me love you, Toby, so much I could hate you for it." She smothered a sob with her palm. "I've never said that to anyone before."

"The part about love?" he asked.

"No," she choked out through tears. "The part about hate."

From that very first kiss, he'd made her feel *everything*—the good and the bad. He brought all her passions to the surface, when she'd worked so long to subdue them. It was infuriating and wonderful and so very frightening. She just didn't know what to do.

Fortunately, he seemed to have an idea.

"I lied," he said, putting his hands on her shoulders. "I'm sorry, but I lied to you again just now. I'm not going to wait for you to do the embracing."

His arms went around her, and Bel rested against his strong, solid chest, shedding tears and soot all over his coat.

"Hush, love," he said, rocking her gently. "It's all right. Haven't I told you, time and again?" He pulled back slightly and tilted her face to his. "You're beautiful when you're angry."

She kissed him. Tightened her arms around his neck, stretched up on tiptoe, and kissed him, in front of everyone. In front of hundreds of gaping spectators, in front of six men with muskets . . . good heavens, in front of her *brother*.

And it was wonderful. Everyone cheered. Even the men with guns.

Well, perhaps not her brother.

"Don't do this," she said, between nibbles at his lips. "It's not too late to withdraw from the race."

"I have to win," he murmured.

"No, you don't. It doesn't matter to me whether or not you serve in Parliament. I won't force you into this."

"I'm not being forced." Putting some distance between them, he took her hands in his. "I know it wasn't my original intention, but now I want to serve, for several reasons. It's my duty as a gentleman of privilege, for one. And I want to honor Mr. Yorke's legacy, for another. In many ways, he was a father to me."

"I'm so sorry," Bel said. "I'm so sorry I wasn't there for you when he died."

"I know. I was sorry you weren't, too—but I knew it was my own fault." He kissed her hand. "But Isabel, the largest reason I want to be elected to Parliament is this: I want to do it for you."

"Haven't you been listening? You shouldn't do this for me."

"Of course I should. I love you, and there's no better reason to do anything."

"But—"

"Shh." He took her in his arms again. "It's my turn to have my say, all right?"

She nodded.

He spoke softly, only to her. "Isabel, you were right about me. I'm capable of far more than this frivolous life I've been leading, and I knew it long before we met. For years now, I've wished for some greater purpose, and you were right to push me to find one. But you don't get to choose it for me."

"No, of course not." She stroked his cheek. "I was wrong to even try. That's why I want you to withdraw from the race."

He shook his head. "No. I'm going to be elected to Parliament, where I will represent this borough with honor. And I will continue to manage my estate. I think I'll prove reasonably competent at both. But my highest goal, my true reason for living, is right here in my arms. It's you, darling. It's us. You are everything I've been yearning for, for so long—a perfect fit for all my natural talents." He smiled, and brushed a tear from her cheek. "Loving you gives meaning to my life."

"Toby." She bent her head, resting her brow against his chest.

He whispered in her ear, "And by God, I will excel at it. I mean to love you so well, so fiercely. To make certain you never doubt what a remarkable, beautiful woman you are. To make certain the world knows it, too. To create a stable, loving home for you and our family. To give you a place where you will always feel safe."

She slipped her hands inside his coat, needing to hold him tight.

"Those may not be the sort of accomplishments that end up in the papers," he continued, "or earn a man society's applause. But they're important, just the same. And as I look around at the world, I realize . . . it's astonishing, how few men are truly good at them."

She lifted her face to his. "You will be magnificent at them. A true champion. I have complete faith in you."

He was right, of course. Toby was a rare man indeed.

In all her life, Bel had never met a person with such infectious warmth and good humor, or his instinctive talent for making those around him feel confident and secure. That combination had attracted her to him from the very beginning. Well, that and the devastating grin spreading across his face.

Oh, she was the luckiest woman alive.

He said, "Then I advise you to get accustomed to this idea, that you are worth any effort. Learn to live with the burden of being adored. Take all that righteous anger, darling, and go forth to battle the dragons of injustice . . . but you must always come home to me." He kissed her nose. "Because I intend to be, above everything, a devoted husband." A sly gleam stole into his eye as he added, "And a doting father."

She gasped. "How did you know? Even I'm not certain yet."

"I'm certain. And I knew it the moment I saw you. I've three older sisters, with ten nieces and nephews between them. I can just tell."

She buried her face in his coat. "I'm frightened. I'm not sure I know how to be a good mother."

"You will be the most loving, patient mother who ever lived." He held her tight. "Except on the rare days you aren't. On those days, I'll take the children to the park."

She laughed into his chest. "How do you do it?" She raised her face to his. "How do you always know exactly what it is I most need to hear?"

"That's easy." He bent to whisper in her ear. "Here I divulge a great secret, darling. I just say whatever it is I'd most like to hear back." His breath warmed her cheek as he murmured hopefully, "I love you."

"Oh, Toby." She melted inside. If there were a better man on this earth—she would still want this one. Forever. "I love you, too."

EPILOGUE

FIVE YEARS LATER

"Well? Did you manage to kill anything today?"

Toby stretched out on the grassy riverbank, reclining on one elbow. "Bagged one partridge. Henry has himself a fine brace of pheasants."

"That's all? I knew I should have gone with you." Lucy looked up at him, the faint gleam of bloodlust in her eye. It was an expression completely at odds with her otherwise maternal appearance. She sat on a quilted picnic blanket, resting her weight on one outstretched hand while the fingers of the other combed her infant's dark curls.

Beside her, Sophia shaded a charcoal sketch of the slumbering baby boy. "Eventually," she said without looking up, "we'll have to stop calling this our annual hunting party. You men so rarely bring anything back."

"True enough," Toby said, watching the play of sunshine and brisk autumn breeze on the stream's dappled surface. "But then, our annual 'tromping-through-the-woods-to-prove-our-manliness party' lacks that certain ring."

"And where are these other exemplars of manliness?" Lucy asked, drawing a thin blanket over her child.

"Felix went up to the manor, I think. Henry took Jem and Gray by the kennels to see his new foxhounds. They'll be around shortly."

"I'm not even sure why Gray goes along with you," Sophia said. "He doesn't like violence."

"Neither does Jeremy," Lucy replied. "He never could bring himself to shoot a single bird. And then there's Felix, whose aim has always been hopeless. Soon Tommy will start begging to go along, and that may put a stop to the hunting excursions completely." She cast a glance toward her older son, who was entertaining a trio of little girls downstream: two fair, one dark. Lucy continued, "Jeremy's determined that no child of his will ever touch a gun."

"That's not wise," Toby said. He could understand his friend's protectiveness, considering how Jem's brother—Tommy's namesake—had been tragically killed. But he didn't agree with it. "The boys will only grow more curious, if he forbids them, and it's curiosity that breeds accidents. In fact, I once knew a girl who secretly followed a hunting party and very nearly got herself killed."

"Oh, really?" Lucy asked, feigning innocence. They both knew he referred to the day they'd met, when young Lucy startled a covey and Toby's shot missed her by inches. They'd been close ever since.

"What an incorrigible child," she continued. "I suppose she came to a very bad end indeed."

"Not at all. She grew into a lovely, elegant countess." He smiled. "Don't worry about the boys. I'll talk to Jem."

A chorus of squeals broke out as young Tommy plucked a grass snake from the rushes and held his wriggling prize aloft. Shrieking, the two blond girls went scurrying up the bank. The third, darker girl held her ground, however, shouting not at the snake, but at Tommy—adjuring him to set the poor creature free.

Toby smiled. That was his Lyddie. She'd inherited her mother's keen sense of justice, along with that dark, glossy hair.

"Drat," Sophia muttered, putting aside her sketch to

chase after her two daughters. "They'll run crying all the way to their papa now."

"So sorry," Lucy called after her. She shook her head and grinned at Toby. "I wouldn't know what to do in her place. It's a good thing I give birth to boys, while she has the girls."

"So far." He flicked a meaningful glance toward Sophia. "We'll see if the pattern holds true in six months."

"Truly? She hasn't said a thing." Lucy's cheeks dimpled with a wide grin. "But I suspected she'd brought home a little memento from Italy."

"And," Toby said cannily, "Sophia's baby won't even be the next."

She gasped. "Surely Isabel isn't—"

"No, no. It's far too soon."

"Well, I know it's not me," Lucy said. Her chin ducked. "Is it?"

"No." He nodded toward two women sitting under a beech tree: their hostess, Marianne Waltham, and Sophia's sister, Kitty. "Looks like Felix has finally hit the mark."

"Oh, thank heavens. Kitty's been waiting so long. For a moment there, I thought you meant Marianne *again*."

They laughed together. Henry, as the first to marry, had them all bested with six children . . . but so far, Toby judged, no seventh on the way.

"Is Isabel up at the house?" he asked.

"What an old, complacent husband you've become. You went all of five minutes without asking after her. Yes, she took the baby for his feeding, a short time ago." She touched the back of her fingers to her own child's cheek. "You will talk to Jeremy, about the boys and hunting?"

"Yes, of course. I have my ways of making him listen."

"I know you do, brilliant politician that you are. And Jeremy would never let on, but I know he respects your opinion immensely." A breeze feathered her dark-brown curls, and she tilted her face to it. "As do I. Now that Aunt Matilda's gone . . . besides Henry and Marianne, this group is all the family we have. You must promise me you'll never stop returning to Waltham Manor each year."

"Are you jesting? Isabel and Lyddie love it here. You couldn't keep us away."

"Good," she said. "This has never really been a hunting party, Toby. It's always been a family party, long before any of us married. And you were always the one who held us together, with your affable nature and warmth. You taught a handful of surly, wounded orphans what it was to be happy and secure, surrounded by people who care." She gave him a self-conscious smile. "That must be why I was so in love with you, all those years."

"Oh, were you?" he teased, remembering the way she'd clung to him all those autumns, like a spindly second shadow. "I never guessed."

"Liar." She lifted one eyebrow. "But here is something I've never told you." Despite the fact there was no one but a sleeping infant to hear, she leaned closer and lowered her voice to a whisper. "Do you know, that year you brought Sophia here . . . I was so desperate with jealousy, I planned to sneak into your room and seduce you, so you'd have to marry me instead."

Toby's jaw went slack. No, he hadn't known that. "Truly?"

"Truly."

"Well, what happened? I suppose you came to your senses in time."

"In a way," she said, smiling impishly. "I somehow ended up in Jeremy's room instead." Her head made a pensive tilt, and she looked up at him, a girlish vulnerability shining in her green eyes. "I sometimes wonder, though . . . what would have happened if I'd found my way to yours?"

"What indeed." He chucked her under the chin. It was a tender, reassuring gesture honed through years of practice—a gesture he often used with his daughter now. "Lucy," he said, "please take this in the kindest possible way. I'm very glad we'll never know."

Slowly . . . gingerly . . . easy now.

Bel lowered her sleeping baby to the bedding. She rocked his cradle gently, keeping one palm flat on his tiny belly until his rhythmic breaths told her he'd fallen into a deep sleep.

Still she stood there, admiring the tiny notch carved in his earlobe, and the sweet curve of his eyelashes fluttering against a rounded, cherubic cheek. Such a beautiful, perfect boy. Love swelled within her, until her heart ached.

"*Duérmete, mi amor,*" she whispered. *Sleep, my love.*

When she'd first married, Bel had been terrified by the intense emotions her husband inspired in her. Gradually, with Toby's patience and care, she'd learned to delight in their shared passion rather than fear it. But nothing could have prepared her for this—the fierce, boundless love a mother felt for her children. There was no controlling this emotion, and certainly no way to separate it from fear.

As she watched her baby sleep so innocently, guarding him with the light pressure of one palm, it pierced her heart to acknowledge that, no matter how she and Toby tried to protect him, no matter how tightly they wrapped him in love—this child would inevitably know pain, illness, danger, sorrow.

But he would never know them at his mother's hand. Of that much, Bel felt assured.

The door creaked softly behind her.

"Only me," a familiar voice whispered. "Don't be startled."

The door clicked shut just as quietly, and moments later, strong arms cinched around her waist.

Toby settled his chin on her shoulder. "Is he asleep?"

"Yes, just."

"Good." His lips grazed the sensitive place beneath her ear, and the kiss echoed in the soles of her feet. Bel released a sigh of pleasure. He always knew just where to kiss her, to set her knees quivering.

"Lyddie's down at the stream with the others," he whispered. "We have some time to ourselves."

She leaned back against his chest, and his hands slid to cup her breasts. They were emptied of milk now—soft, and sensitized at the tips.

"I don't want to wake the baby," she protested feebly, and insincerely.

"We won't," he said, taking her hand and tugging her toward the adjoining bedchamber. "We'll be very, very quiet."

She gave him a mischievous smile. He knew as well as she, it was difficult for her to be quiet when they made love. Being in Toby's arms—it was the safest place in Bel's world, and the one place she released all her inhibitions. He delighted in making her cry out in bed. Sometimes he made her scream. Oftentimes lately, he made her laugh.

And sometimes, like this afternoon, when a sleeping child was nearby and they needed to be very, very quiet—he loved her so gently, so sweetly, he made her weep silent tears of pleasure and joy.

Afterward, she lay in his arms, breathing deep, labored breaths scented with his comforting masculine spice. The afternoon sunlight gilded the sculpted contours of his shoulders and chest and painted amber streaks through his light brown hair.

"You are beautiful," she told him.

"Darling," he replied, "I was about to speak those exact words to you."

Together they floated in that magic, idyllic space between wakefulness and sleep.

"Toby," she asked softly, "will we always be this ridiculously happy?"

"Probably not." His voice was drowsy. "Will you still love me anyway?"

"Yes." She hugged him tight. "Oh, yes."

No sooner had she whispered the words than the baby woke crying. A quarter-hour after that, in came Lyddie with tears in her eyes and two scraped knees. Then an express arrived from Wynterhall, bearing news that meant Toby must leave at once . . . some sort of crisis with the sheep.

Their afternoon idyll was over, the perfect enchantment broken—

But the love remained, beneath it all. Always.

ACKNOWLEDGMENTS

Once again, I owe an enormous debt of gratitude to my two critique partners, Courtney Milan and Amy Baldwin, and others who read various drafts of the manuscript: Lindsey, Terri, Janga, Santa, Elyssa, and Tiffany.

Many thanks to my editor, Kate Collins, and the entire team at Ballantine, including Kelli Fillingim, Junessa Viloria, Linda Marrow, Caitlin Kuhfeldt, copy editor Martha Trachtenberg, and the wonderful art department. I continue to be ever grateful for my agent, the amazing Helen Breitwieser, and for Kim Castillo, who truly is an author's best friend!

Thanks to all who helped me with various facets of research: Sarah, for her horse expertise; Jenny, for the knowledge of opera; Frances, for the theater lighting; and Kalen, for being the go-to on costumes. Any mistakes I've made or liberties I've taken are, of course, mine.

Lastly, I want to thank my family. Writing romance would be much more difficult, had I not always been surrounded by so many examples of caring, respectful, lifelong commitment. And it would be truly impossible if I didn't have the unflagging support of my own wonderful husband and children. Thanks and love to you all!